A TWIST OF SAND

I snapped open the voice-pipe.

"Course three-two-oh. Two hundred revolutions."
I'd get the hell out of this blasted coast, I thought
bitterly.

Then I saw it.

It flashed white and evil, like a guano-covered
fang, out of the sea a few hundred yards on the port
beam. A sick cold feeling hit me in the stomach
after my momentary elation. I had been fooled for
the second time that morning by the current and
fooled more still by the curious light refraction so
that I had not seen Simon's Rock itself, but only
its white-guano-littered tip where the sun caught
it.

"Full astern!" I yelled . . .

GEOFFREY JENKINS

A Twist of Sand

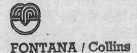

FONTANA / Collins

First published 1959
First issued in Fontana Books 1961
Tenth Impression February 1974

© Geoffrey Jenkins 1959

Printed in Great Britain
Collins Clear-Type Press London and Glasgow

Author's Foreword

It is a fact that the German U-boat High Command tested experimental U-boats in Cape waters in 1941, Captain Johann Linbach, master of the German freighter *Hastedt*, was reported by *The Star*, Johannesburg, on 6th September, 1957: "During 1941, when Germany was testing a new model of submarine engine, six U-boats so equipped were sent to Cape waters . . . only one returned."

The phenomenon of the " double sun " was recorded by meteorologists of the Pretoria Weather Bureau at Swakopmund, South West Africa, on 11th December, 1957.

Adiabatic warming of winter winds is an authentic meteorological occurrence in South West Africa. The colouring of the sea by the autumn bloom on plankton is also vouched for. It occurs in conjunction with gymnodinium, a deadly poison.

I have taken a liberty with the actual date on which the *Dunedin Star* was lost.

Pretoria, 1959

Contents

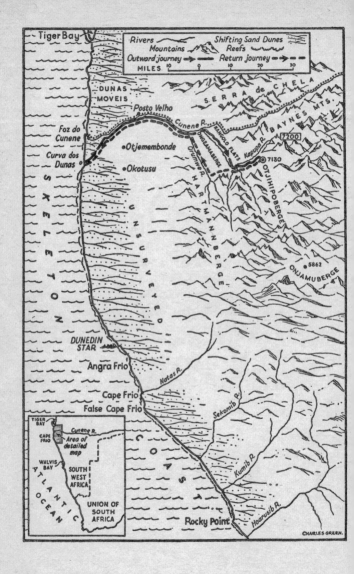

ONE

Skeleton Coast

TWENTY-ONE and a half feet. I shivered.

The movement shook loose from the edge of my duffle-coat a bead of icy moisture which skidded down my cheek and splashed in a tiny bright spangle on the chart under the concentrated glare of the angled light. I shivered again, half in fear, half in discomfort. The fog was condensing everywhere, and I could feel its sharp tingle in my throat. Dawn in fog is the time for any skipper's fears; dawn in fog off the Skeleton Coast is the time of nightmares.

The drop of moisture made a north-westerly digression over the fold of the chart as *Etosha* rolled uneasily. Lying on it, the grey photostat page of the old log, with its neat, Victorian script, looked a little weary, despite its shiny rejuvenation at the magic wand of the camera which had plucked it from forgotten oblivion in a fusty London shipping office.

I slid the photostat of the ship's log under the 18-degree line of the chart as if, by placing it in the exact position where she had struck, I might gain some vital information from its meagre sentences.

"British steam vessel *Clan Alpine*. 13th January, 1890. Bound Tilbury to Cape Town. 5 a.m. Ship, drawing 21½ feet, struck unknown object, thought to be a shoal, 18' 2" S, 11' 47" E. Position 326 degrees distant about 26 miles from Cape Frio. Doubtful. Making water in Number One hold but proceeding at reduced speed . . ." The one page of the *Clan Alpine's* log told all; it told enough; there was nothing later for my purposes.

Twenty-one and a half feet! Hell, that was little enough, and here I was with fully sixteen on *Etosha's* marks and in the same deadly shoal water. Three hundred and twenty-six degrees—that would put the shoal about three to five miles offshore. If that was right—I shook my head unconsciously

9

—and another droplet splashed down in the fug of the chart-room, warm by comparison with the bone-chilling air of the bridge, where only a canvas dodger stood between me and the naked elements.

The old *Clan Alpine* log by itself would never do. I'd snap *Etosha's* back on the same shoal before I knew where I was if I stuck to it alone. The other logs—would they break open the Chinese puzzle? I reached for three other photostats lying on the top right-hand corner of the chart. The heading was uncovered. "Africa—South West Coast" said, the writing. "Bahia dos Tigres to Walvis Bay." Who, I wondered vaguely, gave Tiger Bay that sonorous and Miltonic name? Some old Portuguese navigator? Christ! I thought, I'm just the same as one of those old seamen feeling his way down the same unmapped, uncharted coast of South West Africa south of Angola, the only difference being that I'm using an echo-sounder in this year of grace 1959 instead of a lead-line, as in the year of Our Lord 1486. And mighty thankful I am to have a magnificent modern trawler under me with powerful engines instead of a caravel, unhandy and ungainly, under sail. A sailing ship would be tossing with sails slatting; at least I was holding *Etosha* under the barest steerage way as I probed into the unknown.

I spread the three other photostats out fanwise on the chart below the old *Clan Alpine's* log. Pratt at the Admiralty had really done a good job with the old logs. It was purely for old time's sake in the Navy, I knew that. I certainly had no right to them, under my peculiar circumstances.

"H.M.S. *Alecto*, 1889," written in Pratt's copperplate. I grinned to myself. It brought back memories of his meticulous attention to detail at Gib. during the war. "H.M.S. *Mutine*, 1911" said the second photostat log heading. "H.M.S. *Swallow*, 1879," the third was titled. I knew their contents by heart—a five fathom shoal four miles off the coast, reported *Alecto*; a rock with breakers two and a half miles offshore, reported *Mutine*; eight fathoms, with breakers, three miles from the coast, reported *Swallow*. *Swallow* had added one bit of information. "sand and mud bottom." I grinned wryly. There was something to be said for using a 10-pound lead-line armed with a tallow bottom eighty years ago. It added one tiny little piece to the jig-saw.

I looked at the litter on the chart. By themselves, the inaccurate old logs were enough of a riddle, but the blasted German log threw the whole picture haywire. I wished now I had never dug around in the German archives in Windhoek and never clapped eyes on or heard the name of the German warship *Hyane.* But I had, and here lay the salt-marked log just to prove that all my theories about the location of the shoal were wrong. I didn't have to consult it as it, too, lay on the chart. . . . " Breakers during a moderate SSW gale and a high sea, in a position 282 degrees, distant 2 miles from high pointed hill." Two miles! I couldn't credit it. At that distance from the shore the Kaiser's old battle-wagon would have been a dead duck on the iron-hard sand of the shoal. And probably a rock or two through her armour-plating as well. The bearing, 282 degrees, was just about the craziest I had ever encountered.

I straightened up from the chart table. I was being mocked by the ghosts of ships which had long since gone to their graves. Their tall old-fashioned stacks and yardarmed masts seemed to cluster out of the fog round the modern, sharp lines of *Etosha* like a cerement ushering her to doom. All dead ships—and a shoal of death right under me now.

I shivered again. The dawn made it more morbid still. I looked down at the untidy chart table and cursed them all heartily. I needed fresh air. I cursed the bright light over the chart also: if it had been my old submarine, it would have been red, and I could have gone up on to the bridge without being blind for ten minutes before my eyes accustomed them-selves to the blackness aloft.

It was just beginning to get light. The blackness was turning only slightly grey, but it was sufficient to catch a faint glimpse of sea. Jim, the Kroo boy, was at the wheel. The fog was so thick I could not see the top of the signal halliards, and the great beads of moisture, like sweat urged from a man in a fever, dripped thickly from the lower spokes of the wheel. It fretted in runnels uneasily down the canvas dodger. I glanced at the compass.

"Steer five-oh," I ordered, making a minute correction to the north-east.

Etosha was doing perhaps three knots: I must solve the riddle of the shoal this dawn, or I might not ever get the chance again. John Garland wouldn't always be asleep below as he was now and, as one of the finest navigators in the Royal Navy once, he'd smell a rat before long.

With that extra sense that comes when danger is near, I felt rather than heard the man in the chartroom.

I clattered down the companionway.

John stood examining the photostats and my own chart, with its countless annotations and figures.

We stood looking at one another across the baleful light of the angled lamp. He ran his eyes slowly over the photostats. His voice was hard, but laced with professional admiration when he spoke after a long scrutiny.

"That's a very fine chart, Geoffrey," he said. "For a coast which has never been mapped, or never been surveyed, I'd say, in fact, it was a masterpiece." He leaned over my soundings to the south-west of the *Clan Alpine* shoal. "A masterpiece," he repeated slowly, staring hard at me.

"Where are we now?" he went on in the same voice.

I jabbed a pencil at the five and three-quarter fathom mark. "About there. For what it is worth. It could be nine, or three fathoms."

He blenched. Off the Skeleton Coast a ship's position is every skipper's nightmare. It haunts his mind, waking and sleeping; drunk in a ditch ashore, it is his first waking question.

I had known in my heart of hearts that the showdown with John must come. I would have preferred to have chosen the moment. An icy dawn is not the best time for presenting a case, a shaky case at that, to someone who believes in you.

I made up my mind suddenly.

"John," I said briefly. I drew a line on the chart with the ruler. "I intend to go inside this line. Two things may happen. You may find yourself drowning in the next ten minutes. Or you may find yourself facing a fine of £1,000 or five years in gaol."

"Go on," he said tersely.

" What I'm trying to say is simply this, that this ship is now off the diamond area of the Skeleton Coast. For months I have mapped and charted this coast coming home from the fishing grounds, in your watch below. I bought her for that. Trawling is purely a secondary consideration. It also is good cover. Remember how I insisted that I should take the midnight-dawn trick?" He nodded. " Well, I've faked the ordinary chart, but plotted everything in minute detail on my own special chart, the first accurate one ever of the Skeleton Coast.

John looked puzzled. " You may have hoodwinked me, but what of it? That's not a crime. It's no crime to chart a coast."

I laughed harshly. " It's quite clear you haven't read the Diamond Control Act. I'd say it was the finest combination of threats and penalties I've ever seen. This is the Skeleton Coast of South West Africa, John. Out there——" I gestured beyond the porthole out to starboard—— " are the richest unworked diamond fields in the world. It would mean a fine of £1,000 or five years' gaol, or both, for you and me. That's just for being here. There are plenty of other smaller items in the Act, each costing about £500 a time and a couple of years, which you undoubtedly would find on the charge sheet also."

" So what?" said John. " This ship is on the high seas. We're not ashore pinching anyone's diamonds."

" Ever hear of the three-mile territorial limit?" I laughed without humour. " And if that wasn't enough, there was that judgment the other day in the Appeal Court governing the rights to prospect and mine diamonds : high water marks, low water marks, territorial limits, etcetera, etcetera."

John sniffed : " No bloody South African Navy ship would find you anyway." He grinned for the first time. " You're the most cunning submariner who ever outfoxed a destroyer, and I'd say your hand has lost none of its cunning. Look at this set-up now—thick fog, a coast where only you know where you are, funk holes everywhere. . . ."

" Thanks for the compliments, John," I retorted. " But you're a little behind the times. Ever hear of this new border patrol the South African Air Force flies at unannounced times? Long-range Shackletons. I've seen their photographs of the mouth of the Cunene, the first ever taken from the air. They're good. They've got a coat of arms of a bloody great pelican standing on a globe rising out of the sea. I don't want to be snapped up in the beak of that pelican. There's nothing that would stop me afloat, but a Shackleton would take a photograph and—presto, an exact fix. Inside the three-mile limit. Five years inside for you and me. Irrefutable."

"What are you doing all this for, Geoffrey?" asked John quietly.

"I got kicked out of the Royal Navy—remember?" I said harshly. "I wouldn't say where I was—remember? Well, I've got a particular interest in this part of the world. It might have been just an overwhelming compulsion motive in the ordinary course of things, something to justify myself to myself, but since it ties up with the Skeleton Coast, it becomes highly dangerous and highly illegal at the same time. I'm charting this unknown coast rock by rock and shoal by shoal. The compulsion springs from something very deep in my sailor's make-up, and has also something to do with an old man I saw die. In some ways I'm finishing the job he set out to do. But it goes farther than that also, because I have an interest which I may tell you about some time. The immediate point at issue is, though, do you come in on this? You must make up your own mind."

John fobbed off the question by picking up the *Hyane's* photostat log.

"H'mmm" he mused, casting a glance over the others as well. "Got a problem in navigation on your hands?"

"Here's the shoal where the old *Clan Alpine* is reported to have struck," I said. If John intended to sidestep the issue for the moment, so would I. "These old logs—Pratt got photostats for me at the Admiralty, though God help him if he was found out giving material like this to a cashiered submarine commander—all place this shoal differently. It is the most important shoal on the coast, because it is the southern gateway to this vital piece of water here to the north. If one could penetrate the *Clan Alpine* shoal on the inshore side, it would give a safe passage—although in shallow water—away from a six-knot downcoast current which I reckon ricochets off here, just about the sixteenth fathom mark on the south-westerly corner of the shoal. It is almost impossible to take a ship in close to the coast at all because of that bouncing current. It races southwards through this mass of shoals, rocks and broken ground between here and the Cunene mouth, but I am convinced it doesn't get too close to the shore. . . ."

"My God! Geoffrey," exclaimed John. "This is magnificent!" He studied the annotated chart. His eyes gleamed. He grabbed the dividers and parallel-rules. Then he snatched up the *Hyane's* log.

"I've been over it all," I said coldly. "It's no go."

He straightened up.

"Two hundred and eighty-two degrees," he exclaimed in triumph.

"That bearing's balderdash," I retorted.

"I agree," he went on quickly. "But what if you forgot the first number?"

I saw in a flash what he meant. "You mean—eighty-two degrees? Why, that would have put the Kaiser's old warship . . ."

"Just here!" rapped out John. "*Inside* the channel. Two miles offshore. Dead right. The old *Hyane* found the way, all right, although she didn't know it. Some stupid clot must have altered the bearing from 82 to 282 which would have been quite reasonable since she then would have been safe at sea, even if a little close in. Come on, let's get going!"

"Not so fast," I said. "You haven't given me your answer yet."

"That's my answer, blast you!" he grinned. "You'll need another nautical man for company for your five years in quod . . ."

He stopped short. I felt it too.

The stern was giving a queer shaking motion.

"She's—she's—wagging her tail," he burst out incredulously.

The explosion felt like a huge empty drum dropped on *Etosha's* stern.

We both covered the distance to the bridge in a couple of bounds.

"Port fifteen," I snapped at the Kroo boy at the wheel. John stood by me, trying to pierce the veil, which cloyed

like cerements round our eyes. A heavy bead of moisture ran
off his short brown beard and the condensation on his forehead gave him the appearance of a man literally sweating over
something. His anxious tone did not belie it. The drops glistened on his cap and oilskinned shoulders.

"Where are we?" he asked.

I guestured to starboard. "Gomatom bearing about ninety
degrees, six miles."

"What the hell's Gomatom?" he rasped.

"It's the native name I gave a high pointed mountain
ashore. The name appealed. Sounded like the surf-breaking in
a south-westerly gale."

The Kroo boy's eyes were standing out of their sockets.

"Where did the explosion come from?" I rapped out.

The native shook his head hopelessly.

"Port beam, do you think, John?"

"More on the quarter," he replied quietly. "I've never
heard anything like that before," he went on, craning his head
slowly in a small semi-circle, like a searching radar aerial.

"Nor have I," I said, for it was unlike any explosion, mine,
torpedo or gunfire, I had ever heard. Yet it was an explosion.

Something heavy and wet hit the deck forward of the main
hatch. Near the foremast, I thought, peering into the fog.

"Squid," said the helmsman.

"Keep your eyes on that bloody compass," snarled John.
"Cut the cackle."

"Look-out!" I shouted through cupped hands. "What
hit us forrard?"

The voice came back faintly, as if the man had turned
away as he called back. It had a curious hysterical quality,
but then fog does peculiar things to sound, even a hundred
feet away. Almost simultaneously came another explosion as if
a giant steel drum had been dropped. It was farther away,
but clearly on the port beam.

The Kroo boy at the wheel gave a cry.

"*Bass, die kompas verneuk my!*" ("Skipper, the compass
cheats me!") he exclaimed in Afrikaans.

I was at his side in a flash. The compass rose was swinging
and by the time I reached the binnacle it had travelled through
seven degrees. But the ship's head had remained steady.

" There's a great deal going on that I don't understand and don't like," I rapped out to John, who was looking at the gyrating needle in silent wonder. " I'm going to stop engines and see if we can hear anything. If there's surf dead ahead, we'll hear it. If there's land, we'll smell it."

I rang the telegraph to " stop."

" That'll bring Mac out of his bed," was John's only comment.

" I'm going up above to see if there's anything to be seen from there," I went on. " Did you hear what the look-out said?"

John replied : " Curiously, I thought he said mud."

" Mud?" I echoed. " Mud?"

" That's what I thought."

" Steady as she goes," I told the helmsman.

On the roof of the wheelhouse was an additional deck enclosed by stanchions, where there was a small emergency wheel and, giving the vessel a comically belligerent appearance, a little range-finder which I found extremely useful for my work on the coast. The refraction from the desert dust in the air, however, which took days to subside after a north-eastern blow, was a great handicap to the instrument. I was hoping that by the time we returned to Walvis Bay the small five-mile-radius radar I had ordered would have arrived. The *Etosha* certainly needed radar at that moment.

To reach the upper deck one had to make one's way round the side of the bridge, giving a much wider view astern and abeam. A glow seemed to light the back of the fog away to starboard. A ship on fire? The sun? I couldn't be sure, with the compass playing tricks for no apparent reason, whether *Etosha* was headed north-east or south-west. It might be either. She had practically lost way and was pitching uneasily. The only sound was of my boots on the ladder and the faint squeal of a block on the mast aft as the ship lifted with a short, bucketing, unpleasant motion.

Grasping the rail, I tried to penetrate the fog, but I might as well have stayed in the wheelhouse. If there were surf breaking, I would hear it, for on this coast, except in the winter, roars that great almost perpetual breaking swell from the south-west which seems to bring across hundreds of miles of open sea the lashing anger of the great icefields beyond South Georgia, tossed to hysteria by the great peak of Tristan da Cunha where a jet-force wind never ceases to storm, finally screaming out its anger on the desolate shore under the shifting sand dunes. Many a shipmaster, from the Arab dhow captains who rounded the Cape five hundred years ago, to the nerve-ridden men who drove the tea clippers home from China, had his first and last experiencce on the coast when he heard the breaking surf under his bowsprit in even such a fog as this. The bones of their ships lie in the shifting sands—if you could get close enough to see them.

With the sudden change of temperature which goes with a strong steam heater suddenly switched on, I felt suffocatingly hot and threw open my duffle-coat at the throat. My fingers faltered at the buttons. The swift sweep of warm air cleared the fog and I gasped out loud in amazement at what I saw.

Astern, and on the port quarter and beam, the sea boiled in parturient frenzy. Like a view of the Hebrides I once had from the air, a chain of small islands stretched away, but unlike the calm splendour of the Outer Isles, these were being born; as if merging into the darkness of the womb, they mingled with the bank of fog ahead where the warm air had not yet dissipated it. Each vibrated and trembled—black mud heaved up from the ocean floor; bickering along these strange, new-born, viscous things was a flame of a colour I have seen neither before nor since, a kind of pure white, blotched and seamed with brown and purple. It was as if one of the roses of the ancients had been born from a living body, full of beauty and terror.

Horror rose in me. As I gazed speechless at the spectacle, my seaman's instinct reacted to what I saw. Apart from the chain of gestated islets astern and to port, the coast itself lay not a mile ahead—a dun forbidding shore of low sandhills, eternally shifting under the great winds which come in from the sea, covered here and there with sparse shrub or creeper-like growths. Unknown to us, *Etosha* had broken through into old *Hyane's* channel. Slightly ahead on the starboard bow rose a drab hillock. It stood, calculating and evil, like a huge puff-adder stretched out waiting for the touch of the ship's bow in order to strike back with primitive, coiled-up wrath. The flat hill, dun and serrated on the seaward side, might have been a reptile's flat head and folded throat.

I had only once seen the shore as close from the sea. It struck me that, although the *Etosha* was practically ashore, there was no surf. Then I realised that, in fact, the surf on which one could normally rely to reveal the position of the shore by its breaking was absent. Treacherous always, the coast had betrayed the *Etosha* too. Had I not stopped the engines when I did, she would have been aground by now.

John's footsteps came racing up the companionway and his face was grey as he surveyed our predicament. Landmarks—Gomatom, drab hillocks, characteristic splodges on the dunes—all raced through my head as I tried to place our position precisely.

"Christ!" he burst out. "Geoffrey, where in heaven's name are we? And why . . . he gestured inarticulately at the lack of breakers. Had there been surf, I realised quickly, it would have lifted *Etosha* and torn the bottom out of her by now. It was only because she was lying in calm water that she was not bumping on hard sand and biting outcrops of rock.

"Get a lead-line out: sound! sound! sound!" I roared at the petrified native boy who cowered in pitiful terror in the bows. He reached out numbly for the line with its leather and calico markers. "Sound!" I roared, cupping my hands. "Quick!"

With almost elephantine slowness, he took the line. Its heavy lead sinker might have weighed a ton, he was so slow. He cast forward.

"We must be miles off course," said John quietly. "If she strikes, we'll never come out of this alive. We are hemmed in to seaward by the eruption and the shoal and she's so close in that the sand must be stirring under the screws."

"By the deep three," chanted the leadsman feebly. Out of the corner of my eye I caught sight of several others of the crew who had made their way on deck and were gazing with the fatalistic resignation of the African, at the shore—and at death.

"What sort of bottom?" I shouted back. He picked up the lead and fumbled with the tallow. His moves seemed to be all in slow motion. "Shingle," he replied.

It confirmed what I wanted to know. I turned to John and smiled. "Do you want to know where we are? See that hillock—no, not the higher one, that one bearing about ten degrees? I call it Inyala Hill because you'll see there are stripes of brown and red down the side, for all the world like the markings on an inyala buck's side. It hasn't a name on the chart. And that," said I, pointing to the one towering farther inland, " is Gomatom. With something over three fathoms under us, and shingle at that, do you realise that we are where no ship has ever got before—even *Hyane*—and just because of the lack of breakers? This place is a mælstrom ordinarily."

" The Swallow Breakers," he exclaimed hoarsely.

" You saw the photostat," I said briefly. " *H.M.S. Swallow* in '79."

" But," said John incredulously staring out to starboard, " that means we've been carried miles to the nor-ard. . . ."

" There's no damned time to worry about that now," I snapped. MacFadden, the engineer, joined us on the bridge. He looked without a great deal of interest at the shore, the burning islets and the sea.

" What's this all about?" he asked in his broad Scots accent.

" Mac," I said, " for once your bloody double-action diesels are going to get the chance of their lives. Do you see that dark thing sticking out "—I gestured towards the bows— " about a mile and a half ahead? That's what I've named Diaz's Thumb. You won't find it on the chart either. Nor did Diaz, despite having been here four hundred years before us. Take a look almost due north—there, where the fog has just lifted. You see . . ."

" There's a gap," exclaimed John excitedly.

" Aye, about as wide as a schoolboy's arse," said Mac. " How'll ye ever get her round that rock into a damn near ninety-degree turn, I ask? Fah! Ye're asking me for eighteen knots. This isn't a speedboat."

"Take a look at the alternatives," I said quietly.

"B—— the alternatives," replied Mac. "All I want is to get those diesels at full pelt once before I die. Eighteen knots at three-eighty revolutions." He smiled a thin, cold smile. "Double-action diesels. Fastest things afloat."

He turned and went below to his beloved engines, ignoring the desperateness of the situation.

John and I clattered down to the bridge. I took the wheel from the Kroo boy.

"Full ahead," I snapped. John rang down.

"Any moment that surf may break," I said. "We want every knot we can get out of her. If the wind comes up—and you know how it does out of a dead clear sky here—we're finished. Once the surf breaks under her, you can say your prayers."

"Geoffrey," said John, "there have been times when I started to say my prayers before with you in command, and I feel damn like it now. You know this coast better than any skipper living. . . ."

"Cut out the pretty speeches," I said briefly, spinning the spokes. "I'm taking her on a line with that striped hillock."

Etosha began to tremble like a horse as Mac opened up the great engines.

John laughed suddenly, as he always did in the face of danger. "Mac's whipping 'em up. Inyala Hill bearing green one-oh, speed fifteen," he mimicked a destroyer man. "Enemy in close range. Bearing all round the bloody compass. Director-layer sees the target—and how!"

Etosha was picking up speed rapidly. As her head steadied on the bearing it seemed sheer suicide to be taking her in at speed. Suicide anyway, with a few feet of water under her keel, water which might start breaking at any moment.

"Get the crew on deck," I told the Kroo boy. "Get their lifejackets on, and your own too. If she strikes, it's every man for himself. Make it snappy!"

"John," I said as Jim made his way aft, never taking his eyes from the deadly shore. "You and I are the only two who know our position. For all the crew knows, we're any-where at all." I took my eyes from the shore and gazed at him levelly. "No one is ever to know about this little picnic.

We've never been away from the fishing grounds, do you understand? I want your word on that."

"You have it," he replied. "But the crew will talk."

"What they saw was a submarine eruption which they imagined was the shore—that's the explanation you'll give. Your charts, not those you saw of mine, will show our position at sea—and nowhere near this coast. Is that clear?"

"No need to come the heavy skipper with me," he grinned. "Just as you say."

I knew that *Etosha* was fast, but I did not realise that her slim lines underwater and the fine engines would give her such pace. The coast was tearing towards her bows. Diaz's Thumb looked a biscuit toss away. Beyond, the sea smoked evilly and the angle of the turn looked impossibly acute. I began to have grave doubts whether we would make it.

The air was humid and the islets in their birth-throes gave off a peculiar smell, for all the world like newly-sawn stinkwood—a fetid, half sickly-sweet, semi-acrid pungency, combined with the warm odours of superheated steam.

John stood impassive.

"The scientists say this is the oldest coast in the world," I said slowly. "They say it was here that earth first emerged from chaos. Maybe life also emerged first, here, too. We're probably seeing the same thing before our eyes now as happened on the first day of Creation. . . ."

He took up the speaking-tube. There was a curious exaltation about his voice.

"What is she doing, Mac?" he asked.

The voice came indistinctly back, but John gave a low whistle. "Nearly nineteen," he said. "She's splendid. But if she so much as touches anything now——"

"Get a lifebelt on," I said tersely.

"No time now," he said. "I want to watch the last act."

The water creamed under *Etosha's* forefoot. Diaz's Thumb was now so close that one could see its smooth, wicked fang sticking up a hundred yards away on the port bow. If I could feel any kind of relief, it was that *Etosha* was now—by no doing of mine—north of the dreaded shoal, although still on the shoreward side of it. She'd run through the vital gateway by the grace of God. I gave the wheel a spoke or two and she leaned over slightly towards the rock. Fifty yards now. The crew stood below me on the deck, some cowering beneath the bridge overhang. The ship roared on like an express train. Then suddenly one of them gave a wild shout—it might have been the leadsman—clambered over the bulwarks and jumped into the sea, swimming strongly towards the jagged pinnacle.

John snatched at a lifebelt.

"No," I snapped. "Don't throw it. Let him go. He's finished anyway. You'll only prolong his agony with that. The first surf will smash him to pieces."

John obeyed, but his hand was shaking. One of the crew shouted something obscene at the bridge, but it was drowned in the crash of the bows through the water.

Twenty yards now.

"Take a grip of something," I said quietly. "Here we go."

I spun the wheel hard to port. At the same time I ordered the port screw to "full astern."

At that moment the wave hit us.

Generated by the great south-west winds which strike at gale force out of a sky so clear it might be yachting weather, the sea in these parts works itself up to a demoniacal fury within a space of minutes. This was the wind and the sea which I had dreaded as I put Etosha at full speed across the open stretch of water in the hope that she might get clear before anything struck. The giant wave carried with it not only the elemental force of the sudden gale, but also the punch of the submarine eruptions. No one had seen it towering up astern as we raced towards the Thumb. I caught sight of the massive chocolate-coloured wall, freckled here and there with the white belly of a dolphin or shark killed in the eruptions, and towering above it all a cream-and-dun crest of breaking water. The port screw had begun to bite and the rudder too as the great mountain of sea struck aft the bridge structure.

I felt Etosha's stern cant and sink under the shock of tons of water and the action of the port screw. There was a great rending sound of metal and wood. The transom felt as if it had been mule-kicked. I started to shout to John, but heard no words above the gigantic clangour. I rang the telegraph to

" full ahead." Out of the corner of my eye I saw John snatch an axe and dart aft. The sea poured in over the bridge rails. The stern canted over more steeply.

It is in moments like this that the sailor feels his *rapprochement* with his craft. The mould of iron, the grain of wood, takes on life as the sea seeks to wrest from it the stuff of its being which man has fashioned. The sea on its remorseless anvil seeks to redesign. The sailor, and the sailor only, is the witness of that elemental forging, the fight for a new pattern. The man of the sea expresses it simply : " She was like a thing alive." The whip of strained steel, the near-breaking strain of rope and recalcitrant wood challenge the sea. It is a titan's battle. In those moments a man's love of his ship is born and he hears with pain the rendings of that dreadful accouchement.

A brief glimpse showed me the aftermast canted over and buckled about five feet above the deck. John, up to the chest in water, was hacking at the wire and rigging screws which, fortunately, were secured on the bridge abaft the funnel. The stern tilted, but it seemed to have more life in it. Above the din I heard the thuds of the axe. If only the stays would part! The mast would then go overboard and she might right herself. From the foredeck came screams and shouts from the crew. The axe thudded. With a twang like a huge banjo-string the last of the stays parted. It was followed by a rending, tearing, sickening noise which seemed as if half her stern had gone with the mast. Through my hands on the spoke I felt the slight lightening of *Etosha's* burden of death and then a living movement as the powerful screws thrust. The bow was angled high and the list seemed beyond human power to right. A second later, by the great power of the diesels, I felt she might live if she could only shake herself free. I knew then how my great-grandfather had felt—the story had come down to me as a boy—when the fine-lined clipper he was driving round the Cape of Storms under a great press of sail put her yacht-like counter under the wild seas and he alone had saved her as the water towered over her mizzen chains by cutting adrift the halliards and rigging with his own hands.

Like a cork out of a bottle, *Etosha* leapt free, shedding astern the debris of the mast, stays, boats and stern fittings. Sea and spray cleared. But we had not escaped. Dead ahead, not more than fifty yards, lay a smoking, new-born islet. Beyond was the open sea. The waves out there were white-crested, and, dear God! under them was deep water. A welter of white broke over the shoal—astern. No power could save *Etosha* now. Her gallant fight for life with the huge wave had not saved her. But as the sickening realisation hit me, I saw in a flash that the smoking islet, steam-crested, was not the one I had originally noted when *Etosha* made her great bid for safety. It was new, reared in the few minutes of our travail. As far as the eye could see to starboard now *Etosha* was hemmed in, cut off from the sea by the advancing, inexorable, ever-growing number of islets. The coast had laid a deadly trap.

Etosha checked and I was thrown forward against the wheel and fetid heat rose about me. I waited for the strike which would rip her plating like calico. But it did not come. She lurched slowly ahead, losing speed. Strangely-coloured flames rose and I saw the paint blister. Another lurch—she was cutting through the soft, red-hot mud, as yet unhardened in the sea! Through the steam, a ship's length away lay open water. She slowed more and struggled tiredly. The heat and the steam nearly suffocated me. I saw a wave sweeping in from seawards. *Etosha* was almost at a standstill. Then her bows lifted under the sea. The screws screamed as they rose out of the viscous, turgid mud and bit into water—blessed, salt seawater. She surged clear of the nauseating embrace towards the open sea.

Automatically I rang the telegraph—" Half ahead."

Etosha made her way west—to safety.

John joined me at the wheel, grinning, axe in hand.

" Fried fish for dinner," he said laconically.

" We'll have to open up the hatches and see how much is spoiled," I replied. " But I intend to get clear of this bloody part of the world first."

" She was magnificent," said John warmly.

" Much damage astern?" I asked.

" A complete shambles. The mast and boats are gone and the davits are as curly as a Hottentot's topknot."

" Where's Jim?" I asked. " Take the wheel a moment while I see how the crew's fared."

John's face clouded. "Crew!" he sniffed. "Bloody lot of frightened savages. Do you think one of them stirred a hand to help me? They hung on to anything they could find and prayed for their souls—if they have such a thing."

I looked over the bridge. Even where the force of the huge wave had been slightest, the damage was frightening. The wheel valves on the two winches under the bridge were awry, gear was swept in a wild tangle to starboard and lay in the scuppers in confusion; the crew, with fear in their faces, still clung to their handholds. Paint had been stripped as if with a blowlamp. Curled fragments clung to the blackened bulwarks.

"Helmsman!" I roared. The Kroo boy detached himself and came slowly along the deck. "God's truth!" I shouted. "This isn't an old men's home! Shake a leg!"

He came on to the bridge, sullen and frightened.

"Course south by west," I snapped.

The wheel swung over and the ragged welt of the coast, steaming, turbulent, half mist-shrouded, came into view.

John looked at it ruminatively.

"First round to us—over the Skeleton Coast!" he muttered.

TWO

Rays and Beetles

I BROUGHT the *Etosha* into Walvis Bay towards sunset. John was with me on the bridge. As Pelican Point, a narrow peninsula which juts into the sea at the harbour mouth, came clearly to view about five miles to the southward, the moderate wind to seaward suddenly switched northerly and the uneasy lop of the waves from the south-west indicated that we were in for a couple of days of the great rollers which crash so mercilessly on the coast after a northerly blow, more so at this late autumn season than during the summer.

Etosha eased towards the harbour mouth at seven knots. "If she'd been a sailer, we'd be all aback now," John remarked. His lips were cracked from the wind, and the top of his thick woollen polo-necked jersey was stained with salt and paint. He was tired, too, after the excitement of the dawn. He had been on his feet solidly since.

"I've got some old sailing directions below," I remarked. "It would drive me round the bend bringing a schooner, even under snug sail, up to an anchorage like this."

The wind off the land, blowing powerfully across the direction of the northerly wind outside the harbour, threw up a short, nasty sea.

"Starboard fifteen," I told the Kroo boy at the wheel. "Slow ahead," I rang.

The sun, endowed by the great surge of volcanic dust thrown up by the eruptions, was making a great show of going down. Sunsets are always spectacular on the Skeleton Coast, but this one was out-vying them. Gold spears stabbed heavenwards like molten searchlights, refracted and diffused by the volcanic dust over the sea and the fine particles of sand whipping in from the desert which backs the port.

As *Etosha* edged in towards her buoy, I laid her length parallel with the sandy peninsula.

John laughed. "Not forgotten the tricks of the trade, eh? Put her against the sunset with a spit of land behind and what do our nosey-parkers see from the shore of damage? Nothing. Only blackness. I suppose it's in the blood, Geoffrey—you might as well ask a wolf not to stalk a caribou as expect a submariner not to hide himself!"

I joined in the laugh, although a little cautiously. I was not sure how much the Kroo boy understood of what we were saying.

"You've done such a damn fine job that it's scarcely necessary to conceal the damage," I said.

He nodded. "With a more responsive crew, I'd have had her more shipshape still," he remarked. "We certainly scared the pants off this lot to-day."

John had done wonders. Apart from the missing boats, twisted davits and the mast aft, even the idlers hanging around the quayside (they never seemed to disperse) would not have noticed much amiss. The paintwork had been restored where the blistering eruption had stripped it off her plates like a blow-lamp, although there were still obvious signs on the deck of her ordeal—the twisted winches and bent bulwarks. Nevertheless, I could take her to sea any time. Mac had not reported from the engine room, but I knew he would be along once we had secured. In addition to the repairs, we had heaved about ten tons of fish overboard which had been spoilt by the heat of the eruption.

I brought *Etosha* up to her moorings, which lay well away from most of the other fishing boats anyway, most of them local wooden sail-and-engine craft which (to my mind) have none of the seaworthiness or grace of those fine cutters one finds off the Norwegian coast or on the Icelandic grounds.

The angry sun transformed the harbour, even the ugly Cold Storage works with its tall chimneys and fortress-like structure, to a world of golds, blues, ambers and blacks. The quick late autumn night was falling when we cleared away the crew for the night—I did not allow them to sleep aboard, which they resented, but it was a point on which I was adamant.

John, Mac and I had the *Etosha* to ourselves.

" Come in, Mac," I called from my sea-cabin where John was having a drink with me later.

" Scotch?" I asked.

" Aye," he replied in his dour way. " No water."

" Anything left of your engines after this morning?" asked John.

" Bluidy little," he growled. He turned from the painting of a full-rigged ship which he was contemplating above my desk. Although I had known Mac for more than fifteen years, I still felt a little chilled at his eyes, like a line of surf under the Northern Lights, coupled with his morose dourness.

" Some day," he said angrily, " ye'll go too far, skipper, and you won't have me to haul you out of the muck." He smiled grimly at his inner knowledge. " The luck's been with you, so far, laddie. It damn near wasn't to-day."

I refilled his glass. For Mac to utter more than half a dozen words a day was surprising. This sounded almost like an un-burdening. I poured the Haig slowly and thought, he does know too much. What do I know about him? Precious little. And yet everything a man can learn from another from being in tight corners together and carrying out deeds beyond the arm of the law. Did the same rules apply in the Glasgow gutter where Mac had been born? Was our alliance one of expediency or one of loyalty, the gamin's loyalty to the gang, so long as the leader paid off? Certainly, Mac knew too much.

Mac took the straight drink without a word. "Bit of strain in the shaft, I think, but nothing t' worry about."

"That means that the whole damn thing's as sweet as a nut," laughed John. "What was it like down in your stoke-hole when we staggered through that bit of flame, Mac?"

"Like someone had put a blow-lamp under my backside," he said shortly.

"Everything will be all right for getting out on to the fishing grounds in the morning?" I asked him.

He treated me to one of his hard stares. "Aye," he said slowly, spinning the amber liquid round and round in the glass, obscuring the deep oil stains on the capable fingers. "Where were we this morning, laddie? Anywhere near the old place?"

Blast, Mac, I thought. I had enough on my hands without his raking up what was dead. Certainly he knew a lot too much. I played for time.

"Another drink, John?"

A heavy knock at the door saved my answering.

I opened it. There stood a policeman.

He spoke in Afrikaans. "Which of you is Captain Mac-donald?"

"I am," I replied in the same language. "Come in."

"Venter," he said, introducing himself in the German way. "Sergeant."

Still speaking in Afrikaans, I said : "This is my first mate, Mister John Garland, and my engineer, Mister Macfadden." He shook hands formally.

"Neither of them speak Afrikaans," I said to relieve the uneasy air in the cabin. "Shall we speak English?"

Now was the time for my act, carried out whenever I came to port. I dropped into English with a South African accent, that clipped, staccato form of English which shortens its vowels and studs its sentences with the word "man." They say the first word you hear on arriving in Cape Town from

overseas is the typical "man." Ask a South African to say
"castle" and listen to the value he gives the "a" and you'll
recognise him anywhere. It has none of the twang of Australia,
but has an individuality all its own.

"Have a drink, Sarge?" I said with forced heartiness.
"Whisky, or the real stuff?"

I pulled out a bottle of well-matured Cape brandy.

Venter gazed at the label in admiration. "Jesus!" he said
with a wink. "You sea b——s certainly get the mother's milk.
A nice little *sopie* of that, and you can't say I'm sucking on the
hind tit."

I caught John's amazed eye at this little introduction and
nearly burst out laughing. Mac gazed at him with the sort of
expression I should imagine he reserved for delinquent pieces
of machinery.

Venter took a big swallow, tossed his helmet on the table
and sank with a big sigh into my chair.

"Man, captain," he said. "They sent me to ask about this
bastard of your crew who got drowned."

I glanced swiftly across at John, for I had told him earlier
that I had sent a note with the Kroo helmsman to the police
advising them officially that I'd lost a man overboard.

"I'll get the charts," said John.

"I'll show you the exact place where we lost him. It was
during a volcanic eruption, you know."

"Have your drink first," said the sergeant. "No hurry.
This is bladdy good brandy. A non-European, wasn't he?"

"Yes," I said. "I was making a run at speed to get clear of
a couple of volcanic islands, and the fellow—his name was
Shilling—jumped overboard and swam for a rock which was
sticking out of the sea. I never saw him again."

"Silly bastard," replied Venter expansively. "What did he
want to go and do that for? Not a solitary clue, I'd say."

"There was no chance to go back for him," I added. "I
was moving at full speed and almost at the same moment we
were hit by a big wave."

"Ag, man, the docks are full of unskilled hands—you'll
find another boy quite easily," commented Venter.

"Another brandy," I suggested.

"It's good stuff," approved Venter.

John slipped out and returned with the chart. He had found time even to complete the duplicate. There were the neat crosses and position of the chain of islands, about 150 miles from where we really had been. It would be safe enough, for islands on this coast simply appear one day and disappear the next. No one could dispute it.

"Our position was about twenty degrees fifty minutes South——" he began in a formal voice which took me back to Royal Navy courts-martial.

"Jesus!" exclaimed Venter: "I don't understand that sort of thing. I wouldn't know how even to write it down. Tell me something simple, just for the report."

"Won't there be an inquest?" I asked tentatively.

"Nothing more than just a formality," said Venter. "No, man, just tell me where it was and I'll write it down for the major. That's about all. Bit of a waste of time, I'd say, but there it is."

John looked relieved. I don't think he liked the job of explaining faked charts.

"I should say it was about 150 miles N.N.W. of Walvis Bay. He went overboard sowewhere about six o'clock."

Venter slopped some brandy on to his notebook. He raised it to his mouth and gave it a neat lick, and then went on writing. Mac regarded him with distaste. He laboriously wrote down a few details of the affair. Well, there shouldn't be any questions about where we were to judge from the policeman's attitude.

"Captain Macdonald—what is the *voornaam*—first name?"

"Geoffrey," I replied.

He wrote it down "Jeffrie". That wouldn't do any harm either.

"South African?" he said.

I dropped into Afrikaans with a *bonhomie* which sounded as false as a sham beard to me, but it didn't worry Venter.

"Man, have you ever heard a *rooinek* speak Afrikaans like I do? I was born in the Free State."

"Ag, here," he replied matily. "I'm a Transvaaler. Ventersdorp."

"Parys," I replied cheerily, thinking of the little resort which clings to the banks of the Vaal River with one foot in the veld of the Northern Free State, and the other in the Vaal River.

"This calls for a drink," he said without a blush.

I filled up his glass.

"*Gesondheid!* (good health)," he said. "Man, I'd like to stay and have a party with you boys, but I've got to get back to the station."

Mac breathed a visible sigh of relief. He took his helmet. "Cheerio, heh!" he said. "*Tot siens*, you chaps."

I saw him over the rail.

John was convulsed when I returned.

"How to win friends and influence people!" he laughed. "Well, well, well. He couldn't have cared less, could he?"

"And not a bad thing either," I replied.

"It's a nice little chart you have there," said Mac ironically. "Hundreds of miles out to sea, and nothing to prove it to the contrary. What if they ask the other members of the crew?"

"They won't," I replied. "They could swear blind that they'd seen dry land, but John and I could prove beyond any doubt that they were talking nonsense."

"Aye," said Mac slowly, "You'd prove it to me, too. But just for interest's sake, seeing I saw it with my own eyes, where were we?"

"Off the Skeleton Coast," I said looking into his cold eyes, now a little shaded with the whisky he had drunk. "The Skeleton Coast, Mac."

"Aye," he said. "That was all I was wanting to know."

We all felt the jar as the boat, inexpertly handled, bumped against the *Etosha's* side. In the silence, the unease which had been with me in the morning returned. Who was this now? Was there some further shadow looming? I felt sure it was not the police. Some aftermath of Mac's words remained, the meaningful "aye." He might well brood over the Skeleton Coast. As I might.

Heavy feet clumped on the deck. The three of us stood silent, drinks in hand, waiting for the unknown visitor. The imponderable sense of tension running like a tideway under our lives, made us view the newcomer, whoever he was, as an intruder. We followed the progress of the feet down the companionway; they hesitated for a moment, and then chose the cabin door. Without waiting for the knock, I pulled it open swiftly.

Our preoccupation with the coming of the unknown man to the *Etosha* at night, the sense of indefinable tension which his presence engendered throughout the later tumultuous events, were characteristic of all I ever knew about the tall, slightly bent figure which blinked in the light as I pulled open the door. As a figure, he would have passed anywhere without comment, for his sand-coloured hair had receded slightly from the temples and his grey eyes were those of a thousand other respectable citizens. But it was the strong, cruel gash of the face below the bridge of the nose and his quiet, mirthless chuckle which ever afterwards never ceased to frighten me. I still wake at night sweating when I think of that chuckle as he emerged to kill me on the mountain.

"Captain Macdonald?" he asked with a slightly German accent.

"Yes," I said curtly. I have never approved of sudden incursions into my privacy. That privacy was to be respected, as the crew knew.

He stood a moment in his cheap tweeds as his eyes flickered beyond me, a quick, appraising glance.

"Stein," he said holding out a hand. "Dr. Albert Stein. Not 'Stain' if you please, but 'Stine'."

I didn't ask him in. If he'd come about to-day's business up the coast, he'd go away quicker than he came. I didn't speak.

"May I come in?" The eyes were friendly, but the jaw looked like one of those strange creatures the net brings up out of the depths, snapping at the steel gaff to its last expiring breath.

I stood aside, my ungraciousness apparent.

He looked at John and Mac.

"I haven't also had the pleasure . . ."

"My mate and engineer," I said briefly.

For some reason he held out his hand to Mac. "This is a very fine ship," he murmured. "You must be proud to be the engineer. Fine big engines, eh?"

Mac ignored the outstretched hand. I blessed him for his taciturnity.

" Engines from the Humber," he said. " Would have been better from the Clyde."

" Ah, the pride of the Scot," said Stein amiably. " Two Scots and one Englishman on such a fine little ship."

" I am a South African," I said, underlining it with a heavy accent.

" But the mate is English, yes? And the ship too? Fine, fast ships the English build."

He nodded to the three of us, but his eyes searched the cabin.

" Can I do something for you, Doctor Stein?" I asked coldly. " You haven't rowed yourself out all this way just to admire my ship. Otherwise . . ." I waved a hand vaguely towards the companionway.

" Ah but yes," he cried. " It is about business that I wish to talk."

We remained on our feet.

" If it's a matter of business," I began. " We can discuss it ashore some other time. I sell my fish on a contract basis."

" I am a scientist, not a fishmonger," he smiled and I liked his smile less than a sting ray. " I wish to discuss with you a matter of catching beetles."

Stein certainly didn't look like a crazy beetle hunter, however odd his words sounded.

" The matter of beetle-catching I wish to discuss is private," he said, looking pointedly at John and Mac.

" These men are also my close friends. You may say anything you wish in front of them."

" What a happy little ship," he said encouragingly. " Well, I wish you to take me on a short trip so that I can catch beetles."

John joined in and he laughed grimly. " You don't catch beetles out in the Atlantic, Dr. Stein," he said. " We may catch a lot else, but not beetles."

Stein grinned in his mirthless way.

" Yes, I know," he went on, as if speaking to a child. " But I wish to take your ship and go up the coast to find beetles, or rather, one particular beetle."

I shrugged. I wasn't having Stein, or anyone else, trippering up and down the coast in *Etosha*.

" It's worth a lot of money to you," he said. " Five hundred pounds."

" Where to?" I pressed him.

He hedged. " When I wish to find my beetle, I go to people who know about ships, and I ask, which is the finest ship sailing out of Walvis Bay? They tell me, the *Etosha*. But that is not all I want. The *Etosha* might be the best ship, but it is the skipper who really matters. And who, I ask, knows these waters best of all the fishing skippers? Macdonald of the *Etosha*, they tell me. And here I am. Five hundred pounds for my passage."

I was more amused at the offer than anything. " Where do you expect to go for £500—to South America?"

" No," he said crisply. " I want you to put me ashore on the Skeleton Coast."

I burst out laughing.

" Good God, man, you can't be serious," I exclaimed. " Every policeman knows where every ship goes from this port. I'd only have to tell them what you've said—in front of witnesses—and they'd watch you like a hawk."

" I don't think you'd do that," he said evenly.

" Why not?" I asked.

He looked at me searchingly, and his reply was long in coming.

" I don't quite know," he said, " but I think I am right in saying you won't spread this around. Why? I base my ideas on what I see. I see a fine ship with lovely lines, when big holds are what make a ship pay. Everyone says the *Etosha* must be fast, and yet no one has ever seen her making much above twelve knots. I drop a question to the engineer, and he closes up like a clam, instead of displaying a warm admiration for his engines." He swung suddenly at me. " I hear you lost a man overboard to-day."

I was rapidly losing my temper.

" Yes," I snapped. " And there'll be another one over the side very soon now. Damn you and your impertinence, Stein. Get out!"

He continued to look at me coolly. " My mind is made to inquire and search out the truths of things in nature," he said in a pompous Teutonic way. " If *Etosha* were a beetle, I'd say she was a throwback from her species. But gentlemen, I waste your time. You will not reconsider?"

"No," I snapped.

"Ah well," he smiled while his jaw remained cruel. "Ah well." He turned and went.

The unpleasant taste left in our mouths by Stein's visit was to worsen a day or two later on the fishing grounds into something more sinister, almost a sailor's superstition that he was a harbinger of evil, through a strange incident. I took *Etosha* out into deep water at the spot where I judged the plankton, which comes up in the cold currents from the Antarctic, would be when it meets the warmer seas of the tropics. Judging the right place—in that wilderness of waters—is the measure of a skipper's success as a trawlerman, and it may mean everything between prosperity and adversity. Skippers have their favourite (and jealously guarded) secrets of wind and weather which will bring the fish. One I know worked out his bearings on the fishing grounds by a thermometer trailed in the water astern, at a depth of four fathoms. He claimed it worked, and his holds were certainly never empty.

I had tried in vain to replace the boats smashed in the eruption, but had had to be content with a double-ended substitute which turned out to be a surf-boat. It was certainly quite appropriate to its work in breakers, but not much good for the open sea. The lack of boats was to play a big role in the events which later took their toll of lives.

The net had been out since dawn and *Etosha* was patrolling the great open South Atlantic with the leisurely gait of a policeman on beat. It was about two bells in the first dog watch. And a policeman would not have seen anything to disturb his thoughts in the calm, easy swell, with the sun dropping towards St. Helena far in the west. We'd had a fair haul of pilchard, stockfish and maasbanker, but not what I was hoping for when we met that elusive marriage-point of plankton and tropic waters.

"All aboard for the yachting trip,' said John lazily, yawning and stretching himself on the bridge-rail. He swept the horizon with his eyes. "Not a damn thing in sight—' all alone in a wide, wide sea!'"

The immensity and stillness of the coming evening had put

all thoughts of Stein away and I would not have wished anything but the present idyll of sea and sky merging, somewhere in the east, into Africa.

" I think we must be a little too far south," I murmured. " The water's probably a bit cold for the fish."

" Lucky little planktons," grinned John. " Nothing to darken the shadow of their one-cell lives. Oh happy, happy plankton! Why not try the thermometer trick?"

" To hell with that," I said, falling into his easy mood. " Why don't we pour some whisky over the stern and make them all drunk, and then we can be sure of catching the drunken fish at the end of the bender."

The helmsman eyed me quizzically, not knowing whether this was the white man's humour or not.

" At this rate we'll be out here for a week," replied John. " Hallo, a stranger coming into the nest."

I followed his pointing finger, but it was a minute or so before I saw the flash of white in the south-west. I think the habit of vigilant, never-ceasing watchfulness, the hall-mark of the submariner, had become an unconscious part of John's life. The sea—it always is the enemy.

I reached for my binoculars and focused them on the white triangle rising above the sea.

" Pirates in these waters," I remarked, still in the easy mood of the last hour of daylight. " A windjammer. Stand by to repel boarders."

John watched the sail rising quickly.

" She's crackin' it on, all right," he said, " and I'll eat my boots if she isn't that old Grand Banks schooner from Luderitz."

I kept my glasses on her.

" She's got a wind that we haven't," I said.

I saw the gleam of flying jib narrow, the sun catching it with a yellowing shaft.

" She's altering course towards us," I observed. " She was lying a couple of points nearer north a moment ago."

" I'd have loved to have seen her in her heyday and not under Hendriks," said John watching the lovely sight of a sailing-ship at sea under full sail. " They say, though, he's not such a bad skipper for a Coloured."

"A throwback to some of his Malay ancestors. They love the sea," I said.

The three masts of the schooner were in full view now, although her hull, dark-painted, was not clear to the eye yet.

"He'll sail the masts right out of the old *Pikkewyn* if he's not careful," said John. "I hate his guts for those jackyard topsails, though. Why couldn't he leave her clean, as she was? I never thought I'd see her under three jibs, though. That old hull must have a lot of life in it yet to stand all that sail."

I smiled at John's fastidious appreciation of sail.

The old Grand Banks schooner was a brave sight. The sails were yellow Bushman-ochre on a ground of grey, for all the world like the rock the old primitives used as their desert canvas. The slant of the sun and the distance concealed her age and neglect. She was a lovely, living thing, young and alive in her glory.

"She's coming our way—look at the bone in her teeth," cried John as a flicker of white creamed under her forefoot. "Eleven knots, if she's moving at all."

The old schooner was coming straight at us. Something in my mind sounded a note of warning—that dead straight course, the alteration when she sighted *Etosha* : but I dismissed it as fantasy.

The schooner came on and I could see her fine lines clearly. She was leaning over close-hauled, so far that the boat swinging from the davits seemed almost to skim the water spurting down her rail.

At a mile distance she made no alteration of course. *Etosha* was lying almost at a standstill.

John, too, I could see, felt a little uneasy, despite his enthusiastic comments.

"Shouldn't we get out of her way, Geoffrey?" he asked. "Steam gives way to sail, and all that."

"Give her a spoke or two," I told the man at the wheel. Then I thought of the heavy net trailing astern. "No, port fifteen," I corrected, ringing for a slight increase in speed to swing her bows away from the newcomer.

"That should clear us, all right," I said, "even if Hendriks is fool enough to come racing through the water as if we didn't exist."

"She's put her helm down," exclaimed John with a note of anxiety. "What the devil is she playing at?"

The *Pikkewyn* had allowed her head to fall off slightly and was bearing down straight at us. She was half a mile away.

"Blast!" I exclaimed. "Hard a'port," I snapped. I couldn't ring for more speed because of the heavy net holding us down. Ordinarily, nothing but a warship could have out-manœuvred *Etosha*. But now she was wallowing like a ham-strung horse.

The schooner again altered course and came roaring down upon us. I have never been at the receiving end of a torpedo, but the sight of the old ship tearing down upon me, seem-ingly hell-bent on ramming *Etosha*, gave me some idea of what it is like to see that inexorable track streaking through the water.

I snatched a megaphone. "Cast off that net," I roared, "quick, damn you! cast it off!"

John stood aghast. We were sending over the side our profits just because some damn fool Malay was showing us how he could sail a schooner.

The crew, aware of their peril, jumped to it. The thick hawsers snaked overboard with a splash—away went the catch to Davy Jones.

"Full ahead," I rang, watching the oncoming doom, travel-ling like an express train. Then I saw her lean over as she luffed slightly until her lee scuppers were under water. It was clear she did not intend to ram us. But she was coming as close as she dared. I snatched up the megaphone as she came within a biscuit's toss—it was plain she had meant to cut across our stern and foul the trawl. My anger rose as I saw what she was up to. The fool! Had that light wooden hull, even at eleven knots, fouled the heavy hawsers of the net, her bow would have swung in towards the *Etosha*, and heaven alone knows what would have happened.

I could see Hendriks near the mizzen shrouds, grinning and waving. The figure next to him was Stein.

The stream of invective which had arisen to my lips at Hendrik's deliberate act of provocation was cut short at the sight of Stein. Bracing himself against the angle of *Pikkewyn's* deck, he cupped his hands to his mouth and shouted, but the words were lost in the wind.

John turned to me furiously. " We'll have Hendriks's scalp for this Geoffrey—you can't damn well play about with ships like that. Full ahead and after him?"

" No," I rapped out, for I thought I saw part of Stein's game. " No. She's doing a good eleven knots, and it'll take everything *Etosha* has to catch up with her on that course before night. I think I see what Stein is up to. You remember how he tried to get *Etosha's* speed out of Mac? He's played a double game here—he knew we'd have to cut the trawl for fear of being rammed and then go tearing after him to ask what the hell. No. I've lost the net and my catch and I'm damned if Stein is going to find out what *Etosha* can do. We'll let him go."

The schooner was drawing away rapidly.

" But," said John vehemently, " You can't go attempting to ram another ship on the open sea——"

" He's got the perfect defence," I replied shortly. " A ship under sail has the right of way. Anything under steam must give way to it. We were under way. He was perfectly within his rights. We can't do anything about it."

" Wait till I find Hendriks alone ashore," expostulated John, " I'll teach him. . . ."

" To sail close to the wind," I remarked grimly, nodding my head after the schooner.

A shout from one of the crew, who had been busy watching the antics of the *Pikkewyn*, cut across my anger. A couple of cables' lengths away, as if brought up with the wind of the schooner, was one of the most extraordinary sights I have ever seen at sea. The sea boiled as if from a thousand torpedo-tracks, all running parallel. It foamed, it roared, it churned. Ahead, like a convoy escort, and in perfect formation of threes, a dozen or more huge rays rose, splashing back into the sea with breath-taking slaps. A school of porpoises, helplessly bewildered, were being shouldered along the surface, and my glance of amazement caught a fifteen foot shark struggling to force his way down into the seething mass carrying him along.

It was the barracouta, or snoek, as we call them. The cartoonists' butt from the hard days of food rationing merits more than the contempt poured on the snoek then. He is the finest fighter in the seas, more brutal and relentless than a shark. In these waters the snoeking season generally ends in early winter, but snoek is one of the most important catches in South Atlantic waters.

The sight was like one of those gigantic migrations of springbok in the Namaqualand desert when scores of thousands of buck, moving in gigantic phalanxes a dozen miles across, pour across the countryside, oblivious of fences, oblivious of homesteads, of guns, fire and man. They pour on and on, in countless numbers, and once they threw themselves by the thousand into the sea. Why they do it, man still has to learn.

And the barracouta were the same. As far as I could see, the water boiled with them.

"Get your lines overboard, quick." I roared at the crew. Here was the chance to fill our holds in an hour. Lines flew over the side, scarcely baited. Then the first solid phalanx roared under the ship. The helpless porpoises rolled and kicked, trying to get free of the seething mass. The barracouta ignored the lines but some, like those luckless springbok of the giant herds which impale themselves on barbed wire while the others push until the wire breaks, got caught up in the hooks. There was no catch. Again and again the lines went over the side into the apparently unending mass roaring by, but they were ignored as the huge school, intent on some hidden goal, swept by. They crashed oblivious into the ship's side. They jumped and seethed and milled, like nothing I have ever seen. I stopped the screws for fear of fouling them. Then suddenly, after about fifteen minutes, the water ceased to boil and they had passed. But not quite. Like a destroyer escort astern of a convoy, three giant rays followed.

On the bridge we were too thunderstruck to utter a word. Now the keenness of our disappointment at missing the catch of our lives emerged. It was John who put the thought into words that Stein was the hoodoo.

He jerked his head at the distant schooner.

" Stein's the Jonah," he said. " We'd have got them if he hadn't been around."

Her sails merged into the gathering night.

THREE

Four Beers for the Wrong Man

THE DUST, in suspension with hot diesel fumes from the engine, seeped steadily into the bus. The driver changed down for one of the hummocky dunes across which the road straggles out of Walvis Bay, and the jerk brought in fresh clouds. A bounce against the upholstery of the seat in front was enough to bring on its own little sand-storm, for the whole vehicle was impregnated with it, after doing this route every day for I do not know how many years. The dust in the deserts of South West Africa is laden with fine particles of mica. Normally this is a mixture to be shunned, but add to it blinding heat, sweat, discomfort and thirst, and it becomes an irritant like mild pepper. Not only the nostrils, but the eyes and the ears get choked with the fine, irritating atmos. I have heard hay-fever sufferers (and the majority of people seem to have some sort of catarrhal complaint) sneeze thirty times running. Lower down the coast, near the mouth of the Orange River, there is a settlement where ninety per cent of the wretched inhabitants have tuberculosis.

The bus, run by the railways, swung up the steep gradient and turned left on to the harder desert road. At least on the open stretches the dust would tend to be left behind in the air-stream. Walvis Bay lay on the left as we headed northwards towards Swakopmund. There were half a dozen European passengers in the forward end of the bus, and in conformity with the creed of *apartheid* on public transport, a score or so of Coloureds and natives sat behind the wire-meshed dividing grill. Whether they were dustier or more uncomfortable than the European passengers forward, it is difficult to say. But the grill was certainly not enough to make one unaware of their presence, if such was its intention, for with the dust and oil fumes were wafted in heavy, ammoniacal odours of unwashed bodies, that repellent which may be one of the deep, unconscious roots of *apartheid*. It cuts both ways, however, and a non-European will tell you that he cannot bear the stink of a white (washed) European. Livingstone was the first to find that out.

I caught a glimpse of *Etosha* at her mooring, and the thought of the sweet, clean sea-air made me regret I had not stayed with her for a day or two rather than come ashore. After Hendriks's sailing-ship had nearly cut us down, we spent another five days out on the fishing banks. The hoodoo of Stein persisted, in its effect on the catch. After five days of fruitless, temper-fretting fishing which had yielded a bare four or five tons, I put back to port.

Etosha had to be got ship-shape again, although I was a little perturbed when I found out that the two new boats which I had ordered from Cape Town would not be ready for an indefinite period. Mac wanted to iron out some infinitesimal fault in the engines and the spell in port would give him the opportunity. I felt rather like an admiral without a quarterdeck, so I decided to spend a few days ashore. I must admit that the first day was not auspicious. I started a round of golf in the morning, but in the rising wind it would have taken Bobby Locke to keep the ball in play. In disgust I gave it up. At the clubhouse I rang Mark, who kept the Bremen, a neat little hotel at Swakopmund which was almost a club to me ashore.

" Well, come up," he said. " But you know, Geoffrey, what hell Swakopmund can be when the season's finished. It's June, and there's not a soul about. None of the fine fishing and swimming which make it the Pearl of South West Africa!"

" The fewer people about the better," I said. " And as for fishing—I damn well never want to see another fish again."

Mark laughed. We got along well together.

" What about a new trip to the Brandberg some time?" he said, half-seriously. A collection of Bushman paintings was Mark's chief interest in life, apart from the superb meals he cooked with his own hands for his personal friends. The Brandberg is a great chunk of mountain between Walvis Bay

and the border of the Skeleton Coast where ancient rock paintings, said to be by Europeans of Egyptian or Mediterranean
origin, can be seen if you take the trouble to climb the craggy
heights. The main one is of a woman with red hair, known
as the "White Lady of the Brandberg." I think Mark
was one of the first people ever to see it. He had a truly
Livingstonian passion for exploration coupled with his hobby,
and we had done several trips together, first by jeep, and then
on foot through the giant sand-encrusted, rock strewn mountains to the north.

I fell for his bait. Even if one did not make the trip, half
the fun was planning it.

"I'm game," I said. "What about Oshikuku?"

"Where in hell's that—Japan?" said the voice, suddenly
becoming disembodied as (we always averred) a heavy gust of
wind struck the wires across the desert.

"Middle of swamp—north of Etosha," I yelled.

"Blast it!" replied Mark faintly. "Come up on the afternoon bus and we'll discuss it." The rest of his words
passed into oblivion. Into the sand. Always the sand. The
sand is the master of this world.

The driver changed down. A fresh spate of sand and more
hot oil fumes filled the interior of the vehicle as the force of
the wind caught up with its speed. We ground our way up to
the top of the sandhills, which lie on a level higher than the
shifting dunes lower down and must, however, be traversed
before the hard desert road is reached. I looked eagerly to the
north and north-east, hoping to catch at least a glimpse
(although they are at least twenty miles away) of either Mount
Colquhoun beyond the railway track, or its neighbour, which
stretches up a 2,000-foot thumb like a hitch-hiker thumbing his
way through eternity. The air was too full of sand—swirling,
sickening, everlasting sand—which blotted out even the road a
mile ahead.

The Brandberg and Mount Colquhoun are the pickets of a
great tumble of peaks, broken tablelands, sand-blasted
plateaux, waterless river courses and gullies untrodden by
man since the dawn of time which go to make up the Kaokoveld or, as it is more sinisterly known, the Skeleton Coast. This
territory, without a river, a well, or surface water anywhere

at all, is the size of England. It is closed to man, first, by
Government decree because it is thought it may be rich in
diamonds and a sudden access of the precious stones might
upset world market prices; and, second, more than the decree,
rigidly enforced, is the Kaokoveld's timeless, sleepless guardian
—thirst. And always at his back, death. Plenty of men have
slipped across the forbidden border—it is nowhere marked and
I suppose the nearest to a frontier in the furnace-like world is
in the south, the so-called Hoanib River. It never flows,
although in its broad bed, glistening white like Muizenberg
beach, water can be had for the digging. Elephants and antelope in its wild, untrodden places dig in the river bed and make
their own wells. Man dies before he gets there. The adven-
turers and diamond-seekers who slip away in the night are
never heard of again. Thirst and death claim them.

In its 50,000 square miles there may be one or two white
men. I suppose the little wild Bushmen and their stranger
cousins, the Strandlopers (Walkers on the Beach) do not
number more than several thousands. The Strandlopers,
whom some believe to be almost the lowest type of living man
closest to the "missing link," wander eternally by the shore,
never going far from the moving dunes whose sand rasps and
tears the skin as it blows and shifts under the great sea-
winds. They live on shellfish, dead seals and other creatures
swept up by the huge rollers. Blacker than the tan-coloured
Bushmen, the Strandloper has longer hair, matted with grease
and sand. Their stink is worse than any wild animal. The offal
of the sea they share with the lean jackals and hyenas which
scavenge the desolate seashore engaged on the same relentless,
unsatisfied quest as themselves.

The Skeleton Coast stretches from the Hoanib River in the
south to the Cunene River in the north, the international
boundary between South West Africa and Portuguese Angola.
The territory is about 150 miles long and, at its broadest,
opposite Cape Frio, about the same distance across, although
the width is not maintained, particularly in the south. From
the seaward side it looks like a huge cheetah's head, which
faces south-east into the great sandy tracts which stretch
towards the Kalahari Desert. For fifty miles from the mouth
of the Cunene, it gapes like a shark's mouth, the wicked fangs

jutting into the sea round Cape Frio and running backwards into a savage orifice of mountains which turn the north-eastern shores into a brutal amphitheatre of jagged rock, entered (if that were possible) from the seaward side by undulating, but steadily rising layers of dunes, like the velvet-soft membrane round a shark's lips, while behind them are the death-dealing fangs.

There is no port and, indeed, no seaward entrance to the Skeleton Coast, which well merits its name. The shore is littered with wrecks, from dhow to destroyer, from liner to clipper and New England whaler. The gigantic graveyard does not allow its corpses to rot. The dryness and the sand keep them indefinitely. Men, crazed by thirst, have come back to tell of old ships and treasure chests with dead men sitting round them as they have sat for centuries—but no one risks his life or his sanity to go back, even if he could go legally. Permits to enter the Kaokoveld are given but rarely, and then under very exceptional circumstances. From the sea the Kaokoveld has sealed itself by means of huge rollers and fiendish sandbars.

From the landward side it is easier. The jeep has broken part of the Kaokoveld open. There is an airstrip where a light plane may land at Ohopoho, the administrative " capital " of the Skeleton Coast, where one unfortunate white official lives. There are negotiable tracks through some of the canyons for a jeep or a truck expertly driven, but these are merely the fringes. The whole vast area is for all intents and purposes a closed book. What secrets lurk in the mountains it is impossible to say. One thing is certain, however, the easy talk that Rhodesia might build a railway to the Atlantic is so much hot air. Tiger Bay, say the Rhodesians, is their " natural " port. As a sailor it seems to me that the precarious harbour, locked in by a sandy peninsula which juts into the South Atlantic simply would not be worthwhile. Safe enough in some winds, I can think of conditions when a liner would be as safe at anchor there as running blind among the sandbars of the Skeleton Coast. Like other railways in Africa, it would cost a life a fishplate laid.

All Africa's pent-up hatred of man, of his ways, the cities he has thrown up out of steel and concrete on the veld, of his roads and railways through which her wealth and secrets have been won, stands at bay, fangs bared against the last intrusion,

here in this remote corner of the continent called the Kaokoveld. Round her skirts she has gathered the last untamed
remnants of her once countless herds of antelope, giraffe,
zebra, lion and elephant.

She stands at bay with her back to the wild sea and her face
to the impregnable mountains. Man is puny against this
concentrated might of Africa. The Matto Grosso is as well-
known as Piccadilly compared to the Kaokoveld. Only a few
of the men who dared to enter have ever lived to tell what they
saw, and that has been little enough.

The bus was running more easily now on the hard desert
road. When the winds blow, sand will cover the surface to a
depth of a couple of feet within forty-eight hours. One of the
principal expenses of roads—and railways—is the need to
keep shifting the sand away from them, season after season. It
is a stark reminder that if man's hand were taken away for only
one year, there would be few traces of his occupation left.
With the increased speed, the grains of sand spurted in the
cracks of the steel floor, but fortunately the hot diesel fumes
joined the swirling dust-cloud which marked our path towards
Swakopmund.

Upon Mark and myself the Kaokoveld exercised its lure.
Sitting in the jolting vehicle, my mind went back to the end
of the previous winter. Mark and I had wished to make a trip
northwards to the Cunene and return via the great mass of
swamps and tributary channels which flow into the great lake
of Etosha, probably the finest game reserve in the world, where
one counts the buck in herds of thousands. There the elephants, homeward-bound across the sand-dunes, link trunk to
tail in a " train " which may be a furlong long!

A peremptory official " no " cut across our plans; such was
the suspicion of officials that we even wanted to go to the
Kaokoveld for no well-defined purpose, that we decided it was
useless to try and press it. Instead, we took Mark's Land
Rover and made for a great tableland of unexplored mountains
and peaks along the southern border. It was from a peak
5,000 feet above the Hoanib River that I first saw the wild
tangle of mountains and gullys, shimmering, reflecting, changing colours, like chameleons in the mica-ridden air. The
isolated peak, which had taken us from early till mid-morning

to climb, jutted up on a high peninsula which stood out towards the " river " on its southern side. Using my powerful naval binoculars I could see the green of the tiny settlement of Zessfontein fifteen miles away on my right; on my left the air was clear and one could almost detect the clean sparkle of the sea—a glimmer of white moving, changing, reflecting, seemed to be the remorseless surf shattering itself against the coast, with the whole force of the South Atlantic behind it. Far away below on my left a ragged herring-bone pattern of gullies marking its backbone into the mountains, I could see the " river," the dry sand merely being whiter and more defined than the surrounding dun to which the eyes were accustomed. A 4,000 foot cliff beyond, we had decided were the Geinas mountains, but it was impossible to fix them for the Kaokoveld has never been surveyed.

" Moses viewing the promised land," remarked Mark.

" Like hell! " I replied. " Why would anyone want to go there?"

" For Mallory's reason—' because it is there '," replied Mark.

He scanned the forbidden land with his own glasses.

" Why shouldn't we go on?" he said impetuously. " No one would know. We've both wanted to—look at it!" he cried with a wide sweep of his arm.

" Let's call this a reconnaissance in force," I said, for I had no wish to get tied up with the authorities. " We'll get there —one day."

We had left it at that. Trips with Mark were a joy. As the bus bucketed on, I wondered if he had a new one in mind. We would plan weeks ahead, whenever I brought *Etosha* to port. Mark was a fine climber and an ardent lover of exploring unknown ranges and tracts of country " just because they are there " as the famous Everest climber said. Without his Land Rover, however, it would have been suicide to try. Fitted with twelve forward gears and a Rolls-Royce engine, it was a superb vehicle for the untracked wilderness. The low gearing and four-wheel drive made it ideal for the shifting sand-dunes, where any other type of vehicle, even a more conventional jeep, would have stuck. We would load under the canvas hood food,

guns, tents, lamps, camp beds and the like; water was carried
in special jerry-cans fixed in steel brackets welded to the side;
when it was all packed and lashed down under the canvas
against the sand Jannie, the cross-bred Ridgeback, would leap
on top and we would disappear for weeks at a time. The Land
Rover had a car compass fitted, but Mark was delighted when
I brought a sextant and a boat's compass, for navigation in the
sand is not unlike finding one's way on the open sea. The only
sort of maps of the area are aeronautical, but the scale is small,
and they are full of inaccuracies.

To a sailor it was the incredible silences of dusk and evening which were even more remarkable than the age-old,
saurian-like rocks, fretted by sand and wind until many of the
softer ones eroded like palms bent in a Pacific wind. The
Land Rover would almost merge into the blackness beside
the tiny flicker of fire which elevated us above the wild animals;
the stars looked larger than at sea because of the refraction of
the dust; there might be an occasional, disembodied howl from
some mysterious marauder of the sands which never showed
itself by day, like the black hyena; at the end of a long day's run
gin never tasted as fine as it joined in the great conspiracy of
soothing, selfless silence.

The bus changed gears again, bringing more choking sand
into the interior. Swakopmund lay ahead. In the late autumn
twilight it looked dreary in the extreme, drearier than Mark's
comment that it was dull now the season had ended would have
led me to believe. The cluster of unattractive houses, hanging
perilously between the desert and the sea, seemed lifeless and
neglected. The sea beyond, grey and glassy, held the menace of
a north-west gale which would send every skipper into the
nearest harbour post-haste.

The bus ground to a standstill at the terminus. Stiff and
dusty, I got down. It was only a minute's walk to Mark's place.
As I stepped down my growing sense of frustration and irrita-
tion suddenly blazed. For there stood Hendriks, the coloured
skipper, on the sandy pavement, grinning impertinently at me.
I paused and gazed levelly at the taunting grin.

" *Henriks*," I said slowly in Afrikaans, " *Jou verdomde halfnaatjie*." (" Hendriks, you damned half-caste.") In these parts

the word " *halfnaatjie* " embodies all the white man's revulsion for the half-caste; bastard is a neutral, unbelligerent term by comparison.

Hendriks's grin changed to a snarl. In a flash he came at me at a shambling run. Caution, caution bred of long dealings with his kind, tore my eyes from his face to the hand which flashed into his belt. The knife was raised and plunged at the moment the danger telegraphed itself to my mind. I stepped forward a pace and caught the upraised wrist with my left hand and, in the same movement, slipped my right arm under Hendriks's armpit. Our bodies clashed and the harsh, ammoniacal smell of the coloured man's body made me feel sick. My right arm curled round and gripped my own wrist and locked the plunging downstroke. For a moment I thought the impetus of the stroke would tear his hand free, but the wicked South American grip held. I could feel his arm taut as a steel bar; slowly I applied the savage pressure which gives the grip its notoriety among the back streets of Montevideo and Buenos Aires.

Someone in the throng of passengers shouted hoarsely, but the duel between Hendriks and myself was silent. My wristlock tightened and I saw the sweat and fear start out in his face. The savage beauty of the grip is that a man cannot use his left hand either. Ruthlessly I threw in all the strength I had. I heard the muscles of his shoulder start to tear. I gave a final twist and his shoulder gave, just as one rips the leg off a Christmas turkey. Hendriks never uttered a sound, but hung from his shoulder in my grip in a dead faint. I slipped free and he fell, an untidy bundle of rags, at my feet. I kicked the knife away.

When I looked up Mark was standing there, his face white with concern.

" Good God, Geoffrey," he burst out. " He would have killed you!"

" Not a man who can look after himself like that," grinned a husky Afrikaaner farmer who had been on the bus. " Man, I'll give you fifty pounds to teach me that grip."

I felt sick and angry with myself when I saw the pathetic bundle of rags on the pavement.

" Get a doctor," I said harshly. " Tell him he'll find the

shoulder muscles torn and ligaments probably damaged. Send me the bill."

"Nonsense," said the farmer, "If a man pulls a knife, he's got all that's coming to him."

My revulsion welled up and I turned upon the farmer. But I checked myself.

"Mark," I said, "let's get out of here. I need a drink and a bath."

A voice stopped me as we turned away.

"Captain Macdonald," it said smoothly. "As well as congratulating you on your sailoring, may I add that a hold like that is the acquisition of a very determined—or a very desperate man."

It was Stein. The ugly jaw was smiling. For a moment I felt like putting the hold on him.

"At least," I rejoined as calmly as I could, "it will prevent your friend for a while from taking you for joy-rides out to sea to smash up my trawl."

Stein continued to smile.

At the bar after a quick bath, Mark having brought me a siff whisky-and-soda, I could not shake off the sense of foreboding and depression which the unpleasant incident of Hendricks had occasioned. I felt no qualms at having disabled Hendricks, although I was prepared to admit that I had been more savage than I need have been. Still. . . . there was Stein. Subconsciously I felt that it was he who was behind something that I could not fathom. No, he could not have known about me, it was all too long ago. Had he penetrated my façade, I would have seen it when he first came to the ship. How could he suspect anything? But, the thought followed quickly, who is Stein anyway? He might be anything from an insurance broker to a civil servant. That cruel mouth was the clue. I really couldn't imagine Stein docilely sitting behind a desk in the South West African Administration.

My eyes roved round the bottle labels as I turned the problem over in my mind. My gaze fell upon the eel in the case between the bottles. I grinned to myself. It was Mark's boast that the old stuffed eel was the finest weather prophet on the coast. A grey metallic colour normally, Mark averred it turned a steel-blue when the winter north-westerly gales were due, and a peculiar shade of dun when the summer south-westers came. He had another gunmetal shade for fog—the joke of it was that he often seemed right. I walked over to have a closer look at the weather-eel when four Germans came in.

" *Bier*," cried one gutturally. I took him for one of the post-war newcomers. The previous German residents of the territory seem to have soaked out some of their native arrogance in the desert heat. I went behind the bar to serve them. Mark had gone off earlier to the kitchen to cook one of his superb meals. All four of the Germans looked tough, and one had a slightly vacant stare. Perhaps he was half-drunk. The others were noisy enough. One of them slapped down the money on the bar counter and they sat round a table in the far corner. I couldn't get the drift of what they were saying, but they certainly seemed to be on the way to having a night out.

" *Besatzung stillgestanden!*" roared the vacant one. The others leapt to their feet and all four stood at attention for a moment and then collapsed with laughter. " *Bier!*" shouted another. I got four bottles down from the shelf and was about to open them when a word in the rowdy conversation caught my ear—" *Der Pairskammer.*" Now " *der Pairskammer* " is as much part of the jargon of U-boat men as " uckers " is to British submariners. " The House of Lords " is the quarters of German seamen ratings in a U-boat. I looked at the four beery Germans with renewed interest. It was the vacant-looking one who had used the term. He seemed launched on a war-time reminiscence, while the other interjected, apparently pulling his leg. The vacant one, whom one of the others addressed as Johann, thumped the table and the others guffawed their disbelief. There was no one else in the bar, but the four of them were making enough noise for a whole room full. I went across with the beer.

" *Hier is jou bier*," I said in Afrikaans. As I set them down I noticed that I had forgotten to uncork one.

I pulled out an opener from my pocket. With it came something else that fell on the table in front of Johann.

He got to his feet, horror in his eyes, and started to scream —a ghastly, penetrating, maniacal scream.

Stein stood at the doorway, watching.

FOUR

" Utmost Priority "

THE TINY thing, as it lay on the beer-splashed table in front of the four Germans, was the avatar of death, destruction, shells, torpedoes, fire. It brought like a manifestation as fresh as yesterday into my memory after seventeen years the ghastly torment of war, death always at one's elbow as one lifted it— and drowned the thought in gin.

The tin contortions of the object might have been the contours of Malta's beleaguered and embattled island itself. It symbolised, since it was our emblem, the hectic and wonderful days in *H.M. Submarine Trout.* The thin high scream of the drunken German as he stood transfixed staring down at it, his three drinking-companions stunned into sober silence, called back from the past the death-whine of the Stukas as they plummetted down remorselessly on the convoys to the fortress at bay, or on the Dockyard itself.

As he screamed and screamed, a choking, sobbing gurgle started to strangle his vocal chords. His eyes were wide and staring; they had the look not only of an imbecile, but of a maniac. The gurgle might have been the sinister chuckle the torpedo gives as it leaves the tube on its death-dealing mission, followed by the long, lover-replete sigh of compressed air from its intricate mechanism.

I was transported from the pleasant Swakopmund bar whose peace was now so torn to nerve-searing hysteria by the petrified German, back again seventeen years.

War. Mediterranean. 1941.

The graticules of the periscope cleared, fogged, and then cleared again, like consciousness trying to break through a curtain of sleep. Then the tip of the attack periscope was clear of the water, and the giant Littorio class battleship lay in my vision.

"Bearing now and range?" I asked, my eyes glued to the rubber eyepiece.

"Director angle green two-oh," came the calm reply.

"Range six thousand."

A longish shot, but a battleship like that was worth any risk, particularly as the firing angle was good.

I kept my eyes riveted. I could feel the rising tension in *H.M. Submarine Trout*, although all of us were battle-hardened. For this was war, and the shallow Mediterranean had been the grave of many a fine British submarine. My orders had been explicit—and difficult. After Taranto the Italians had patched up their battle fleet, badly damaged by the daring of the Fleet Air Arm in the famous night strike against the port, and Intelligence believed that one of the least damaged, the Littorio class now running into my sights, was to undergo trials. My orders were simple : sink her on her trials. No other targets, however inviting, which might come my way. I was to patrol off Naples, round the islands of Ischia and Capri, and sink the battleship when she came out.

I smiled grimly at the casual rider which had been added to my orders : "Air and surface cover will be heavy."

Across the calm sea it proved to be all too true. The battleship, her bow-wave creamy against the blue sea, was surrounded by destroyers. I counted eight or nine, but it seemed there might be even one or two more on the far side. Four Cant flying-boats hovered protectively. They meant business. So did *H.M.S. Trout*. I had had the torpedoes set at twenty feet, so that they would pass underneath the destroyers if they were in the line of fire. John Garland was at my elbow in the control room, calm, assured, as he always was under attack.

"Take a quick look," I told him.

He bent down and when he rose his eyes were eloquent, but he said nothing. No use working up the crew unnecessarily. The battleship creamed into my sights. I touched the firing push.

"Fire one!"

The boat jumped, and there was the tell-tale pressure on the ears as the compressed air escaped and the torpedo leapt on its deadly mission.

"Down periscope."

"Fire two!"—five seconds intervals only, for the battleship was making twenty-eight knots.

"Fire three! Fire four!"

"Four torpedoes running, sir."

"Course two-seven-five. Full ahead."

Trout dived. The next fifteen minutes would tell whether we would live or not. It would also tell whether my hunch regarding the shelf off Ischia was right. The dice were cast.

I went to the chart table and called John over. I pointed to the soundings.

"We are just here," I said, almost as if he didn't know as well as I did. "If you look along here, you'll see there is a rough line of equal soundings. Over towards Ischia the land intrudes and it makes, in fact, almost a shelf. Over the shelf is another deeper patch."

John leaned over and grinned wryly: "Only 110 feet."

"It's enough," I said curtly. "If we can get *Trout* into this little hollow, those Itie destroyers will have to come mighty close to get at us. The shelf will break the force of the depth-charges, and over here"—I stabbed the chart—"there'll be such an echo back from the land that their Asdic won't pick us up. Same thing with the hydrophones. . . ."

There was a thump from outside *Trout*. Another. And another.

"Three hits, sir!" exclaimed young Peters. The tension broke. Everyone was all smiles.

"Well done, sir!" John was jubilant.

"Going up to have a look?" he inquired tentatively.

"No," I said briefly. "Unless you want us to get scuppered on the turn. I give it five minutes before the ashcans come."

Trout drove on towards her one slim chance of safety. Waiting for a depth-charge attack is probably as bad as the attack itself.

"H.E. bearing dead astern sir," came the report.

We waited for it. The destroyer was on our tail all right. I wanted those extra minutes of the submarine's speed, however. I would wait till the last minute. The crash shook us all over. Pieces of cork fell down, but the lights remained on.

"One hundred feet. Slow ahead together. Silent routine."

Now I could hear, as everyone else in the boat could, the

crash of propellers overhead. The destroyer was overshooting us, but soon the rest would be round us like flies.

I tore my thoughts away from the attack.

"No evasive action," I ordered.

That shelf and the shallow depression beyond were really my only hope. The water all round was too shallow to stave off an attack by eight or more destroyers, even given the luck. Three-quarters of a mile to relative safety. Three knots only. Only a whisper from the men. Overhead the crash of more propellers.

"Discontinue asdic bearings," I whispered.

The rating looked amazed. But my course was dead ahead. I wasn't going to try and outwit the destroyers—yet. With a little luck, they might plump for the evasive routine.

Crump! ! !

A pattern of five reverberated, slightly on the port bow. The destroyers, now between us and the hole in the sea-bed, had believed I would turn away after the first attack.

He had chosen port, but he might as easily have made it starboard. It was anyone's guess. More thrashing of propellers slightly astern, followed almost at once by a pattern of five depth charges. This one would call up his fellows to make short work of us.

Half a mile to go. I held *Trout* due east. Soon I would have to rise to eighty feet so as not to stick my nose into the shelf. Twenty precious feet—it could mean life or death.

They were really on to us now. Three patterns broke all the lights, and the deadly cold little emergency lights came on. Dust seemed to come from everywhere.

"Eighty feet," I ordered in an undertone; John passed it on.

Young Peters blinked in astonishment. I could see what was in his mind—"no use going to meet it; why not stay down here?"

I had to risk the noise of the ballast tanks blowing. As they blew a deep pattern exploded next to *Trout* but, as luck would have it, the moment we rose. At our previous depth it would have been fatal. *Trout* glided over the hummock in the sea-bed.

" Hard-a-starboard!" I said tersely. " One hundred and ten feet."

Trout settled on the sea-bed. Three more patterns of depth-charges followed, but mercifully farther away to starboard. *Trout* would have to do better than just lie in a deep declivity. I pumped more water into the starboard ballast tank and she leaned over. Ten, fifteen degrees. As close as I could judge, I laid her against the shelf in the sea-bed, tilted against it like a man cowering for dear life behind a small bank. From the ragged and distant patterns it was clear the destroyers were out of touch with us. All that remained was to stick it out and hope for the best.

For nine hours the destroyers came close, over and beyond, but they never located us. For nine interminable hours came the crash and thump of heavy depth-charges. I think the Italians must have blown up everything between *Trout* and Capri.

Seldom were there fewer than five hunting, and often I think there must have been more.

Everything became strangely quiet. It was after midnight. I decided to give it an hour more in case the searchers were " playing possum." At one-thirty, tired, red-eyed, our ears still tingling in the unaccustomed quiet, I brought *Trout* to the surface. The night was dark, and if the destroyers were there, at least I couldn't see them, nor could they see me. I intended to beat it out of the Tyrrhenian Sea as quickly as I could.

I set course for Malta at full speed.

Malta gave *Trout* a heroes' welcome. We surfaced inside the deep minefield, made o. r recognition signal, and cruised slowly across the blue Mediterranean water towards the beleagured island, looking strangely tranquil in the morning light. The crew, grinning hugely and thinking more of a run ashore in the rum shops than glory, were snodded up in their best; on the port side of the conning-tower, young Peters, overalls over his shore-going rig, was busy with a paint brush and pot adding to *Trout's* score. The main feature of this rather curious design was a hand, rather a strange-looking hand, which half-cocked a snook at our tally of merchantmen and destroyers, and now the battleship.

Peters got the idea from the mascot I always carried with me —one of those things one sees in southern Germany, a root-fern, I think it was, contorted by nature into a replica of a human hand. I had seen it in a little village called Loffingen, near the Black Forest, in the summer before the war. Loffingen is one of those tiny, quaint little places where an iron-work German eagle hangs on an iron lattice-work above a fountain in the market-place where a bronze boy, on some indefinable errand, clutches a spear. I went for a drink at the inn and, dodging the cluster of bicycles at the entrance, saw the " little lucky hand " (the German notice said) in a tiny shop window adjoining. I carried the little hand in action, and Peters had reproduced it (with liberties) on the conning-tower. *Trout* was even affectionately known as " The Hand " at the Lazaretto base.

I felt unutterably weary as I brought *Trout* alongside. The cheers, the sirens, and even the presence of the commander of the base and Dockyard failed to cheer me. Battle fatigue, I thought tiredly. It's when you feel like this that they get you. Even the thought of a long bath and a long gin did not lift the depression which had settled on my spirits.

" Wonderful work, Geoffrey! " exclaimed the C.O. as he came aboard, his quick ebullience spreading round him like an aura. " Come and tell me all about it—no hell man, don't worry about a written report yet. This is just for my private ear."

He looked at me keenly, noting probably the tight lines round the mouth, the stubble and the typical submariner's pallor.

" I've also got some news for your private ear."

He hustled me away, leaving John to do the donkey work.

In his cabin he poured me a stiff gin. I sank into the soft cushions of his own favourite chair, the softness wrapping round me like a cloak.

He jerked out : " When I detailed you for the job, I thought you might get her. But I didn't think you'd make it back."

I looked at the tonic fizzling slowly up in the glass. Like breaking surface on a dull morning, I thought. I wondered how many shells, or even how many lives, this one bottle of tonic had cost to bring to Malta.

" I didn't think you'd make it back," he repeated, flashing a quick glance at me. I could see what he was thinking; I was powerless to cover up : " He's done too many patrols; punch-drunk; he doesn't hear the ashcans any more until they're close —too close. Once more—then it will be too late."

" Look," I snapped suddenly, so suddenly that my subconscious told me how jangled my nerves really were. I meant to tell him about the shelf on the sea-bed, the long weary hell of depth-charging and waiting, but something inside me balked.

" It was a bit tough, but the Ities didn't get too close. Broke some of the fittings. I'll send you a report of the damage," I said offhandedly.

The commander gazed at me steadily. " *Trout's* seaworthy, then?"

" Good God, yes!" I exclaimed impatiently. " This gin tastes wonderful."

" Yes, I suppose it does." His probing, assessing gaze irritated me.

" Look sir," I burst out, " I'll give you the low-down, charts, position, damage and all the rest of it after I've had a bath. A night's good rest and I'll be ready for sea again."

He got up and stood by the porthole, swilling his drink round and round. Then he faced about suddenly.

" You're not going to sea again."

The shock of his words penetrated only dully. Punch-drunk.

" Not going to sea again?"

" No, Geoffrey."

‾ I laughed grimly : " Battle fatigue—and all that. No re-action. Shaky hands." I drank down the gin at a gulp.

He burst out laughing. " So that's what is eating you! No, it's not that." He waved a signal slip. " Read it for yourself."

" . . . to report immediately to the Admiralty in London. Special air transport to be arranged for this officer." I gazed in wonderment at him. " What have I done?"

The other man laughed again. " Search me. But," he added, " the Admiralty certainly saved me a tricky decision. I have lost one of my best fighting men."

"You might have anyway," I rejoined.

"When do I start?" I asked.

"You're still under my orders, and you're spending a couple of days catching up on sleep. The Admiralty will slap on another gong for that little business you've just done, but they can't give you sleep. I can. Lieutenant-Commander Geoffrey Peace, D.S.O. and two Bars, etc., etc. Cheer up man! Meet me in the bar later."

I did. After the utter heaven of a bath and a shave and a complete change of clothes, I felt more like a human being again, although the odd feeling of looking at the normal world through the wrong end of a telescope persisted.

"Utmost priority!" The Royal Air Force officer, suitably moustached, threw back his head and roared with laughter. "Christ!" He turned angrily to me. "What do any of these bloody brass hats know about utmost priority? Have you seen the airfield? As full of craters as a whore's face! And I have to give you top priority to fly out of here! I couldn't fly out a flippin' boy's kite, let alone a naval officer." He snorted and drained his glass.

"Do you know what's going on here?" he went on. "We're so bombed to hell that the Ities and Jerries only need to really come over in force and we've had it. Why, one parachute regiment would write off the airfield."

He signalled frantically for more beer.

"You naval types just don't know what's going on around here. A few bombs at sea, but *you* can always dodge them. And then—home with top priority—out of Malta! Hell!"

The C.O. leaned across to him and I saw the flicker in his eyes. He said quietly: "You're talking to the man who sank the Littorio battleship. Confirmed by air reconnaissance. Your crew rather jumped the gun with that emblem on the conning-tower."

"My God!" he roared. "So you're the . . . who sank that load of old iron! Torpedoes right up her arse!" He thumped me on the back and the others in the bar turned and grinned at the little comedy being enacted. ". . . me! And I start a penny lecture about bombs! Barman! Line 'em up for the Admiral!"

At any other time I might have enjoyed his discomfiture and friendly amends, but to-night I wished him as deep down as my victim. Above all, I was aware of my curious sense of separation from the events going on, almost as if I had been a spectator to my own half-tentative efforts to reciprocate. I'd better get drunk, I thought, and when I wake up with a monumental hangover I'll really feel I've done something to justify my double vision.

We drank to my success.

"I'll get you out of here top priority even if I have to fly the bloody thing myself," roared the R.A.F. man. I saw a rating standing nervously in the door and, more nervously still, he made his way through the officers to our group.

"Signal, sir."

"What the hell——' burst out the C.O. "Can't a man have a drink in peace——" His voice tailed off as he saw the look on the man's face. He jabbed his finger more nervously than ever at the superscription on the signal—"most secret."

The C.O. ripped it open and his right eyebrow rose a little. It was the only form of surprise he ever allowed himself. Otherwise his face, if not his eyes, remained inscrutable.

"Here, Blacklock, this concerns you too."

The R.A.F. man glanced at the signal form. He gave a long whistle. His eyes riveted on me and he made a little sideways gesture of the shoulder to the C.O.

"He might as well know about it, seeing it concerns him most of all."

Blacklock threw down the signal in front of me. "Admiralty to Flag Officer (S) Malta. Lancaster bomber S for Sugar leaving Maddocksford 0400 G.M.T. for Malta to transport Lieutenant-Commander Geoffrey Peace to London. Utmost priority. The expeditious return of this officer must be treated as overriding consideration. . . ."

Blacklock was a sound enough man to keep his mouth shut in the bar, but I could see he was thunderstruck.

"Have to make arrangements to get that damn great plane in here without wrecking itself in the bomb-holes. More joy for the pick-and-shovel brigade." He looked at me with respect.

"You must be quite a boy in your own way," he said.
"Fancy sending a special plane out to fetch you. Personal
service in war-time —— me!"

The C.O. looked thoughtful. "When do you think the
Lancaster will arrive?"

Blacklock laughed. "He'll have time for a night's sleep. I'll
give you the E.T.A. when Gib. signals it. I don't know which
will be worse, trying to bring her in at night, or during the day
when the Jerries are sure to pick her up. We could get her
away better at night, though," he mused, "but, Christ! can
I get her off that piddling little runway? I hope they have
the good sense to fill her up at Gib." He turned to me
with a grin. "You'd remember it all your life if Malta fell
because we used up all our petrol to fly out one of the
Admiralty's favourite torpedo-boys."

Blacklock excused himself and shot off, with characteristic
energy, to cope with the physical problem of handling the big
machine. The C.O. was silent for a long time.

"Why do they want me in London?" I asked. After all,
the Admiralty doesn't send a special plane for a submarine
officer just because he sinks a battleship. Other submariners
had done every bit as well and there were other men just as
capable, if not more so, than myself. My tired brain, a little
muzzy now with the gin, simply balked at the mental jump and
would not go over it.

So I said to the C.O.: "Tell me if you can, why should the
Admiralty want me in such a hurry? They don't just want to
pat me on the back for being a good boy."

"Geoffrey, I don't know any more than you do. I could
think of some reasons, but they're obscure and I'm sure they
don't fit. But you can take it from me, if the Admiralty can
take the trouble to arrange and send out a bomber—and if the
R.A.F. is willing to let it go at this particular juncture of the
war—then you're a damn important personage, make no mis-
take. Just think of the paper work alone to get the R.A.F. to
lend one of its precious bombers to the Navy! It looks like a
decision which couldn't have been made except at the very
highest level—maybe even the chiefs of staff. I could imagine
the hell any service head would kick up at being told to send
one of his fighting units for the purpose of picking up just one

man. You're in cotton-wool from now on, Geoffrey. No risks. No courageous wanderings when there's a raid on. You'll take orders from me to keep yourself as safe as a new-born prince."

I grimaced : " Yesterday I was simply a submarine commander who felt he'd done a job of work. I hadn't had a bath for three weeks. Now I feel unclean with all this limelight focused on me. I felt better on the bridge of the *Trout*. In the light of all this," I burst out, " it's a pity the Ities didn't get *Trout*—to hell with ' utmost priority ! ' "

The C.O. said harshly : " You can keep that sort of maudlin talk for somewhere else. Those boys of yours are a damn fine bunch, and I wouldn't like to think of them at the bottom of the sea just because you're facing something you don't know." He stood up and eyed me unrelentingly. " You'd better get a good night's rest. We'll try and get you out of here sometime to-morrow if the raids are not too heavy."

I suppose that at that time there were fewer drearier places than the huts grouped round Malta's much-bombed airfield. For the hundredth time I changed my position on the scuffed, hard chair and pulled up my greatcoat collar, not only to keep out the chill, but the unrelieved glare of the unshaded lights. The place looked stark, kicked about; indeed it was. It was no fitting portal of glory for the men who, day after day, set their faces against the impossible odds of the great bombing squadrons which sought to destroy not only the airfield, but Malta itself. Blacklock had been hovering around, but his main concern was chivvying the weary workers filling in bomb craters from the last raid of the day, and trying to get a few precious extra yards of runway to help the heavy Lancaster bomber off the field. I could see he was inwardly dubious. Gibraltar had given us a short signal about five hours ago that the plane had left there; we weren't likely to have any more news until she arrived after the long 1,000-mile haul from the Rock.

The pulsing of heavy engines cut the thick silence of the early hours.

Blacklock joined me. " I hope to God they don't pile that monster up on my runways," he said. " It's bad enough having to give them our precious petrol, but it would be hell if they chewed up what's left of the airfield. Besides," he added,

" after these top priority signals, I've got to swaddle you in cottonwool. If they don't get that bloody great thing off the deck again, I feel they'll court martial me. You'll probably be beyond the powers of court martial if she doesn't lift." He grinned, but he was nervous.

The flarepath came on.

" All in your honour," said Blacklock. " I wouldn't dare use it unless it were vital. As it is, it might bring the Stukas in post-haste." He glanced anxiously round, a man naked to his enemies.

The cumbersome shape teetered down on the extremity of the runway. It ran on and on. I thought it would never stop. Blacklock drew the breath between his teeth. The giant slowed, creaked, and turned towards the apron, the propellers cutting arcs of pale light.

" Bloody fine landing!" exclaimed Blacklock. " Bloody fine! Fine being the operative word. They've sent you a good pilot, laddie, if that landing means anything. Get those lights out," he shouted to someone in the darkness above in the control tower.

Before the great bomber had stopped rolling the airfield was in total darkness. Blacklock and I went forward while he shone his torch on the crew's entrance. Four men emerged, walking with that stiff, uneasy gait a man has after a long flight.

Then a fifth pair of legs emerged and an Australian voice said : " Malta, the jewel of the sterling area! Holiday in sunny Malta! See Malta and the worst bloody airfield I've ever seen! Push it over the cliff, chum, push it over the cliff!"

Blacklock went forward to the rangy Australian squadron leader.

" That's what the Jerries are trying to do. I'm Blacklock." He turned to the ground crew. " Get her fuelled up. Anything else needed?"

The Australian looked at him in astonishment.

" What do yer mean, fuel her up? I'm getting fuelled up myself before I take this cow back. I want a bath and a night's rest." With heavy sarcasm he wheeled on Blacklock. " We've been flying chum, remember? Fifteen hundred miles to Gibraltar way out to sea, and another thousand here. See?"

I admired Blacklock then, and saw what had got him to the top.

"You're taking that bloody great thing out of here just as soon as I can get her filled up. Two hours, maybe."

The Australian turned away truculently. "Bugger you," he said.

Blacklock didn't argue. "See here," he said evenly. "If you are not fit, or your crew is not fit, I'll put another crew aboard, but that Lancaster is going to be on its way back to Gibraltar before daylight. Out of the way of the Jerry bases on Sicily and the mainland. Make up your mind."

The Australian faced about, and in the stronger light I could see the lines of fatigue round his mouth. But he changed his tune in the face of Blacklock's stiff line.

"What's the hurry?" he demanded. "Who's this bastard we've got to get back without so much as an hour's rest? Churchill's younger brother? Why can't the bomber stay here for to-morrow at least?"

Blacklock was fast losing patience. "First, because I say so. Second, because that plane will be bombed to pieces in the first raid to-morrow morning. Third, I don't want more of a mess made of my runways than necessary. Fourth, because this is the man you're taking back. Lieutenant-Commander Geoffrey Peace. 'Utmost Priority,' that's why they sent you in the first place."

The Australian looked round with his eyes narrowed with weariness. "O.K." he said. "Fill her up. Call me when it's done. She's O.K. otherwise. I suppose we have time for a cup of coffee?" Then his manner changed. "Don't let those bastards of a ground crew into the plane before we get the stuff out of her."

"What stuff?" asked Blacklock suspiciously.

"There are three crates of whisky and three of gin in the bomb-bay," he grinned. "And about the same number of tinned food. I figured you miserable bastards would need something to cheer you up. 'Utmost priority'" he mimicked.

Blacklock slapped him on the shoulder. "Sorry about this, Aussie. We could have had a party."

"Ah, well," sighed the Australian.

Two and a half hours later the big bomber stood quivering

at the end of the runway, brakes hard on with the great Rolls-Royce engines roaring defiantly. Spurts of blue flame flickered over the cowlings as the Australian revved them up to almost full boost against the brakes. Then the flarepath came on momentarily, the brakes were released, and we catapulted forward. Had it not been for my strap, I would have been thrown from the metal-backed seat on to the mattresses the crew had slept on on the floor. The great machine bucked and roared as the pilot fought to get her off the tiny runway. The tail came up but it seemed an eternity. Then it slowly lifted and with the Rolls-Royce engines bellowing, we lifted clear and swept out to sea. Even as I looked back, the flarepath went out, and we were alone over the sea for all the long flight back to England.

FIVE

Suicide—by Submarine

" THE THIRD man is dead," said the Flag Officer (S). " You'll take his place. The list is short. The others are beyond telling the Germans."

An old submariner himself, the Flag Officer (S) did not waste his words—or his time. The Admiralty looked bleak and cold in the late London spring; chill it seemed to me after being used to the friendly bite of the Mediterranean sun. Bleaker still looked those eyes over the top of the desk. They reminded me somehow of Rockall, the lonely isle in the Atlantic—they only changed their shade of greyness, sometimes stormy, sometimes still, but always grey and bleak with the chill of the near Arctic.

I did not reply. The sudden transition by air from one place to another has always left me feeling as if a part of me had been left behind; it requires time to catch up again.

" Are you tired, Peace?" the level voice snapped.

Dear God! Was I tired of people telling me I was tired! First at Malta, where I had been fussed over—sleep and rest!

And now the Flag Officer (S) himself. Something inside me tightened.

"Of course I'm tired," I replied savagely. "I sank a battleship and had God knows how many depth-charges dropped on me for God knows how many hours. I come straight off patrol and I fly for God knows how many hours in a cold uncomfortable plane with everyone swaddling me in cotton-wool. I *am* tired, but I can be a damn sight tireder. If you had hidden behind a shelf of sand for nine hours. . . ."

The hard look which struck terror into the hearts of so many, and my own now when I realised the folly of such an outburst, changed to one of surprise and the Arctic eyes became slightly less grey.

"What's that?" he whipped out. "What's this about a shelf of sand? There's nothing in the report."

"They probably didn't consider it worthwhile burdening the air with so much detail," I replied. "It was this way, sir . . ." I told him about *Trout's* long ordeal and how I had chosen the undulation on the sea-bed as my protection. I must admit I made it longer than I normally would have done, but while I kept talking I felt he might overlook my nervous outburst.

When I had finished, he said quietly : "I owe you an apology, Peace. When I saw you there I thought I was seeing what I have seen so many times : a fine officer, but his battle reflexes shot to hell. I had three submarine commanders on my list for this job, and it was the battleship that tipped the scales in your favour. A moment ago I had doubts. Now I am ordering you to do it." He smiled slightly. As a once brilliant submarine commander in World War I, he still knew that you can only push a submarine man so far and then—the enemy gets him.

He leaned back in his leather chair.

"Three men know about this thing. I will tell you who they are : myself, and the Director of Naval Intelligence, now you. One other man knew, but he is dead. The Gestapo saw to that. I tell you that the fate of the whole war at sea depends—and I do not say may depend, but depends—on the success or otherwise of the mission I have for you."

He pressed a button and lapsed into silence, but the cold eyes watched me, probing, mesmerising, seeking out the hidden weakness of the instrument he had chosen.

" Show in the Director of Naval Intelligence," he said.

I got to my feet as the grave, sad-eyed man came in.

" Hallo, Peter," he said. He spoke like a world-weary diplomat. He seemed to have reached a stage beyond sadness at human ferocity and had only compassion left. He looked at me. " So this is your man?" It was a different type of scrutiny, a subtle, diagnostic friendliness but not less deadly than the scalpel-like probing of the Flag Officer (S).

" Tell him," he said curtly.

The newcomer sat on the edge of the desk with one leg swinging idle. He lit a cigarette and gazed for a moment at the cold view beyond the windows, as if mustering his thoughts.

" You will see," he said didactically, " that I have no papers with me. There are no papers. All I have is a message sent by our agent at the Blohm and Voss yards. It was a longish message, and that is probably why they caught him. His Majesty's Government will never have the opportunity of rewarding him." He said it without a trace of irony, but rather with pity. It might have been an epitaph for a Spartan.

" You may guess," he went on, " although you may not know, that the Germans have been working on forms of sub- marine propulsion other than conventional methods for some time."

I shook my head.

" You've been too busy sinking things to keep up to date," he murmured reprovingly. " What would you say were your two main problems in a submarine? You, as a practical exponent of the art?"

The schoolmasterly chiding held no hint of the venomous subject it treated : slow coughing to death in a steel coffin in fifty fathoms of water; no hint of our excruciating passion for more speed to evade the hunter.

" Fresh air and speed," I replied.

" May I congratulate you on your man, Peter? I suppose a submarine commander doesn't have much time to waste his words."

" Fresh air and speed," he went on quietly. " Yes. Four

words tell the whole story. The Germans are getting the answers, too. They are well ahead of us."

The Flag Officer (S) stirred slightly in his chair. The burden of that terrible summer and its more terrible winter in the North Atlantic lay heavily on his heart. Half a million tons a month sunk, they said.

"They seem to have given priority to air," the easy voice went on. "They are working on a kind of hollow tube which will supply air to the vessel while it remains submerged." He consulted his mind. "The Dutch had something of the sort at the outbreak of war. They called it something like . . . ah, yes, snort or snorchel."

I listened in amazement. "Why," I exclaimed, "give a submariner a thing like that and, and . . ."

"Precisely," he smiled. "And one poses a whole new series of tactical problems of the gravest import. Fortunately I am not called upon to counter these things. I am simply a glass through which the rays of information shine, I hope, not too dully." He smiled faintly at the stern-eyed man at the other side of the desk.

"Now the Blohm and Voss people"—he said it as one might name a favourite tailor of close acquaintance—"have evolved a prototype which they are calling Type XXI. It is fully streamlined and is fitted with what we will conversationally call a snort. It will do sixteen knots submerged, has six bow tubes and carries twelve spare torpedoes. I evaluate its firing power at eighteen—I think kipper is a distressing piece of naval slang—in thirty minutes."

The man behind the desk stirred again. That schoolmasterly voice meant, translated into the practical, a burning hell of tankers sinking, men dying in agony, or freezing to death in perishing seas. The cold eyes were so cold that years later I was still to remember them.

"The Type XXI also has a new kind of range-finder—again, well in advance of us or the Americans—which enables him to fire his torpedoes from thirty-five metres down without using his periscope at all."

I jumped to my feet. "No, that's impossible! !"

My informant looked at me mildly. "By no means, my dear Lieutenant-Commander. It is a reality. By this coming winter in the North Atlantic there will be scores of the Type XXI at work. I assure you you have no reason to doubt my information."

I looked at the glum face of the man in the chair and accepted, as best I could, what the chief of Intelligence was saying.

" Air and speed, you said Lieutenant-Commander," he went on.

My words tumbled out : " But the Type XXI solves them both sir—all the air you want, and all the speed."

" By no means," he replied. " Both are a step forward, but by no means absolute."

" What do you mean by absolute, sir?" I asked with heavy humour. " My boat might make a single burst of nine knots in an emergency, but three or four would be more like it. I'd have to charge batteries the next night when the air was foul anyway. This Type XXI—why, it's unbelievable."

" Your problem," he replied dogmatically, " is having to come absolutely to the surface, stop and recharge, or run on the surface. The Blohm and Voss beauty sits below at snort depth, runs her diesels and charges her batteries. She is still vulnerable, and that snort is vulnerable, too. Her motive power is only an improved version of the old—ours, for example."

" Give me a boat like that, and I'd go damn near anywhere, sir," I said vehemently, for the idea fired me. Think, if I had had a fast manœuvrable ship like that for the battleship attack . . .

" I say the Type XXI is quite vulnerable," he said quietly, " and I am sure with—ah developments—we shall be able to cope with it."

This high-level talk was sweeping me off my feet.

" But you know, Lieutenant-Commander, the Germans are an imaginative lot. If we had had the initiative to develop the Type XXI, we would have concentrated exclusively on it. Developed it, streamlined it a little more, improved the engines and so on. We might have even got eighteen knots underwater. But the German is a perfectionist. He wants something better than that. So instead of concentrating, he diversifies his energies. Air and speed. Absolutely. I can say that the Type XXI is obsolescent."

Astonishment robbed me of speech. I gestured feebly at the Flag Officer (S). He nodded curtly.

"Not that she won't go into service," went on the evenly modulated voice. "She is quite lethal, you know."

Of all the gross understatements, that surely took the biscuit, I thought. It made *Trout* and her like seem like things used in the Napoleonic wars.

"What do you know about hydrogen peroxide, Lieutenant-Commander?"

A flippant reply about ladies' hairdressers rose to my lips, but died without utterance at the abstracted face before me.

"Only what I learned at school, and that I've almost forgotten," I replied.

"The Germans are using it to propel yet another experimental type," he said coolly. I wondered if the effects of the depth-charging and the long flight were really making me rather addle-headed. Hydrogen peroxide!

"We have good reason to believe that they are using hydrogen peroxide as a main fuel, and then feeding it through a complicated system of burners, mixed with oil fuel, and driving U-boat turbines."

"Air and speed?" I asked wryly.

"Not quite," he smiled back. "But damn nearly. Without boring you with what few technicalities we know, I can say that this type—we just call it HP on our files—is faster than the Type XXI. The air problem is almost solved, for she can remain submerged——"

"But the air to burn the fuel . . ."

"In the hydrogen peroxide," he said. "She doesn't need a snort for her engines, but there are a maze of technical problems to be beaten (I should say) before she becomes really operational. Although she might be fundamentally sound, she might still be too complicated to build more than a few. I doubt whether they could mass-produce them with any degree of success for some years. And then there's the R.A.F. bombing to take into account also."

"I feel that I would have the same chance against one of these hellish things as I would taking *H.M.S. Victory* to sea against the *Scharnhorst*," I said grimly.

The Flag Officer (S) tightened his compressed lips.

" They aren't invincible," he said with a grate in his voice. " You don't know what they have coming to them in the Western Approaches."

I suppose his cold rage was more terrifying than any bombast or bluster. Here was a man who weighed up the facts. He was interested in facts only. The weight of one fact against the other. Death and counter-death. An icy level of cold command, I thought, wondering why I as a mere submarine commander ever had cause to feel the isolation of command.

" Why are you telling me this?" I asked the Intelligence Chief.

" I haven't finished telling you," he rebuked me gently. In his prim voice he went on, " As you see, the Type XXI is lethal, but suffers from the conventional maladies which have beset submarines since their inception. In truth, I would call it more of a submersible in the strict sense than a submarine. To my mind submarine means a permanent ability to operate *under* water. The surface is only incidental to it."

My mind reeled. When I thought of the ordinary things which surrounded *Trout*, the need for intensive training and engineering skills in her operation compared with these dreadful weapons, I could have wept.

" The U-boat which I really fear is the one I want to tell you about," he said.

Fear and terror take many forms. All my life I have been used to associating them with violence, actions, events, turbulent emotions. But that calm, didactic voice speaking of fear as if he had been discussing the merits of a long-dead Greek play struck a chord of horror in my heart which I have seldom known before or since. And I am not a man easily frightened; death had been near to me too many times for me to shudder at the thought of a sudden rending of flesh, or suffocation by salt water.

A hush fell over the room. Both men, unconsciously, gave full drama to the pause. I remember the incidental noises still —the faint hoot of a car, and the muted drone of a squadron of high-flying bombers overhead. Neither moved. The one was lost in the technical problem, the other pondering his next words to put it plainly to a seafaring man. And why, in God's name, send for me in the Mediterranean to tell *me* all this? This was stuff for the Cabinet and the Prime Minister, and certainly not for very many others less elevated.

" Air and speed," he said, and there was a note of tiredness in his voice which heightened my feeling of fear. Fear of something gigantic, unknown, prescient of the thing that was to warp my whole future.

" Even the German High Command won't believe that they have, in fact, solved it—absolutely." ,

" Absolutely?" I said stupidly.

He almost drew his schoolmaster's gown about him. " Blohm and Voss have their assembly yard at Wesermunde," he said without expression in his voice. " One of their top engineers there is a man called Werner. He designed a U-boat which can do twenty-two knots under water, is silent, and doesn't need to come to the surface. She can fire acoustic torpedoes from about fifty metres almost parallel to a convoy, and she will outrun the ordinary escort group ships in the North Atlantic—submerged. Only a destroyer is faster."

" Impossible," I said.

" Thank God, that is what the German High Command also say—still. But Werner is a man of parts. He is not only a practical engineer with the greatest appreciation of what is needed; he is also somewhat—more than somewhat, if I might interpose Runyon in this conversation—of a scientist. Do you know anything about nuclear physics?"

For the only time the cold mask behind the desk relaxed. " Give him a chance, George."

" Not only from Werner's little goings-on, but a lot else which I won't burden you with, I believe that the Germans have solved the problem of propulsion—whether by sea or in the air—by what I call, if I may coin the phrase, nuclear propulsion. I suppose only a handful of men in this or any other country have heard of using the energy generated in splitting atoms for propulsion. It is enormous. And Werner has designed an engine using steam and nuclear power. He shoved it into a U-boat, a huge U-boat of about three thousand tons. The atomic radiation needs a lot of shielding. It's so revolutionary and so in advance of anything we or anyone else have ever thought, that the German High Command simply doesn't believe it. But don't think Blohm and Voss don't. To prove their point, they have built—a lot of it at their own expense—an experimental U-boat with these fantastic abilities. The High Command still thought it a crackpot idea, fraught with all kinds of difficulties and dangers—as well it might. But Blohm and Voss prevailed to the extent that they persuaded the High Command to let NP I—nuclear propulsion Number I—go operational on the longest route in the world, with Hans Tutte "—he smiled—" you'll have heard of him—in command. NP I has all the answers, as our American friends would say."

The fear and foreboding which those grim words sent down my spine grew when the man behind the desk got up and crossed to a huge wall map.

He jabbed his finger at a spot in the South Atlantic. "On 29th November the *Dunedin Star*, carrying tanks and war supplies to the Middle East, reported a mysterious underwater occurrence. Her captain beached her here on the coast of South West Africa. Total loss. Hell of a to-do about the passengers. The South African Air Force did some fine, if damn foolhardy things to try and get them out. Overland expeditions, drama in the desert and all that. But all I am interested in is—was it NP I which sank her? I have the details of the attack here. Nothing—except a muffled crash which tore a huge hole in her. No sign of an attacker. I think NP I sank the *Dunedin Star*. That was over three months ago."

The D.N.I. interrupted. "I might add that this voyage of NP is a proving voyage. If she comes home with a bag as full as I think she will get, the Germans will concentrate everything on building scores of her type for the North Atlantic. Their virtues—on paper at least—are innumerable—high operational speed for indefinite periods; no need to surface; stealth of attack . . ."

"There is nothing she doesn't have!" I broke in. The futility of British submarines, their wearisome little technical faults and the simple problem of operating them without straining their conventional machinery—it seemed to me like comparing a turbine with a lawn-mower.

"No," said the schoolmasterly voice. "There you are wrong. There is one thing they certainly do not have. That is, radar anything like as good as ours. Their FuMB counter-radar really isn't up to much. Our V.H.F. is years ahead of theirs. So is our underwater radio reception and asdic. When our ships in the Western Approaches have these installed . . ."

He trailed off at the stern eye of my senior and shrugged. " In for a penny, in for a pound. He knows more now than anyone else; it won't harm him to know about the radar also. Besides, we'll install it in *Trout* in order to give him the best chance."

His matter-of-fact words struck a new chord of fear in me. *Trout?* What had she to do with it? Were they going to send me out against this futuristic submarine in poor little *Trout?* I still remember the prolonging of the minutes; somewhere down below there was a slight screech of rubber on the road as a driver braked carelessly; from the Thames came the mournful siren of a tug. The Flag Officer (S) stood with his face half turned to the great wall map. He and the Director of Naval Intelligence both realised that the cat was out of the bag.

" Surely . . ." I gasped.

The cold eyes never looked colder, and his voice sounded like backwash on sharp shingle.

" Your orders are to take *H.M.S. Trout* and sink NP I."

I looked from one to the other hopelessly. The *Trout* ! A piddling little " T " class submarine against a 3,000 ton non-surfacing, super-efficient U-boat which was so good that even its creator could not believe it was true ! Here was the straight, unswerving road to suicide !

I said flippantly, for after all they had signed my death warrant as certainly as they stood before me :

" Just tell me where to find her, sir."

The note in my voice certainly jarred on both of them. The icy eyes flickered only for a moment. His next words dumbfounded me, even if I was capable of feeling little else but bitter, hurt anger.

" I don't know. You will have absolute discretion. The whole South Atlantic is yours."

I turned hopelessly to the Intelligence man.

" Surely, sir, you must have some reports about where she is based ? You can't tuck a huge submarine away like that without a trace. What about some unfrequented harbour along the South West African coast? The Germans there are well disposed towards the Nazis. Perhaps. . . ."

He was smiling, sadly. " My dear boy," he murmured. " A submarine like that doesn't need a regular operational base. I estimate that she can travel about fifteen months without refuelling. She can carry all her own stores. She only needs to go home when she's shot off all her torpedoes. She carries plenty of them, too."

His words felt like the final body blow to a boxer. Neither of them said any more. I suppose several minutes must have passed.

Then I said feebly : " Briefly, then, I must take *Trout* to the millions of square miles of the South Atlantic, find and sink a U-boat capable of doing eighteen or more knots submerged, no base, no silhouette. Am I correct, sir?"

The icy eyes remained ice. " That is correct."

Their minds were made up and there was little I could do about it—except make my will.

" I am bringing *H.M.S. Trout* to Gibraltar. The new radar will be fitted there. It is not to fall into enemy hands, do you see, Peace? It will be fitted with special demolition charges. If you are in any immediate danger from the enemy, you will blow it up. If necessary, you will blow up *Trout* also."

They were certainly making sure of my death.

" And if I catch up with NP I, what are my orders, sir?" I asked.

" You will sink her with torpedoes. You will bring home positive proof that she is sunk. There must be no half-measures."

The quiet voice joined in our conversation. " Once she is sunk, and does not return to Bremen after a period which the German High Command thinks appropriate, I feel certain they won't go ahead with building others. Remember, they are not even half sold on the idea. This mass of complex, highly dangerous nuclear machinery doesn't appeal to the men who know ordinary U-boats. But if NP I comes home with a string of sinkings and a world cruise behind her, they'll go for it." He glanced at his watch. " I feel all I can wish you is good luck."

He looked at me in his gentle way, and then averted his head sharply. He knew he was looking at a dead man. "But," he said crisply, "remember that radar. You can pick him up at thirty miles. It's the only Achilles heel I know he has."

He turned and walked out.

The Flag Officer (S) had seated himself again. "I'll see you get all the necessary charts, stores and so on. I shall have you flown out to Gibraltar, and from there you will go to Freetown and then to the Cape. Your plans are your own after that. You can have a clear run ashore for a month before you go to Gibraltar. Haven't you got some relative who is ill somewhere?"

"Yes sir," I replied. "My old grandfather had a stroke at his place near Tiverton. I would like to see him before he dies. He hasn't got much of a chance according to the local medico."

"Leave your telephone number, then," he said briskly.

He hesitated for a moment. "You may be wondering why I didn't turn this job over to a hunting group of the North Atlantic boys."

I grinned wryly. "I don't wonder at anything any more, sir."

"In a future war," he said, standing looking out across the pale scene, "the submarine will be licked by the submarine. That's a radical theory which no one—not even the Prime Minister—would accept to-day. The hunter becomes the hunted. Stealth will steal up upon stealth, and destroy him by stealth. You are the first of the new hunters," he said without facing me. "You will see more of what I mean when you have time to think over what a nuclear submarine means in terms of future sea wars. You will report back personally to me. There will be no signals if you encounter or sink her, understand? *Trout* will have a free rein anywhere in any port of the free world. You must come back and report to me—personally. You have the honour of being the first of the new hunters."

I had heard that he was a man who seldom spoke, and never revealed his mind.

"Or the last of the old hunters," I replied.

He wheeled round and gazed at me, and the Rockall of his eyes softened.

"You believe in your heart that I am sending you to your death, don't you, Peace?" he asked.

"Yes, sir, I do," I replied levelly. "And there are sixty-five others in *Trout* who are going to their deaths. Not one of them is afraid to die, but there are no odds in this case. The certainty of death in a submarine is not a pleasant thought."

"If you feel that way, I shall not wish you the submariner's usual *au revoir*. Good-bye," he said and held out his hand.

I shook it perfunctorily.

When I reached the door, he said softly : "If you are thinking of getting drunk to-night, Lieutenant-Commander, do. There will be an Intelligence man by your side every moment until you sail from Gibraltar. He'll save you from yourself—or knock you down if you say a word too many."

SIX

South of North

"LUFF! LUFF! LUFF! Get the sails off her, you sons-of-bitches! By the mark four! God, only four under her and it's coming up from south-west! See that over there, Mister Mate? No, not there—326 degrees? Yes? Looks like porridge, but they're breakers. *Clan Alpine*. *Alecto* was there the year before too. No, you can't see it ordinarily, and *Clan Alpine* didn't either. Of course we're going in! No damn you, we had a good sight of the sun at Ponta da Marca and I reckon by now I can smell the *Clan Alpine*. Three hills. Magnificent bearing. Here—look at the chart. Don't be damn stupid, this is my own chart; the Germans think they know the coast; but this is my own and not even the Admiralty knows. Captain Williams! Bah, that chartman! I know Captain Williams. Farilhao Point . . . must make southing to-night or else we'll beat against the inshore current all day to-morrow. . . ."

For hours the old man had been rambling. I sat by the bedside of my grandfather, old Captain Peace, who was indeed making his last landfall the hard way. Doctor Chelvers had told me when I arrived from London the previous night that by rights the old captain should have been dead days ago. Coronary thrombosis, not a stroke. But he was fighting it out to the last, although he had made his number to Lloyds.

I sat in the quiet room and listened to the old sailorman's phrases of the sea, in sharp contrast to the lovely Exe Valley, where everything was of that tender young green which one sees nowhere in the world except England, and nowhere lovelier in England than the Exe Valley.

Doctor Chelvers had said that morning that it might only be a matter of hours before old Captain Peace died, or it might be days. I looked at the weather-beaten face against the pillows, and thought of *Trout* and what was waiting for her. No peaceful sick-bed at the last for me! A sharp rattle from a depth-charge, or more likely the quiet, lethal whisper of a torpedo screw in the hydrophone operator's ears coming nearer . . . nearer . . . nearer. . . .

London had been a failure. I had taken my chief's advice and tried to get drunk. I had given it up in disgust. Somewhere in the club had been that Intelligence man, but I never saw him. I had rung Wendy with the firm intention of spending one last night with her. Half-way there the air raid sirens went and the mood of depression became so strong that I never got as far as her flat. The thought of the sheer hopelessness of it all overwhelmed me. The absolute secrecy was a further burden. The prospects if the Germans made use of their frightful new weapon in the Atlantic, as they were bound to when NP I returned from her successful cruise, were appalling. I decided to get out of London and see old Captain Peace before he died. The sight of the old sailor dying so manfully, with a flood of nautical phrases and oaths on his lips, affected me more even than unburdening my secret would have done. The old captain had been delirious off and on since my arrival the previous night. Now the salt of a sea life blew like spindrift through the sick-room.

The nurse came and took the dying man's pulse. She looked across at me and shook her head slightly. She was middle-aged, bosomy, and kind. I have never yet encountered the blonde, glamorous nurse of the cinema sickroom. The more crow's feet at the corners of their eyes, the better nurses they have been.

"It's a wonder he has lasted all this time," she said. "He must have a constitution like iron. You know, if thrombosis doesn't kill in the first attack, they sometimes linger on. The following fortnight is the dangerous time."

"You don't think he'll make it?" I asked. Death seemed everywhere.

She glanced at me keenly. "No, he can't. He is very near the end, now. You should take some rest yourself."

My laughter rang harshly in my own ears. Rest! I'd soon rest throughout eternity.

She came round the bed and stood looking down at me as I sat. "I don't know what your job it in this war, but you've been through it, I can see. Forget what has happened."

"Look," I said. "You're very kind to show an interest in me. All I can say is that I envy that old man dying in his bed."

Tears filled her eyes and she hurried from the room.

NP I *must* have a base. That thought went through my mind, over and over again. The two naval chiefs were sure that she had not. I sat in the pleasant morning sunshine by old Captain Peace and turned the problem over in my mind, while from the bed came half-incoherent oaths, sailing-ship directions, mutterings all about winds and tides.

I tried to put myself in the place of the U-boat commander. The first thing, I thought, must be to rid myself of the fear which had engulfed me of this new frightful weapon. Was it, I asked myself again and again, quite as awe-inspiring as the Intelligence man had made out? Where was the flaw, the flaw of human fallibility? He had spoken of her radar as the Achilles heel. Well, that was one card in my hand, and likely to be a trump if well played. I projected myself into the skin of the U-boat commander Hans Tutte. Before I left the Admiralty I had asked for everything they had about him. Certainly the pipsqueak clerk had resented giving me the top-secret Admiralty appreciation of Tutte, but with my backing it seemed that I could ask what I wished. So also, I thought grimly, can a man on the eve of his execution.

Tutte was not the flamboyant extrovert that the great aces like Schepke and Prien were. The training of these great U-boat aces, their successes in early years and so on had been very similar. But when it came to attack, Tutte was different. There had been survivors' accounts of that dreadful blood-and-oil bath in the North Atlantic, some hysterical, some non-committal, but on putting them together I found that Tutte, daring, brave, resolute, was a master of the calculated risk. There was a fierce precision about his sinkings, even amid the tumult of burning ships, star shells and thudding torpedoes. It did not surprise me to read that his father had been a professor of mathematics. There had been throughout the momentary holding-off while he assessed the rate of risk and either he held back altogether, or struck with a rapid, deadly blow. His crew idolised him; there was warmth in the man to his crew and record of humanity towards boat survivors. One merchant first mate noted how, eight hours after Tutte had sunk his ship in one of those hideous mêlées in the North Atlantic at night, Tutte had surfaced alongside and passed a Thermos of coffee, some hunks of bread and a bottle of rum into the boat.

" The North Atlantic is a bastard," he had said in excellent English. " We sailors all know that. Steer such and such a course."

Imagine yourself such a man fresh from the North Atlantic, I told myself. Here is what Blohm and Voss says is the perfect U-boat. Reaction? First, call in your battle-trained officers and examine the new submarine in detail. I could imagine that conference in the as yet unliving control room of NP I.

Hans Tutte listens.

" Too big," says the first officer. " The new British corvettes and frigates turn on a sixpence. They'd get you in a clumsy big thing like this."

" All right for a straight fight with twenty knots, though," said the second thoughtfully. " Fast run in, no noise, torpedoes away, fast out again."

The engineer is both thrilled and subdued. " Wonderful, if it all hangs together. But burn anything out at sea, and it would be a dockyard job."

" If the Royal Navy ever let you get home," said the first grimly.

" But she's big, and she'll be wonderful for the crew. The lack of confined space will keep up their morale wonderfully."

Hans Tutte leans against the periscope housing and weighs up the experience of his veteran U-boat men.

He says suddenly :

" How long do you think men can stay submerged and retain their fighting efficiency? Number One?"

" You mean, sir, in relation to this, or the standard U-boat?"

" This."

" No surface, no action, just submerged?"

" Yes."

No. One pauses. " At a guess, I'd say twenty days."

Tutte surveys him judicially. " Number Two?"

" Maybe a month, but they'd be no match for anything when we came up."

" Engineer?"

" It's easier in the engine-room, sir. There's always something to keep my men fully occupied. Small things go wrong and need fixing. But a month is a long time. . . ."

" Gentlemen," says Tutte coldly. " I have orders to carry out a cruise—without surfacing at all if possible."

The others gaze at him silently. He knows what is running through their minds, and the same doubts about morale and fighting efficiency are in his.

" No base," he added.

Number One coughs discreetly. " And the length of the cruise, sir?"

Tutte eyes him grimly. " The equivalent of once round the world—with action."

The U-boat service is too well disciplined to vent its surprise and dismay. Then Tutte smiles the smile for which his crew would follow him to the ends of the earth.

" I think, too, we must have a base, if it's only to surface and relax and see the sun. Not necessarily a naval base, for we have all our stores and torpedoes, but a base to relax in. The U-boat Command disagrees with that. Perhaps——" he grins knowingly at his trusted officers—" once we are at sea the High Command might relent."

I sat long with this imaginary scene in my mind. Was it wishful thinking? I asked myself. I for one would have put forward the argument, as a submarine captain, of the need to relax and surface. What would happen in the interior of a submarine after a month under water? True, in the NP I the air would not foul as in ordinary craft, but what about the stink of humanity, the accumulation of refuse if operating in enemy waters, and the green slime which would coat everything inside the U-boat? What would happen to the physical state of the men themselves? Would they get sick from some as yet unknown effects of long submersion? And—this was a wayward thought—was NP I quite foolproof in her machinery? Might there not be some poisonous exudation from this new-fangled nuclear propulsion? It came to me as I sat there in the pleasant sunshine that, perfect though NP I might be mechanically, the human element, particularly the human element trained in more conventional craft, would not stand up to the strain of the war at sea as well as her designers thought. NP I *must* find herself a haven, a nook away from the world. If I were Hans Tutte, that is what I would do. Somewhere safe to let the men smoke, swim and tan their bodies in the warm sun. This, I convinced myself, was the true Achilles heel of NP I. A base, a haven, a hidey-hole . . . she must have it.

The relief of having made some positive contribution to my problem was so great that it was some time before I realised that old Captain Peace was talking rationally. I saw that he was rational and his eyes had lost their uncomprehending look.

He stretched out his hand. " Geoffrey!" he exclaimed with pleasure. " Blast me, I never expected to have a real sailor at hand for my last voyage."

I muttered something about everything being well.

"Balls!" he said heartily. " I'm a dead duck, and you know it. What have you been doing with yourself? Why are you in England and not at sea? You didn't leave your submarine just to come and watch an old man die, did you?"

He rose up against his pillows with a burst of violent energy which had characterised him throughout his life.

England's enemies, beware of men like old Captain Peace, I thought to myself.

"No," I said steadily and I saw it cheered him at once. " Special orders."

" No tell, eh?" he laughed.

What the hell, I thought suddenly to myself. Why not tell him? He'd probably be dead before nightfall anyway. Somewhere in that vast accumulation of sea lore there might be something which would help me sink NP I. It would also help me, the unburdening of this terrible secret. I got up and closed the door.

I told him about my mission. I told him the details, the pros and the massive cons; I told him about Hans Tutte and what I would do in his place; I told him that I was convinced that NP I needed a base—of sorts. The old man's eyes gleamed and then filled with tears.

"Geoffrey," he said in a whisper. "It breaks my heart to know what England has against her, and I can't do a mortal bloody damn about it." Then the self-pity died out of his voice and he asked strongly: "Where is NP I going to operate?"

"In the South Atlantic," I replied.

"If only I had a ship," he exclaimed. "God, I know it like my hand. None of the islands. Plenty of skulking holes in South America, though, but not the place for a rest cure with that climate. I'd go for Africa, if it were me. Too many people around, too, and the Navy is not so stupid that it wouldn't search across the trade routes to Buenos Aires. That's what put Harwood on to the *Graf Spee*," he chuckled.

"Africa has the same disadvantages," I pointed out. "Bad climate in the tropics, too many people. Even if they are blacks."

"South West Africa," cried the old man waving a pyjama-ed arm. He was very excited.

"Not a harbour worth a damn between Tiger Bay, Walvis Bay and Cape Town," I said, bitterly disappointed now that I had mentioned the operation to a wandering old man on his death-bed. "I mentioned it to the Admiralty."

"God's truth!" roared the old sailor. "Admiralty! Why, that Captain Williams hydrographer-bastard wouldn't even look at my soundings. Get me a chart, boy—in my desk. No, not the Admiralty one—there's one of my own. What size is NP I? Three thousand tons? By the Lord Harry, she'd just about make it!"

He looked very excited and I slipped from the room. His desk was pure chaos. Papers, charts, maps, old ship chandler's orders, all kinds of nautical junk littered it. I rummaged about and saw a handwritten "last will and testament of Simon Peace, master mariner." I found what the old man must regard as "his chart"—it looked, at first glance, like a stretch to the south of Angola, heavily annotated with figures. I went back.

The moment I set foot in the room I knew what had happened. A glance at the mottled, congested face told its own story. I ran swiftly to the door and called for the nurse. He lay back gasping and coughing, like a seaman full of chlorine gas.

"He's trying to say something to you," said the nurse gently.

He spoke loudly.

"North?" I echoed. It sounded like north to me, but his voice was going.

"Twenty miles—north." He just couldn't get his failing voice round the last word. "North—north—north——" but it wasn't quite north, the way he said it. "Twenty miles south of north—big rock—twenty miles south of . . ."

The death rattle severed the last word.

Then to our utter astonishment, he sat up straight and said quite clearly and strongly: "A twist of sand, boy. It's your damn property anyway."

The nurse was crying. She put down the limp arm.

"His heart had stopped before he said that," she whispered.

SEVEN

On the Tail of a Whale

THE LONG South Atlantic afternoon ebbed out westwards towards St. Helena. From the conning-tower the ocean stretched away, apparently limitless, across steamship routes forsaken for years of their peacetime traffic. War made the South Atlantic lonelier than it is in peacetime, and that is lonely enough. Sun-tanned, wearing shorts, off-duty men played Uckers on the casing near the gun. The swell from the south-west scarcely had energy enough to reach up the steel deck. Between Mossamedes and St. Helena we seemed the only craft afloat on the great waters.

John Garland, white shirt open at the neck, and tanned as an advertisement figure, looked down lazily on the group below.

" If this goes on, Geoffrey, we'll all be so bored that we'll be betting on the Uckers men too—despite Navy regulations."

I said nothing. I was worried. I could see the signs of slackness, the canker of the present easy life, eating into my veteran, battle-tried crew. Sun-tanned beauties don't return from submarine cruises. It had all been so easy, and so un-warlike, that even the ghastly shadow of why I was here at all on a sunny afternoon in the South Atlantic seemed far away. I had flown out to Gibraltar and found *Trout* waiting. She was ready fuelled, ammunitioned and stocked up. On someone's orders—someone high-up who smelled the danger of the *Trout's* mission without actually knowing it—cases of Canadian and American luxury foods had been sent aboard, a case or two of Scotch for the officers, and even a dozen of the finest Tio Pepe especially for me. For those about to die. . . . I thought grimly to myself.

There was no doubt at Gibraltar and at Freetown, where we fuelled, and again at Simonstown, Cape, that *Trout* was priority. Nothing was too much trouble, and no request was refused. The crew got on to it quickly. But, Navy-like, they forgot what danger must lurk behind these unusual gestures, and were content to live like lords. I overheard one of my ratings, half drunk, say at Simonstown: "Whisky, my boy; no piddling drinks for the *Trout*-men—only the best is good enough for *Trout*."

At first I had not seen the softness, but the long weeks of solitary cruising up and down, down and up, through the vastness of the South Atlantic was robbing the crew of their super-sharp vigilance. That is the difference between life and death in a submarine. As the afternoon wore on, I was more and more jarred by the easy-going air of life aboard *H.M.S. Trout*. I had done the conventional thing. I had ruled the South Atlantic off into tight little squares. I had plotted the position where the *Dunedin Star* had first been rent under water; I had patrolled day and night, night and day. For weeks I had not even seen a ship. There was, in fact, nothing. Not a ship, not a sail.

John's remark jarred. I could not go on carrying out practice attacks, dives, dummy shelling and the rest of it day after day. *Trout* seemed to have reached a point of crisis, a crisis of deadly boredom. All war is boring, but this was boring beyond any war. My orders were explicit: to locate and sink NP I. Where in God's name, I thought desperately, gazing round the limitless sea about me, could she be? Had she simply blown up and disappeared without trace? Would *Trout* continue her ceaseless patrolling until two men at the Admiralty became convinced that she no longer existed? Or would they recall me peremptorily, asking for an account of the failure of my mission?

I cast a mental eye over the charts. There was nowhere where NP I could hide. I thought of every remote anchorage from Walvis Bay to Pointe Noire in Africa; the South American coast was too long to even consider in relation to this damn-fool square-search pattern. And I meant to go on doing it for months yet!

Through this mangrove tangle of conflicting thoughts the look-out's voice came like a bucket of cold water.

"Bridge, sir! Tripod masts bearing red one-oh."

Heavens! The relief of spotting a ship! It surged over me even as I pressed the alarm. The Uckers men gazed at one another in disbelief. I really think they had forgotten what an emergency dive was like, I spoke into the voice-pipe.

"Eighty feet. Course three-two-oh. Clear the bridge."

My soft sailors clattered down the hatch like men possessed. It was good to see that danger had given them a shot in the arm. I closed the conning-tower hatch and clipped on the catches, not avoiding a few dollops of water as *Trout* went down steeply.

"H.E. bearing green one-five," reported the hydrophone operator. He added tersely : "Warships. Big ones."

Trout swung on to an attacking course. The "fruit machine" fed by information from two officers, gave the course and speed of the warships.

"Twenty knots," said John.

"That's fine," I said. "I'll fire into the sun. Lovely silhouette. I'll go up and have a look. Stand by," I ordered. "Up periscope. Thirty feet."

The dripping glass thrust its baleful eye out of the South Atlantic. I looked at the masts in disbelief. British warships! Two cruisers, with a nuzzle of four destroyers.

"Take a look at that, John," I said.

The tension ebbed at once in the submarine. An alert crew is extraordinarily sensitive to the smallest change of inflexion in the commander's voice.

"Jesus!" exclaimed John. "Shall we . . . ?"

"Yes, take her up," I snapped. "But be bloody careful to get off the recognition signal pronto. Signalman! Send this——" and I prefaced it with the usual code and recognition signals—"Use the shortwave," I added hastily, remembering the explicit radio ban. I felt I couldn't let a group of British warships go by without hailing them. *Trout* seemed a bit of a pariah on the seas, even if she was a pariah living in luxury.

The water wasn't off the plates before John and I were looking out at the cluster of warships.

The destroyers rippled as if a nerve had been touched.

John grinned : "Look at that, Geoffrey. They've certainly spotted us." His hand moved towards the recognition flare trigger.

"Don't fire that damned thing," I said shortly. "It could be seen twenty miles away."

Long patches of white creamed under the destroyers' bows.
They fanned out. And, ghastly to see, the barrels of the six
and eight-inch guns on the cruisers all moved, as if endowed
with powers of thought, at *Trout*.

"Western Approaches stuff," grinned John, but a trifle nervously. "Those boys are really on the ball."

They well might be, I thought grimly, remembering NP I.

Despite the fact that the signal had gone off, the destroyers
were not taking any chances. They came round in a wide
circle, doing every bit of thirty knots. An Aldis lamp clattered
as I sent off a visual recognition signal.

"Stop both," I said down the voice-pipe.

John looked at me inquiringly.

"I'm taking no chances."

"Funny," murmured John. "They should know we are
in this general area." Would they? I wondered. My guess was
that *Trout* was on her own—desperately on her own.

She lay down, pitching in the swell of the destroyers.

The signalman handed me a message.

"If you are *Trout*," it read, "what are you doing here? No
notification of your presence from Admiralty."

I handed it to John, who started at its contents.

Reply: "Even the best fish, including *Trout*, must rise to
breathe occasionally."

We waited. The cruisers hovered. Then one destroyer
detached itself and came within hailing distance. The metallic
bark of the loud-hailer came over the water.

"*Trout* . . . is that who you are?"

I was seized with impatience. "Damn it, of course I am.
Do I look like a U-boat?"

The loud-hailer chuckled. "All right, all right. But remember . . . Look, I'm carrying mail for *Trout* addressed to
Simonstown. I'm sending a boat with it."

She came close in and dropped a boat. The sub-lieutenant in
command grinned over the couple of feet of sea separating us.
"Shall I throw them across, sir?" he asked.

"Yes," I replied, thinking of what mail at sea, delivered at
sea, would mean to my jaded, bored crew.

"Everything all right?" he added curiously. "No one
expected you around these parts."

"It doesn't look like it," I grinned, waving a hand to the wary destroyers.

"Doesn't look so good at the receiving end," he rejoined. He tossed the packets of mail over. "Good-bye sir, and good luck."

"Thanks," I said. "Call the dogs off now."

A wave of the hand and the boat pulled away to the destroyer's side.

"Good luck!" said the metallic voice.

The group of warships drew rapidly away southwards. The sun began to dip.

"Night stations," I said to John. "Clear the bridge. Sixty feet."

"No moonlight picnic to-night," he teased.

"Everyone will be happier well below the surface to-night reading about wives and sweethearts. Moonlight will only revive old memories."

He glanced at me sharply. There was an edge to my voice.

Trout dived under the darkening South Atlantic.

My share of the mail, in my tiny cubbyhole of a cabin with only its worn green curtain separating me from the rest of the submarine, looked uninspiring. There didn't even seem to be a personal letter among the lot. I felt depressed at the stark little pile of letters and papers, all typewritten. No loving hand to smooth my way, I thought grimly. The whole depression of the mission hit me again. In London it was *Trout's* lack of even a sporting chance that had shaken me; deep under the South Atlantic to-night it was the awareness that the chance was never likely to occur at all.

I ripped open the mail. One bore the superscription "Hodgson, Hodgson and Hodgson, Lincoln's Inn Fields, London." It was from my grandfather's lawyers. The dry phrases seemed utterly sterile. "We have to inform you, as the sole legatee of the late Captain Simon Peace . . ." It seemed the old man had left me about £500 and a miscellaneous collection of old nautical instruments and charts. I'd taken some of the old charts with me from his desk the day he died, anyway. I'd not looked at them.

Then came a rustle amid the dry legal phrases : "You will

notice from the enclosed copy of Simon Peace's will that you have been bequeathed, in terms of it, the island of Curva dos Dunas, stated by the late Captain Peace to lie in 17′ 30″ S 11′ 48″ E. A title deed, apparently legal, filed with the former German Administration of South West Africa, is attached. Owing to war-time restrictions on the availability of charts and maps, we have been unable to establish the identity of this island. The Admiralty states that it cannot disclose any such information in war-time but added, confidentially, that it was unaware that any islands existed in that part of the South Atlantic. The Admiralty, however, refuse to disclose what specific area of the South Atlantic it was referring to. However, we enclose a copy of the title deed for your perusal and suggest that when conditions are more settled, a thorough investigation may be made into the whereabouts and value of this property. We await your instructions as to its disposal at a later date."

The old bastard! I thought amusedly to myself. So he had an island tucked away and no one knew anything about it! Well, it was easy enough for *me* to find out. I went through to the navigation table and pulled out an Admiralty chart " Bahia dos Tigres to Walvis Bay " with the annotation " principally from the German Government charts to 1930." I checked off the position in the letter with the dividers. It was about twenty miles south of the mouth of the Cunene River. There was no sign at all of an island. Curva dos Dunas? I double-checked the position. There it was—a foul-looking piece of coast, if ever there was one, with broken water and shoals all over the place, but no sign of Curva dos Dunas. There were plenty of isolated rocks which pass as islands south of Walvis Bay, but nothing so far north, or near the mouth of the Cunene, which is the international boundary between South West Africa and Angola.

I was puzzling over the little mystery when the hydrophone operator's voice reached me clearly.

" Captain in the control room," called John.

" What is it, John?" I asked.

" Bissett's getting some odd noises," he said. " He just can't identify them."

" H.E?" I asked.

"No, hell," laughed John. "Elton says it's all Bissett's imagination, but you know Bissett is the best we have."

"I'll go and have a look and listen myself," I said.

Bissett had the earphones over his head and Elton, his relief and junior, was standing by, looking rather bored and amused.

"Listen to that, sir," said Bissett, giving me one earpiece.

At first I could hear nothing. Then there was a kind of gurgling noise, very faint, and then a slight, resonant hiss, almost like a bubble slowly bursting under water. It kept repeating in a kind of cycle. In the background there was a slight churning noise.

I simply couldn't make it out.

"Propellers!" I asked tentatively.

"No, definitely not," replied Bissett. "But it's moving sir. Left to right, about ten knots, I reckon."

"About south-east," I reflected aloud.

"Sounds to me like a whale farting," commented Elton.

The remark stung me, epitomising as it did the slack attitude of the crew on this warm-weather cruise.

I turned savagely on Elton: "Another remark like that, Elton, and you'll find yourself in serious trouble."

"Sorry, sir," he muttered, but the contemptuous amusement was not entirely gone from his face.

"It's slowing, sir," said Bissett.

"I'm going to follow it," I told him. "Keep on to it and don't let me lose it. If it speeds up, let me know."

I went back into the control room! "Steer one-six-oh," I told John. "Seven knots."

"Aye, aye sir," he said. "Plot?"

"No." I said. I drew him on one side. "Frankly, John, I haven't a solitary clue what we are following, but I can't stand this bloody square search a moment longer. Anything is better than that."

"Aye, aye, sir," he grinned.

I took the chart from the navigator's table and went towards my cubbyhole: "Call me at once if we catch up on that noise."

John nodded.

In my solitary cabin I started to unfold the chart I had brought with me, but my mind was against Simon Peace's little mysteries, and I threw it down in disgust. I glanced through the remaining letters. A bill or two and a neatly wrapped copy of *The Times*. I opened it and saw that the " deaths " column had been ringed with blue pencil. I could see the precise circle being drawn by the school-masterly hand. The news was like a cold douche. So he was dead! He had deserved to die with a deck under his feet, had old Arctic-eyes. " Killed in an air raid . . ." It left the Director of Naval Intelligence and myself. The only two who knew about NP I outside Germany. That neat circle of blue was both a courier of news and a warning. My little cubbyhole suddenly seemed unbearably stifling. It was quite clear; it needed no words, no admonition, to convey to me the meaning of the man with the pedantic air and heart full of secrets.

I tossed the paper aside and went through to Bissett.

He looked up inquiringly and nodded as I came in. " Still there, sir. Steady seven knots, maybe eight. I just can't make out what that noise can be."

" Steady course, no deviations?"

" Absolutely steady, sir."

The control room boys were chattering between themselves as I came through, but they were on the job all right. I had a feeling of unease which I coul ' not explain.

I threw myself down on my unk again, but I couldn't sleep. I got up and reached for a cigarette and then cursed my forget-fulness. On the handkerchief-sized table lay Hodgson, Hodg-son and Hodgson's letter. Curva dos Dunas! I took the navigator's chart and checked again on the position. I remem-ber that I had crammed a couple of the old man's charts into my grip. I rummaged round and found them, crumpled, but not in bad shape really.

At that moment I knew I had NP I in the bag.

Curious how one's mental processes range apparently with-out purpose or pattern and then suddenly crystallise. When I saw old Simon Peace's chart—criss-crossed with soundings and annotations—I knew that I had been right in what I had intu-itively reasoned before—that NP I must have a base.

And there it was : *my* island, Curva dos Dunas, exactly where old Simon Peace had positioned it. Curva dos Dunas—a Twist of Sand !

I looked at the formidable stretch of coast about twenty miles south of the mouth of the Cunene—what a fool I had been about the old man's dying words! Not south of *north* as I had thought. But south of—and there it was plain on the older chart—south of what the river used to be called, the Nourse. Twenty miles south of the Nourse lay the island, amongst the worst shoals and foul ground that could be charted anywhere. Most of them weren't anyway, not on the Admiralty map.

I studied Simon Peace's map in utter fascination. It was obvious that he had surveyed and charted the whole area himself. There, like a jewel set amid broken patterns of ore, was Curva dos Dunas. Guarded from the south by a needle-shaped rock ("ten feet at high tide, eight fathoms under" said the precise lettering in old Simon's hand) and protected farther south still by the *Clan Alpine* shoal, Curva dos Dunas was the most perfect hide-out anyone could wish for. North of it lay a series of shoals: the water shallowed with incredible abruptness from thirty-two to five fathoms in one place: on the landward side was a rock-strewn, hilly coast surmounted by high shifting dunes; a three-topped hill guarded a tiny beach marked "only sandy beach." This lay half at the back of the island, which seemed only a short distance from the mainland itself. This mainland is known to sailors as the Skeleton Coast, a coastline beaten by high, thundering surf from the south-west; low, wind-blown scrub relieves the utter baldness of the dunes, and everywhere are the wicked shoals. The high dunes, stretch northwards almost to the mouth of the Cunene (or Nourse as old Simon called it). The mouth itself is guarded by a most wicked constellation of shoals.

All this had been carefully charted, a labour which must have taken the old man years. The thought that he might have done it all in a sailing ship along that coast of death made me shudder and marvel at old Simon's intrepidity.

Curva dos Dunas! The name rang like a bell.

I looked at the soundings and shuddered. It meant that I would have to go in through the shoals and pick off NP I as she lay there. "Discoloured water," said the chart. God! I knew what that meant: sand, stirred up from the shallows, and obscuring what little view there might be of channels. Channels! That was what I needed. There must be a channel in from the entrance—was there such a thing as a harbour? I checked the meticulous array of soundings. Seven, four, eight, fifteen, thirty fathoms—all in a jumble. If I took *Trout* in there I'd have her aground before I could say NP I. How did the Germans know about Curva dos Dunas? Well, that was probably easy enough to guess—the Admiralty charts were based on German ones compiled during their long occupation of South West Africa. I remembered that a German warship had done a survey before World War I, and the thorough German mind must have tucked away information like Curva dos Dunas for all the intervening years.

I knew quite instinctively that that was where NP I was lying low. I looked at the map again. On the seaward side of the stark little beach where the neat lettering said " three-topped hill," were two words. They said simply : " see inset." So the old man had made another map of the island, too? Where the devil was it? A brief look through the other crumpled charts and papers in my grip assured me that it was not there. I looked at the stiff parchment map : no, there was no inset. True, the chart would take me there, but on that wicked coast I would need more than just that. For by now the conviction was firm in my mind that I would take *Trout* in, whatever the cost.

The chart, laid out on the tiny table, crumpled itself and automatically I straightened it.

Then I saw.

The thick parchment had been split on the lower right-hand corner. With trembling fingers I felt. They met another edge of thin paper. Scarcely able to control my fingers and dreading that I should tear it, I slipped it out. I could have wept for joy. Silently I blessed old Simon. Curva dos Dunas! —a large-scale map with the entrance channel close to the ten-foot rock which I had first seen on the other chart.

The one I was now examining was a little masterpiece of cartography. The old sailor had taken bearings of the three-topped hill and the entrance channel in relation to the rock in the sea. Small wonder he had called it Curva dos Dunas—a Twist of Sand. The entrance channel curved like the whorls on a man's inner ear, swinging sharply north from the entrance and away from its first easterly direction, then doubling back almost on its own course; in between was a bar of what was marked as " hard sand." I thought what a brief end that sand-bar would make of a ship. The channel then swung round northwards in an irregular semi-circle—north, east, due south and then west again, debouching into a " harbour " contained in the enclosing arms of sand. It was thirty fathoms deep in places. It was something like the Jap base of Truk, in the Pacific, on a much smaller scale. What a funk-hole, I thought to myself. You could not winkle a submarine out of there with a can-opener, and it would be way out of range of the odd sea-search bomber of the South African Air Force at Walvis Bay. To the north lay neutral, largely unknown territory, and to the east the mainland appropriately known as the Skeleton Coast. Yes, that was where NP I was! I'd take *Trout* down that tortuous channel and sink the super U-boat with torpedoes in the deep water inside! Thank God that interminable box-search was at an end! I'd make for Curva dos Dunas and lie in wait for NP I.

Excitedly I got a ruler and made a rough calculation of my course to the island from *Trout's* present position. One hundred and sixty degrees. That would bring her nicely to the ten-foot rock—I'd call it Simon's Rock, in honour of the old sailor who might yet be my salvation—and, for that matter, the salvation of the fighting fleets and merchantmen in the North Atlantic. The thrill of the chase welled through my veins as I turned again to the beautifully drawn map of the channels into the " inner harbour " of Curva dos Dunas. My island! And in occupation by the most lethal submarine in the world! I could be there by late to-morrow. . . .

The appalling significance of it struck me like an icy sea down the conning-tower hatch. One-six-oh! That was exactly the course we were steering! And we were on that course because—dear God!—could it be? Bissett had said the course was steady, and the sound was travelling steadily ahead of us at about seven knots. Course one-six-oh! The homeward-bound course of NP I to her base! *Trout* was, in fact, trailing along merrily, without any attempt at concealment, behind a nuclear-powered submarine!

I broke out in a cold sweat. The noise, that bursting bubble effect—it could well be that the Germans, with all their ingenuity, had abandoned the ordinary propeller and were using a form of hydraulic jet propulsion which ejected the water in exactly the same way that a squid sucks water into its gills and expels it again under high muscular pressure, thus providing its enormous speed and motive power. The thoughts tore through my brain. For a submarine fitted like that—and apparently all the power in the world with which to expel the water—it would be at a double advantage, for those death-dealing, tired, trigger-happy men of the North Atlantic escort groups were accustomed to ordinary propeller noises and this new one would deceive them—at least at the outset. I knew hydraulic jet propulsion had been tried out with great success on shallow-draught small craft, but its application to anything else—well, that was a brand-new lesson for the North Atlantic.

Christ! How many precious minutes had I wasted in thinking this out, and for every one of them *Trout* was in mortal peril! Or had NP I simply not heard us because her hydrophones, listening dead astern, might be confused by the upsurge of ejected water. She had only to change course slightly, and she would hear *Trout's* asdic, as sure as little fishes were waiting for us at the bottom of the ocean.

I bounded towards Bissett, leaping through the control room as I did so. John and the others there gave me a startled glance.

" Switch that infernal thing off!" I roared to the astonished Bissett. He flicked a switch. I could feel the sweat moistening on my face.

" Same course, same speed?" I snapped.

" Aye, aye, sir," he replied, wonderment written all over his face.

" How long have you been listening to that—that—noise?" I whipped out.

" Ever since you . . ." he began, but stopped at the look on my face. " Nearly two hours, sir," he replied woodenly.

" You could identify it again?" I asked.

" Why, yes sir. . . ."

" Shut off everything, then. I may want you to listen later.

But you will not use any of this listening gear without my express permission. Understood?"

" Aye, aye, sir," he replied. There was equal astonishment as I whirled round and entered the control room.

" I'll take over, Number One," I rapped out to John.

" Slow ahead both! Silent routine! Shut off as for depth-charging. Absolute silence. No talking. And if anyone so much as drops a damn thing on the plating, I'll have his guts."

John gave me a penetrating look and rapped out a series of orders. *Trout* eased away from her deadly ocean paramour.

" Course, sir?" asked John.

" Hold her steady on one-six-oh. What's her speed now?"

" Three knots, sir."

" Hold her at that for ten minutes. And then I want just enough way on her to keep her even. Not a fraction of a knot more."

" Shall I sound action stations, sir?" asked John.

" You heard my orders," I snarled. The sweat was trickling down inside my shirt. I took a handkerchief and wiped it away. I saw young Fenton eyeing me apprehensively.

The minutes ticked by. The control room was as tense as if we had been under attack. Six, seven, eight, nine, ten. . . . John gave an order in a low voice.

" Barely steerage way, now, sir."

We waited. I must give her a good half an hour so that we were well out of hearing before I broke surface.

" Take over for a moment," I said to John. I went back to my cubbyhole. I decided that I would navigate myself using old Simon Peace's magnificently annotated chart. Even far out in the ocean his soundings were better than the Admiralty's.

I knew exactly what I had to do. I must steer a course away out of immediate danger from NP I. I must also get to Curva dos Dunas before her. That meant a course as close as pos-sible to the deadly one-six-oh degrees which I must assume she would follow. I would now take *Trout* to the surface and make a break at high speed for Curva dos Dunas, hoping to get there before NP I. I did some quick sums in my head. They had said NP I could do twenty knots submerged. Well, she might, but she had been cruising along gently at seven for the past few hours. I could catch her shortly after daybreak entering the channel, which would give me a good light for firing: it is always tricky firing on a hydrophone bearing alone. I took the detailed map of Curva dos Dunas. There were sixteen fathoms at the entrance and it was very deep all the way in, although here and there buttresses of sand projected, like waiting claws, into the channel itself. There must be a hell of a tide to scour these channels, I thought. But . . . how many years ago had these soundings been taken? The Skeleton Coast is notorious for its upheavals, and even whole sections of coastline have changed their contours overnight. I couldn't think about that. I pored over the entrance. I would lie just southwards and . . . what depth would she come in at? Perhaps on the surface? Only the event would tell. She wouldn't know a thing until they heard *Trout's* torpedoes running; then it would be too late.

Were they quite oblivious of us? There was the sudden slowing-down which Bissett had noticed. What did it mean? Had they . . . no, I rejected the thought desperately. They couldn't have seen *Trout's* rendezvous with the warships! Dear God! I put myself in the boots of NP I's captain. He is lying in a good position to sink a couple of British cruisers, and what happens? Suddenly a British submarine breaks surface and the warships sheer off like startled cats. His whole firing plan goes to maggots. He takes a cautious look and sees a strange sight indeed. The destroyers about as hostile as could be—towards one of their kind. But they would *know Trout* was in these waters, he argues. And what in the name of all that is holy is a submarine doing lying motionless on the surface while the destroyers circle and one goes in and drops a boat? Hunted as he is, he must jump to the immediate conclusion—these warships are looking for NP I, and so must the British submarine be. So they know about me! A cold chill runs down his spine. Must I justify NP I at all costs? Sink that nearest destroyer and the submarine? No, that would be too easy, and the others would be right on the trail. Beat it at high speed? Yes. Eighty feet, high speed away to Curva dos Dunas! And by the merest chance, I added grimly, *Trout* takes an identical course and bashes away merrily in the wake of the deadliest thing afloat, with not a caution or a care in the world! The thought of it made my insides turn over.

I'd had the let-off of my life, I thought without humour, and it's going to cost every man of that wicked U-boat his life. The half-hour was up. I picked up the Admiralty chart to give to the navigator as a formality only. I left my own—old Simon's—in my cubbyhole. After all, I thought with the first lightening of spirits since the enormity of the whole thing had struck me, it is *my* island, and I'm going to protect *my* property, so why should everyone know about it?

John looked expectant as I came in. It was just after nine o'clock.

" Diving stations. Stand by to surface," I said briefly.

" Check main vents," rapped out John.

" All main vents checked and shut, sir."

" Ready to surface, sir."

" Surface. I want you on the bridge with me, Number One."

" Aye, aye, sir."

The hatch was flicked open and the usual sea, warm it seemed to me, slopped in. I scrambled up and immediately searched the horizon. Everywhere the sea was bathed in bright moonlight. And a good thing too, because neither I nor the men on watch had had time to get their eyes accustomed to the different light.

" Nothing in sight, sir," reported John formally.

" Good," I said, drinking in the beauty of the night, and looking half expectantly ahead, as if to find our lethal fellow-traveller along the line of *Trout's* forestay. The South Atlantic was as empty as it had ever been.

" Group up," I ordered. " Start the diesels. Full ahead together. Three hundred and twenty revolutions. Course two-five-oh."

Trout veered away at right angles to the previous course —NP I's course, leaning to the full power of the massive diesels, and tore away into the silver night.

EIGHT

Curva dos Dunas

THE MOON'S silver began to give way to the first grey of the yet unborn day. *Trout* tore on. Sleepless and keyed to a high pitch, I remained all night on the bridge. My eyes were red with watching, and they always strayed back to NP I's imaginary track, now well to the north and west of *Trout*. John had come up during the night in cheerful conversational mood.

"What's all the buzz, Geoffrey?" he asked in his easy, competent way. "Making a real mystery of things, aren't you?"

I regretted to have to do it, but I resorted to that funk-hole of the man in command, rank. I simply said nothing but stared ahead into the night.

John at first did not catch on.

"Brushing up the old navigation all by yourself, too?" he laughed.

I realised that I would rouse some comment by navigating myself, but I simply refused to turn old Simon's maps over to the usual navigator. I said nothing in reply to John's sallies. Out of the corner of my eye I saw him freeze when he realised that we were no longer on the chummy basis on which we had always gone in to the attack. John had always been excellent in giving the crew a loudspeaker appraisal of a tricky situation, and I expect this was his way of putting it to me. He froze into immobility and, except for a few terse, necessary words changing the course after we were well away from NP I's track, there had been silence between us for the rest of the night.

I decided that I would approach Curva dos Dunas from the south, turning north and east once I crossed the seventy-five fathom mark. The more I looked at the ghastly coast, the more thankful I was for old Simon's charts. It was a hopeless conglomeration of broken water, shoals and rocks; everywhere were the terrorising words, "discoloured water." Once across the seventy-five fathom line, I decided to turn *Trout* north-east and thread my way to within fifteen miles of the coast, and then try and pick up my two only sure landmarks, the ten-foot projection which I had named Simon's Rock, and the distinctive three-topped hill with another high hill about seven miles to the nor'ard. If I could spot the tiny beach marked " sandy, white " on the chart, it would be a great additional help; otherwise the old sailorman's only direction on the landward side were " *dunas moveis* "—shifting dunes.

I crossed to the voice-pipe.

" What depth of water have we under us?"

" Eighty-seven fathoms, shoaling, sir."

" Call them out as she goes."

" Aye, aye, sir. Eighty-five. Ninety. Seventy-seven. . . ."

God, I thought, what a coastline to be approaching! Rough as an uncut diamond.

" Seventy-five . . . eighty, seventy-four. . . ."

" That'll do," I snapped out. I had crossed my rubicon. Well, here goes, I thought.

I turned to John who, with the exception of the watch-men, was alone with me.

" Clear the bridge," I said. I felt the tremor in my voice.

" Diving stations, sir?" asked John, shooting me a curious look.

" Clear the bridge," I repeated. " I'll give my orders from up here. Alone."

The ratings on watch glanced nervously at each other as they scuttled down the hatch. John followed. He paused as his head was about to disappear. Apparently he thought better of it and I could almost see the shrug of his shoulders.

" Course seven-oh," I ordered and heard John repeat it. " Speed for ten knots."

The shudder died as *Trout* slowed. I searched the horizon with my glasses, looking every way for the twin sentinels on land which overlooked NP I's hide-out.

I felt completely naked. A warship is a lonely place anyway, but when one has sent everyone below, it seems more so. The gun, unmanned, pointed forward, lashed, with its muzzle to-wards where the land must be. The light anti-aircraft weapons on the conning-tower had the same forlorn look. The quiet sea washed across the casing. All around the darkness was lightening, bringing with it that depression peculiar to early dawn. I swept the horizon in a slow arc with my glasses. If I were fool enough to have no watchmen with me, at least I could be careful enough not to have *Trout* caught with her pants down, so to speak. I could imagine what sort of short shrift I would get from a court-martial, driving a warship in war-time towards a dangerous coast without a single man on watch. And the enemy in the vicinity!

Then I saw the Skeleton Coast for the first time in my life.

I have seen it many times since, but I suppose I shall never forget the primeval awesomeness of that first sight. It was a trick of refracted light from the desert behind, I suppose, but it sent a spine-chilling thrill through me. Against the far rim of lightening east, a shaggy dinosaurus, tufted by shaggy bush and a dun tonsure of sand, rose and gazed hostilely at the lonely submarine. It was, as I have said, a strange trick of the light which gave me that forbidding first cruel glimpse of sand, sea and dune-starved shrub, for *Trout* was, I suppose, every bit of fifteen miles away. Light refracts and plays the strangest tricks in the mica-laden air. I gazed at the strange revelation. How many times had it shown itself in this way to old Simon, laboriously—and with superb seamanship—toiling up and down charting Curva dos Dunas from his sailing-ship? I leant forward to take a bearing.

The Skeleton Coast reached for *Trout's* throat.

I saw the discoloured water as I leant forward and, God knows, even at that stage of my ignorance of the Kaokoveld, I knew it for what it was—sand, shoals, death! I could even see the dun sand swirling in the sea under the thrust of the screws.

"Stop both!" I screamed into the voice-pipe. "Full astern!"

Almost in slow motion *Trout's* way diminished. The sand swirled forward past the casing as the screws bit astern.

"What depth of water under her?" I asked weakly.

"Five fathoms sir," replied the disembodied voice from below.

Five! I marvelled, and reached a trembling hand for the chart. Another cold chill ran down my spine. *Trout* was over the dreaded Alecto Shoal, about fifteen miles south of my objective. Alecto! I didn't know what it meant then, but later I was to discover that *H.M.S. Alecto* reported this piece of particular horror in 1889. I realised, too, that I was only two miles off the coast—two miles! I thought I was five at least

" Stop both," I ordered. " How much water under us?" a question which I came to ask almost automatically later.

" Twenty fathoms, sir."

Well, that was safe enough. Looking at the chart, I estimated that I had almost run *Trout* aground on the north-western tip of the Alecto Shoal. I decided to swing her round and keep away from the general north-westerly trend of the shore-line.

" Speed for six knots," I ordered down the voice-pipe. " Course three-four-oh."

" Aye, aye, sir."

Trout edged her way round the shoal. Then the light came. I was aghast. I seemed to be almost on top of the land. The sea was quiet, with no sign of the dreaded heavy south-westerly swell. The sun, starting to rise redly against the backdrop of dune and sand, looked as if it had a hangover. I felt something like that myself. I took *Trout* seawards for a while and changed course inwards again. The chart said " foul ground " —and foul, indeed, it was. *Trout* ran on slowly. Out to port the quiet sea merged into the peculiar light haze; to starboard loomed the long line of dunes topped by the bibulous sun. I switched my glasses to the north, but I suppose the refracted light destroyed some of the magnification, for a moment later, when I looked with the naked eye, I saw the three-topped hill, unmistakable, against the dun background. The entrance to Curva dos Dunas! I altered course slightly to keep me clear of a sudden four-fathom hump to the south-west of the three-topped hill.

Trout, at funereal pace, moved towards where I knew Simon's Rock must lie. And—beyond lay *Trout's* objective, Curva dos Dunas! A ten-foot rock sticking out of the sea is a difficult enough thing to see at any time, but in the peculiar inshore light, one might well pass it by—and be wrecked on the shoals at the entrance to the island. Old Simon's chart showed it bearing 330 degrees from the three-topped hill.

I began to sweat; nothing showed as the bearing approached. All those doubts which I had rigidly refused to consider when I had made my decision to break away from the box-search assailed me. If all this was merely chasing a will-o'-the-wisp. . . . The line of the bearing fell across the 330 degree mark. Nothing! There was nothing either on the landward side—nothing that remotely looked like an island.

" Stop both," I ordered, struck by the harshness of my own voice.

I consulted the chart again. I was almost exactly—if any navigator can hope to be anything like exact on that coast—where the rock should be. While *Trout* wallowed in the slight swell, I swept every inch of sea between myself and the shore.

There was nothing. No rock, no breakers, not a living or dead thing.

I scanned every inch of sea where I knew Curva dos Dunas should lie. Nothing!

So, I thought bitterly to myself, an old man's illusion and a young fool's dream turned out to be nothing but a stretch of empty water! I could take *Trout* through without a thought of wrecking her, if I wished.

Even to myself I could not answer the questions which arose about NP I—or rather the noise which I fatuously believed was the hydraulic jet machinery of NP I. Who had ever heard of a submarine being propelled by the expulsion of water anyway? Who would believe such a cock-and-bull story? It looked lamer every moment. I had made a complete fool of myself in front of my officers and my crew, standing a watch alone—in wartime—and conning a ship without a single soul aboard knowing where she was. *Trout's* log would look lovely before a court-martial! No entries, and the captain unable to say where he was. I looked round me, cursed the Skeleton Coast and cursed NP I and all the blasted fools who had given me this impossible mission.

I snapped open the voice-pipe.

" Course three-two-oh. Two hundred revolutions."

I'd get the hell out of this blasted coast, I thought bitterly. Then I saw it.

It flashed white and evil, like a guano-covered fang, out of the sea a few hundred yards on the port beam. I had been on the *inside* of the damned thing and I had been searching landwards! A sick, cold feeling hit me in the stomach after my momentary elation. I was in the wickedest stretch of foul ground. The fathom line was contorted like a switch-back at Blackpool. I had been fooled for the second time that morning by the current and fooled more still by the curious light refraction so that I had not seen Simon's Rock itself, but only its white-guano-littered tip where the sun caught it. I was like a blind man rushing through a roomful of glasses trying not to knock them over.

" Full astern ! " I yelled in the voice-pipe. " No, stop both ! Give me continuous depth readings."

" Echo-sounder reports four fathoms, sir," came up John's quiet, untroubled voice. What the hell would he be thinking about my hysterical commands screamed down from the bridge where there was no one else to tell him what was going on?

" Asdic reports obstructions bearing ah . . . hem . . . almost all round the compass, sir." The calm voice had a tinge of irony. " Hydrophones report all quiet, sir. No transmissions."

Trout lay in the troughs of the waves while I tried to make up my mind. It was easy enough to know where I was. I had Simon's Rock at my back, and the three-topped hill ashore to give me a fix. I pored over the annotated chart and saw that if I turned *Trout's* head I could get her into the position I had originally intended, a piece of deep water flanking the entrance to Curva dos Dunas. Curva dos Dunas ! Where the hell was it ? The sea was calm, almost oily, and there were no breakers. There should have been, looking at old Simon's annotations. " Breaks. Six fathoms. Breaks occasionally. Possibly less water. Heavy breakers. Surf."

I gazed hopelessly around for the sand-bars which must mark the channel into Curva dos Dunas. There simply *must* be ! With trembling hands I took a bearing and cast my binoculars along the line of it seeking my island. Nothing ! Had it disappeared in all the years that had elapsed since the chart was drawn? But, argued my sailor's mind, the rest of it is accurate enough. So damn accurate that had it not been so you and *Trout* would have been dead ducks already. Again I cast my eye along the line of the bearing. Suddenly I felt terribly afraid. My palms sweated. I knew why they called it the Skeleton Coast. I knew the terror of the men who drove in to this fearful, bland, cross-eyed shore and were called crazy when they got back to port—if they did. I shivered, despite the growing intensity of the sun. I noticed *Trout's* head beginning to swing away landwards. God, what a race there must be here! The thought shook me out of my nameless terror. I would take *Trout* outside Simon's Rock and make a reconnaissance of the so-called entrance to Curva dos Dunas : if the soundings proved to be the same as on the chart, I would follow my original plan. The part about Curva dos Dunas simply not being there— I'd forget it, for the moment.

"Slow ahead both," I ordered. "Give me continuous soundings. Tell Bissett to keep his ears skinned."

"Aye, aye, sir," came John's voice.

I eased *Trout* round and she made her way slowly through and over the wicked sand-bars only a few feet under her keel. Had the water been breaking, I thought grimly. Now we were in deeper water. The soundings suddenly deepened—from five and six to twenty-nine and then forty-seven and sixty-one. I breathed freely again, knowing we were safe for the moment but remembering what the bottom looked like in case we had to dive. Dive! I thought of NP I. With this coast under us, we would be like two men fighting between themselves and a third at the same time. Certainly the Skeleton Coast would give neither of us any quarter.

I brought *Trout* round in a shallow circle and ran in towards where the entrance to Curva dos Dunas should lie. Using Simon's Rock and the three-top hill like a man in a fog holding on to one patch of light, I brought *Trout* in.

"Bottom shallowing, sir," came John's report.

I blurred a spot on the chart with a pencil where *Trout* lay. Thirty fathoms here, said old Simon's handwriting.

"Thirty fathoms, sir. Hydrophone operator reports no transmissions. Three knots."

Dead right. I felt the sea catch *Trout* by the tail and as she swung I felt the correction. Someone was certainly on the job down below. But it showed there was a tide race. Thirty, twenty-seven, twenty-five, twenty-three, twenty-five read the chart.

"Thirty fathoms, sir, twenty-seven, twenty-three, twenty-five. Asdic reports obstructions port, starboard and ahead. Clear astern."

God! The old man was right!

Then I saw Curva dos Dunas.

I think it must have been the slight gust of wind from the south-west—sailors on this coast mutter south-west in their dreams, for from that quarter come the waves and the wind to drive you against the ruthless shore. A ripple spread across the calm surface of the sea. I saw a sudden flicker of white. A rapid whorl of white, convulsed and turning like a man's inner ear. I saw the sand-bars curve and twist like the charted lines. The wind had whipped the sea against the wicked, waiting sand for a moment.

Curva dos Dunas had revealed itself, a veil rent aside only for a moment.

I couldn't see the inner anchorage clearly, but what I saw told its own deadly tale. Here was an anchorage—the only anchorage for a thousand miles, and it lay behind a convolution of sand-bars, completely hidden in calm weather but visible in anything of a breeze, when any sailor worth his sense would shy like a frightened horse at spotting those lines of broken surf. I marvelled at the guts of old Simon Peace at taking a sailing-ship in there; at his courage at winding his way through those broken lines of surf, now snarling as the wind broke the water across their half-concealed fangs; at his tenacity at coming back again and again to chart it. No wonder he had screamed on his death-bed! Sand, bars of sand, every one of them death at the touch of a keel. To take any ship, even under diesel or electric engines, into what appeared a broken holocaust of surf, would require a heart as steady as the three-topped hill away to starboard now. I looked with grim satisfaction at my island, my only landed possession in the world. It was a gift worthy of the old dead sailor: surf on this coast is death, but an anchorage is life. He had shown me where I could find NP I, if she was to be found.

I changed course and cruised across the entrance. No Navy hydrographer could have done a better job than old Simon. The swirl of the tide must have kept it swept clean all these years, and was likely to do so long after I was dead. I checked my original plan and made for the southern side of the entrance where there was deep water. From there, I had planned, I would sink NP I as she entered the channel. Now, however, I changed my plan slightly. Sink NP I I would, but slightly farther away and not block the one safe anchorage on all this wild coast. If only they had given me a couple of mines! I could have mined the channel and simply sat back and watched NP I destroy herself. Or would I? I asked myself now. Would I have blocked the entrance when only her skipper and I knew of the existence of one of the best-guarded maritime secrets in the world? I didn't bother to answer myself. I hadn't the mines anyway.

I manœuvred *Trout* into position. I would lie on the sea-bed until I heard NP I and then sink her quickly. For the first time in days I grinned to myself. I reached for the voice-pipe. NP I might be almost upon us, but she wouldn't find *Trout* unprepared.

"Dive!" I ordered curtly. "Action stations."

The atmosphere in the control room was plain to me even as I clipped the hatch above me and received the familiar dollop of water as *Trout* slid under. John was meticulously correct and formal, and God help anyone under him who erred. But I could tell from young Devenish, the sub's, face, that the officers considered their skipper had gone round the bend—perhaps even now he was going up the creek by this apparently ridiculous order for action stations after a couple of hours of fooling around which would have caused any would-be officer to be sacked from his training course. The crew, battle-hardened, were alert and on the job, every man where he should be. If the officers thought I was crazy, heaven alone knows what the crew thought. Blast them all, I thought savagely, it isn't for them to think. I'm doing the thinking, and I'm carrying a burden of responsibility which may well decide the fate of the entire war at sea. They just have to sweat it out.

"What's the sounding?" I asked briefly.

"Fifteen fathoms—a shade more, sir."

"Steer three-five-oh," I ordered.

The helmsman spun his wheel and *Trout* swung her deadly snout towards the spot where I knew NP I must enter that fearful channel.

"Depth, eighty feet. Lay her gently on the bottom."

The planesman manipulated expertly.

"Torpedo settings for eight and ten feet," I continued. "All tubes to the ready."

"Down periscope." I had taken one last quick look round. The shallow settings on the torpedo were tricky, but I was working on the assumption that NP I would come in on the surface. I gave the plot for the attack and the fruit machine went into action. In my mind's eye I saw the whole situation. The old thrill of the chase and the consummation of the attack swept over me. The bastard, I thought without rancour.

"Course for a ninety-degree track?"

"Three-four-five degrees, sir."

Well, my rough estimate of three-five-oh had been near enough; good enough with a spread on the torpedoes.

Trout planed down to the hard, sandy bottom of the Skeleton Coast. There was a faint bump. The one and only time, I said to myself, that I hope to touch the sand of the Skeleton Coast. *Trout* lay with her nose, fanged now and waiting the venomous thrust of compressed air to lash its deadly cargo into life, pointing exactly where NP I must cross her path. The range was easy, and all we had to do was to wait. NP I would be a sitting duck—and she couldn't come in there at twenty knots, even if everything I had been told was true.

"Stop both," I ordered. "Silent routine." I gestured to John. "Tell them over the loudspeaker that I want absolute silence. Absolute. Do you understand? Their lives depend on it."

"Aye, aye, sir," he replied, but his glance was a mixture of curiosity and compassion. I know what he's bloody well thinking, I told myself. The skipper's imagining all this. He's fighting the old battles all over again. He knows the drill so well, you can't fault him. But the sea's empty and there isn't a whisper on the hydrophones. He's playing possum with his thoughts on some remote African beach; he's told no one where we are. They'll let him down lightly when this gets out because of his war record. But he's crazy; he is still in command.

I saw it all on his face.

A deathly hush settled over *Trout* after the impersonal crackle of John's voice over the loudspeaker. All pumps and all machines were still, and not a man said a word. One could almost hear the crunch of the hard sand under *Trout*.

Bissett's voice came muffled.

"Hydrophone operator reports no transmissions, sir," said John. His voice was almost a whisper.

"Unless there is something to report, tell him to keep quiet," I said. Blohm and Voss alone knows what listening apparatus NP I has. I couldn't afford to take one slightest chance.

I stood by the periscope, its clipped-up handles making it look vaguely like a spaniel with its ears tied back above its head. The operators stood by their unmoving dials, and in the immobile engine-room I could see Macfadden gazing, apparently with the vacancy of a lunatic, at the dead telegraphs. Mac was very much on the job, however, and I couldn't have hoped for a better engineer—or a more stable man under attack. *Trout* lay under the sea like the puff-adders lie in the desert sand—immobile, asleep, coiled, but quick as a dart when trodden on amid their dun surroundings. So *Trout* lay —waiting, listening for that strange bubbling, thumping noise which I construed to be NP I's engines.

With the air conditioning machinery switched off—for what it was worth—the sweat started to trickle down the back of my neck. John's face glistened in the high humidity. The clock hand moved round. Silence. A great silence, only broken by the occasional soft thump as *Trout* nuzzled the unfriendly sand under her. An hour passed. I was almost startled to see one of the crew move silently to request permission to visit the heads—he had removed his shoes and socks and was padding about barefooted. In the engine-room men had stripped off their shirts, and the sweat ran in runnels from their bare, browned torsos—legacy of the cruising days in the sun. Let them sweat it out, I thought unfeelingly.

Two hours. Three hours. We stood to action stations without exchanging a word. The heat was becoming very oppressive. No one had eaten anything since the call to action stations. I called John and gave him instructions to have bullybeef sandwiches served all round.

"Tell the cook," I added, "that if he so much as drops a knife, he'll stop right away and no one will get a morsel."

"Aye, aye, sir," John said formally.

The sandwiches provided a welcome break in the long vigil. It was now past noon. The smell of humans, mixed with oil, so characteristic of submarines, hung heavy in the staling air. My own sweat stank rank; it stank of fear. You can smell a frightened crew, but this one wasn't. But their commanding officer was—terribly, frightfully afraid.

As the afternoon wore on, the fears which had gone underground since I had actually located Curva dos Dunas raised their heads, each one with two more heads attached to the original one. Suppose I *had* smelled out NP I's lair—was there any guarantee that she would return soon, even reasonably soon? With her apparently unlimited cruising range, she might be away weeks. I swore to myself that if I had to wait a week, or even two, I would do so. I had waited before. The French saying came to my mind : "Patience is bitter, but its fruits are sweet." In the balance of my doubts, I had the one great concrete fact : I had found a hide-out capable of being used by a marauding submarine which no one knew about. That it was navigable, I had only old Simon's charts to rely on, but they had proved themselves accurate enough. And there had been the strange noises which *Trout* had followed— I was still convinced, almost to her doom.

We waited.

Another hour ticked ponderously by. John stood like a statue, and the others might have been hypnotised into frozen flesh, except that they were sweating more heavily now. Once I caught a fleeting exchange of glances between the sub at the "fruit machine" and the navigator. They still thought I was crazy, maybe even crazier after a silent action stations vigil of more than six hours. Up above the sun must be starting to sag towards St. Helena. For hours I studied the small inset chart of Curva dos Dunas, until I think I knew every fathom mark, every obstruction, every sand-bar. I glanced at the clock. After five! Weary with the long inactivity, I decided to speak to Bissett myself. After hours at the hydrophones, even his sensitive ears—and they were the keenest in the boat—would be deadening. I edged into his cubicle. My rubber-soled shoes made no noise. Elton was lounging next to Bissett.

I caught his whispered words before he saw me.

" . . . crackers. Up the creek. Reckon Jimmy the One thinks so too. You've been listening for eight hours—for what? A farting whale. If that isn't plumb crackers . . ."

" Elton," I said softly, and he froze. He turned swiftly and faced me. There was a half sardonic grin on his face which triggered off the accumulated tension of hours of nerve strain within me.

He opened his mouth, but he never said what he intended to. I hit him across the side of the neck, a savage blow meant for a street fight, a muscle-ripping, cruel lunge with the edge of my forearm. He sagged like a rag doll and sat down with a heavy thump, his senseless eyes rolling back with fear.

Bissett looked aghast and did the sensible thing by concentrating on his job. I felt sick, and deeply ashamed of myself. The savagery of my pent-up feelings had mute witness in the sorry picture half propped against the bulkhead. I felt his pulse. Well, I hadn't killed him.

Suddenly a ripple ran through Bissett, like a pointer sighting his game.

" Sir! sir!" he whispered urgently.

" What is it, man?" I rapped out.

He didn't hear me. His whole being was listening.

" Confused noises bearing red one-five," he said slowly. " Getting stronger."

I could barely utter the words. " Is it the same. . . .?"

He nodded.

He looked up and smiled.

" Coming this way all right, sir. Lot of ground echoes, but quite clear. Same as last night."

I snatched an earpiece and listened. Yes, there it was, the same deadly thump, like a man dragging a leg.

I knew all I wanted to know.

I shot through to the control room.

" Continuous readings," I snapped as I left him.

" Group up, slow ahead. Revolutions for four knots. Stand by all tubes. Plot? Firing angle? Range? Enemy course? Speed?"

Trout was galvanised. The attack routine went into deadly efficient action.

" Thirty feet," I said. That would give me the opportunity to fire either by periscope or on the hydrophone bearing, although I preferred the former.

" Slow ahead." I'd close the range as near as I dared in the shallow water. There was the danger that *Trout* might break surface if I fired a full salvo.

The planesman spun his wheel and the water blew.

Trout rose silently off the sand and glided upwards.

Then it happened.

The inclinometer went mad. *Trout's* bows lifted like a mad thing and she spun half on her side, throwing John and myself together in a heap under the " fruit machine."

" God's death!" I swore. Davis was fighting like a maniac with the planes, but *Trout* bucked and kicked like an untamed broncho. He was cursing, softly, but with horrible fluency. If *Trout's* bows reared out of the water—it would be the end of us.

Then her nose dipped and the compass card swung madly. With a sick realisation I knew that the tide-race had us inexorably in its grip. My attack plan had gone haywire in a matter of seconds.

" For Christ's sake!" I screamed at Davis. " Get her under control! Keep her bows steady. . . ."

Loose things fell about the conning-tower and I kicked away with savage anger a pair of shoes which seemed to materialise and try and attach themselves to me. The inclinometer bubble swung berserkly.

" God's teeth!" I raved and screamed, all my nerves shot to hell. NP I in my sights and *Trout's* trim so impossible that I simply couldn't fire!

" Blow the main tanks," I shouted. " No, belay that."

I knew I was beaten. There was only one thing to do. Get down on the seabed and try and sort things out while the deadly foe went on his way—unharmed. But at least I would have a look at him.

"Up periscope." I gripped the handles.

The tip burst wildly through the water and for a moment my eyesight reeled before a drunken, swinging vista of sky and white water. With that up top, it was scarcely any wonder that *Trout* was behaving like a madman below, in the shallow water. The periscope lifted fifteen feet out of the water in a horrid swaying arc, and I prayed silently that the look-outs on NP I wouldn't spot it. Through the white water and blue sky, deepening in the coming evening, I caught a glimpse of NP I. The narrow conning-tower stood up frail and delicate like an aircraft wing, and in that split moment I saw how lovely her lines were. She headed unwaveringly towards the entrance to Curva dos Dunas.

"Down periscope," I ordered briefly, calm now that the great moment was passed.

"Take her down," I said briefly. "Eighty feet."

The Skeleton Coast had won. NP I had got away—almost in my sights. As the water poured into her tanks, *Trout* steadied up a little and then, almost magically below sixty feet, regained her composure. The boat was a shambles.

"Take her down," I said, almost abstractedly. "Clear up this bloody mess."

Bissett's voice came through clearly.

"Stop that bloody row!" I snarled. What he could tell me would be of no use to me now. I knew where NP I was headed.

Trout subsided with a faint thump, like a breathless athlete.

"Take over," I said to John. I wanted time to plan a new course of action. "Break off the action. Crew to normal stations."

"Aye, aye, sir," came the reply.

I went to the cubbyhole which passed for my private cabin. I sat down wearily, and as I did so the fetid smell of sweat came up. The sweat of fear. Yes, I was frightened; that delicate, airy conning-tower of NP I had struck the fear of God into me. For a split second I felt almost glad that the Skeleton Coast had intervened and prevented my firing the death-dealing salvo. I pushed the thought aside. I had missed my big chance—through no fault of my own—and now the odds would be twice what they were. Bitterly I cursed the tide-race and the variable density of water which had sent *Trout* rocketing about. I had never reckoned on it.

Anyway, there was nothing I could do about that now. What I had learned was that the Skeleton Coast always laughs last.

I took old Simon's insert chart of Curva dos Dunas and laid it before me on the minute scrap of wood which passed for a table. Mines! I could slip back to Simonstown and load with mines and finish off NP I. It would mean leaving Curva dos Dunas unguarded, but then, either inside or out on a cruise, NP I would sink herself in the channel. Neat and easy, and no danger to *Trout*. I had almost sold myself on the idea of mines when I remembered the tide-race. No, it would be quite impossible to lay mines in the channel with the race sweeping out seawards. *Trout* would blow herself up—since they would sweep down on her as she laid them. To lay them from the inside would be equally impossible, as *Trout* would then be bottled up by her own mines.

The Skeleton Coast had won again.

I glanced at my watch and I took the decision which I had, through fear, kept rigidly at the back of my mind.

I would take *Trout* in after NP I.

I felt unutterably weary. I shuddered as I glanced at those fearful whorls on the chart, guarded by the remorseless sand-bars. Peering at the welter of soundings and curt annotations, I suddenly found myself amused. Before the final whorled channel into the anchorage in the centre was marked "Galleon Point." And, minutely under it in the faded Indian ink, "spar shows at low water. Five fathoms." A galleon! The thought was too much for my tired mind. I laughed to myself and the laughter, like a balm, soothed my failure and crystallised my new attack plan. It was almost dark now. I had two choices: I could try and take *Trout* in on the surface and risk discovery and almost certain sinking by NP I—there was no room to manœuvre—or go in at periscope depth, using Simon's Rock, the three-topped hill and another high hill to the north to steer her by. My heart sank when I looked at the channel. A mis-

judged order, one mistiming, a swing of the tide-race, and
Trout would be jammed against the sand-bars and wolfish
breakers. It would be moonlight. I'd take *Trout* in, even if it
killed me. Once in the inner anchorage, NP I would get her
delayed salvo of *Trout* torpedoes, although I hoped the
explosion wouldn't damage *Trout* as well, the distance was so
small. Anyway, that problem could wait. If I could take
Trout safely in, it would be the most fantastic piece of navigation I had ever attempted. I would also have to bring her out
again. And, I thought, the Skeleton Coast alone knows what
the water densities are in that channel, sweeping in from warm,
shallow water to the cold South Atlantic outside. The only
other alternative had already been lost—to have tried to follow
NP I in on hydrophone bearings. I would have had to take
Trout so close behind, however, that she must have heard us.
Here goes, I thought grimly. I laughed as I tossed down the
dividers.

John was looking at me. I hadn't heard him come in, I had
been so engrossed in the plan of attack. He had heard that last
laugh of mine, and I guess it didn't sound too good to a man
who thought his skipper was running off the rails.

We faced one another. John's air of anxious care nettled
me. Humour the patient, I thought to myself.

" Well?" I said curtly.

John spread his hands slightly. " Look, Geoffrey. . . ."

He stopped hopelessly when he saw my face. " You've been
without sleep for two days and nights. Have some rest. I'll
set a course for Simonstown—if you'll tell me where we are."

I took refuge in my command. " There's a new attack
plan. I don't want it fluffed, like the other."

John made a gesture of despair. So low that I scarcely could
hear, he said : " What were we attacking before?"

His loyalty, his despair, his obvious conclusion that I was no
longer in a fit state to command *Trout* roused me. I laughed.
A hard, brittle, nervous laugh. It drew a sharp look from him.

" I'm attacking the most dangerous enemy in the most
dangerous waters in the world," I said.

He looked at me disbelievingly. I went towards the entrance and for a moment I thought he was going to stop me. I
brushed past into the control room.

"Diving stations," I ordered. "Twenty feet. Up periscope. Group up. Both ahead together. Revolutions for six knots."

I intended to rush through the patch of rough, low-density water, and—I hoped—be shallow enough to avoid the turbulence, and get fixes on old Simon's rock at the southern entrance, and on the two hills before I committed *Trout* to the channel.

At sixty feet *Trout* bucked madly again, but at twenty feet all was quiet.

"Up periscope."

There was Simon's Rock, still white tipped in the near-dark. I had a clear view of the three-topped hill bearing 105 degrees and the northern mountain, almost masked now against its dun background, on seventy degrees.

"Course one-oh-oh," I said, committing her to the entrance. It was about three-quarters of a mile to the first big swing in the channel; it then turned back almost parallel to the entrance.

Trout glided towards Curva dos Dunas.

I raised the periscope higher and was appalled at what I saw. Against the dun backdrop of the dunes, touched now with the last light of day, a gale creamed in from the south-west, breaking berserkly on the bars at the entrance, bared now like fangs. I was steady on my bearings however, and old Simon's chart was a marvel. All round creamed broken water.

The sweat trickled down my neck.

"Hydrophone operator and asdic report confused noises to port, starboard and ahead, sir," John reported, his face a mask of formality.

"Switch the bloody things off," I snapped.

"Aye, aye, sir."

"Course one-oh-five degrees," I ordered. The helmsman made a minute adjustment. Beyond the seething water straight ahead I could see the strange three-topped hill. I only had to steer for that until the high hill to the north bore sixty degrees, when I would make my first great change of course as the channel turned back on itself.

Trout crept slowly towards the bearing. I swivelled the periscope round—Simon's Rock had been lost in the whiteness on the starboard quarter. One of my lifelines was gone. I

must have enough light to keep the high northern hill and the
three-topped hill in view just till the moon rose.

The bearing neared.

Here it was.

"Course three-two-oh," I said without expression.

John jumped like a scalded cat.

"Three-two—oh." Very slowly : "Aye, aye, sir."

"Helmsman, course three-two-oh."

Trout swung round. I waited without breathing for the
tell-tale bump which meant the end. It did not come.

The control room was tense. By the unknown grapevine
the buzz had gone around the boat and most of the men, of
their own accord, had taken up action stations.

The sweat poured off me. Up above, the mælstrom of white
water was more terrifying than ever. Nowhere could I see unbroken sea. It was lashed to foam, aided by the strong south-
westerly gale. I was getting to know my Skeleton Coast. I was
also getting to know what courage it had taken the old sailor
to *sail* a ship in there, and take soundings. *Trout* edged back
almost the way she had come in the new channel. The light was
dying on the three-topped hill, and its outlines were blurred.
God, for that moon which would silhouette it for me, I prayed.

She came on to the bearing for the next wide, shallow turn
to the north; the channel then veered almost due east, and
again towards the south and west for the final entry into the
anchorage.

The hill was more blurred and my heart sank as I decided to
change course.

"Steer three-oh," I said. The rank sweat coursed down
inside my clothes.

"Three-oh, aye, aye, sir," said John. But his tone reflected
the growing anxiety of every man on board as *Trout* swung and
veered down the channel.

"Sir. . . . " he came forward anxiously.

I could spare him this moment. And, by God, I thought,
I'll teach him to think I'm crazy.

I stood back from the eyepieces, wiping the sweat on a
stinking towel. I gestured him to look.

He bent down. Every eye was upon him. At last, I thought,
they're saying Jimmy the One is getting a look in and, if the

skipper's crazy, at least he'll get us out of this mess—whatever it is.

I watched his face. I saw the white bracket form round his mouth as he saw the inferno of breaking water. The crew saw it too. Under his tan, his face went deadly pale. He slowly turned the periscope through a full circle, and then back again. I touched him on the shoulder. He pulled back, formal, but his face and lips were bloodless. The effect was not lost on the watching men. It was the face of a man, inwardly terror-struck, who was doing everything in his power to keep his face from showing it.

"Thank you, sir," he said.

I wiped the streaming rubber eyepieces.

I changed the course slightly again, praying for the moon to rise behind the three-topped hill. I would have to wait for that, and the present gentle curve of the channel seemed as easy as any. I reduced speed to bare steerage way. *Trout*, at only twenty feet, seemed to be making good progress; the tide rip must be deep underneath, I puzzled. Farther on I would call the crew to action stations. There was about another four miles to go to the anchorage after that.

"Dead slow ahead," I ordered. Hoping for the moon, I could pass safely through this section—with luck. It was only a matter of five minutes. Five minutes, and I would be opposite Galleon Point. The tide was high, so I would not see the spar marked on the chart.

Then *Trout* struck.

As if an unseen hand had given her a push, she yawed to port and stuck firm. There was no warning, and not much concussion. Her head simply swung and stuck.

I rapped out a rapid command. The engines stopped and there *Trout* lodged, slightly canted, but not bumping. I swung the periscope round. She didn't seem to be right in among the breakers. Could this be some new obstruction since the days when old Simon had mapped it?

"Half astern," I ordered. If she came off, she wouldn't slide too far backwards. The engines woke up. *Trout* remained stuck.

"Full astern!"

No result.

John had checked and apparently there was no damage. *Trout* didn't seem in grave danger, but her stern now swung inwards with the current. I took the chart between sweat-soaked fingers and saw that *Trout* must be hard aground off Galleon Point. What had pushed her sideways? There was nothing on the chart. I swung the periscope round and studied the broken water to the south. Then I saw. There was a slight clear patch running directly into the main channel. It was a kind of overflow channel through which the water sluiced when the tide was nearly high, like now, and invisible at low water. The situation was serious, but by no means hopeless. I could blow the tanks and probably shake her loose, but that might mean giving away my position. But in this near-dark? A submarine's silhouette is small at the best of times, and it was not likely that she would be spotted if she broke surface only for a moment. . . .

" Blow the main tanks," I ordered.

Trout strained as she became buoyant. Strained, held—and tore free—free! She leaped to the surface.

" Twenty feet," I ordered.

She dived like a mad thing. As the words left my lips I knew that her hydroplanes were damaged.

" Surface."

" Aye, aye, sir."

Trout came up raggedly, very raggedly.

" Try and keep her awash if you can," I said to John. His clipped, curt commands showed that he knew what danger *Trout* was in—he had looked through the periscope.

There was only one thing now—to take *Trout* in on the surface and hope that she wouldn't be spotted before I could deal a lethal blow. There was also the moon. A sharp look-out aboard NP I and we were doomed. On the other hand, a submarine's conning-tower, with the rest of her almost awash, is not easy to see—unless a sliver of moonlight reflecting off the wet casing gave us away.

I reached for an old reefer jacket.

" I'll con her from up aloft," I said. " No look-outs."

Then the thought struck me.

With one foot poised on the steel rung, I remembered my explicit orders. " You will destroy. . . ."

"Fuse the demolition charges to blow her up," I said.

Davis at the hydrophones blanched. I turned to John and looked him in the eyes.

"If you fail to receive word from me within five-minute intervals, no one is to venture up aloft. Is that clear? You will blow the demolition charges."

"Escape drill for the crew, sir?"

I thought of that pitiless waste of waters. They would be better off in one short, sharp explosion than trying to battle it out against the inexorable sea.

"No escape drill," I replied. "You will blow the charges. That is all."

He looked at me bleakly. I knew he would do it.

"Aye, aye, sir."

The salt spray smarted on my lips up aloft. Curva dos Dunas might have looked grim through the periscope, but from up here, with a view all round of the terrifying breakers, it was truly horrifying. *Trout* seemed stuck in the middle of a welter of creaming white water, with the salt spray and spin-drift tearing up from the south-west across her, half-sub-merged. In fact, I could scarcely see the full length of the casing, or distinguish where it started and ended. It would need a very keen pair of eyes to pick us up from NP I in that driving mælstrom. Radar—but that was her Achilles heel. I felt a little easier. Then, through the broken, spume-laden air on the landward side, my two mountains, like things primitive when the world was young, reared their dun crowns as the moon rose behind them, pale and strange in the queer refracted light which the salt-laden air of the sea, meeting the mica particles of the desert, had contrived. The moon itself looked distorted, sick. The feeling of being utterly alone, dominated by the wild elements of sea and desert, wiped the fear of NP I from my heart. It was not NP I who was the first enemy, but the Skeleton Coast. Alone, I shivered.

"Steer one-one-oh," I ordered down the voice-pipe.

Trout headed down the channel. There was almost nothing to distinguish it from the rest of the white water. The spume tore across the slowly-moving submarine.

The two mountains gave me a new bearing, and I altered course sharply to the southward, the land being now close by on my left. I could even see, in the strange light, the scrub on the corrugated sandhills above the rocky beach. *Trout* had not suffered much—for surface running at any rate—but I reckoned, looking at old Simon's chart, that we must have struck at Galleon Point. She may have even fouled some old wreckage there.

My eyes were riveted to the south-west, where I knew NP I must lie in the inner anchorage. The driving, salt-laden gale made it impossible to see any distance. About a mile and a half to go. . . .

"Action stations," I ordered. "Bring all tubes to the ready. Settings for four and six feet. Gun crew at the ready. When I give the word, I want them to fire on a bearing I will give them immediately before. Is that clear?"

"Aye, aye, sir," came John's disembodied response.

I altered course again, due south now. The channel made one last swing before the anchorage. I felt my heart racing, for now it was all or nothing. I couldn't dive and I felt sure that in a gun-fight *Trout* would be outclassed.

Then I saw the long causeway leading ashore.

For a moment I couldn't believe my eyes. There it was, almost awash in the tide, but a dead straight line between the anchorage and the shore! There was nothing on my chart. Had these thorough Germans built themselves a concrete runway to link themselves with that inhospitable shore, a back door to the funk-hole?

I looked closer and saw it was hard-packed, iron-hard shingle, a natural causeway as perfect as anyone could wish. But there was no time to admire. We were almost there.

"Course three-two-oh," I ordered.

Trout swung through the last great whorl and I noticed how much calmer and oilier the water was. I still felt reasonably safe from discovery.

The anchorage!

There was NP I on the far side, wraith-like, beautiful.

She was big—every bit of 3,000 tons, I guessed quickly. She was painted white—perfect camouflage in the breaking waters —which gave a fairy aspect to her lovely clean lines and the wing-like, streamlined conning-tower.

"All tubes ready?" I asked.

" All tubes ready, sir. Settings for four and six feet."

" Course one-nine-oh," I said.

NP I was a sitting duck. I didn't need all the elaborate para-phernalia which are vital to attack: all I had to do was point *Trout* at NP I and fire my salvo. The danger really lay in damage to *Trout* herself at that short range. She'd have to risk that.

" Stand by," I said. " Target bearing dead ahead."

Trout pointed her deadly snout across the salt-impregnated anchorage. To my amazement, I saw that NP I had a small light rigged and there was a group of men doing something to the casing—andd I thought I saw more men on a strip of sand-bar beyond.

Then *Trout* gave her fateful lurch.

I do not know whether it was one of those hellish cross-currents, or a sudden change in density of the water, but she lurched. I grabbed to steady myself. My grasping fingers clung, caught and tugged as I struggled for balance.

I fired *Trout's* recognition flare.

The flare soared across the anchorage, lighting everything, drowning the moon. German faces whipped round on NP I and stared, first at the flare, and then in horror at the clear out-line of *Trout* at the entrance. I stood speechless, aghast. By a million-to-one chance I had given away all chance of conceal-ment, and surprise. It wasn't going to be a clean kill now.

The flare arched over and plunged down, burning brightly. At growing speed it plummeted towards the surface of the anchorage. It struck.

The sea exploded in flame.

How long—or how short—it took I shall never be able to calculate. My mouth was on its way to the voice-pipe to send the torpedoes on their deadly way when the sea burst into flame all round NP I. She looked beautiful before the first savage flames soiled her. The stupid clots, I thought, they've been discharging oil and petrol: they felt so safe in their funk-hole. I saw figures running, and then the flames shot up high over her bridge.

The flames came tearing across the sea towards *Trout*. We were in deadly danger.

"Break off the attack," I yelled down the voice pipe.
"Course three-oh degrees. Full ahead both."

As the screws gripped *Trout* swung while the deadly flame
chased across the anchorage. I *had* to get into that channel. It
seemed an age before the water began to break to starboard
and I knew there was a sand-bar between us and the fiery sea
of flame, now shooting skywards. I could not see NP I now.
Miles of sea seemed ablaze. She could not survive. I felt weak
and limp.

I had destroyed NP I.

The flame flickered at the entrance channel, but came no
farther. I gasped as *Trout*, off course, headed towards the line
of breakers to starboard. I quickly altered course for the
middle of the channel. We were almost abreast the causeway.

Two figures came racing along the sand, waving frantically,
arms tearing the air in terror. I could no longer see the causeway, however. The tide had covered it. The two men—sailors
from NP I—tore along a narrow spit of sand, while the flames
reached at them from behind. *Trout* was a biscuit-toss away.

"Slow ahead both," I ordered.

When the one sailor, glancing in terror at the flames
behind him, saw me lean forwards to the voice-pipe, he sank
on his knees and stretched his hands out in a frantic gesture
of despair.

In broken English he screamed: "For the love of God,
Herr Kapitän. . . ."

No, I thought. There will be no one except three men who
knew about NP I, and only myself to remember her fate.

I swung the Oerlikon on its mounting.

I fired a burst into the sailor's sagging face.

That face haunts my nightmares.

NINE

Trial at the Cape

" MOST IRREGULAR," interjected the president of the court martial.

His cherubic face, which I had once known to become as mischievous as a schoolboy's when arranging a secret drink before lunch at Admiralty House, was stern.

The five officers, divided by the rear-admiral in the middle, formed the proscenium, as it were, to the glorious backdrop of the Cape mountains behind Simonstown. Through the long windows behind them I could see a great wash of white arum lilies—they grow as wild as hedge-flowers in England during the Cape spring—for all the world like surf against the blue sea and the mountains, to which Drake paid immortal tribute when he rounded them four centuries ago.

Elton stood, faintly self-conscious but smirking at being in the limelight, at the improvised " witness box " which had been rigged for the court martial. I and my defending officer, Lieutenant Gander, sat behind a table facing the two captains, the two lieutenants and the Rear-Admiral Commanding South Atlantic. Elton was enjoying telling them about my savage assault on him before *Trout* went in to sink NP I.

The court martial was, of course, inevitable. It followed my arrival as surely as the breakers of Curva dos Dunas snarl over the burnt-out remains of NP I at this moment. I suppose my return navigation of the tortuous channel—alone, utterly alone with nothing but my own thoughts—was one of the most automatic things I have ever done. Through the creaming welter of death I had conned the damaged *Trout*, past the invisible causeway to the shore, through the twisted whorls of the channel to the open sea. I have, to this day, no clear recollection of that night. Probably the reaction of seeing NP I come to such a ghastly end, followed by my own action in massacring a terror-stricken wretch with a machine-gun, had been too great. Vaguely the death-dealing breakers and sand-bars glided by and, my eyes aching from the whiteness of the surf under the whiteness of the moon, I stumbled down the conning-tower hatch and gave John a course for Simonstown.

" Full ahead," I had told him in a toneless voice.

I fell upon my bunk and slept like a dead man.

There is, however, no escaping the vigil of the Royal Navy. I had sinned—or they thought I had—and the court martial was the natural sequel. Half a day after *Trout* had tied up in Simonstown and the signals had flown between Simonstown and London, I was relieved of my command. The Commander-in-Chief had decided that there was certainly something very fishy about *Trout* and her skipper.

Elton was doing nothing to disillusion the court martial on that score.

" When," asked the bland voice of the prosecuting officer, " did you have doubts about Lieutenant-Commander Peace's er—ah—mental state?"

" The night we 'eard the whale. . . ." his voice trailed away uncertainly.

The Commander-in-Chief gazed at him questioningly. Certainly the court martial was providing its quota of surprises.

" Heard a whale?" snapped the gold braid at the high table. " What d'ye mean—heard a whale?"

" Well, sir," stumbled Elton, growing pink round the gills. It came out with a rush. " I don't like to say in front of the lady, sir." He gestured towards the Wren who was taking the proceedings down in shorthand.

" You mean . . ." the rear-admiral snorted, incredulously. " Anything you have to say, say it, by God, and let us hear, even in front of a lady."

" Well, sir," said Elton. " The night we heard a whale farting over the hydrophones."

A slight tremor in her pencil was the only indication the Wren showed that the shock had not passed unnoticed.

" Heard a whale . . . er . . ." gasped the rear-admiral.

" There seem to have been some strange occurrences in *H.M.S. Trout*," said the senior captain, his voice like a file.

" Explain yourself, Elton," said the Commander-in-Chief.

" Well, sir, we was listening, Bissett and me, on the

'ydrophones and there comes this noise. Strike a light, I says, that bleedin' whale must be getting the same sort of grub as we get in *Trout*. 'E's got a guts-ache, all right."

The Wren's pencil faltered, but she carried on gamely, brown head bent over her notebook.

Elton paused while the drama sank in.

But the old seadog presiding wasn't going to let him away with it.

" And then?" he asked in his quarter-deck voice.

" Lieutenant-Commander Peace come in and he seemed to think it was a U-boat." The contempt for my judgment was obvious.

" Could it not have been H.E. muffled, or distorted?" asked the senior captain.

" Not a . . . beg pardon, no sir," replied Elton. " I never 'eard H.E. like that.'

The junior captain on the other side chipped in.

" You're not the senior hydrophone operator in *Trout* are you?"

" No, sir," said Elton, " but . . ."

" That's all," snapped the officer. Here at least, I thought wanly, was someone with a judicial turn of mind.

" Yes, and then?" asked the rear-admiral, usurping the prosecuting counsel's function.

" The skipper, I mean Lieutenant-Commander Peace, told Bissett to keep on to it. I 'eard 'im giving orders to follow it."

" Thank you," said the prosecution. " We shall now pass on to the occasion when *Trout* stood at action stations for— how many hours, Elton?"

" Must 'ave been about eight hours, sir," he replied.

" Between the time of your first hearing this extraordinary noise and the time you stood to action stations all day, did you have any cause to suspect that Lieutenant-Commander Peace was not himself."

" Oh yes, sir," smirked Elton. " We all knew 'e was nuts— shouting and screaming orders down the voice-pipe, and 'im up alone there with no look-outs. . . ."

The Commander-in-Chief and the senior captain exchanged whispers.

" I presume you will be bringing evidence on this point, Lieutenant?" asked the president.

" Yes, sir, I am afraid so," he replied.

" Don't be afraid," snapped the old seadog. " I want the whole story of *Trout's* mission." I knew what was passing through my unwilling tormentor's mind—I've got a cast-iron case against this poor bastard in the dock, but he's had a bloody fine record and I'll let him off the little bits as much as possible.

The judicial captain on the rear-admiral's right came to my rescue.

" Elton, did you have any actual orders from Lieutenant-Commander Peace during this time?"

" No, sir," said Elton, falling into the trap. " 'E kept Bissett going something cruel, sir. Said Bissett 'ad the best ears in the boat."

" So all this you are saying is merely crew's gossip— Lieutenant-Commander Peace in fact never gave you personally orders during this period?"

" No sir, but . . ."

" That is all I wanted to know," he said and leaned back. I needed a friend pretty badly, too.

" Now, Elton, tell us about this alleged assault," said the lieutenant.

Elton darted a venomous glance at me. They said he'd been unconscious for two hours after I'd hit him.

" We'd been at action stations all day, sir, and not a sound on the 'ydrophones," he said. " Then the skipper—I mean Lieutenant-Commander Peace, sir, comes and I seed in his face . . ."

" Only the facts, Elton," said the junior captain.

Elton bridled. " I was saying to Bissett, sir, that the skipper wasn't looking too good and 'ere we'd been eight hours listening for a fartin' whale. . . . Then the skipper—I mean Lieutenant-Commander Peace, sir—was standing there looking as if he'd bloody well murder me and then 'e 'it me. When I comed round we was moving."

" What did you say to provoke Lieutenant-Commander Peace into such an extraordinary act for a commanding officer?" asked the rear-admiral.

Elton coloured. " 'E overheard me saying 'e was crackers," he mumbled.

The senior captain cut short his narrative, which, told thus coldly in court, sounded too damning.

"You were with Lieutenant-Commander Peace in the Mediterranean, were you not, Elton?"

He looked suspicious. "Yes, sir, I was."

"He was a goood commanding officer and—if I may say so at this stage—a very brave one, too, was he not?"

"Yes, sir, 'e was."

"Is it true *Trout's* crew had a nickname for him?"

"Yes sir. We called 'im ' The Mountie,' because he always got his man."

The court smiled. One up to me, I thought. A past record would only count in mitigation.

"A very brave and daring commanding officer, with the D.S.O. and now two Bars?" persisted the senior captain.

"Yes sir."

"And you never had occasion to query his actions then?"

"No sir."

"And why in this instance, then?"

Elton shuffled. Perhaps he remembered the sinkings and the glory in the Mediterranean.

"I don't want to say nothing against Lieutenant-Commander Peace," he said haltingly. "But this time 'e was different—I thought . . ."

"You thought, if I may use colloquial language, that he was round the bend?"

"Yes, sir, that's it. I ain't saying nothing against him. . . ."

"Thank you, Elton, that will be all," said the president.

Elton looked across at me half apologetically as he came out of the witness box. He's said enough, I thought.

Bissett, supremely uncomfortable, took his place. After the routine questions, the incident of my striking Elton came to the fore.

"You were the only witness to this extraordinary action," said the lieutenant. "Tell the court what happened—in your own words."

"I'm afraid I can't sir," Bissett said hesitatingly.

"You can't?" echoed the prosecutor, glancing at his sheaf of papers.

"No, sir. You see, I was busy on the hydrophones. I couldn't hear what was being said between Lieutenant-Commander Peace and Elton, sir. The earpieces were over my ears. I only saw him against the bulkhead afterwards."

Good, loyal Bissett!

The Commander-in-Chief surveyed him with frosty eyes.

"Is that all you have to say about it, Bissett?"

"Yes sir."

The admiral knew his ratings well enough to know Bissett was lying like a sick baby. His glance travelled slowly between Bissett, the prosecuting officer and myself. We all knew.

"Very well," he said coldly. "Get on with this question of the whale."

The lieutenant refreshed himself from his notes.

"The night before the long stand-to at action stations—when did you first hear this extraordinary noise on the hydrophones?"

"It must have been about getting dark up above," said Bissett. "I heard noises and so I called the captain."

"Why?"

Bissett looked puzzled. "Well, sir, any extraordinary noise and I report it at once. That's the way it works in a submarine." His gibe touched the lieutenant.

"What was different about this noise from any other—you could have been mistaken, couldn't you? Might it not have been a confused echo back from the warships—the ones which stopped and gave you mail?"

Bissett smiled, the smile of a man who really knew what he was talking about.

"No sir, definitely not; I never heard a noise like that—before or since."

"Can you describe it?"

"Yes sir. It was a sort of regular gurgling—a sort of thumping and a gurgle, but quite regular, sir."

The judicial captain leaned forward.

"Not once or twice—like ah . . . a whale?"

The Wren's pencil trembled slightly.

Bissett smiled. " No sir. I listened to it moving left to right, travelling at first maybe at about ten knots. Then it slowed."

" Did Lieutenant-Commander Peace hear it too?"

" Yes sir, he listened at the hydrophones. Then he changed course and we followed it."

" How long?"

" Nearly two hours, sir."

" Now tell the court, when Lieutenant-Commander Peace heard it for the first time, what was his reaction?"

" He seemed interested, but puzzled, like I was, sir."

" Was there anything—er—abnormal about him at that stage?"

Bissett's face grew red.

" There ain't anything wrong with the captain," he broke out. " He's the best bloody skipper I ever sailed with . . ."

" Bissett!" growled the gold lace in the middle.

Bissett swung and faced him. " It's true, sir. Ask any of the crew. He's on the mat because young Elton here got what he deserved. We still dunno what he was up to, but any of us would go to sea to-morrow with him if you asked us."

The judicial captain said ironically : " A very fine spontaneous tribute and I hope it was not too quick for the record. We want facts, Bissett. The court will ask for your opinion if it requires it. Meanwhile you can save it."

" He saved us often enough," said Bissett rather wildly.

The Lieutenant stepped into the breach.

" Now, Bissett," he said. " You had been following this strange noise on a steady bearing for two hours, correct? Then what happened?"

" Lieutenant-Commander Peace rushed in, excited-like and told me to switch off everything."

" What was he excited about?"

" I don't know, sir. He don't usually consult me about an attack. I'm only a rating."

A heavy frown split the Commander-in-Chief's face at this uncalled for sarcasm. But he kept quiet.

" And then?"

" After I had switched off, he told me not to use the hydrophones again without his express permission, sir."

" What would you deduce from that?"

" That *Trout* was in danger—in big danger, sir. He knew what he was doing."

" The court will decide that," said the lieutenant grimly.

" And when did you next use the hydrophones?"

" Next day, when we went to action stations."

" What did you hear?"

" No transmissions, sir" said Bissett woodenly.

" Until when?"

" After he knocked Elton out, sir. The transmissions was the same. Lieutenant-Commander Peace was with me at the time."

" Same as what?"

" As the previous night, sir. No mistaking it. Regular gurgling. Not H.E., sir."

" And Lieutenant-Commander Peace intended to fire a torpedo salvo on this bearing?"

" I dunno what the skipper was going to do, sir. All I know is that the noises were the same."

The prosecuting officer sighed. Bissett was certainly no help to him.

" Was Lieutenant-Commander Peace quite normal when he heard the transmissions again?"

" Yes, sir, quite normal. We were both pleased."

" Why were you pleased?"

Bissett looked at him contemptuously. " We'd found the enemy again, that's why."

The judicial captain leaned forward.

" You say ' enemy,' Bissett. What makes you say that?"

" It was the enemy all right, sir," muttered Bissett, nearly caught.

There was a short silence.

" You must think over this next question very carefully before answering," said the captain. The way he said it sent a thrill through the court. Bissett felt it, too. I hoped he wouldn't be stupid and try and cover up for me again.

" You say enemy. That means what you heard was—machinery?"

Bissett looked across at me, hopelessly. There was a long pause. Bissett shuffled and then looked up suddenly.

" Yes, sir, it was machinery."

The tension broke.

" But not H.E?"

" No, not H.E, sir."

The rear-admiral smiled frostily at my counsel.

Bissett went, with a last appealing glance at me.

The prosecuting officer fumbled with his papers for a moment, producing the necessary air of drama before the entrance of his key witness.

" Lieutenant John Garland," he called.

Someone at the door repeated it and I heard it again down the corridor. Since the moment I had " frozen " John on *Trout's* bridge that night, we might have been strangers.

John came in and made his way, smartly uniformed, to the witness box. He was sworn and looked aloofly round the court. His preliminary answers were dry, clipped, official. He looked as cool as he always was under fire.

Then came the questions about what had happened after Bissett had first heard NP I. I would have to cure myself of thinking of the noise as NP I, in case it should slip out, I thought grimly to myself.

The prosecutor consulted his notes.

" On orders from Lieutenant-Commander Peace, you altered course sharply, did you not, Lieutenant?"

" Yes, sir, I did," replied John.

" Why?"

" Because I was ordered to do so."

" That's no answer, Lieutenant—what was the reason for the sharp alteration—it was nearly right about face, wasn't it?"

" There was a suspicious noise on the hydrophones and Lieutenant-Commander Peace decided to follow it."

The prosecutor scanned his notes. " Did not Lieutenant-Commander Peace use these words : ' I'm sick of this bloody square-search and I'm trailing a whale with alimentary ailments?' "

John looked him in the eyes, lying magnificently.

" Those words were never used to me, sir."

"Are you sure, Lieutenant? Confirmation might be in Lieutenant-Commander Peace's favour when his mental state comes to be considered."

John wouldn't fall for that sort of blandishment. "They were never used to me," he repeated.

"I shall bring two other witnesses to swear they were used to you, Lieutenant Garland."

John shrugged slightly. The prosecutor saw he was wasting his time.

"Now some time afterwards Lieutenant-Commander Peace rushed through the control room in an agitated state and shouted for the hydrophones to be switched off immediately—correct?"

John smiled slightly. "Lieutenant-Commander Peace stepped through the control room—I was unaware of an agitated state—and ordered the hydrophones to be switched off."

"Why?"

John flickered a glance at the Commander-in-Chief. "In submarines an asdic transmission, or any untoward noise, can reveal one's presence to the enemy. The order was perfectly logical to me."

"The enemy, lieutenant—what enemy?"

"The sound at the other end of the hydrophones."

The prosecutor began to enjoy himself. "Both you and the chief hydrophone operator have used the term enemy without the slightest reason to suspect there was anything at all making a noise—not even a whale, with or without alimentary ailments."

The sally left John as cool as before.

"To me, sir, strange transmissions at sea, in war-time in a submarine, are the enemy. Until they're proved otherwise."

"A curious attitude," remarked the prosecuting officer. "In other words, fire first and ask questions afterwards?"

"Yes, sir," replied John.

"And then Lieutenant-Commander Peace ordered silent routine—why?"

"Normal precautions when in contact with the enemy," said John with a ghost of a smile.

"Logical, rational orders?"

" Yes."

" When a noise, which could not be identified by anyone on board, let alone Lieutenant-Commander Peace, was heard?"

" Logical and rational battle orders, sir."

" And you would consider equally logical and rational Lieutenant-Commander Peace's ordering you off the bridge and navigating himself, without reference to his senior officer?"

John remained silent. It was all he could do.

The prosecutor had me in the bag—and he knew it.

" I quote you," he said : " ' What's the buzz Geoffrey—and brushing up on the old navigation all by yourself too.' "

My defending officer was on his feet in a trice.

" If the prosecutor wishes to question his witness on the point, he is at liberty to do so. He cannot say ' I quote '."

" I withdraw that, then," replied the other but to the naval minds unused to the niceties of the law, I could see that my case had been further damaged.

" Lieutenant-Commander Peace made another sharp alteration of course before steaming all night at high speed?"

" Yes, sir," said John miserably, and gave technical details of course, speed and so on.

The prosecutor tapped his pencil lightly on the table. " And when you approached a destination—still unknown to you— Lieutenant-Commander Peace ordered you off the bridge, as well as the watchmen?"

" That is correct, sir," said John.

" Why did he do that?"

" I do not know, sir."

" Were those ' logical, rational orders '?"

" I was surprised, I admit, but Lieutenant-Commander Peace has always had an individual touch. I remember——"

" No reminiscences, please, Lieutenant. Stick to the facts."

" After which, from the bridge, Lieutenant-Commander Peace gave a series of course alterations at short intervals?"

Thinking of my navigation off the Skeleton Coast, that was a superb understatement.

" Yes, sir."

The prosecutor looked at him. " Please produce to the court your chart showing them."

This was the left hook to the jaw.

"There was no chart," he replied simply.

"No chart?" exclaimed the rear-admiral. "What do you mean, Lieutenant Garland?"

"I mean, sir, that Lieutenant-Commander Peace was navigating from a chart of his own, which he did not reveal to me. The log is here, though."

The old fighter behind the table eyed John severely.

"You have no idea where you were?"

"No, sir, not to this moment."

"Or what you were following?"

"No, sir."

"Or what the alterations of course were for?"

"No, sir."

"No idea at all?" he barked out.

"We must have been close to land, sir, because of the echo-sounder readings."

"And then *Trout* lay at the bottom of the sea at action stations for eight hours with torpedoes at the ready?"

The prosecutor flicked over several pages of notes to draw this further damaging conclusion.

"Yes, sir."

The log book was passed up to the main table. The rear-admiral peered at it intently for a moment and then threw it down with a snort of disgust. I probably would have too.

The judicial captain chipped in.

"Lieutenant Garland, if you were presented with this log book with these apparently unrelated changes of course—extreme changes of course—what would your interpretation of it be?"

John looked across at me, the first time he had done so. There was no compassion in that look, such as I had seen when he came in and found me laughing after I had decided to go in and sink NP I in her hide-out.

He replied firmly and without hesitation: "I would have said they were the work of a madman."

The Commander-in-Chief let out a faint sigh. My best friend had made the most damning statement yet before the court.

"So," said the prosecutor and I could see he was hating it,

" in other words, you would say your commanding officer was mad?"

John looked at him squarely. "I did not say that, sir," he rejoined firmly. Even the judicial captain lost some of his detached air as the sense of drama heightened.

"What I did say, sir, was that if such a log book were presented to me here in court, I would say it was the work of a madman. What I did not say was that I was there. *I* looked through the periscope. *I* saw what he was doing."

The prosecutor reddened. "There is no record of this vital piece of evidence. . . ."

John brushed his words aside.

"I looked through the periscope," he repeated slowly as if every single breaker of that wave-lashed holocaust were living again before his eyes. "I saw the most fantastic welter of broken water that ever terrified a sailor out of his wits. It frightened the living hell out of me. I still dream about it. All I know is that until that moment I thought my commanding officer was . . . to say the least . . . suffering from battle fatigue. I thought so when I heard him laughing to himself. I thought the attack plan was all a figment of his imagination. I thought the torpedo settings were so shallow as to be crazy. I thought his action in standing watch alone on the bridge was near madness. I have no words for his course alterations and the soundings. But when I looked out and saw *Trout* among the breakers, I knew that he was sane beyond sanity, and he proved it by bringing us out alive. No one else could have done it. But for him we would all be dead men. There wouldn't be any court martial. I don't know to this day what he was doing, but I believe if he said there was an enemy, there was."

There was a long silence. The Cape mountains looked lovelier than ever. A tear splashed from the Wren's cheek on to her notebook and she dabbed hurriedly at it. John never looked across at me.

The Commander-in-Chief cleared his throat.

"Lieutenant Garland," he said, "if I ordered *Trout* to sea to-morrow with Lieutenant-Commander Peace in command, would you be prepared to sail with him?"

"Yes, sir," said John simply, "anywhere."

He cleared his throat again. "No further questions? Thank you, Lieutenant."

I smiled wryly to myself. John had convinced them I was sane all right, but if I was fully responsible for my actions, then what in heaven's name was I doing? It really weakened my own case. How could I answer the unanswerable questions about NP I? I knew the line I would have to take.

"Any more witnesses?" asked the gold braid.

The prosecutor grinned wryly. "I'm afraid that if I brought every one of the crew, they might say the same sort of thing. No, sir, I have a number of affidavits here which can be referred to if the court feels there should be oral evidence in clarification of various points, but in point of fact there is no dispute about the general facts. Unidentified noises were heard, an attack was mounted, *H.M.S. Trout* was damaged, there were a series of the wildest alterations of course and depth soundings, *Trout* was apparently in grave danger, there was a complete failure on the part of her commanding officer to notify his officers what he was doing and even where his ship was. I have discussed these points with the defence "—indicating my defending officer—" and they are not in dispute."

"Most irregular," sniffed the rear-admiral.

"In fact, your case is complete against Lieutenant-Commander Peace then?" asked the judicial captain.

My defending officer was on his feet in a trice.

"I cannot allow such admissions," he snapped out. "Lieutenant-Commander Peace is on trial on the most serious charges. It is only right that he should be heard in his own defence."

"He admits the facts, but has some explanation of them?" asked the Commander-in-Chief.

My defending officer shuffled. "Unfortunately, sir, I am not in the accused's—Lieutenant-Commander Peace's—confidence regarding his explanation. But he has a right to be heard, nevertheless."

The old sailor nodded and I was duly sworn. I could see them all eyeing me closely.

"Before you begin, Lieutenant-Commander," said the C.-in-C., "there are a number of points regarding *Trout* which the court wishes to clear up before we go into detail regarding this . . . ah . . . attack. Commander Peace will answer them, since I must confess I am seriously at a loss myself. First, Commander Peace, who ordered you to take *H.M.S. Trout* to sea? I have signalled the Admiralty and I can find no authorisation—whatsoever—for your ah . . . mission."

So, I thought, those clever two never wrote down anything at all. The net was closing fast.

" I was ordered verbally by the Flag Officer (S) in the presence of the Director of Naval Intelligence. I was flown from Malta and briefed in person."

A ripple of incredulity ran through the court. All five officers stared at me from the dais.

" In that case, then," said the judicial captain levelly, " there will be a record of your briefing which will be available in your defence to substantiate what you say."

" No one else was present at the meeting," I said. " There was no record."

" You mean to tell me——" snapped the rear-admiral. " Rubbish!"

" Even admitting it were so," said the judicial captain, " it must have been a matter of considerable secrecy for two officers of their rank to discuss it with you—in private?"

" It was," I said grimly, remembering the look in those Arctic eyes when he thought of his precious convoys and the battle-stained North Atlantic.

" What was it?" snapped the C.-in-C.

" I cannot answer that question, sir," I replied.

" My God!" he shouted. " You stand there like a schoolboy and tell me you can't say?"

There was no avoiding the blow much longer. In a moment, in a moment, I told myself, steeling myself for the inevitable.

" Not under any circumstances," I said.

That brought him up all standing.

He gave me another moment's respite.

" You mean to say that you received a secret briefing for a secret mission and that none of the usual form was observed—no record of your conversation, your orders, nothing?"

" That is correct, sir."

The judicial captain flicked through some papers at the table.

"I notice, sir," he said to the president, "that all authorisation for *Trout's* stores, fuel and so on are on the personal instructions of the Flag Officer (S)."

"Where were you when you made this remarkable attack —and on what?" snapped the old seadog, now thoroughly angered.

"I'm afraid I cannot answer that, sir."

"Are you prepared to answer anything at all?" he snapped sarcastically.

My moment had come.

I remembered the schoolmasterly voice and the precise muster of sentences. I remembered the compassionate, the professionally compassionate farewell. He would shake the hand of the bright boy at school when he gave him the prize in the same gentle way, probably with a slightly pedantic chiding. I imagined that he would tend the roses in his country home just like that too, and talk them over with the locals at the annual rose show. To him I was not a cypher, I was something to be wept over, but not to be mourned. He'd passed beyond ruthlessness into compassion, beyond compassion into ruthlessness. I remembered his farewell. Had he gone so far in man's barbarity to man that he no longer felt, or was it his professional manner to shield himself—what did he think deep down? It was all justified, in his view, justified because Britain was in danger . . . I jerked myself back. Even if I opened my mouth, he would . . . he'd have to . . . deny it all. I remembered the slight sad droop of the eyes. It was his job. He'd sold me down the river, the river of death or ignominy that bleak day at the Admiralty. We both knew the rules. He knew what he was doing, and I knew what was being done.

Here it was.

"Sir," I said, "I wish to admit all the charges against me."

"What?" roared the rear-admiral.

I think even the Wren forgot to write it down in the general sensation. The judicial captain eyed me coolly and I could see that he had made up his mind that I was certainly on my way to the madhouse. The other members of the court martial whispered between themselves. The tanned face in the middle was purple.

"The defence . . ." bleated my defending officer helplessly. "The defendant . . ."

I was almost oblivious of what was going on. I was living again the holocaust at Curva dos Dunas, the anchorage blazing and the distant thud of explosions, the one German with his hands upraised and the bloody, unrecognisable mess the Oerlikon had made of his face. The resolution never to mention or reveal Curva dos Dunas dropped crystallised, clear, inexorable, into my mind. I had done what old Arctic-eyes had sent me to do : that delicate, wing-like conning-tower would never show its deadly dorsal fin in the turbulent wastes of the North Atlantic now. Blohm and Voss would never know what had happened to her. She was a risk, an unjustifiable risk at best in the German naval mind, even before she sailed, and her non-return would set the seal on others of her kind. She had been destroyed through the knowledge old Simon Peace had given to me—and he was dead. The man who had ordered me to destroy her—he was dead. The Director of Naval Intelligence—well, his mouth would always be as closed as if death itself had sealed it. There would never be any hint at all of NP I if I kept my mouth shut.

The president, who had half-risen, seated himself again with a thump. He gazed at me for a long time. No one else said anything. I had admitted the most serious offences. There was nothing more to be said. Only to be done. And that was clear enough. They'd have to kick me out—kick me out right on the peak of my naval cap.

"The court will adjourn," said the old man savagely.

I have only the vaguest recollection of the rest of the proceedings. It was only a question of disposing of the corpse, so to speak. I felt quite unmoved by it all. I remember John coming to chat with me, and then to plead, half-quizzically, and again with a measure of friendship which I did not realise he had for me. But the die was cast. Curva dos Dunas and I must keep our secret—until death do us part.

The sentence was a formality. The old C.-in-C. saved me some of the disgrace. The words had an almost Miltonesque quality : " In view of this officer's gallant and even glorious service in destroying the King's enemies at sea . . ." I wasn't kicked out, but ushered out of the Royal Navy, rather.

I took a vow to go back to Curva dos Dunas.

TEN

A Nymph Rejoins her Ancestors

" IT IS ONLY a very small request, and I shall pay you well," murmured Stein blandly. The shadow from the light above his head in *Etosha's* saloon did not conceal, but rather accentuated, the cruel mouth. The mouth was twisted ingratiatingly, but the eyes and the face were deadly cold.

The faint movement of *Etosha* at her buoy rocked the whisky in my glass. I focused on the amber liquid to compose my thoughts. I was angry, furiously angry, at Stein again pushing his way into *Etosha's* cabin when Mac and I were having a drink together, as we always did after the crew had gone ashore. It was a month since that dreadful scene in the bar at Mark's. The drunken German was removed screaming like a madman and shouting obscene threats at me. Stein had just stood and stared at me as if he were trying to sort some mental jigsaw into place. The whole thing still jangled on my nerves. I hadn't seen Stein since, but the sight of him back in *Etosha* brought forward all my latent fears and caution. What did Stein really want of me?

Mac sat under an open porthole, his face inscrutable.

" Stein," I said and my voice rasped at the goading of anger and whisky. " Once and for all, I shall *not* put you ashore on the Skeleton Coast, even for a thousand pounds each way."

" I am a scientist," he replied, ignoring my mounting anger. " All I ask is the opportunity to collect a beetle which has been lost to science for many, many years."

" To hell with you and your precious beetles!" I swore. " Now get out and leave me alone."

" I repeat," said Stein and the cruel gash of a mouth grinned more sardonically than ever, " I am a scientist. So when a man starts to scream in a bar for no reason at all, I say to myself, there must be a reason. Not so?"

" What has a drunken sailor got to do with my taking you to the Skeleton Coast?"

Stein evaded the issue. His voice became prim.

" I say to myself, a man does not scream for nothing. There must be a cause. Could it be the little thing which fell out of Captain Macdonald's pocket? I ask myself. And what is that thing—a little lucky charm which we have in southern Germany. Surely that alone would not reduce a man to a frenzy and send him into a mental hospital afterwards?"

Stein was smiling again. He had some good cards somewhere, and he was playing them skilfully. I bit down my anger.

" A mental hospital?"

" Yes, Captain, a mental hospital." He gazed at me as though I were a scientific curiosity.

" The psychiatrist is a good friend of mine, and he finds the case of the German sailor very interesting. He has what you call a fixation about a hand. Captain Macdonald's little lucky charm triggers off the malady all over again."

I began to sweat, even in the cold early winter night. I poured myself another Haig. Mac did the same. I didn't offer Stein one.

" So?" I asked.

" Ah, Captain, that is much better," smirked Stein. " You may even become so interested in my story that you will offer me a drink next time, eh?"

" Perhaps," I said grimly.

" So, both of us being scientists, we go into the case history of this Johann. A curious case, in fact. We find that Johann is, in fact, an orphan—his life only begins after 1944."

" What the hell are you talking about?" I asked.

" I will be frank," continued Stein. " Johann has no past. He was found with a tribe of Bushmen on the Khowarib, near Zessfontein, by a missionary in 1944. He was brought to Windhoek and spent two years in hospital. They never found out who he was. But one thing is clear—he is a sailor, a U-boat man. He knows nothing of how he came to be wandering with a tribe of dirty little wild men. He lives in mortal fear of a hand."

I thought of the victory hand painted on *Trout's* conning-tower. The whisky I was drinking might have been water for all the stimulus it gave me.

" Johann improves daily, however, and he will soon be back at his old job again in Windhoek," smiled Stein. He rose as if to go. He turned back at the doorway. He was playing me as a cat does a mouse.

" I was interested in Lieutenant Garland," he said casually. " A friend of mine in Cape Town checked on a Navy List, and I was fascinated to know that he also once commanded *H.M.S. Trout*, a British submarine, with a most distinguished war record under her first captain, one Lieutenant-Commander Geoffrey Peace."

I had not heard my own name in years and it sent a cold shudder down my spine. So Stein was going to blackmail me with my past in order to force me to take him to the Skeleton Coast. It was impossible that he should know about Curva dos Dunas.

Stein came a pace back into the saloon.

" Lieutenant-Commander Peace was discharged from the Royal Navy after a court martial," said Stein in a harsh voice. " And the emblem of *H.M.S. Trout* was a hand painted on her conning-tower. Strange, I said to myself, a crazed U-boat sailor who sees the fear of death in a hand, and a British submarine whose victory emblem was a hand, and a South African skipper who carries a lucky charm around in his pocket in the shape of a hand."

It was Mac who precipitated the situation. His attack on Stein was as swift, unheralded and savage as a wolf's. Like a striking mamba he was behind Stein and had grabbed a handful of loose skin under his left ear and with his right—I never saw the movement, it was so swift, but only heard the tinkle of the broken bottle—thrust the neck of the broken Haig bottle into the other side of his neck.

Involuntarily I struck at Mac's fearful weapon, even as it broke the skin. I saw the blood run, but it was not the death-spurt of an artery. Where Mac had learned that filthy trick, I do not know. As I grabbed his hand, Stein writhed loose and slipped from Mac's grasp.

The Luger never even trembled in his hand as he stood back against the padded locker by the porthole. He smiled mirthlessly.

" Two very desperate and dangerous men," he said, eyeing Mac and myself with respect almost. " I watched Captain . . . ah . . . Macdonald twist Hendriks's arm off with the dirtiest hold I have ever seen. I myself nearly fall victim to an even worse trick from his engineer. You gentlemen must have been brought up very badly indeed."

Mac did not say a word. The dour mask remained unpenetrated. I measured the distance carefully to see whether I could jump Stein's gun. It seemed a slim chance. Mac would certainly provide the follow-up.

Stein spoke to Mac although his eyes were as wary as a lynx.

" I shall kill you in my own good time," he said quite dispassionately. " But not now. Now would not be the time, when we are having such an interesting discussion about Lieutenant Garland and his former skipper. Where is Lieutenant Garland, by the way?"

" He's ashore with friends," I said, looking for any chink in the man's vigilance.

" I have friends ashore too—good friends," continued Stein conversationally as cool as though death had not all but touched his jugular vein. There was a faint runnel of blood down his collar, but that was all. The Luger covered us steadily.

The plan to murder Stein dropped into my mind then.

It was just too simple. All I would have to do was to agree to his plan—and the Skeleton Coast would do the rest. I did not like the way he had been digging into my past. The merciless sands of Curva dos Dunas would be all that would hear his death-cries. I decided to play it softly, for he was a cunning devil.

" Are you going to threaten me at pistol-point to take you to the Skeleton Coast?" I asked sarcastically. " Beetle, my Aunt Fanny! Is it a packet of diamonds you are going to pick up?"

He eyed me blandly. " Strangely enough, Captain . . . ah . . . Macdonald, it is a beetle. I want that beetle more than anything else in the world. I am prepared to force you to take me there—at pistol-point if necessary—but somehow I don't think it will be necessary."

I didn't like the way he said it, but I let it ride.

" You have the whip-hand of me," I pretended to admit. " All right, I'll take you—but £500 is not enough. I want at least £1,000 and specific guarantees that there will be no leakage to the police."

Stein looked at me contemptuously and waved the Luger, not threateningly, but to emphasise his words.

" Five hundred pounds was the original offer, Captain, but now it is much less. In fact, I think I shall ask you to do it free, gratis and for nothing."

I thought I had bluffed him, but I hadn't. I took a pace towards him, but the Luger swung up at my stomach.

" Neither of you," said Stein ironically, " is likely to be scared by the mere sight of a Luger. Oh no, Captain Macdonald, your capitulation was much too quick. Perhaps with a less—shall we say, determined and resourceful—man I might have been persuaded. No histrionics, I beg of you. No, you shall take me to the Skeleton Coast and put me ashore just where I wish to be put ashore."

" The hell you say," I snapped.

Stein was enjoying himself. " Say you are Lieutenant-Commander Peace, the famous war-time commander of *Trout*. Assume that it is so for the sake of my argument. What of it? What good would it do either me or Lieutenant-Commander Peace, alias Captain Macdonald, to noise it abroad from the housetops that he is now a trawlerman operating from Walvis Bay? Good luck to him, they'd say. To quote the newspapers, he would have rehabilitated himself. The English sense of fair play. He'd taken his rap and got kicked out, why throw it up again in his face, even if he's got a different name and says he's a South African—and even speaks like one? It would not serve any useful purpose whatsoever. Nor would a man in that position on the mere threat of throwing open his past agree to do a job which might involve him with the law once again and wash out any chance at all of leading a decent life in the future. You agreed far too suddenly, Lieutenant-Commander Peace."

I inwardly cursed my own bungling. What did he mean? His use of my own name and his veiled references left me uneasy, very uneasy.

"So what?" I still tried to bluff it out. "Say I am Lieutenant-Commander Peace. What should the Navy care about a man kicked out and treated like dirt after what I'd done for them and the way I risked my neck? I tell you I got a raw deal and a man who has gone through that doesn't sniff at the opportunity of making a little on the side."

"Nicely taken," sneered Stein. "But when I first saw this ship I asked myself, where does a man like that get the best part of £200,000 for a modern trawler like *Etosha*? Why the double-action diesels? Why the yacht-like lines when they should be tubby to hold fish? I hear rumours ashore that Captain Macdonald knows the Skeleton Coast better than any other skipper sailing out of Walvis. They say in the waterfront bars that he keeps to himself. Why? Is he running diamonds from the Skeleton Coast? Is that what those fine lines and fast diesels are for?"

"Ah, bulldust!" snarled Mac, drawn by the reference to his engines.

Stein turned to him with a cold smile.

"That is what I said to myself—bulldust," he remarked agreeably.

He let it sink in and gestured sociably with the Luger.

"Don't you think we should sit down? We have so much to discuss—details of the trip to the Skeleton Coast and so on?"

"There is nothing to discuss," I said flatly, knowing perfectly well that there was. "I won't take you to the Skeleton Coast—under any circumstances whatsoever. That's flat. Now get out—and if you come back again, I'll throw you overboard."

"Brave words, Captain Peace—or is it Lieutenant-Commander? I can never be quite sure in a situation like this," he sneered. He sighed theatrically. "You force me to use cards I don't want to. Macfadden," he said harshly, anticipating a move by Mac, " I swear before God that I will kill you on the slightest pretext."

Mac saw that he meant it, too.

" Now, Captain Peace," he went on. " To get back to this very fine ship. Could it be that this fast, well-found ship is a diamond smuggler? I don't think so."

" Thanks for damn all," I said sarcastically.

" The point is, looking at this ship, that the man who bought her must have made his money before, not after. If you can afford a ship like this, you don't need to smuggle diamonds, do you, Captain?"

I felt the sweat trickling down my shirt. The swine was playing with me.

" I don't know the purpose of this ship yet," he said quietly. " But I intend to find out."

So he hadn't heard of Curva dos Dunas. I'd see that he never did—or never came back to tell about it.

" I became very interested in Lieutenant-Commander Peace," he went on, " and so I asked an acquaintance in Cape Town if he could find out something more about this famous submarine commander. I discovered, in fact, that he was drowned at sea eventually—after the court martial."

The cold fear tingled across my heart.

Stein put the Luger back in his pocket. It was a gesture of victory.

" Lieutenant-Commander Peace took an old merchant ship to sea in—when was it? April, '45. You remember the old Phylira, Captain? Fancy Georgiadou calling an old wreck like that after an ocean nymph! But then the Greeks, even old Georgiadou, are a sentimental lot, are they not?"

Automatically I poured myself another drink. So the Phylira was calling from her grave—and the twenty-seven men of the crew with her! Icy fear gripped me. So Stein knew about the Phylira, and had found out that I was her captain. By all the rules I was dead—the Phylira sailed from Cape Town for Tangier and was never heard of again.

" The old Phylira's engines were as bad as they come, weren't they Macfadden?" taunted this evil incarnation of a past which I thought I had buried alongside NP I on the sand-bars of Curva dos Dunas.

Stein laughed.

"A brilliant submarine commander as the skipper of a rotten old merchantman, and a brilliant engineer to keep her old engines going—just as long as they needed to be kept going, eh?"

There was pure murder in Mac's eyes. Stein knew he had us. He didn't even bother about the Luger any more.

"What did you do with her, Captain Peace? How can a man make away with a whole ship and twenty-seven men without a trace? And how did he disappear himself without a trace, to come back with a small fortune? Georgiadou would be terribly interested to know. No one could have been more heart-broken than that unsentimental shipowner about the loss of an old ship, for which he got more than her value in insurance, anyway. If he hadn't been so cut up about the loss of the *Phylira*, I'd have sworn he'd paid an enterprising, ruthless captain like yourself to get rid of her. But he still mourns the loss of the *Phylira*, Captain Peace. I'm sure he'd be only too keen to renew acquaintance with his erstwhile Captain and the Scottish engineer. Tangier, too. What was her cargo?"

"If you know all this, I'm sure you've seen *Phylira's* manifests," I rapped out harshly.

"Of course I have," he said smoothly. "Canned fruit, brandy, wool—nothing in the least exceptional. But why Tangier? I ask myself. And in '45 when anyone and anything shady could be bought in Tangier."

I'd often wondered how Georgiadou took the loss of his packet of uncut stones, all £200,000 of them. From what I heard later, Georgiadou, under his respectable merchant trading cloak in Adderley Street, was the biggest rogue south of the Congo in organising the smuggling of uncut diamonds from South West Africa, Sierra Leone and West Africa through Tangier mainly to Iron Curtain countries. I can still see the look on the Greek's face when he handed me over a tiny parcel, carelessly done up in a small carboard carton with the King's Ransom "round-the-world" label still on it.

"You will deliver these to Louis Monet in the 'Straits' bar in the Rue Marrakesh," he said incisively. "There are over £200,000 worth of uncut diamonds in that parcel. Many a man has had his throat cut for a tenth of that amount, Captain, so don't get any ideas about private enterprise, see?"

It was Georgiadou's own remark which sowed the seed.

Far to the south of Curva dos Dunas, off the mouth of the Orange River, the old *Phylira* wheezed along. It was a close night and my cabin was hot and stuffy from the dry wind coming off the land. Somewhere beyond the night out to starboard across the water the searchlights would be playing back and forth across the barbed wire which guards the Forbidden Area of the Diamond Coast. As I glanced out through the porthole, I could almost imagine I could see their reflection against the night sky. In that barren wilderness the policemen sent to patrol the desert go mad; they never see a woman in two years' shift of duty; they don't worry about the seaward side which the devilish sand-bars make so safe.

Except for Curva dos Dunas, I thought grimly. That thought triggered the whole idea off. What in God's name was I doing skippering a floating wreck and relegating myself to the status of a pariah when I held sole title to the only harbour except Walvis Bay, from Cape Town to Tiger Bay? I and I alone knew of the existence—and more particularly, the navigational hazards—of a harbour which either Rhodesia or South Africa would give millions of pounds to own. Curva dos Dunas was mine, but no government would even listen to a sailor's tale without proof. Proof! I could picture myself in the cool arched corridors of the Union Buildings in Pretoria being shifted—ever more impatiently—from one civil servant to another, fobbed off with evasive, ever-less polite answers to a man they would consider a crackpot—unless. Unless I had a ship of my own. A ship! I would have to go back and chart the place in case the tides and currents had closed or altered it since I sank NP I. I must have a ship. My own ship.

Perhaps in that lonely, stuffy cabin the ghost of old Simon Peace came to insinuate the idea into my mind. Above all, his challenge. Curva dos Dunas had cast its spell over him, and I likewise had been bewitched. Without formulating my ideas, or even putting them into rational form, I knew it was the lure, the challenge to me as a sailor and a man, as much as the other thoughts of a key harbour to which I alone held the secret, which drove me on.

I stared out of the porthole. Curva dos Dunas! The Achilles heel of the whole Skeleton Coast! What a magnificent hidey-hole to smuggle out diamonds!

The thought hit me with such force that I smacked my palm down on the table. Why not smuggle them *in*, not *out*? Georgiadou's precious parcel! Private enterprise! Two hundred thousand pounds would get me the sort of ship I wanted —fast, eminently seaworthy, handy. My thoughts tumbled over one another as it all fell into place. A fast trawler, putting up a front of fishing. I could operate out of Walvis legitimately, and no one would suspect my operations on the side at Curva dos Dunas.

Private enterprise!

The first thought that rushed into my racing brain was to run the old *Phylira* ashore at Curva dos Dunas and slip ashore. I thrust it aside. I couldn't leave Mac and twenty-seven innocent men to die a hideous death, not for all the diamonds in South West Africa. Automatically I went over and tapped the scuffed old Kew pattern barometer hanging on the bulkhead. It was almost a reflex action, for the weather would be a vital factor in my plans. I didn't like the sultry night. The long swell under the old freighter portended a stiff blow from the west-south-west if—but then one never can tell on the Skeleton Coast. It might remain fine with a heavy sea for days, or, in line with the subtle alchemy of cold South Atlantic currents and hot desert air, to say nothing of the fickle and unpredictable elements which a land breeze might throw into the weather's chemistry, a raging south-westerly gale might descend out of a clear blue sky and whip up the sea in the opposite direction, throwing up a barrage of wind and water which would nullify any plans I might have of getting ashore. Olafsen, the mate, in his drunken state would not know how even to keep the old wreck afloat under conditions like that.

I wiped the sweaty stickiness of my palms, opened a leather suitcase, and took out old Simon's annotated chart, the one I had used when I sank NP I. I spread it out and measured off the distance from Curva dos Dunas to Tiger Bay. About fifty miles as the crow flies, but I would skirt round the Portuguese post at Posto Velho and avoid the track along the seaward dunes running from the outpost on the Cunene River boundary to Cacimba, at the southern end of Tiger Bay. I might have to walk anything up to eighty miles on the detour, if I could get ashore. I hadn't any fixed plan yet. I would come in to Cacimba from the east, not the south. No one would then suspect I was a shipwrecked sailor.

And the *Phylira* herself? I felt quite certain Olafsen would put into a Portuguese port once he was sure I was missing—Lobito, probably. He would never attempt Tiger Bay with its tricky entrance. By that time I'd be well out of the way. Certainly Georgiadou wasn't the man to spread it around what the *Phylira* was carrying; I was quite sure, looking at the scruffy crew, that there was not a man among them who was the wily Greek's watchdog over me.

I flicked through a table of tides. The causeway would start to flood slowly from about four a.m. onwards with the rising tide. I could get ashore in the half-light of dawn and even if *Phylira* had the temerity to hang around, they would see no link between the sea and the shore except a line of breaking surf. My bet was that Olafsen would head her straight out to sea as soon he he saw that, if he waited that long looking for me.

I bent over the chart again and was stepping off the distance carefully between Curva dos Dunas and Cacimba when I sensed more than anything that I was not alone.

I wheeled round.

There was Mac. He was grinning—a curious, one-sided, evil grin. In his hand he held a massive wrench. His eyes were without a trace of mercy.

"Aye," he said slowly, glancing at the chart. "Aye, I thought so right from the start. Lost without trace at sea, eh? Nice insurance for that Greek bastard."

I saw the way to do it, then. With an accomplice it would be easy, alone it would be near impossible.

I nodded.

"Almost, Mac, but not quite."

"Including the Scots engineer who deserted the Royal Navy to be with his skipper?"

He said it without rancour. His morals were those of the gutter. He understood, instinctively, what I was about, though he didn't know the details. The killer instinct, beggar-your-neighbour, morals of the gutter.

I glanced at the heavy wrench. I'd toy with him a moment. I don't think he was offended, even while he thought I was about to leave him to drown. It was what he would have done in my position. We understood each other perfectly. My action, as he saw it, didn't even violate his code of loyalty to me.

He jerked his head at the chart.

"Going back to where all the fuss was over the court martial?"

"Yes, Mac," I replied evenly.

He hadn't got my drift, but he had assessed the measure of the lure that Curva dos Dunas had for me. He did not know, however, on the one hand the age-old challenge which old Simon Peace had faced—and won up to a point—and which he had bequeathed to me, and on the other the material prospects of a valuable harbour to which I held sole title.

Mac looked at me squarely.

"With some men it is women, and with some it is whisky," he said. "With me it's machinery. With you, skipper, it's some God-forsaken piece of land or sea, I'm not quite sure which. It's ruined you once. Why not leave it alone now?"

Mac would be in this now, I decided: up to his neck in it with me. There could be only one way to get his assistance and that was by telling him everything.

I took the battered King's Ransom carton from the suitcase and locked the door. Mac looked interested as the key turned, but he knew he could batter me into submission with the wrench. I tipped the contents, the dull uncut stones, on to the table.

Mac made a curious gesture as he flattened the pile down with the palm of his hand.

"That's very expensive whisky," he said. It was the only time I had ever seen Mac shaky.

"Enough," I said briefly.

"You taking them out?" he asked.

"No," I said. "I'm taking them in. You and me Mac.

Two hundred thousand quid's worth, if I guess right. Maybe more."

"Do you want me to open the valves?" he asked cryptically. I knew he was in on it now as much as myself.

"No, Mac," I said, as if we were discussing a minor engine defect and not the biggest thing in diamonds since Cullinan. "In a little more than twenty-four hours from now you will stop the engines and report to me that something has come adrift in the steering gear—the rudder pintles have gone, or any other bloody technicality you like. You'll think up something, or you'll put it wrong yourself."

Mac grinned. He knew exactly what I meant.

"I'll lay the *Phylira* against the current. The Trout current, I call it, just for old times' sake."

Mac winced. I didn't think it would touch him so deeply.

"If you've got some real whisky somewhere, I'd find it useful," was all he said.

I pulled a bottle of my special Johnny Walker Black Label from a locker. Mac took it straight.

"You've a lot of very fine whisky in this cabin," he muttered.

"The Trout current sweeps down here at anything between four and six knots, close inshore," I told him. "You'll have to leave enough way on her to cope with that. It swings and weaves through these rocks and shoals like a matelot on a bender. It'll be damn tricky, even if the weather is calm. This swell is enough in itself."

"I don't get it," said Mac. "I've stopped the engines with just enough way on to hold her against the current and I report to you on the bridge that the steering gear's amiss. What then?"

"We go over the side to inspect the fault," I said crisply.

Mac tapped the edge of the whisky glass with the wrench until it rang dully, like a bell of doom.

"What time is all this?" he said slowly.

"About three-thirty a.m," I said.

"And then?"

"I'll have this old wreck lying a bit to the nor-ard of where I intend to land," I said. "As soon as the boat hits the water, the Trout current will sweep it away from the *Phylira*. In two minutes we'll be lost in the darkness. I know the way after that. I'll give a course of three-one-oh degrees just before we make our ' inspection.' That'll take the *Phylira* well out of the way.',

Mac shook his head. " They'll simply turn round and search for us. A couple of hours and it will be full daylight. They'll find us, sure as nuts."

" You're wrong, Mac," I said quietly. " The Royal Navy never found the U-boat I sank. And no one in this rotten old tub, let alone that soak Olafsen, will find you and me where we are going." I smiled grimly at his set face. " I give you my assurance of that, Mac. I *know*."

Mac eyed me for a long time. " So it was a U-boat then? You never said so at the court martial."

" No, Mac," I said. " And the reasons still hold good to-day. There are others also."

Mac was as sharp as quicksilver.

" The . . . whale noises . . . special machinery?"

" Special machinery," I said, looking hard at him. " A lot of men died because of that special machinery."

" But you never fired a shot," Mac protested.

I heard the harsh grate in my own voice. " I know how to kill men without using torpedoes or bullets, Mac. The sea and I. See that chart?" I deliberately put my hand across it so he wouldn't see the whorls and the depth readings. " That's a murder weapon, Mac. I used it once to kill men. It's also worth more than all those diamonds, if I get back to do what I want to do. I used it once and I'm going to use it again—and you and I will be rich men."

" You're a more ruthless bastard than I ever imagined," he said slowly. " But I'm with you. This Skeleton Coast is eating into you, Skipper. If it's as bad as I think, it'll also get you in the end. Is that the plot?"

" Not all," I said. " It's all deadly simple. Once we're clear of the *Phylira,* I'll take you in to land. Can we use the small boat with the engine? Is it working?"

" If it's like everything else on this ship, it isn't," he said acidly. " But I'll make it work by to-morrow night." The thought struck him.

"But the sound of the engine—they'll pick us up easily . . ."

I heard the harshness in my voice again. "They bloody well won't because it will be drowned by the thunder of the surf. We'll be right close in, Mac, so close that it'll probably scare the pants off you. I want that engine working—well. I don't fancy the idea of taking anything in under sail through a deadly channel at night."

Mac flicked another measure of whisky into the glass.

"I saw Garland's face when he looked through that periscope," he said, his eyes shadowed. "He was as scared as a man could be. I'll get some water and food into the boat now. You've worked out the plot and I know there won't be any snags. A completely ruthless bastard," he repeated.

But there were snags.

As the boat with only Mac and me hit the water that inky night, Curva dos Dunas hit, too.

It was a savage right cross from the wind, followed by a brutal left hook by the sea. *Phylira* never stood a chance.

Except for the long swell, the sea was relatively calm as I gave the order to clear away the falls of the boat. It had been hauled up forward earlier so that it would run the length of the starboard beam before getting clear. This would give us a lee from the ship's side which would enable me to get her well under control—engineless until we were clear of the ship— as the swift current gripped her. A few minutes before Mac came to the bridge with his faked report about a rudder fault, I had altered course so that the old freighter lay with her head pointing slightly away and parallel to the land. This would get her clear to sea out of danger of the rocks and shoals. On her new course, *Phylira* now lay with her port beam square to the south-west.

The right cross of the gale struck with untamed ferocity out of the south-west, without warning. It was so violent that at first I thought it was a squall, but it was to blow for days afterwards. *Phylira's* whole length lay open to the blow. As the boat with Mac and me felt water under her, *Phylira* reeled under that gigantic elemental punch.

One moment *Phylira* was peering ox-like out to sea, the next I was staring horror-struck at the red-painted, rusty side swing over the tiny boat, alive and electrified by the galvanic force of

the blow. There was nothing Mac or I could do. In the lee of
the ship we were protected from the thundering charge of spray
and frenzied wind which tore over the ship. *Phylira* hung
poised over us.

Mac, one hand on the tiller and the other on the starting
handle, gazed awe-struck as thousands of tons of rusty old steel
bent right over us, a moment's hesitation before the death-
dealing roll which would take her and us to the bottom.

"Christ!" he screamed, and began to swing the starter like
a madman. It stayed dead. But the Trout current already
had us in its grip and we were swept as far as the engine-room.
Phylira leaned still more over us and loose gear began falling
in the water. Part of the deck came into view, so sharp was
the list. *Phylira* was about to fall right on top of us.

Then the sea dealt its left hook. The savage mountain of
water recoiled off the northerly point of Curva dos Dunas. It
was almost the place where I had first seen the graceful, deadly
dorsal fin of NP I. The sea staggered back from the iron-hard
sand-bar. The Trout current threw in all the weight of its six
knots behind the recoiling wall. The current had already
swung the old ship's head from north-west almost round to
north-east. I could see *Phylira* sag as it burst all over her bows
and, even above the scream of the wind, I heard the whimper
of torn metal. Our cockleshell shot high into the air and we
slid by the canting stern into the mælstrom. *Phylira* disappeared in the darkness.

Mac got the engine to fire as we swept past like a surf-boat,
but it was a puny thing. The boat swung round in the grip of
the enhanced current and made madly for the surf. I baled
frantically. Then suddenly the water was calmer. We had been
swept inside the northern entrance arm of Curva dos Dunas.
In the small boat, half full of water now, but afloat, we were
safe inside the sand-bars, despite the screaming wind and
driving spume.

The King's Ransom packet lay soggy, but safe, in the water
sloshing above the floorboards.

From the beach next morning we looked at the wreck of the
Phylira through my binoculars, wiping them clean of the blowing salt every few minutes. We disposed of the boat by staving

in a few planks and weighing her down on the causeway, where the next tide covered her. *Phylira* lay against the southern entrance—heaven alone knows what combination of sea and wind put her there. Her masts were canted over and from the way she lay I could see that her back was shattered. I spent the morning searching the rigging for traces of the crew, but there were none. When the causeway cleared at the next tide Mac and I got within a few hundred yards of the wreck, but there was not a sign of life.

Curvas dos Dunas would keep Georgiadou's secret well.

Stein's voice cut into my line of memory.

" It must have been brilliantly executed, Captain Peace," he sneered. " Georgiadou would love to know the details. You and he should become partners, you know. On the one hand, a Greek with a tortuous, greedy mind, and on the other a sacked Royal Navy officer with a flair for brilliant, ruthless execution. It would be a great team, Captain Peace."

I said nothing. So he thought I had deliberately disposed of the *Phylira* and her crew. Well, even to deny it wouldn't send me up much in Stein's opinion. With hellish ingenuity this German bettle-hunter—so he said—had put together a chain of unrelated things and found out just who and what I was. Would any man go to those lengths just for the sake of finding some extinct species of beetle? Curva dos Dunas! There lay my trump card, and I intended to play it. Let him think what he liked about the *Phylira*. It seemed that Curva dos Dunas was the only thing Stein had not unearthed, that and the fate of NP I.

Stein looked at us both blandly. He jerked his head generally at the *Etosha*. " Lowestoft?" he remarked, knowing perfectly well that she had first tasted water on Oulton Broad.

He was enjoying himself enormously. It was simple enough, of course; he could have seen the brass plate by the bridge companion. But with his evil air, it smelt to me of black magic again.

I nodded briefly.

Stein rose and fingered the panelling in the saloon. He hummed and then broke into a surprisingly clear tenor.

> " In Lowestoft a boat was laid,
>   Mark well what I do say!
>   And she was built for the herring trade,
>   But she has gone a-rovin', a-rovin', a-rovin',
>   The Lord knows where!"

"Kipling had a way of putting these things, did he not?" he went on urbanely. " The operative words being, of course, ' the Lord knows where!' The Lord and Captain Peace know where!" he mocked.

Then the mockery died in his voice and he rapped out:

"You will be ready to sail at dawn to-morrow, Captain Peace. I shall be here and I shall want room for my assistant, too."

"You can go to hell!" I retorted. "You and your beetles. Garland isn't here, won't be until to-morrow afternoon and I'm damned if I sail without my first lieutenant."

"You have no choice at all," Stein replied smoothly.

"I must wait for the boats," I replied. "Mine got smashed up in a heavy sea. They'll take a couple of weeks to get here."

"Don't play for time," sneered Stein. "You can't bluff me like that. We sail the morning after to-morrow, then. Garland can be safely back on duty. The rest is unimportant."

He turned by the companionway and smiled.

"No need to see me off the ship, Captain Peace," he said. " It's a dark night, and accidents can always happen. This has been a most instructive and informative evening. I can understand why the Royal Navy respected your talent, Captain Peace. I do too, or else I would not be asking you to take me. Gentlemen, to the Skeleton Coast."

With a melodramatic wave of the hand, he disappeared.

ELEVEN

A Lady for Onymacris

" IT LIGHTENETH," observed John biblically. He raised his
night glasses from their strap and rubbed off the moisture
with the tip of his elbow, heavily swathed in an off-white
sweater.

And almost a biblical figure he looked, too, in his thick
sweater and balaclava cap dripping droplets of moisture, the
whole picture slightly out of focus in the swirling fog.

I glanced at the compass card.

" Christ!" I exploded at the Kroo boy. " Can't you keep on
course without swinging a point or two either way!"

He looked truculent. More truculent than scared, although in
his hands lay the fate of *Etosha* and us all, ripping through
this cursed darkness with all the power of the great diesels. The
telegraph stood at full ahead; she had her head, striding out
through the murky water almost dead into the light breeze from
the nor'-nor'-west. She had been doing gloriously since I rang
down to Mac hours ago when *Etosha* slipped out of Walvis into
the fog. The winter fog was ideal cover for our movements,
and if the wind did not freshen from the north-west, it would
hang around until the middle of the afternoon.

I steadied the wheel over the Kroo boy's shoulder. The fog
came in through the open bridge windows, wet, clammy, but
fresh with the sea—unlike the land smog with its tale of filth
and cities.

" When do you think we should sight it?" asked John.

" In about ten minutes, if this black bastard can keep his
mind on the job that long," I replied acidly. " Bearing oh-five-
oh. You can't miss it."

" You can miss anything in this fog," rejoined John.

" No, you won't," I said. " I've been keeping her about six
miles offshore all night . . ." I saw him wince as he thought of
the shoals and the rocks as close in, and the wicked currents
which come and go along the Skeleton Coast . . . " and in about

ten minutes the sun will be at a sufficient angle to refract under the fogbank. You won't miss the hill in Sierra Bay. It's about six hundred and fifty feet high, and you'll catch a glimpse of white water as the sun glances off the fogbank."

" Neat as a problem in physics," laughed John.

" Oh, for God's sake!" I burst out. Then I regretted it. My nerves were shot to hell, tearing through a fogbank like this at sixteen knots and never being sure that I was not taking *Etosha* to a sudden and dreadful death. " Sorry," I said. " But this isn't a pleasure cruise to me—and you know anything can happen on this coast."

John grinned. " Forget it," he said. " I'm only an unskilled help. You're the backroom boy—you've got it all in your head. I must say it frightens the pants off me."

" Well," I said, mollified by his calm which was always a tonic to me in a tight corner, " I had to get well clear of Walvis before any of the fishing fleet started cluttering things up. At this speed, if *Etosha* hits anything, we will all take a nose-dive to the bottom. I'm making like a bat out of hell for Sierra Bay, and I think I'll get a fix on the high hill there. About eight miles to the north-west will be Cape Cross and when we spot the white water there I'll change from this course nor'-nor'-west to nor'-west. But I'm holding her close in so that we'll be in fog most of to-day, and by this afternoon when it clears we should be somewhere around the Swallow Breakers."

John winced again. " Where I put up my classic boob and nearly had us ashore."

I looked at him sombrely. " I can't promise you I won't do exactly the same. I hope to get another fix there, and then we'll beat it for the mouth of the Cunene." I dropped my voice. " That's where our friend is going to be dumped."

John looked at me; the fog distorted the size of his eyes.

" Dumped?"

" Put ashore," I hastily corrected myself. I wondered if John guessed I had no intention of bringing Stein back alive.

" Tricky," he said, turning away and raising his glasses.

" Watch this boy," I told John. " I'm going up above to see if I can get a glimpse of the breakers."

" Aye, aye," said John.

The fog seemed thicker up on the " flying bridge." I

strode over to the starboard wing and my anger and frustration at the whole project boiled when I saw a duffle-coated figure looking landwards. If I was going to taxi Stein around this perilous coast, at least I wasn't going to have him or any other of his party on my bridge.

I grabbed the coated shoulder.

"Get off my bridge," I snarled. "Get the hell out of here back to the saloon."

The hood fell back as the figure turned. It was a girl. Even in my anger I noticed that the long, red-brown hair seemed more to tumble out of her hood than anything else in its profusion.

I looked at her in stupefaction. The fog perhaps distorted her eyes, but I can see the look in them still. She gazed at me silently.

"As you wish," she said in a low voice.

She started to brush past me. All my pent-up anger at Stein and his machinations broke loose.

"What the bloody hell are you, a woman, doing on my ship?" I burst out. "If Stein thinks he can bring along his home comforts on a trip like this, then, by God, he's mistaken!" A plan flashed through my mind. Cape Cross! Yes, I'd send her ashore in the surf-boat under cover of the fog—there was a primitive settlement there—and she could have a look at life in the raw.

"Out there," I snapped, waving my hand landwards, "is a series of shacks round a saltpan. I'm putting you ashore there—and you'll bloody well like it, understand? I'm not having any woman on board my ship on a trip like this."

She eyed me coolly and it may have been a gesture of nervousness, or a woman's instinct, that made her fumble to undo the top button of her duffle-coat.

"I think we should discuss this question with Dr. Stein, don't you?" she asked levelly.

"I won't discuss anything with Stein," I snapped back. "I'm not having his bloody woman on my ship. Having him is quite enough."

"Stop saying 'his woman'," she retorted. She stared at me hard and I remember still that there was a slight crumple of flesh between her right eyelid and eyebrow as she frowned.

"So you are the famous Captain Peace," she went off at a tangent.

I started to reply, but John's hail came floating up.

"Breakers bearing oh-four-oh, six miles. Geoffrey! Geoffrey!"

I stood, torn between my anger at finding Stein's woman, and the imperative need to con *Etosha*.

She smiled. "Go on, Geoffrey," she mocked. "You can deal with me later. Your ship needs you now."

I went.

"I just caught a glimpse of it," said John, "there, I think, bearing now oh-three-five."

I waited for a moment for the refracted light to strike back.

"No," I said, "I don't think so. Oh-three-five is too fine. I think it must have been a mirage off the smaller saltpan, which lies just south of the point. How much water under her?"

John flicked a glance at the echo-sounder.

"Nine—and a bit, shallowing."

I grinned at him. "Oddly enough, it's not shallowing just here. As we come opposite the point we'll get up to thirteen fathoms. I wish we would get a bit of sun, though."

Etosha tore on. John, I could see, was plainly nervous. So was I. Toying with a trick of the light for a reliable bearing on the Skeleton Coast is about as safe as playing Russian roulette.

The fog dripped, but it was lighter to the east. If I missed this bearing, I would, at best, have to fumble my way northwards to Palgrave Point and Cape Frio and beyond that, in the foul ground towards Curva dos Dunas—I felt myself sweating even at the thought.

I trained my glasses on a fixed bearing. At thirteen fathoms under *Etosha*, that should be just about right.

"How much water under her now?"

John's voice was surprised.

"By the deep twelve."

"Good. Take the helm, will you, John? We should pick it up in a moment. It'll be tricky. I don't want that Kroo boy spoiling things."

A flicker of light, like a halo, twitched across the landward side of the fog. Here it comes . . . I thought.

A bright shaft, almost like a searchlight, struck the outward opaque edge. The sun, as I had assumed, had glanced off the startling white surface of the great saltpan north of Sierra Point; along its beam I hoped to see the bald, eroded hill which stood out at the back of the two saltpans.

Like a revelation, the fog opened and my landmark was as clear as day.

" High hill bearing red oh-three-three," I grinned at John, enjoying the complicated problem in navigation.

But my professional pleasure was spoiled. Stein was on the back of the bridge with the woman.

" You see, my dear, what I mean when I say that Captain Peace knows the Skeleton Coast quite as well as they say in the bars at Walvis. Look! no charts, no references—it's all in his head. It looks so very simple, does it not? But do you realise that if he didn't know exactly what he was doing he'd tear the bottom out of her in three minutes?"

The girl said nothing. I couldn't worry about them now.

" Steer three-four-oh," I said in a flat voice.

Etosha came round in a sweeping arc, blinking into broad sunlight for a minute as she cocked a snook at the dun coastline with its balding fringes of windswept weed here and there.

" Steady as she goes," I said to John. " Put the Kroo boy on now."

I had my fix and *Etosha* was set for Cape Frio. Beyond that . . .

Fortunately it was just as suitable for dropping a boat off Cape Cross.

I turned to Stein.

" In half an hour," I said acidly, " I shall stop the engines and drop a boat over the side. This woman of yours is going ashore." I looked at the composed face under the duffle-coat hood.

" You've got twenty minutes to get your things together."

Stein grinned his ray-like grin. This was the sort of situation he loved.

"May I introduce," he said calmly, "Dr. Anne Nielsen, of the National Zoological Museum in Stockholm."

I gazed at her in cold rage.

"You're losing time," I snapped. "If your things aren't ready, I'll throw them over the side after you."

"Dr. Nielsen," Stein continued, "is the only scientist in the world—at least in this generation—to have actually examined the species Onymacris in the flesh, or shall we say, in the shell?"

I still did not catch on.

"What all this mumbo-jumbo has to do with me, I am at a loss to know," I retorted. *Etosha* was cutting through the fog and it gave an eerie air of making everything a little larger—like her eyes.

"Shall I explain, that Dr. Nielsen is my principal assistant on this trip and she will accompany me in order to establish whether or not the Onymacris beetle lives on the Skeleton Coast. It will be a discovery of the first importance, both to science and the world. Captain Peace," he said and his voice hardened, "you will understand that there is no question of putting Dr. Nielsen ashore? She comes with me."

The thought gave me a jolt. If I did away with Stein, she'd have to be a victim too. I must have been pondering this deeply until suddenly I was aware that I was staring at her; the only sound on the bridge was the click of the ratchet on the helm.

I looked from her to him.

"Very well," I said, "but I hadn't bargained for a woman. On a ship like this there's not much room. You'll have to find a corner somewhere. Mister Garland will see to that. And—Stein—if you have any more surprises in your party, you'd better tell them to me quickly, or else . . ." I left the sentence unfinished.

Stein said smoothly. "My personal bodyguard and general factotum is, of course, Johann."

"Johann!" I gasped. "That mad U-boat rating! God's truth, Stein, what is this?"

"It's my expedition and you are going to put us ashore at a spot which I hope sometime to-day you will be good enough to show me on a chart. My objective on land is slightly west of the Baynes Mountains."

I stared at him in open disbelief. The woman first, the mad German rating second, and the Baynes Mountains third.

" The Baynes Mountains!" I exclaimed. " You're crazy, Stein! No white man has ever set foot inside them."

" Except Baynes," retorted Stein.

" And do you really expect me to hang around the Skeleton Coast while you traipse off to the Baynes Mountains—you'll take a month at least to get there."

" Depending," interrupted the girl, " where you put us ashore."

" That's fair enough," I replied. The freshening wind blew back the hood. Her hair was very lovely. " But when I undertook to convey you to the Skeleton Coast, I understood that you were making a quick run ashore—at the most two or three days. There was no mention of a specific objective."

" You will fetch us in a month's time, depending on where you are putting us ashore," said Stein. I didn't like the way he said " will."

This new development meant I must disclose the whereabouts of Curva dos Dunas—at least vaguely. Well, I ruminated grimly, they've all signed their own death warrant. Pretty girl or no pretty girl, Curva dos Dunas was mine. I salved my conscience quickly. I could perhaps arrange a " leak " through Mark and the police would soon round them up, but then I would be involved if Stein spoke—and I felt quite sure he wouldn't hesitate if he found I had turned the tables on him. I shelved the question for the moment.

Stein was speaking again.

" I think the best plan is if we go to the saloon and I shall indicate exactly where I am going."

I nodded. The girl went first.

I found myself alone in the saloon with her. She slipped off the unshapely duffle-coat and I was surprised at the slim figure underneath. She wore corduroy slacks and a tangerine shirt. It looked as if it had come straight from the laundry. Her breasts barely filled the curve of the shirt.

She caught my glance and smiled.

"Not exactly the rig for the Skeleton Coast, thinks Captain Peace?"

"I don't think this coast is any place for any woman at all," I said gruffly, half irritated at her close scrutiny of myself. I hadn't shaved as I had been on the bridge all night and I could feel the sticky mixture of salt air and fog moisture on the bristles. My eyes probably looked like a drunk's.

"Cigarette?" she asked, pulling out a packet of Peter Stuyvesant.

"I don't smoke," I said, "or practically never."

There was a reserved, mocking smile on her lips.

"Spoils the ability to smell where you are off the Skeleton Coast?" she asked lightly.

I looked at her, but there was no laughter in my reply.

"Stein didn't tell me he was bringing a woman along with him. Particularly an attractive woman. I just don't like the whole idea."

There was no laughter this time from her either.

"Your idea or his idea?" she asked penetratingly.

I fenced it off, but it gave me the measure of her intelligence.

"The two ideas must necessarily combine. I supply the landing-point—so I thought. That is my business. Where it is is also my business. I wasn't bargaining for a return pick-up in a month's time."

"Return pick-up sounds awfully like some kind of tart," she grinned.

But she cut short my return grin and I found myself feeling rather inane with it hanging on my lips. She took a quick draw on the cigarette—I noticed she had almost smoked half of it in our brief conversation—and said crisply, as if she regretted her sally: "You're Captain Macdonald, alias Lieutenant-Commander Peace, aren't you?"

I didn't like the way she said it.

I nodded.

"That's right," I sneered. "Lieutenant-Commander Geoffrey Peace, D.S.O. and two Bars, Royal Navy, cashiered. Now a fisherman. At present engaged in dubious unspecified activities off the Skeleton Coast."

"I just want you to get it quite clear what my position is in all this," she went on decisively. " Let's get the record straight before we start. The first thing that springs to your mind when you see me is that I'm Stein's woman. Those were your own words."

" What else was I to think?" I rejoined lamely. " An attractive young woman . . ." My words petered out.

" Exactly," she snapped, grinding the cigarette savagely. " To you a woman means only one thing—and you had the impertinence to say it to a complete stranger. Get this clear; I don't like Stein any more than I like you on first acquaintance."

" Then there's nothing more to be said," I snapped back.

" There's a great deal more," she said. " I know the sort of man Stein is, and I know the sort of people he hires to work for him."

We stared across the table in open hostility.

" If you know all about slumming, why come along?" I sneered back. " Why dirty your lily-white hands with all this human offal?"

She lit another cigarette angrily.

" Don't you *know* what a living Onymacris means to science?"

" No," I replied, " and I don't give a damn either. Stein is no more hunting an extinct beetle than I am. I don't see him as the scientist in his ivory—or is it uranium—tower devoting his life and fortune to restoring one little beetle to the sum of human knowledge."

" I was absolutely right in my assessment of you," she said. " Tough, ruthless, self-centred, no gain but my gain. You wouldn't know what it felt like to have a leading ideal about a thing like this."

I was more curious than angry now.

" And you have—of course."

" Look," she said, " I was born during the civil war in China . . ."

" Is this autobiography really necessary?" I asked.

The barb went home. She flushed. She turned away to the porthole.

" It only is because it illustrates why I am here," she said. " I haven't got any illusions about Stein—or about you, for that matter. Or this expedition. But Onymacris matters—matters, oh, so much."

I wasn't going to let her get away with all that.

"There must be something darkly Freudian about conceiving a passion for a beetle," I said.

"Damn your cheap flippancy," she snapped. "When did you last speak decently to a woman?"

"I never do. It was one of the charges when they cashiered me."

She ignored this. "My father was one of the world's leading authorities on beetles," she said. "Without boring you with tales of hardship and being only one jump ahead of death for months on end, ahead of one opposing army or the next, he and I eventually got to the edge of the Gobi Desert. Mother, who was English, died long before that. He rediscovered Onymacris there. When at last we escaped from China, he died one night suddenly of a heart attack aboard a sampan near the Yangtse mouth. I didn't know about it till morning. The body had been robbed by the coolies. His precious beetles, which we'd kept alive when we thought we'd die of starvation ourselves, had been stamped flat. Just a couple of squashed things at the bottom of an old shoebox. A lifetime's work for science crushed out by some careless foot. I'm going to find Onymacris again—for science. I've got to. That's why I'm here."

"It must sound a pretty obvious question," I said. "But why not go back to the Gobi and get some more, if you're so keen?"

"First," she said a little didactically, and I could see now that she was a little older than her looks and figure would seem to indicate, "it's behind the Iron Curtain. Second, the place where we found them is now a prohibited area, anyway. Probably a sputnik launching site. An Iron Curtain behind an Iron Curtain. I know. I've tried."

"It seems a tough proposition," I agreed.

She came back shortly: "Onymacris is a tough proposition, Captain Peace. And I expect to find only tough circumstances where it is. That's what makes it so precious to science. It's not one of the things you find by chance on a Sunday afternoon walk. You've got to work for it. It's a tough proposition."

" Like this outfit," I said ironically.

She looked at me levelly. " Like this outfit, Captain Peace. Like yourself, Captain Peace. Like this coast, Captain Peace, which I am told you know so well. I'm after something tough, just like you, that's why I accepted Stein's invitation without hesitation. You can forget about the woman-comfort side of things. I thought I'd explain this clearly to you before you start showering your protective instincts on a helpless female."

" I don't see how you could be a doctor of science at Stockholm . . ." I began.

" Why not?" she flashed. " Every moment of my life I've slept, eaten, talked beetles. What's so strange about it? My father taught me everything—and more—a university ever could. A doctor's degree is a necessary appendage, that's all. It couldn't have been easier. A piece of cake." She lit another cigarette. She came back at me remorselessly.

" Why are you so cagey about this whole landing affair? Why don't you think it's safe?"

" Listen," I rapped out, fast losing patience, for she was so damnably sure of herself and her precious beetle. " Everyone loves this blasted beetle so much, you'd think it was pure gold. You'd think each one of us was acting within the law, when we're just as far outside it as could be. I'm putting you ashore —illegally—at an illegal spot on the Skeleton Coast. You and Stein have absolutely no right to be there. You yourself admit it isn't going to be easy. I say so too. I'm aiding and abetting a crime."

She looked at me cynically. " Stein will be paying you well enough."

I couldn't let it go.

" I'm doing this free, gratis and for nothing," I snapped. " I'm not getting a penny for this joyride."

" I don't believe a word of that," she retorted.

Her composure rattled me. What did a hint—or more—of the truth matter when it blackened Stein?

" I've been blackmailed into this trip," I said curtly.

" Blackmailed?" she said incredulously.

So Stein hadn't told her.

" Yes," I retorted. " I'm the sort of man you can blackmail

—tough, self-centred, anything for personal gain. You said so yourself."

I had shaken her. I rubbed it home.

"You're dealing with tough people. I quote you again. You must expect these things."

She shook her head. "But . . ."

"There are no buts," I retorted. "If anyone gets word of this trip, you're in it as much as Stein or myself. If anyone is missing for a month from Walvis, or Windhoek—it's a small place—the police smell a rat, and they're very good at that. Or someone passes the word to Ohopoho that a white man—and a white woman—are in the Skeleton Coast."

"Where's Ohopoho?" she asked.

"It's a God-forsaken spot near the Ovambo border," I said. "It's the headquarters of the one official in the Skeleton Coast. There's an airstrip. He's got a radio-telephone. All he needs is a suspicious buzz and they'll send out a couple of jeeps and a truck to round you up without further ado."

She parried the thrust of my attack by switching her ground.

I watched you up on the bridge," she said. "I would have said—for a moment—that you were almost happy."

I'd learned enough about her in a short while not to fall for that one.

"Thanks," I replied dryly. "A sharp problem in navigation is always prescribed for the patient in the Royal Navy."

The rapier-point flickered.

"Before or after cashiering?"

This woman with the red god hair certainly knew how to cut across wounds with a scalpel.

She followed up the punch, but this time I was ready for it. Ready, like an old windjammer, under snug canvas for the squall.

"And you left her and followed the course of duty? And made yourself into a human chuck-out, a sort of maritime beachcomber."

"You've got your metaphors mixed," I stabbed back. "What interest is it to you to know how tough men spend their off time? If you really want to know, I went to her flat to sleep with her before going on a suicide cruise—for the last time—but I wasn't in the mood. In fact, I never got there."

Stein broke it up. He bustled in carrying a cardboard cylinder. He looked suspiciously at us both, but said nothing. He took a map from the cylinder and spread it out.

" Here is my plan," he said briefly.

It was a small map, much smaller than my Admiralty charts, and was headed " Ondangua, World Aeronautical Chart."

Maps have always fascinated me.

" I've never seen this map before," I said.

It covered an area roughly from the Haonib River (which is really the southern boundary of the Skeleton Coast) to Porto Alexandre in Angola. It went as far eastwards as the great Etosha Pan, that inland lake where the elephant are counted in thousands and the antelopes thunder by your jeep like the charge of the Light Brigade. It showed the Cunene River, international boundary between South West Africa and Portuguese Angola, for hundreds of miles into the hinterland.

Stein smirked.

" I'm glad there are some maps of the Skeleton Coast which you haven't seen, Captain Peace. As a matter of interest, you can get this one for five shillings from the Trigonometrical Survey Office in Pretoria."

He put a couple of ashtrays on the corners to hold it down.

He jabbed his finger at a light brown patch on the map below the Cunene.

" That is where I am going."

The map showed a great welter of mountains on the southern side of the great Cunene River marked " Baynes Mountains." Some figures in a neat oblong read " 7200 feet." Before one reaches the Baynes Mountains there is another huge range of unfriendly mountains marked Hartmannberge.

I could not but admire Stein's courage. No white man except Baynes has ever been inside those broken fastnesses. For hundreds of miles inland from the coast and along the shoreline itself the map says simply " unsurveyed." Only the highest peaks are marked. In between might be almost anything.

I shook my head. I was aware of Anne's eyes on my face.

She seemed so self-reliant, so remote. Perhaps her early hardships had given her that air of detachment, almost Oriental acceptance of things as they occurred.

" What is your route?" I asked Stein flatly.

" Where are you going to put us ashore?" he countered.

I looked at the stark map, just about as bare as a Skeleton Coast dune. I had already made up my mind. Curva dos Dunas was my secret and was going to remain so.

I pointed to the mouth of the great river. There wasn't a single shoal or sand-bar marked. God help anyone who took this official map for his guide!

" About there. Where it says Foz do Cunene."

In fact, Curva dos Dunas lay about twenty miles to the south. Stein was pleased.

" That is excellent," he said. " It ties up nicely with my route. You see, I intend using the river bed as my road into the interior. It's dry at this time of the year. Here, look."

His enthusiasm was almost catching. Anne came round and loooked over my shoulder. The fresh perfume of Tweed mingled with the musty smell of the thick map paper. Nothing ever gets wholly dry in one of these fogs.

" I'm going to march up here, past Posto Velho—that's the Portuguese guard post—and the river provides me with a gap right through the Hartmannberge. It cuts past the Ongeamaberge, which are right on the river itself. You see these huge wadis coming down from the mountains from the south to the river itself? Well, when I get about seventy miles from the mouth of the river, I'm following one of them by turning south too—at the Nangolo Flats, they call it. See this thin blue line? —that's the Kapupa River, probably only a dry bed anyway. That's my dagger into the heart of the Baynes Mountains. Here's a seven thousand foot peak, the Otjihipo. That's my immediate objective."

The northern side of the river, the Portuguese side, looked even less hospitable than the southern, or South African side.

The girl seemed to catch my thoughts.

She ran a painted nail round a gigantic cluster of tumbled peaks and mountains on the Angola side, completely unmapped and unsurveyed, but with a single title for an area the size of Scotland, " Serra de Chela."

"It looks just like a rabbit," she mused. "See, here's his tail, opposite our turn-off at the Nangolo Flats."

The remark caught me off balance. How much of her façade was real, I wondered. She said it gently, humorously, a side of the girl-scientist which was new. I found it attractive. She held my eyes until I dropped them from her steady, level gaze. I took refuge in the job on hand.

"You'll need all the luck, including a rabbit's tail, that you can find once you get inside those mountains," I said briefly.

Stein smiled mirthlessly.

"Captain Peace is a great believer in luck, my dear. Ask him. His luck's so strong that it drove a man off his head."

She looked at me with a kind of remote disbelief. The cards were down anyway, so I pulled out my little lucky hand. As it lay in my hand she motioned to touch it and then drew back in horror.

"It really looks like a tiny little hand, shrunken. . . ." she backed away in fear . . . "You didn't, did you. . . ."

"Oh, for God's sake, stop regarding me as a monster! All right, if you like, I cut off the hand of one of my victims and by a process unknown to any white man but me, and learned in the course of my nefarious career when I was a pirate off South America. . . ."

Stein stemmed my outburst.

"You get them in German villages, particularly in the Black Mountains. But that's not to say no one has died because of that hand. I would say that quite a few men have died because if it; not so, Captain?"

Stein always waited for the thrust in the back. The fool project he was indulging in, and probably because there would be more blood on my hands before it was out, brought my anger welling up against him. Somehow it wouldn't spark against the girl. A moment before, something of the adventure of the whole thing had taken me out of myself for a moment; now it all backfired.

"I land you there," I said harshly, stabbing at the mouth of the Cunene. "After that, you can go to bloody hell for all I care."

"It's just to avoid that unfortunate circumstance," replied

Stein smoothly, " that I have come to discuss my route with you."

Anne had drawn away at my outburst.

" I land you, and I fetch you—in a month's time," I said restraining myself.

" You also supply the expedition," Stein went on.

" What do you mean?"

" It could not have failed to meet your keen submariner's eye," Stein continued sarcastically, " that even though my party came on board at night, they were without camping equipment, food, water or provisions for a trip which you yourself regard as hazardous."

I had scarcely given it a thought.

" I have a list here," and he drew it from a pocket, " of what I will require from your ship's stores. You will give instructions to that effect."

" But . . ."

" There are no buts, Captain." He added impatiently: " Did you want all Walvis to know what was going on—tents, equipment, food, all being loaded aboard your ship? You would never have been allowed out of port without the police coming aboard."

I said nothing, but took the long, old-fashioned pair of ivory dividers with its pearl-inlaid top and needles of porcupine quills instead of steel—something which I had found amongst old Simon Peace's things—and stepped off a twenty-mile circle from the mouth of the river. The old dividers looked as if they had originally been in an Indiaman in John Company's service.

They were plotting the mathematics of my strategy at the moment. Anne was looking at them curiously. The map did not show the great cataract about twenty miles from the river's mouth; it was so great, according to old Simon's chart, that the river sagged like a great intestine to the south in overrunning it. I followed the course of the river with the old dividers. The second cataract, too, within fifty miles of the coast—well, they were Stein's affair. His plan had the virtue of great simplicity, but those mountains would never have remained inaccessible for half a century of white occupation to the south and north if the path to them were simply up the dry bed of a river. Where Curva dos Dunas lay was simply an unsurveyed light brown patch on Stein's map, which showed an even coastline, sand-hills and escarpment rising through steps of 1,000 and 2,000 feet to the grim fortresses of the Hartmannberge, the first sentry of the Baynes Mountains beyond. The Portuguese cartographers had at least added the words " dunas moveis "—shifting dunes—on their side of the frontier.

" What are you working out?" asked Stein keenly.

I must have been completely lost in my own thoughts, for the girl was looking at me also.

" You see where the river turns northwards right as the mouth?" I asked.

They nodded.

" Well, the mouth is actually one mass of sand-bars and often after the rainy season the delta changes its complexion considerably. Depending on the sand and the state of the mouth, I shall decide on the spot where exactly to put you ashore," I lied.

I'd give them a course for the river from Curva dos Dunas and, after half a day's march, they'd never find it again. It would take a skilled navigator to recognise it anyway, and I was prepared to bet that from the landward side it resembled an anchorage even less than it did from the sea.

" You mean, you don't know a channel into a landing-spot?" Stein asked suspiciously.

I laughed. " Look at your map," I retorted. " See any landing-spots?"

" Of course not," said Stein. " That's exactly why I got you to bring me to the Skeleton Coast. You have it all in your head."

My round, I thought. " I have the mouth of the Cunene ' in my mind,' too, if you want to know, and that's why I shall decide when we get there. There is also the question of the wind, and the tide, plus inshore currents," I elaborated with equal untruth. " You can't judge these things until you are there."

" I don't like it," frowned Stein. " I thought you'd do

better than this, Captain. Any clever skipper could do what you are intending to do."

"Then let's turn back and you can get another—with pleasure," I snapped.

"What's going to happen if the wind and the currents are not right when you come to pick us up again?" he went on.

I was enjoying myself.

"That'll be just too bad," I said. "You'll have to wait for the next slow boat to China."

The cruel mouth tightened. Stein seemed abstracted for a moment or two. I was not to know that my sally was to cost an innocent man his life.

Etosha tore on through the day. The fog scarcely lightened. In the middle of the morning I left the bridge to John.

"Call me when it begins to lift," I told him. "I'm going below to catch up on my beauty sleep. We should be somewhere off Cape Frio when it disperses."

"That's a long day's fog," murmured John, looking at the endless moisture.

"Damn good for this sort of job," I replied.

"About Cape Frio, then?" he repeated.

"Or sooner, if it starts clearing. But I don't think so with the wind in the north-west. Barometer's steady. Not that that means much off this coast. If it starts to blow hard, call me. It could mean we're in for a swell which will shake the guts out of us all."

"In other words," grinned John, "if almost anything happens to the sea, the fog or the wind."

I grinned back.

"You've got it dead right," I said.

When I reached my cabin I kicked off my shoes and lay down fully dressed. I didn't sleep right away. I told myself it was the girl's red-gold hair, but my sub-conscious told me I was lying. She had shown me the picture of myself as I was. "No gain but my gain," she had sneered. Tough, like this expedition. Never a leading ideal. She hadn't believed I'd ever been anything else. I thought of the first days of my command in the Mediterranean. I turned restlessly. So easy to say, they made a killer of me. Kill, or be killed. I was prepared to believe her ideal about Onymacris. The fire of hardship had burned away almost everything else—you could see it in the tight lines about her mouth, although youth was holding everything in check.

I fell asleep wondering what sort of person she really was.

The look-out's cry cut across my sleep. I suppose a sailor develops some sort of "third ear" which always listens, even when his mind is unconscious.

"Steamer on the starboard bow!"

It was wrong, all wrong, my mind told me even as it shook off the curtain of sleep and rose to the surface. A steamer on the starboard bow inside the six-mile limit of *Etosha's* course!

I had my shoes on and was already half-way up the companionway when I heard John repeat the look-out's call down the speaking tube to me. I was on the bridge in three bounds. The fog was lifting, as I had told John it would in the middle of the afternoon. I found myself half-blind and blinking in the pale, almost sodium-yellow light.

John lowered his glasses for a moment in puzzlement.

"I can't see her, but the look-out did spot her through a patch. It's lifting. I'll be damned if I know how any ship could be inside us. . . ."

I moved to the engine telegraphs and cannoned into the girl. I hadn't seen her.

"Sorry," she said almost contritely. "You said I shouldn't come up here, but you were asleep. . . ."

Her eyes held the previous challenge, but there was also a smile. I parried the challenge and accepted the smile.

My last thought before falling asleep was with me. "Just keep out of the helmsman's way and everything will be O.K." I said.

The challenge softened and the smile warmed, although her lips did not move. She stood back watching.

"Slow ahead," I rang down. The eager pant of the great diesels and the angry susurration of their firing, carried through steel plate and rivet to the soles of the feet, slowed. Mac was on the job all right.

"We're running clear of it, I think—I hope," said John. A day's growth of beard, the white yachting sweater, cap and old serge trousers gave him almost a naval air again.

"Where are we?" I asked him. "What's the sounding?"

" Forty-three, twenty-five, twenty-eight—and shallowing."
" Any fixes?"

He shrugged expressively at the fog.

" Cape Frio, by dead reckoning. But the operative word here is dead."

Suddenly the fog blew back westwards, like a curtain-shift at a slick American musical. The whole scene was laid bare to our eyes at the flick of an invisible curtain-hand.

There was the steamer, a liner, with her bows pointing south and east. Beyond was a flat beach, beaten punch-drunk to an off-white by the surf, backed by low dun-coloured sand-hills, trailed here and there with a wispy tonsure of grey-green naras plant. I could even see its yellow fruit, something like a melon, rotting away in the sun.

I was astonished to find the girl at my side, tugging at my arm.

"Do something!" she cried. "Only you can save her, Captain Peace! Tell her how to get off the rocks! She'll be ashore in a minute!" She brushed round to be in front of me and in doing so I felt her breast against my forearm. She looked beseechingly up at me. "I don't want to see any more pain and death, do you understand? I've seen enough in my lifetime. Do this one thing and it doesn't matter . . . the past. . . ."

I led her across to the side of the bridge and said gently: " She's been ashore for years. That's the *Dunedin Star.*"

She gave a little sigh.

"Thank God for that!" she exclaimed. This time her lips smiled too.

Stein joined us.

"They beached her after she struck a sunken object at sea. Everyone had great fun and games getting the passengers off that beach. The South Africans seemed simply to throw away tugs and planes and lorries to reach them."

The ill-fated liner, her smoke-stack still gamely erect, held grimly on to her never-never course.

"Look," I said to Anne, handing her my glasses, "you can still see the emergency floats lashed to her decks."

"I can see a locomotive—and a tank," she exclaimed with a note of excitement in her voice. Until now it had been level and controlled in her conversations with me. "Can't we go in closer?"

John looked dubious as I slowed still further and altered course to take *Etosha* nearer the famous wreck. Anne's suppressed mood gave a holiday air to the bridge.

"I can see more tanks and guns and look at that huge pile of tyres—I think it's tyres—on the beach."

Stein said heavily: "She was carrying tanks and guns to the British in the Middle East, as well as tyres for the Eighth Army. Her loss must have hit them pretty hard at that time, I guess."

Anne gave him a long, considered look. It almost seemed as if she thought as little of him as I did. I could see him mentally rubbing his hands. His gloating satisfaction rather sickened me. Somehow the thought that she wasn't on Stein's side pleased me. One way and another, Onymacris must be quite a beetle.

Etosha came closer in and we could see the pitiful abandon of a ship left to the waves and the birds.

"It was a stroke of luck, her hitting a submerged object like that—for the Germans, I mean," went on Stein in his mincing voice. "The court of inquiry thought she smacked on to an outlying spur of the Clan Alpine Reef. You'd think the British captain would have kept away from a coast like this instead of coming in so close. Not unless Captain Peace was in command. He must have known he was taking a big risk."

"If you'd really like to know," I said quietly, "the *Dunedin Star* was sunk by a German torpedo."

"Rubbish," snapped Stein. "It was a reef. Slipshod. If he'd been a German captain we'd have shot him. The *Dunedin Star* was off course. There was never any mention of an explosion."

Etosha circled her dead friend of the sea. Stein knew a lot about the *Dunedin Star*. I wondered to myself how much he was concerned in knowing her movements—in time of war.

"Did you ever hear of the Type XXXI U-boat torpedo?" I asked.

I had Anne's and John's full attention now.

"No? Well, Blohm and Voss developed it. Acoustic, of course. The torpedo that sank the *Dunedin Star* was fired from a secret type of German submarine. I'll reconstruct it for you. What went through the U-boat commander's mind when he saw the *Dunedin Star*, laden with weapons of war, in his sights? He didn't press the button and send her to the bottom. Sooner or later—probably sooner—there would have been a hunting force up here looking for him. So he just tagged along behind the *Dunedin Star* while he drew the main charges from his Type XXXI's because he knew that at fifty knots—and they did every bit of fifty knots—a close salvo would tear right through any liner's plating like butter. There'd only be a dull thump. Four little beauties and a hole like a house, and a deadweight cargo that would take her to the bottom like a load of lead. The U-boat skipper went even one better. He waited until *Dunedin Star* was among the worst foul ground in the world. Then he fired. The whole world believed that the *Dunedin Star* struck a hidden reef and tore her bottom out. I would have liked to have met that U-boat man."

Stein gazed at me like a man entranced.

"By God!" he said. "It would take a German to do that."

Anne's dry interruption gave me the measure of her thoughts about Stein. In words at least, it aligned her on my side.

"You forget, the solution has been worked out by a British submarine captain." She looked levelly from him to me. "Very ingenious, Captain Peace. No wonder they loaded you up with decorations." She must have sensed something of the drift of my thoughts, and the barb followed with all the flickering speed of the Bushmen's arrows out there in the desert behind the wreck. "But I'd really like to know something about your last fling that didn't come off."

I thought our truce was peace, but I was wrong.

"Course three-one-oh," I snapped savagely at the Kroo boy. I rang the telegraphs.

"Half ahead."

"I'll take over," I went on to John, quite unreasonably. "You get some rest, unless you really want to tag along here. I'm going outside the *Clan Alpine*. The chart says sixty fathoms, but I'd swear it's nearer six at fifteen miles offshore. There's a lot of discoloured water and breakers between the shoal and the coast. I don't want to risk it—particularly as it will be dark quite soon."

Stein left.

"You said I could stay . . ." Anne began.

"Yes," I retorted curtly and I saw, to my surprise, the hurt in her eyes. "I repeat, you can stay. But don't get in the way of anybody. And any fortuitous comment will be out of place."

She went over to where she could see the coastline—for what it was worth—and leaned out across the starboard wing of the bridge. For an hour or more *Etosha,* her port bow towards the lowering sun, shook herself free of the grim tentacles of the Skeleton Coast—the innumerable, shifting shoals of sand, the uncharted, hidden rocks and the sailor's nightmare which is put down on charts in the classic understatement of "foul ground, discoloured water." The late afternoon was clear but cold—even in midsummer, let alone midwinter, the mercury falls owing to the peculiar juxtaposition of desert and Antarctic air which comes on the wings of the perpetual south-westerly gale. The afternoon's wintriness and the morning's fog arise from the warmer, moist air which sweeps in in June and July from the humid, tropical seas to the north, creating a fog similar to that of the Grand Banks of America.

Anne stood alone without looking round for that whole hour. The coastline was clearer than at any time during the morning and in the far distance I could see the ragged tumble of blue which marked the mountains of the interior, anything up to a hundred miles from *Etosha.*

I jammed myself on the opposite side of the helmsman away from the girl. It needed all that cold, fresh sea air to dampen my anger against her. What damnable nerve! I brooded to myself. I was angry at her unconcealed opinion of me and at the same time puzzled when I thought of the other side of her I had seen for a moment when she believed I could do something about the *Dunedin Star.* Then the holiday mood on the bridge—which was real, the cool, self-poise, or the holiday mood? She seemed to have an ability, a kind of psychological homeopathic flair, for bringing pain. I thought the old wound was healed. Why should I put up with her anyway? I asked myself savagely. I thrust myself back on the smooth surface of the stool and almost slipped over backwards. How she'd laugh if I did, I told myself with unnecessary heat. Why should I find myself snarling; what the hell did it matter what she did or didn't think? I glanced overtly at the slim back and line of her buttocks beneath her corduroy slacks. I couldn't tell myself she was just one of Stein's minions—she'd made it perfectly clear she'd come on the expedition with her eyes open—wide open—to both Stein and myself. And yet I couldn't reconcile her devoted scientific attitude, her " keep-off-the-grass " line to me, with those moments looking at the old wreck. She'd come out in my defence over the sinking of the *Dunedin Star*—if that meant anything after what followed. I'd handed Stein the black spot, and that meant her too, I brooded, taking my eyes from her back. It was a fair fight between Stein and myself but Anne was so obviously in a neutral corner. . . . The wide expanse of sea seemed weary with the day's care. The strange light did nothing to alleviate my mood. Too much sea and too much Skeleton Coast!

I got up suddenly and joined her at the rail. She said nothing. She seemed scarcely aware of me. She continued to stare out towards the coast.

I fumbled for something to say.

" It gets cold towards evening. You'll want something more than that thin sweater," I said lamely.

She barely glanced towards me. An opening gambit like that deserves it, I told myself in a moment of introspection.

I was wrong. She gestured towards the dimming coastline. I felt as lost among her vagaries of mood as I once did among the shoals of Curva dos Dunas.

" It tends to get a hold on one, doesn't it?"

She turned without straightening so that she looked up from the level of my chest into my eyes. The movement caught a wisp of hair and blew it across her forehead. The underside was more red than gold.

She followed the movement of my eyes.

" I'll shave it off, and that will shake you when you pick us up again," she said. The sun, at its sinking angle, cast the left side of her face into faint shadow. It showed me, for the first time, the lovely disproportion of the two sides.

I wasn't going to lay myself open again. I started to say

something about sending my razor ashore with her, but it died on my lips and I turned shorewards under the scrutiny of her calm gaze.

She leaned her elbows on the rail. There wasn't a landmark or a hill worth mentioning to break the conversational impasse.

She surprised me by doing so.

" That was a lovely old pair of dividers you had in there," she said. " I'd like to have a closer look at them."

My surprise must have shown on my face.

" I'll do it on an exchange basis," she smiled, and it flashed across my mind how wonderfully it lit up the muscles which seemed to be more in the power of pedantry or self-defence when in repose. She dug a hand into the pocket of her slacks. She took something out and held it behind her back. It was almost the teasing attitude of a small girl. I would have fallen for it right there, had I not been forewarned. " I'll show you what's in my hand if you'll go and get the dividers."

" Of course," I replied guardedly. " Stay here, and I'll slip below and get them."

" I couldn't run very far, could I?" she responded lightly.

I took my time about going down the bridge ladder. She seemed such a mass of contradictions. I returned with the dividers.

She took the instrument from me and held it by the mother-of-pearl tip. She ran a finger down the ivory and stopped in surprise at the bottom.

" Why," she said, " they're so old that they haven't even got steel points. What is it?"

" Porcupine quill," I replied.

She opened her own hand. There was a tin Chinese figure of a water-carrier, done in ivory. It was yellow and dis-coloured. The water-jug was gone.

" Just as you carry your lucky hand, so I carry this round," she said. I couldn't fathom this unburdening. " See, the water-jug got broken. It was in a fire when the soldiers first burned down our home. We were always on the run after that for years."

With a deft movement she put the dividers in the empty socket of the little water-carrier and swung them round and round.

She eyed me.

" Measurement, calculation, plot. . . ." she murmured. " I suppose there comes a time when measurement becomes all-important, becomes an end in itself. The same with calculation."

I tried to laugh it down. I remembered the " keep-off-the-grass " sign.

" I'll bet the old John Company captain never thought his dividers would become part of a moral tale. Particularly in the abstract."

She didn't laugh.

" Calculation is important in your life, isn't it?" she said.

" If it weren't, you might be swimming for it now," I replied flippantly.

Her next remark came out of the blue.

" Have you killed many men, Captain Peace?"

" Thanks for the memory," I said bitterly. The grey light, the mica dust-blinded evening, made it all grey. I needed a drink.

The wind flickered a wisp of hair across her face. The crumple of her eyelid was accentuated. *Etosha* creaked against the night swell.

" You can feed any sort of information into a calculating machine," she went on. She seemed to be weighing something almost judicially in her mind. " I remember seeing a ' Zebra ' computator, one of those electronic brain affairs, which could work out things to sixty-four decimal places. It also worked out how much a worker did or didn't do in a life-time's employment. Equally, it gave the exact radius blast of a hydrogen bomb. It had all the answers, and it didn't matter to it whether it was people dying or people living. It didn't hear them scream. When you live close to a thing like that you begin to see things the way it does, only as a matter of computation, no other issues." She swivelled round on me.

" You've lived a long time with the Skeleton Coast, Captain Peace."

" Yes," I said, " a long time." My anger wouldn't ignite.

" Listen," I said, " I'll show you to-morrow. You ask about

killing men. You'll see the corpses. Seventy-five in one beautiful steel coffin and twenty-seven in another."

"You—were responsible?"

"The first lot," I said harshly, "I would do it again for the same reasons—and the same consequences. Those seventy-five men had to die if thousands more wanted to live. That's fair enough. They took their chance, like I did. I won."

"But, from what I hear, the Royal Navy didn't seem to think so."

"No," I said shortly.

"But you had a defence?" she probed.

"For God's sake, yes," I burst out and I caught a glimpse of the helmsman's eyes flickering sideways at me. "I had a defence all right. It . . . it lies out there."

I gestured to the north-east, to Curva dos Dunas.

She missed nothing.

"But you took the rap? And that's where we're going—going ashore?"

I nodded.

"What does it matter?" I snapped, for she had brought pain from what I thought was a dead wound. "After all, what does an ultimate weapon matter now? The dead men are history. Lieutenant-Commander Geoffrey Peace is history. Or maybe he's dead, too, in a sense."

She eyed me for a long time.

"Down in the Antarctic," she said, "on those little gale-lashed islands like Heard and Marion, the ordinary housefly has so adapted himself to conditions that he has shed his wings, so the continual gales can't blow him away. It's an entomological fact. You've become so part of the Skeleton Coast that you are just pure computation, nothing else."

"A sort of living computing machine," I sneered. "Only I can't work out sixty-four decimal places."

"No," she answered steadily. "But whatever fact is fed to you, you digest it . . . purely for plot and counter-plot, measurement and counter-measurement. What I like to think is that, like those flies, you once had wings."

I was shaken.

"If you have a cigarette," I said, "I'll break my non-smoking rule and have one."

She passed the carton of Peter Stuyvesant without a word. She lit mine, and one for herself.

"If the first was a fair fight, I gather you think in your own mind, the second—the twenty-seven—wasn't?"

"It was an old Greek freighter," I said quietly. "If there'd been anyone left to put an obituary notice in *The Times*, you could have looked me up. Presumed lost at sea. She didn't stand a chance. . . ."

Anne was looking at me calculatingly.

"Look," I went on rather desperately, "I wasn't responsible, or only indirectly. Even if I'd been on the bridge that night I couldn't have saved them."

"But you weren't on the bridge, and so indirectly you were responsible," she said.

"You don't know the facts," I hurried on.

"I don't suppose anyone ever will, if what I hear about you is true," she countered. "I suppose it was all illegal?"

I shrugged and turned away. "Like this little jaunt, it was well outside the law. Only one man would be interested now and he would deal with me—outside the law—if he knew. Stein promised to tell him."

She looked at me and her voice was tired.

"I thought it would be something like that. I didn't know the details. It simply confirms my ideas about Stein."

"And about me, too," I followed up.

She evaded it.

"I am sure you can find some neat analogy from the great world of nature," I said sarcastically.

"Yes," she replied. "Yes, I can. It was in my mind even before you spoke. Out in those dunes there lives a blind beetle. It once had eyes like any other beetle. It always lived on the shadowed side of the dunes, digging down deep out of the sun. It has now completely adapted itself to its environment. But it's quite blind as a result." She stared at me. "Quite blind, do you understand? It can't even see its fellows, but all its other senses are doubly developed. It lives by its senses. But it will never see again."

"Why do you tell me all this?" I asked.

It may only have been a last dart of light from the sun that caught her eyes.

" Purely in the interests of science," she said.

I looked squarely at her, but the face was withdrawn, full of a sadness as weary as the eternal vigil of the shoals and the desert of the Kaokoveld.

" And so Stein doesn't come back either?"

I reached out and touched her shoulder. She tried to pull away, but I gripped it and I felt the crescent of her collar-bone under the wool. I turned her gently round until she faced me. I knew what I had to do, then.

" You weren't meant to either," I said softly.

TWELVE

Madness of the Sands

STEIN SAW the white death in front of him and blenched. His face turned a sickly green and he pulled out the Luger.

" Get back!" he screamed. " Astern, astern!"

He groped madly for the telegraph, pitching John, who was at the wheel, on to the plating of the bridge. Anne retreated, her white face accentuated by her scarlet polo-necked sweater and matching lipstick, to the head of the bridge ladder.

I wasn't afraid of Stein, but I was scared to death of the sand-bars of Curva dos Dunas.

" You bloody fool!" I shouted, making a grab at the spinning spokes as Etosha yawed twenty degrees off course. As I spun the wheel back I hit Stein across the face with the back of my left hand and he went reeling to his knees. Anne picked up his gun uncertainly.

Well, if that's the way he wants it, he'll get it, I thought grimly. " Full astern " I rang on the telegraph. Etosha slowed to a halt, like a horse about to take a jump, and then reined back almost in mid-flight.

It was Etosha's sudden emergence from the fog which threw Stein off balance. I wasn't surprised, although my stomach was turning over. It was the morning after my talk with Anne and Etosha had torn north-westwards through the night to be

in position off Curva dos Dunas by mid-morning. She was only
doing six knots when she broke through the encumbering
gloom into bright sunlight maybe five miles offshore, sunlight
reflecting more whitely by contrast as it came off the creaming
surf. Back in the fog I had watched the soundings plummet
from sixty-five to forty-seven fathoms, and I knew exactly
where I was. Off Curva dos Dunas. I'd played the Benguela
current off all night against a small local stream, narrow but
powerful, which forces its way from the mouth of the Cunene
River through the wild welter of broken, discoloured death
traps southwards to the Clan Alpine shoal. The great Benguela
current is cold, majestic; it has made its way past a thousand
obstacles from South Georgia and Tristan; it is broad, life-
giving with its countless myriads of living plankton for the
fish; the narrow but powerful down-coast current from the
Cunene, which I called the " Trout," bounces and races south
and south-west at fully five knots and scrapes along the landward edge of the kingly Benguela, but it is wicked, diabol-
onian, fickle, and turns the entrance to Curva dos Dunas into a
sailor's idea of hell. When I took *Trout* in against NP I
I hadn't known it existed, but all the time since I had patiently
spent charting its vagaries in *Etosha* made me sweat at the
thought of my ignorance at that time. I'd brought *Etosha* to
Curva dos Dunas with the Benguela under her stern and the
Trout under her bow, and I was not a little pleased when the
65-47 soundings came up, familiar as Table Mountain.

And now this madman Stein threatened to spoil it all as he
saw the savage breakers hammering at the sand-bars of Curva
dos Dunas. Admittedly, it was a staggering sight under the
lash of a wild south-westerly blow. The run of the sea, thundering against the fang-white sand-bars, threw up acres of
water, smashed to white, high into the air; the Trout current,
tearing down past the entrance, provided a more flexible, if
not less formidable barrier, and the sea also broke wildly out of
reach of the sand itself, well out to the fifty fathom line.

Etosha lay bucking at this stupendous vista while my eyes
sought, automatically, my lifelines—seawards, Simon's Rock to
the south, and on land the three-topped hill a little to the south-
east, and the mountain in the north. With those three, and

daylight, and my soundings dead on, I'd take her in just as I had taken *Trout* in that unforgettable night.

Stein's mouth was wet and whether he stammered slightly from fear or the blow as he crouched, I could not have cared less.

"Captain Peace, I forbid it! Do you hear, I forbid it!" His voice rose. "You want to kill me, I know. But I won't let you."

"Pull yourself together," I snarled. My attention was only half on him. The three-topped hill was beginning to bear— one hundred, and *Etosha's* head was easing, one hundred and three. One hundred and five degrees! She was dead right for the entrance, with the great northern pile steady on seventy degrees.

"Hold her like that," I rapped out to John.

"Soundings?"

"Thirty, twenty-seven, twenty-three. . . ."

"We're bang on," I exclaimed, and the magic of it came upon me. Perhaps that is the deadly fascination for the Peace sailormen of Curva dos Dunas. The one degree error that spells death, the foreknowledge of what cold, low-density water will do against warm, high-density currents, in juxtaposition with wind, sea and tide. Not a problem in navigation, but a primitive problem of survival. A deadly throw of the dice, man against the sea.

"Take a look," I said harshly to Stein, who had got to his feet. "That's what you wanted, wasn't it—to go ashore in safety? I'm taking you ashore. . . ." I grinned at his patent fear—"through that lot. A moment ago I could have stopped, but it's too late now."

Stein said quickly : "I never expected . . ."

"Of course you didn't," I retorted without sympathy. "But if you have to hang over the side retching your guts out, I'm taking you inside."

Through Stein's fear came a flicker of reluctant admiration. He made a ghastly attempt at a smile.

"They all say you are the best skipper on the coast Captain Peace," he replied. "Now I think so too."

I rang "slow ahead."

"Watch those bearings," I said to John, who was back at the wheel. "You miserable bastard," I said to Stein. "I'm risking my ship and all our lives for you, but I'm going to show you what keeping a bargain means. I hope you like it."

I couldn't see the line of the channel as such, the confusion of water was too great. There was no quiet water anywhere. Old Simon must have been a genius as a sailor.

"Steer one-oh-oh," I said tersely to John. The dun coast lay deadly quiet, poised like a giant Anglosaurus lizard about to strike.

Etosha went in. I could hear Stein's breath rasping faintly. Anne came over to the pelorus and when her hand rested on its stand, I could see the fingers trembling. I adjusted the line of my bearing.

"One-oh-five," I said to John. John stood there, his face like granite, withdrawn, remote. I was taking her in towards the first great swing in the channel, which then doubled back almost on its own tracks. The bearings from the night of NP I's doom were indelible on my mind. Spray began to blow across the bridge in fine clouds from the breaking water. *Etosha* crept on.

Suddenly Anne gave a cry. "Look, a ship!"

Every eye flashed to the spot where she pointed. The old bluff bows of the *Phylira* looked as ugly in death as I had seen them that first day when Georgiadou had taken me down to the Table Bay docks where she lay in an out-of-the-way corner. I was surprised to find myself quite impersonal. That wild night seemed to have no connection with myself, somehow.

Stein was beside me, his face intense.

"Georgiadou would be very interested," he sneered. "A fine piece of wrecking, if I may say so, Captain. And a colossal nerve it must have taken to do it there too."

"You may say so, but I don't know what you're talking about," I rejoined. Circumstantially, there was only one answer —they would say I had wrecked *Phylira* and sent the crew to their deaths in the creaming holocaust. So Stein thought, anyway.

"Come, come, Captain Peace, that's the ship you put ashore. You can't bluff me."

I stared him out of countenance.

"Do you see her name, or any identification?" I asked. "What makes you think I know anything about that wreck? I don't. Georgiadou wouldn't thank you for that kind of information. She's probably been there for years."

There was almost admiration in Stein's tone when he replied.

"It is clever, Captain, too clever. As you say, Georgiadou wouldn't thank me for it. I couldn't even say where this wreck was, and if I could, how would one ever get close enough to look—unless Captain Peace showed them how? How did you get out alive, Captain, from——" he waved at the breakers—"that?"

Anne looked at me tight-lipped. "I don't believe it," she said slowly. "No one could ever come out alive."

If racing drivers have their brains in the seats of their pants, then I think some of mine must be in the soles of my feet. Some slight movement, something out of accord, warned me. Concentrating on the grave of the *Phylira*, I'd missed a trick. The bearing had passed.

"Quick," I rapped out to John. "Steer three-one-five." Simultaneously I rang "Full ahead." *Etosha* juddered. Sand? I wasn't sure, but the screws and full wheel would bring her round, if anything would.

John never raised his eyes, but his face was set. He spun the spokes. *Etosha* bucked. Looking at the creaming surf through salt-stung eyes, it was impossible to judge whether or not we were against the far side of the channel or not. I thanked God that we were afloat—just. One slight lapse, and the Skeleton Coast would trump your ace.

I glanced at the bearings of the two hills ashore and then swung right round to Simon's Rock. Not so bad. I breathed easier.

"Three-two-oh," I said, tension making my voice grate.

I waited for the tell-tale bump which would spell the end, just as I had waited for it in *Trout*. Two minutes—three minutes—four. *Etosha* was clear in the channel again!

She was running back, slowly now, almost parallel to the way she had come, her stern now pointing at the coast. Out to sea, the perpetual morning fog hung like a shroud. She had

T.O.S.   G about fifteen minutes' steaming to the next, wide, shallow turn to the north.

I straightened up. John met my eye; he looked the way he had done when I thought he had turned against me at the court martial.

"Five minutes' clear?" he asked in his best quarter-deck voice.

I nodded.

"Those bearings and the course, they are exactly the same, aren't they?"

I nodded again. I didn't look at him.

"You took *Trout* in through this after—something?"

"Yes," I replied, inaudible almost to myself.

"Geoffrey," he went on remorselessly, and his tone drew Anne into the circle too. "All these years I wondered—did you sink her? Or," and his eyes looked at mine and I saw pain and doubt which I had never suspected, "was it something in the mind that sank you—for always—that night?"

I turned slowly round until I faced east-nor'-east. Straining through the blowing spray, I thought I caught a glimpse, a momentary glimpse, of the object.

"What is it?" Anne burst out. "What is it?"

Doubt was written all over John's face. I could see it all in his attitude: "I've opened up the old wound, and now he's round the bend again—poor bastard."

I came back and gripped one of the spokes of the wheel. My voice was unsteady.

"I sank her," I said simply. "The wreck bears about one-two-oh degrees at this moment."

John was too good a sailor to take his eyes off the course.

"I'll see her again when we get inside this lot?"

"Yes," I replied. "You'll see her all right. On the far side of the anchorage."

John's glance didn't waver. "Was it as important as all that—important enough that you kept your mouth shut? Who were you shielding?"

Stein joined us. He was lapping up the drama avidly.

"See here," I said to the three of them. "It's history now, and I want the record straight. It's history now, and that's why I can tell you. An atomic submarine is nothing new to-day.

But in the early war years it was God's answer to the U-boat Command. All it had to do was to prove itself. Blohm and Voss made one. She sank the *Dunedin Star* with torpedoes from which the warheads were drawn. She came back here. I went in after her. I sank her."

Stein goggled : " You mean we—Germany—had an atomic submarine and it was never used in the Atlantic?"

I rounded on him. " Yes," I said. " The U-boat Command were dubious because they thought it too much of a break with the old, engine-driven U-boat. So they sent it out on a trial raiding cruise. They thought it would blow up. Two men in England besides myself knew about it. My orders were to destroy the new U-boat. I did. She's lying—or what's left of her—a couple of miles away inside this channel."

Stein looked unbelievingly at me. Then he said slowly : " So it was Lieutenant-Commander Peace, D.S.O. and two Bars, that did more than any other single man in the war to win the Battle of the Atlantic! Why, we would have torn England's throat out with atomic submarines! And you sank her! God's truth, how?"

John butted in. " Yes, how? *Trout* never fired a torpedo."

I laughed in their faces. " I sank her with a recognition flare."

John thought I had gone off my head.

" A recognition flare?"

" She was fuelling and the burning flare fell in the fuel. She went up like a Roman candle."

Stein looked at me, still in disbelief.

" No survivors?"

I looked at him squarely ; the nightmare of the men on the sand-bar came back to me.

" I shot down the survivors with a machine-gun."

" No, Captain Peace," said a voice, ragged with menace from the head of the bridge companionway, " you didn't. One got away."

The three of us, even John, swung round electrified. Johann stood at the back of the bridge. He carried a heavy wooden bar, called a kierie, we used to kill the snoek. Gone was the vagueness, the hesitancy of the man whose dazed mind fumbles. Curva dos Dunas had jerked him back to reality. The eyes had lost their blurred perception and were blazing now —with the lust to kill. There was no doubt that Johann had come up on to the bridge to kill. It was his deadly quiet which frightened me.

"You fired the gun in our faces," he said slowly. "I can see you now as you swung the barrel round, Captain. And now I am going to kill you. But there won't be any doubts about this kill. For three days I lay on the sand. It was all sand, all sand and salt. The bullets got me here"—he pulled up a sleeve, never taking his eyes off me in case I jumped him—and showed me the underside of his left arm where almost all the flesh was missing. It was a hideous wound.

"I prayed to die, Captain, out there on the sand. I prayed that you would die slowly, like me. I went back to the U-boat —you'll see her just now, because I know this part of the world better than you. I should do. It is a trap. You die slowly here. I walked every inch of sand looking for a way out. There was not one."

I couldn't credit that he had missed the sand causeway to the beach. Perhaps the pain and mental shock of being all alone in this wind-driven hell had deadened his faculties.

"I went aboard the U-boat when she had cooled down." He laughed and the high note revealed the mind on the verge of being unhinged again. "They were all cooked, Captain. All my friends were cooked. But it was easier to eat my friends cooked than raw, wasn't it?" He gave a high giggle and Anne shrank back at the sound.

"And now, after all that cooked meat, I must have some raw, not so?" He came forward with the kierie. I could see he had the strength of a maniac. Out of the corner of my eye I saw Stein glance anxiously over the side.

"This is a fascinating story," he said and the mouth was as cruel as a sting-ray with its victim under its eyes. "We have now added war crimes to Captain Peace's long—and often nefarious—record."

I saw the sudden tautening of Johann's muscles. It telegraphed the warning, but there was little I could do about it. With lightning speed the kierie flickered upwards, but Stein struck first with the deadly venom of a cobra. Even in that moment of mortal peril it made me wonder where he had learned his trade. The Luger hit Johann high above the ear, just where the hair leaves the scalp. He stood swaying in front of me, the eyes unconscious. He slumped at my feet.

"Don't waste your time on him, Captain, or on thanking me," whipped out Stein. "We'll be ashore in a moment. Get your bearings, or whatever you do, in God's name!"

I swung the pelorus with hands that trembled. I gave John a new course. We were almost opposite Galleon Point. I could see the spar out to port where *Trout* had gone aground. I nodded towards it.

"That," I said to John, "is where we damaged the hydroplanes."

He didn't reply. I could see that the deadly swiftness of Johann's attack had shaken him. His helmsmanship remained masterly.

Stein kicked the still figure without compassion.

"All this makes him a better bodyguard than ever, doesn't it," he grinned evilly. "With a score like that to settle, particularly."

He bent down and examined the unconscious man's head. "He'll be out for another hour at least," he said. "Will that get us safe into the anchorage? If it won't, I'll make sure that he doesn't wake up for another couple." He took the kierie and looked questioningly at Johann. The cold precision of it revolted me.

"It'll be enough," I said.

"In this channel you're far more valuable—for my life in particular—than this," he said kicking the still form again without compunction. "But there may well be occasions when the position is reversed."

The high hill to the north, clearly visible, and the three-topped one to the south, peered down at the ship making her way in. The dun beech and the dunes, tonsured by clinging, wind-torn shrub, were half opaque through the driving salt. There was still enough glare, however, to make the eyes wince. I gave John the course. As *Etosha* came abreast Galleon Point I could see the tall spar rising from the sand. A sailing ship's mast? A landmark? A beacon? Even at a couple of hundred yards it was impossible to know. One never would know. In silence, John, Anne, Stein and I watched the scene. *Etosha* swept round the last great whorl of the channel and again turned parallel to the way she had come in, facing due west now. The hammering of the sea eased. The wind continued to lash out blindly.

Etosha was safe inside Curva dos Dunas.

" Course two-seven-oh," I said.

She headed across the anchorage. Through the opaque light I saw what I had been looking for. NP I. The high, fin-like conning-tower was black with rust, the ethereal quality of it as I had seen her that night now gone, like the colour which dies when a lovely deep-sea creature is brought to the surface. The fin was slightly canted, but the merciful salt and whiteness still blanketed the wounds which sank her. I included John and Stein in my nod towards her.

" There's the atomic U-boat."

Stein went forward and I could see how white his knuckles were as he gripped the top of the dodger.

" The ultimate weapon," he murmured almost to himself. " And a British captain with an ordinary submarine sank her with a recognition flare!" He turned to me and his voice rasped with bitterness. " Congratulations, Captain Peace! It is so like the British to reward their heroes with the boot."

John relaxed at the wheel. He grinned a little.

" I'll never forgive you, Geoffrey, for not letting me in on this," he said. " Now you can be reinstated."

" Rubbish!" I said sharply. " There's no question of reinstatement now. That's all in the past."

Anne surprised me by agreeing with John.

" If you're innocent, then the court martial can reverse its findings." She turned to John. " It's up to you to tell them."

John nodded.

I rang for slow ahead. I'd anchor near NP I and then send the party ashore in the boat.

" Now see here," I said. " This particular place happens to belong to me. In that sense it's private. And NP I is part of its private history. You, John, can go and tell your story to the Admiralty—if you like. They'll want some proof. And where will you get it? Do you think the Admiralty is going to believe a sentimental, unlikely little story about a hidden anchorage from a friend who feels sorry that his former chief

was kicked out of the Service years ago? They'll want proof."
I turned to Anne. "John's a sailor. He couldn't find this
place, let alone bring in a ship. There's only one man living
who can do that, and that is me. The only other man to do it
was the skipper of the U-boat, and he's roasted. I expect
Johann ate him into the bargain."

The anchor clattered over the side. Eight fathoms and a
bottom of hard sand. Good holding ground.

Anne said, a trifle judicially, "I seem to remember an
American lieutenant in that famous old-time battle off Boston
—what was it? . . ."

"Shannon? Chesapeake?" said John.

"Yes," said Anne. "That's it—Chesapeake. They reinstated him donkeys' years later. . . ."

I smiled grimly when I thought of the Director of Naval
Intelligence. One played that game by their rules—until death
do us part.

She might have been arguing for the man, not the cause.

Stein, however, aligned himself with me.

"Captain Peace has too much of a past to let him feel comfortable," he said amiably. "The present is what matters.
The Afrikaaners have an expression—'Don't haul dead cows
out of the ditch.' With Captain Peace in particular they are apt
to stink."

Anne turned to John.

"You could send a radio message. There's nothing to stop
you."

"Except," I said acidly, "a squadron of American ships
which is cruising around here somewhere recovering guided
missiles fired from Cape Canaveral. They've got aircraft with
them, too. Go ahead. Broadcast to the world our illegal
mission. They've got the latest radar and radio-interception
devices in the world. Even so, they won't find *Etosha*. Not in
this anchorage, anyway."

Stein glanced at me in veiled admiration.

"This Captain Peace would be a great poker-player—always
a new ace up his sleeve."

"See the sand blowing across from the sand-bars there?" I
said. It billowed like a windsock of snow from the summit of
Mount Everest. "That sand is laden with mica and chemical

salts. You remember a thing the U-boats used in the war—
Bold, they called it? They used to release a film of chemical
components which hung like a curtain in the water and foxed
our asdics. The same thing happens with the sand. Radar
will simply not penetrate inside here." I turned to Anne
with more vehemence than I really meant. "Go ahead. Get
John to signal your American friends. And explain all this
away too."

A flush came up on her cheeks, already bright with the
wind.

"Computation—you remember?" was all she said.

"Are you ready to go ashore?" I asked Stein.

"In half an hour," he said. "I've got the stores all
packed."

"You'll have to put up with the surf-boat," I said. "The
others got smashed . . . er—at sea in a blow. I'll send the Kroo
boy, he's the best surfman amongst the crew."

Stein's mouth hardened.

"You're going to send us ashore at the mercy of a single
kaffir? What does he know about this anchorage?"

I almost felt sorry for Stein then. It was like dropping an
unwanted puppy in a bucket of water with a brick round its
neck. But he knew too much. The girl—well, I had a plan for
her.

"Of course I'm coming," I said. "How far do you think
you'd get without me?"

Stein relaxed. I refused to look at Anne.

"Get the boat alongside," I told John. "Detail the Kroo
boy to come with me. Get some of the others to load the stuff
into the boat. Smack it about."

Stein had certainly helped himself liberally to *Etosha's*
stores. With typical thoroughness he had labelled everything.
Jim, the Kroo boy, stood in the tossing surf-boat with its high
prow, and the crew passed down things to him. Stein had even
roped up some canvas—for a tent presumably. He came up
with a Remington high velocity in one hand and the Luger in
the other. He was like a child off on a picnic.

"Arms for the man," he grinned. He'd also stuck a Bowie
knife in his belt. "This will stop almost anything," he patted
the Remington affectionately. "For personal protection, there's

nothing at all to touch the old Luger. Perfect balance in the hand."

Anne had changed into a thicker red sweater and a duffle-coat. She was very silent.

Stein knelt down and listened to Johann's breathing.

"Tie his hands and throw him in the boat," he said callously. "He may come round on the way to the beach. He may cause trouble if he finds you in the boat also."

Johann was heaved like a sack of potatoes into the boat. The native crew looked on goggle-eyed. The surf-boat looked very deep in the water, but I thought she would be all right.

I jumped in. Anne stood at the open rail and looked down into my face.

"Come on," I called. "Jump. I'll catch you."

It may have been the blowing salt, but her eyes were wet. The right eyelid was slightly rumpled. She gave a ghost of a smile and leapt lightly down, scarcely making use of my proffered hands.

Stein came last. I noticed the bulge of ammunition in his pockets. Well, he'd need it, every round of it, to get him out alive. You can't shoot the Skeleton Coast.

"Cast off," I said.

"Back in two hours," I called to John.

The Kroo boy cast off expertly. If he was something of a duffer at *Etosha's* wheel, he certainly was in his element now. He guided the heavily-laden boat expertly as I headed her towards the channel. Our course lay roughly across the causeway, now submerged, to the beach, which meant the boat would have the protection of the sand-bars for the tricky run in through the surf. Since they guarded the beach against the south-westerly swell, it shouldn't be too risky. A dollop of water came aboard and Anne gave a slight gasp. Curva dos Dunas certainly looked more terrifying from the low level of a boat than from a ship's bridge. The surf creamed on every side, but with the boat's compass I took a quick bearing and then headed her almost directly towards the high hill to the north. Once inside the channel it became smoother and the water turned white with a pale blue backing—like the colour of a Lazy Grey shark. Satisfied that I was now over the causeway proper, I turned the boat directly shoreward.

" How's your surf-riding?" I asked Anne banteringly.

" Not so good," she replied, putting on a brave show, but I could plainly see she was terrified of the line of creaming surf ahead.

" This Kroo boy is as good as they come," I said. " He'll take her in like a ski-boat."

" It would solve a good many problems if we all got drowned," she said sombrely. She shivered inside the dufflecoat, now glistening with a faint film of white salt.

Stein was silent. Johann had given a stir, but his eyes remained shut. The Kroo boy, wearing only an ancient pair of Jantzen trunks, had unshipped the tiller and was steering with an oar. He was grinning with animation. It was a challenge to his skill. The ragged fringe of beard—all southern African natives are vastly proud of even a few wisps of a beard for it is a sign of virility—whipped back across his left cheek.

" I put her ashore—any pertikler place, baas?" he shouted. The boat bucked with the first of the inshore breakers.

" Anywhere you think best," I called back. " Anywhere on that beach."

" Good-oh," he yelled, remembering some sailor's expression.

Now that the beach was closer, I could see that it was not fine sand, but coarse, broken here and there by rocks fretted and polished by the wind.

The Kroo boy yawed slightly. I had not noticed the big comber building up about twenty yards to starboard. But he had, and in a moment we were carried majestically, high above the surrounding sea. Then the nose of the boat tilted downwards and, with the water vainly clutching at both gunwales, rushed at something like twenty knots for the beach. Anne sank down by one of the seats and closed her eyes, clutching at the wood.

" Steady as she goes," I ordered, quite unnecessarily, to the Kroo boy. The sea had given him life. The underfed figure was proud and tensed under the whip of the wind and waves. The black face, usually sullen and unwilling, had become alive.

The great breaker streamed in towards the beach. If we touched anything, let alone the iron-hard beach, it would tear the planking out like matchwood. Even a strong swimmer wouldn't last five minutes in the mælstrom. But the oarsman knew his job. Suddenly the boat lurched sickeningly to port, into a welter of foam. Another great wave ahead of ours had crashed on the beach and was hurtling itself back seawards. The spindrift, thick as foam, enveloped the boat, and I had to peer to see above it. The boat's motion was stayed like a turbo-prop engine in reverse. She touched once, touched twice. In a second the oarsman was over the side, up to his waist and hauled her in towards the beach. I jumped out after him, haul-ing on the other bow at a short painter. The sea slopped inside my half-boots. Without looking back—we both knew the menace of that twenty knot wave even a biscuit-toss from the shore—we hauled the boat up on the tough shingle.

" Out ! " I yelled to Anne and Stein. Their feet crunched on the beach. We hauled the boat still higher. The Kroo boy and I were panting, and my peaked cap was floating in an inch of bilge-water.

" My God ! " said Stein.

" How'll you ever get back?" shuddered Anne, her face pale.

" It's like Sputnik," I grinned back. " It's much easier going than coming."

There was a nervous air about Stein.

" Get Johann out and lay him here on the beach. Untie his hands," he said rapidly.

I stared at him in surprise. After his earlier attitude, it wouldn't have surprised me if he'd thrown him overboard. Now he was fussing like a hen over a chick.

The Kroo boy obediently hauled him out and laid him on the sand.

The touch of the gritty shingle electrified the unconscious man.

Without opening his eyes, his hands, as if of their own volition, reached out, fingering the shingle. Then the hand moved slowly up the side of the face, as if exploring the beach against his cheek. He gave a terrible scream and sat upright. Thank God his hands are still tied, I thought.

Stein jabbed him with the Remington, while the Kroo boy, aghast at the wide eyes and screaming mouth, like a gutted barracouta, cringed against the boat. I was glad to find Anne close to me.

"Shut up, you bloody fool," he shouted. "*Besatzung Stillgestanden! Attention!*"

Johann rose, U-boat discipline still automatic in his make-up, but he whimpered and gathered up another handful of sand. Sand had made him mad. It wasn't any wonder, looking along that desolate beach with the granules of hard sand chafing like sandpaper. It never seemed to blow away. There was always more.

Stein cut the ropes and gestured with the rifle to the boat.

"Unload," he said harshly.

Blindly, as if only his motor impulses and not his mind were working, Johann stumbled across to the boat. Without waiting, the Kroo boy started to pass the stores to him and together they piled them up a little way up the beach, out of reach of the sea.

Stein, obviously tense, made a movement of his hand towards Johann.

"A living Nemesis of your misdeeds, Captain Peace," he sneered. "You should have made a good job with the machine-gun. See what the touch of the sand does to him."

I saw the fret of the wind and the sand and could sense the utter desolation the mad sailor must have felt when, somehow or other, he had got ashore—alone, utterly alone, with my ghastly machine-gun wound in his arm. The blowing sand made for a grey light, even with the sun shining and the white reflection off the surf; the sand had a quality of stinging which, after some time, would be like the drip of water in Chinese torture.

The muscles tugged at the corners of my mouth and eyes. I sensed, too, what Anne was feeling.

"Poor devil," she said softly.

We watched the two men unload the stores and heavy tarpaulin. They had to drag it up the shingle by the ropes. The pile of wrapped pieces looked utterly forlorn and pathetic. In a few moments the drag-marks had been obliterated by the blowing sand. Everything seemed too inadequate against the mighty forces which were apparent on every hand. Johann came over to join us while the Kroo boy went to fetch one last thing out of the boat. I think it was my cap. He was about fifteen yards away. He was bending over, the underfed hip-bones projecting from the ragged trunks.

Stein walked quickly over towards him. The boy's back was towards us. He couldn't have heard Stein coming.

Nor did Stein hear Anne's scream as she started towards him. Some sixth sense must have told her what he was about.

As it was, it was so unexpected that it hit me like a blow in the stomach.

Stein pulled out the Luger and shot the Kroo boy through the back of the head.

The wind carried the sound of the shot away, adding to the ghastly unreality of it all. It was like something happening in slow motion, miles away. Anne, sobbing, with arms out-stretched, reached for the weapon. I saw Stein turn, in the same ghastly slow motion, death for her in his eyes too. He hadn't heard her until that moment. The black figure pitched forward slowly and lay raggedly half in and half out the boat.

One life more or less didn't matter at that moment to Stein. I think the madness which I saw in his eyes had obliterated all comprehension who it was reaching for his Luger.

Thank God my cap had fallen off in the boat. I was able to tear the heavy binoculars in their leather case from round my neck without obstruction and, using the strap as a sling, cast it at Stein.

The soft, harmless thump in his ribs jerked the kill-lust from his eyes. A split second before Anne was a dead woman. As she clawed at him for the gun I saw the mighty control he exercised over himself. He turned the barrel away almost as if he feared his own reflexes would beat his mind to the draw. At the same moment I saw his left forearm with its heavy watch crash into Anne's cheekbone. She fell sideways on to the shingle in an untidy heap.

I leapt forward.

Stein swivelled the Luger at my stomach. "Back!" he shouted hoarsely, "Get back! Johann!" He threw the Rem-

ington by the barrel away to his left. " Get that rifle, Johann!
Kill him if he makes a move!"

The mad sailor's face creased in a grin. He grabbed the rifle
and flicked the bolt expertly.

" Now, Herr Kapitän?" he grinned.

" No, soon," said Stein soothingly, as if talking to a patient.
" Soon, see?"

" You murdering bastard!" I rapped out, " I'll . . ."

Stein had regained all his composure in a few brief seconds.

" On the contrary, Captain Peace, I have you to thank for not
committing me to that reprehensible category. If you hadn't
thrown that case, I might have forgotten myself—just for the
moment. The consequences to myself, but more particularly to
this expedition, would have been immeasurable. Without our
scientist, all our best efforts would have been put to naught,
not so?"

It seemed hardly possible that this bland, self-controlled
man had just killed in cold blood.

" I'll get you back to Walvis to hang for this," I snarled.

I knelt down by the crumpled form on the beach. There was
an ugly mark on her cheek. She moaned slightly. She
wasn't badly hurt. She'd be round in a moment.

" Very touching," sneered Stein. " Sir Galahads have always
got me down, even from the original prototype. But get this
quite clear, Captain Geoffrey Peace. You've just saved this
expedition in a way which you couldn't have foreseen. You
wouldn't have got off this beach alive to-day but for your
quixotic gesture. You are not going back to Walvis. You're
coming with me."

" Like hell I am," I retorted.

I didn't like the look of the Luger, or the Remington. The
girl moaned quietly. She was still stunned.

" You don't think," he sneered, " that I was going to allow
you to go back to your ship merely on the promise that you
would come back again, did you? Give me credit for a little
assessment of your character, Captain Peace. You're a functional aid to this expedition, no more. Just like that silly
woman there. She's a dedicated woman, Captain Peace, but I
must say this little effort of hers took me unawares. She has her
uses, just like you. Again I must thank you for what you did

—it would have been too bad to have ended her functional usefulness prematurely." He half-bowed mockingly. "If I had allowed you back on board, all you had to do was to forget about Stein and his party, and the Skeleton Coast would do the rest. You don't think I—to quote a military phrase—would allow you to keep your lines of communication open while cutting mine?"

So Stein had anticipated my moves. All my neat plans for getting Anne back to *Etosha* and leaving Stein and Johann to their fate, a horrid fate, had been trumped.

He must have seen the look on my face, for he burst out laughing.

"You made me shoot that kaffir," he said, without pity. "You can't get the surf-boat back by yourself. It's the only boat in *Etosha* anyway. Garland has simply no option but to wait for our return. He couldn't navigate the channel out to sea. So you'll come along, whether you like it or not. I'll watch you every moment, so don't try any tricks. You'll guide the party to the Baynes Mountains."

"Without instruments or a compass?" I asked.

"The boat's compass is good enough, and you're an expert," he replied. "I don't want positions of exact latitude and longitude. You'll navigate—where I want to go. Johann will be your personal bodyguard. His finger's just itching on that trigger."

Anne lay quite still.

"And—the girl?"

My gesture must have had more in it than I thought.

"Ah, the girl," he said. "Scientist to spitfire in a flash! Chivalrous Captain Peace! She is, as you might say, a hostage to science. She is the only living person who can positively identify Onymacris, and as such she is absolutely indispensable. She comes along—unharmed. You are the only person who can get in and out of the Skeleton Coast without anyone else knowing. Johann is a hostage, a hostage to your past, Captain. He certainly won't let you forget that!"

Anne opened her eyes.

"Thank you," she whispered.

"Get some water," I said briefly to Johann. He paused, but Stein waved him on.

"Not the water-bottle," he added. "Just enough in a mug."

I played for time.

"You can't expect me to hike a hundred or two miles inland in this rig," I said.

"Why not?" he retorted, his eyes wary for some trap. Anne drank a little of the water from the mug. She sat up. I faced Stein. If only I could get him to remain near the beach until nightfall, when the tide would roll back the secret of the causeway, he'd get the surprise of his life. Anne and I were both merely expendable ciphers in his master-plan, whatever that was.

"You've got on a perfectly good pair of boots. Your clothes will do, even if the occasion isn't as nautical as they would seem to indicate."

I cast round: "I can't go far without a hat of some sort. Within twenty miles I'll have sunstroke."

Stein laughed. "Keep him well guarded," he said to Johann. "Shoot him if there's any monkey business—him or the woman." He'd put her firmly on my side now.

He walked over to the boat and came back with my cap. He was about to hand it to me when he paused. There was a ghastly stain across the white.

"How these kaffirs bleed," he remarked indifferently. He bent down and waggled it to and fro in the surf. Then he tossed it at my feet.

"Wear that," he said. "We'll start right away."

I glanced at my watch. It was nearly midday.

"Aren't you going to arouse suspicion aboard *Etosha* if all of us are seen trekking away from the beach? Garland will be watching through his glasses."

Stein wheeled round. "I'm giving the orders from now on, Captain. We start at once. You know where this beach lies, and you know my route. You'll give Posto Velho, near the mouth of the river, a wide berth." He didn't know it was the best part of twenty miles away. "You'll aim to strike the main river flow away from the mouth somewhere near the first cataract. No nonsense."

I looked round despairingly at the desolate beach, with the grey gloom over it all. Through the murk to the north I could

see the hilly plateau which runs westward from the high
northern hill which was one of my landmarks. Macfadden and
I had tried that way after the wreck of the *Phylira.* We returned exhausted after ten miles, for the jagged hills came
right down to the beach and, if one wanted to get by, it was a
question of dodging between the tide as it came in and a
narrow strip of soft sand in which one sank halfway up to the
knees. We had probed the back of the beach like two hounds
tufting up a scent, and after two days we had found a narrow
gap about four miles south and east of the causeway through
which we had floundered. We had almost given up at the
sight of the high shifting dunes on the far, or landward side
of the neck, but our salvation was a path, hard and compacted
by elephants' feet, leading northwards.

Stein still held the Luger and kept his distance. Once
away from the beach, he could let me run away—to certain
death. The only water was in a couple of canteens he had. I
was his prisoner—if he could get me away from the beach.

"The loads are divided into thirty-five pound packs, and
twenty-five pound for the girl," he said briefly. "You first,
Captain."

I glanced at Anne and saw the misery in her eyes. I shrugged
my shoulders and found a series of parcels—but no water—
neatly marked "Captain Peace."

I shouldered it. It felt like lead. The wet cap on my head
added to my general discomfort.

"There's no water," I said.

"Not for you," grinned Stein. "When they take a man
prisoner in war, they take away his pants. Metaphorically
speaking, water is your pants. You won't get far without it."

There was nothing to say.

"We strike south for a couple of miles," I said harshly.
"There's a track on the other side of these hills. And sand.
The track is hard."

"Why not north?" demanded Stein.

"I've tried that way," I smiled grimly. "There's no way
through."

"I'll keep the compass until we get on to our main line of
direction," said Stein. "Get the boat's compass," he told
Johann.

"We go south and then almost due east through a gap in the hills," I said again. "You'll just have to take that on trust."

Stein looked wary.

"I trust you only when you are away from the sea," he said. "The sea is your ally, somehow. I don't feel safe when you and the sea are near. You've won together too many times, Captain Peace. So we'll get away from the sea as soon as possible."

Anne and I fell in together with the other two behind. Our feet crunched on the gravelly shingle. The boat, well above the tidemark, left a trail in the sand culminating in the forlorn figure of the Kroo boy. The strange nocturnal prowlers of the Skeleton Coast would leave nothing but his bones by morning. The day after, his bones, too, would be gone. *Etosha* was screened from view out in the anchorage.

I took a line on the three-topped hill. We struck into the Kaokoveld.

THIRTEEN

500 *Years of Love*

"HALT!" ordered Stein.

The cup of thick white sand, protected from the perpetual south-westerly gale, looked a good spot for the night. It seemed like a gigantic child's sandpit about a quarter of a mile each way, nestling against the westerly side of the peak which I had used as my northerly bearing to bring *Trout* and *Etosha* into Curva dos Dunas. The trails of naras creeper would provide some sort of fuel for a fire. The hard-packed game track we had followed all day branched off to the right, skirting the cup, but I felt sure that the soft sand must have been used by the elephants as a giant dry-cleaning shop. There had been no sign of a living animal all day, but that didn't mean to say they weren't around. Passing a low group of shrub some miles back, our noses had been assailed by a tangy game smell, and the elephant droppings along the track did not appear to be more than a day old.

Stein and Johann had marched behind us all day. Stein still kept the Luger ready, but every mile we drew away from the beach, he relaxed. He still kept his distance, however.

I slid the heavy pack from my shoulders and dropped it on to the sand, flexing my stiff shoulder muscles. Anne sat down with a sigh, releasing her pack too.

" A good day's run, as they say at sea," grinned Stein. He must have been in training, for although his face was streaked with sweat, he looked pretty fresh. Far too fresh to try any consequences with. " How far do you think we've come?"

" About fifteen—maybe eighteen, miles," I replied wearily.

" Good," he said.

He took the map from his pack and studied it.

" You're sure we're not near Okatusu?" There was a note of deep suspicion in his voice, for what he didn't know was the point we had started from.

" It's only a geographical expression, anyway," I replied, feeling utterly weary and frustrated.

" We must be somewhere between Okatusu and Otjemem-bonde," he said.

I sidestepped his little trap.

" I'll tell you when we hit the Cunene," I said off-handedly. " Now go to hell."

He hesitated a moment and then shrugged his shoulders. He knew he was wasting his time. He strolled off to collect some naras bush for a fire. I noticed that he had tucked the Luger away in his waistband.

I sat in the comfortable sand. I couldn't say where my thoughts were. Anne jerked them back to the moment.

" Geoffrey," she said, " can you manage another couple of steps?"

The use of my Christian name made me roll on to my elbow and gaze at her in astonishment.

She looked at me levelly.

" From that hill we might see the sea."

" It's not far away," I agreed cautiously. " A few miles as the crow flies, maybe."

" Shall we have a look-see?" she persisted. " One never knows."

I nodded and rose stiffly. I called to Stein, for I didn't want a bullet following us. " We're going to have a look at that hill over there."

He grinned and waved his hand in a wide gesture. He's damn sure of himself, I thought. I knew myself that we couldn't get far. The only escape road was the way we had come. Even if I made a break for the beach, he'd find me there before the next tide revealed the causeway.

Anne said nothing. We trudged together across the deep sand. Before we reached the western edge we were blowing like two spouter whales. We lit a cigarette each to still the pounding of our hearts and climbed up the gnarled flank of the hill. We reached the top. There, about five or six miles away, was the sea. There seemed to be a bank of cloud far out.

I waited. She fenced for her opening.

" So near and yet so far," she said, twisting down the corners of her mouth.

" Very far indeed," I said. She'd come to say something. She'd kept up magnificently all day, despite Stein's blow. There was a faint mark under her cheekbone. Let her make the opening herself. I pointed to the jagged fret on the seaward side of the hill. " Those projections are like razors. All summer the south-westerly gale eats away at the solid rock, and then in winter the easterly wind comes scouring down from this side. It's quite remarkable, really—it's not a high altitude wind. It sticks close to the desert, picking up the warmth of the sand as it goes. I've felt the grit in my mouth miles out to sea. When it hits the cold sea—fog, nothing but fog. You saw for yourself."

" Geoffrey Peace," she ruminated. " Those two names go well together. Peace is ironical for a man of war and violence, though."

I said nothing. She came up close to me.

" You saved my life this morning," she said, almost accusingly.

I laughed it off. " It was one of those things," I said.

" It was not ' one of those things '," she retorted vehemently. " Take it as read that my life did not matter one way or another. I'm looking at it from your point of view. You had nothing to gain at all by doing it. In fact, if Stein had shot me, it would have given you a moment of diversion in which to

cope with him—and Johann. You wouldn't be here now. You
would have been sitting pretty. You could have made
both of them prisoner. . . ."

I remembered our first encounter.

"No gain but my gain," I said ironically.

"No, Geoffrey," she said. She repeated it as if the sound
pleased her. "No, Geoffrey."

It sounded good to me.

"A person can do many wrong things for right motives, but
eventually they get so caught up in the doing that the rightness
of the objective gets lost sight of," she said. "That's the way it
is with you. The U-boat, the old freighter, your secret landing-
spot—it all fits into the pattern."

"Anne," I said. "You're just trying to excuse me. You're
trying to rationalise away a whole past—and a present—which
doesn't bear looking at under a spotlight. It's not very pretty.
You may be right about motives. But the means I have used
would outweigh the ends."

"If you'd run true to the general picture you're trying to
paint of yourself, you would never have done what you did
down there on the beach," she argued. "I refuse to accept it."

"You're just grateful to me for saving your life," I rejoined.
"The confessional makes allowance for the pendulum swinging too far the other way. That's the way it is now. There
comes an inevitable levelling-out. But it was nice to know."

She shook her head.

"In fact, I'm curiously ungrateful for your having saved my
life. I might be a little resentful about losing it if I had something to care about which would make it worthwhile not losing.
Even Onymacris has its shortcomings, you know. Does that
sound terribly mixed up? But I am curiously grateful for what
that incident has shown me of you."

"I thought you'd seen quite enough," I mocked.

She rounded on me angrily.

"What are you doing wasting yourself—a man like you,
chasing some will-o'-the-wisp you won't confide, and some
resentment from the past you won't concede? What are you
doing here on this isolated coast when, in the great world
outside, things could be so full, so complete. . . ." Her voice
trailed off and she threw the cigarette butt away savagely.

"I've adapted myself—like the blind beetle."

"Oh, for God's sake stop quoting the rubbish I said then!" she snapped. "I still believe you are tough, but you're not evil, like Stein. I believe *in* you, that's what I'm trying to say. . . ." She broke off suddenly and smiled. I saw that the rumple of her eyelid was quite smooth. She came right up close to me and looked up into my face. "You wanted analogies from the great world of nature," she smiled. "I suppose one of those wing-less flies down on Marion or Heard would find it damned hard to understand if someone put their wings back again."

She slipped her arms through mine and ran her finger-tips up my shoulder-blades. "I wonder how one sticks wings back on to flies full of prickles?" she asked.

Her lips brushed mine; as they did so she stiffened as her eyes went seawards.

"Look!" she gasped. "Either I'm drunk, or seeing double —do you see what I see, Geoffrey?"

She slipped out of my arms and pointed at the setting sun. There were two. There was a thick layer of cloud, although there was a very narrow band of clear sky between it and the sea's horizon. As we watched in amazement, one sun dropped slowly from the layer of cloud, while the other sun rose out of the west towards it. Like lovers who cannot wait for each other's arms, the two suns, the male sun reaching down and the female reaching up ecstatically, melted together, merging along their lower rims first, and, in passionate embrace, merged wholly together. Then only the one, descending, remained, and it hastened towards its sea-grave, throwing out great bars of triumphant reds, russets and purples.

"There's pure magic in this Skeleton Coast of yours, Geoffrey," she said. All the tiredness had gone from her face. "No wonder you love it. But how on earth. . . . ?"

"It must be something to do with the temperature and humidity layers," I replied. "I've never seen anything like that before. I suppose I have seen more magnificent sunsets off this coast than anyone has the right to claim, but never two suns, one rising and the other setting."

"It's the most beautiful thing I have ever seen," she replied, radiant. "I can forgive your Skeleton Coast, Geoffrey, its brutality, its primitive cruelty—like that killing this morning."

She dropped her eyes. " I might even rationalise the whole situation and forgive—you."

I turned and faced her, but the moment was gone.

" Look! " she cried. " It's becoming more beautiful still. Look at the sea, there out beyond the surf! It's the loveliest yellow I've ever seen! Where can that shade of lemon come from a red sun?"

She was on her feet now, smiling like a girl.

I smiled too.

" That isn't light, even refracted light," I said. " That's fish."

" What! " she exclaimed. " I simply don't believe you!"

" Well," I grinned back, forgetting all about Stein and the unholy adventure we were engaged on. " Not exactly fish, but bloom on fish."

" You're just teasing me," she replied. Her face had caught something of the afterglow; I never saw it lovelier.

" If you want science to step in and ruin beauty, well then, here it is," I said. " You know the plankton—the minute things the fish live on—come up with the cold current from the Antarctic. In autumn and in early winter they bloom, just like grapes. It's called gymnodinium, and it's deadly poison. The plankton get that exquisite lemon-flush on them—I think someone told me once that the gymnodinium organism is five thousandths of an inch long. But when you get millions of plankton together. . . ."

" I just don't want to hear any more of your dull scientific stuff," she said smilingly. " All I see is that it is lovely beyond description." She came close up to me so that I could smell the sweet sweat of the day's march, mingling with the acrid tobacco. She ran one hand inside my reefer jacket.

" If I'd never met Geoffrey Peace, I would never have seen such beauty," she said. " You'll remember that, won't you?"

I didn't touch her. She seemed as intangible as the bloom on the plankton.

" Yes," I replied slowly. " I'll remember that. I'll remember that you forgave Curva dos Dunas and the Skeleton Coast. I'll remember, some future day at sea when the plankton bloom, that you forgave me too."

She stepped back and looked long and quizzically at me.

"Food!" she said with a complete change of mood. "I need food if I'm going to tramp all day to-morrow again." Then she stopped impetuously and came back to where I stood, for I had not moved.

"No," she said. "To hell with food. I want to know about this great secret love of Geoffrey's, the Skeleton Coast. Give me another cigarette."

She sat down and blew a burst of blue smoke seawards. She pulled me down by her side.

"Come on," she said. "Wave your magic wand. Make your plankton bloom for me again. Make one sun into two."

I caught her mood.

"It's really all very simple and easy to explain scientifically," I said. "You see, this is the only place in the world where the Antarctic and the Tropics meet."

"If you told me this hill was solid diamond, I'd probably believe you," she replied.

"It might be," I responded. "If the diamond pipes of Alexander Bay continue up here, there's no reason why you should not become a sort of female Dr. Williamson."

"I have no intention of sublimating myself into diamonds," she smiled back. "I always felt sorry for Williamson—every golddigger in the world after his money."

"It's quite a simple explanation, although it sounds a paradox," I said. "You see, the Benguela current comes straight here off the ice. The Skeleton Coast is tropical, with a desert thrown in. One day, when I was close inshore, I saw a lion tackling some seals on the beach north of Cape Cross. Can you imagine—a tropical hunter like a lion living off an Antarctic creature like a seal?"

"Cape Cross," she frowned. "Why Cape Cross?"

"One of the earliest Portuguese navigators—I think it was Diego Cao—made his landfall there, way back before Diaz. He took one look at the Skeleton Coast and said to himself, if this is Africa, I'm on my way home. So he beat it back to Prince Henry the Navigator without going for the Cape."

"Is it the same sort of climatic mix-up which made us see two suns?"

"Yes. If we'd been lucky we might have seen some flamingo

this evening too. You get huge flocks of them at sunset. Just think, a red sun, lemon sea, flamingo sky."

"You sound like something in *Vogue*," she replied. "Think what a seller it would be—Skeleton Coast black, with a flamingo stole."

We laughed and she threw down the butt of the cigarette.

"Now you've really made me feel uncivilised," she exclaimed. "My face must look like one of those jagged rocks there, from the feel of it. Come on now, food. No more lovely fairy tales until to-morrow."

She took my hand as we slithered down to the sand basin; it was hot and sticky and I could feel the tiny grains of sand between her fingers. Where the sweat had soaked through her sweater there was a line against the general dustiness of her breasts, emphasising their curve. The cheekbones were flushed —from the filing of the windblown sand, I thought.

We trudged back to camp.

The grey monotony of the sand changed to white, white so dazzling that when I looked through my binoculars, my eyes crimped up under the magnification. I was leading the four of us next afternoon, Anne behind me, silent, lost in her thoughts, Stein next and Johann bringing up the rear. Occasionally he cursed softly in German at the weight and heat of the Remington. Stein had pocketed the Luger now; I was safe inside the sand prison.

"What is it?" said Stein coming up to me.

I gestured towards the whiteness.

"See that extra whiteness of the sand?" I said, moistening my lips and feeling the grate of the sand on my teeth.

"That's the river."

"Ah!" he exclaimed with deep satisfaction.

"Give me your glasses, Captain."

He took them and gazed for a long time at the whiteness about five miles away, below the level of where we were standing. The unbroken, savage ridge of hills and cliffs on our left as we slogged all day in the burning heat never repented. At the closest we must have been five miles from the sea, and at the farthest eight. We followed the hard track, sweating blindly. Once in the far distance ahead we saw an

elephant—or thought we saw one—but otherwise the remorseless countenance of the Skeleton Coast remained unrelaxed.

" I don't see water," said Stein.

" And you're equally unlikely to," I said. " The Cunene is
dry at this time anyway. It's probably dry all the year. About
once in five years it comes down in full spate and it's twice the
width of the Orange."

" How far inland are we hitting it?" asked Stein.

" About ten miles from the mouth, I reckon," I said.
" There's a cataract a few miles above. I've not seen it, though.
I don't know if we can get by. But for some unknown reason,
the course of the river widens below the cataract—it looks just
like the advertisements you see for colonic irrigation."

Stein ignored the sally.

" Why shouldn't we get past the cataract?" he asked.
" What do you know that you are keeping up your sleeve,
Captain Peace?"

" Oh, for God's sake!" I said. " I've simply never been
there, that's all! I know the river bed is there because I've
walked across it. Every bit of three miles wide, but it's hard
and much easier going than this. All I know is that if it had
been as easy to get into the Skeleton Coast by using the dry bed
of the Cunene as a track, lots of people would have tried it
already. I don't know why they haven't."

" We'll find out," he replied tersely. " Nothing is going to
stop me now."

I looked at the cruel face, sweat-stained. I believed him. I
took the lead again. We marched towards the river.

I thought at first they were elephant or buffalo, but they were
trees. Glorious, welcome shade after the lidless blaze of the
past two days. I am a sailor and I suppose one's eyes get used
to the endless monotony of the sea, but desert is different. The
sand fretted at the eyes. It seeped into every crack, it made its
presence known at every footstep. Anne had plastered her face
with cream and she looked like an Everest climber in reverse.
She was limping a little, but still game.

No word had been spoken since we first sighted the river.
Now, although the cataract was not in sight, we were at the
wide sweep of sand, still unbearably bright, which is the
Cunene. There was no sign of water. In a shallow bay of

sand were half a dozen huge trees whose roots, on the edge of the sand, were eroded like primeval things. By some sort of tacit consent, Anne and I flopped down under one and Stein and Johann under another, about thirty yards away. They were near enough to guard us, but far enough away not to be able to hear what was being said.

Anne stretched herself back and faced away from the sun. "I couldn't care less whether there are half a dozen suns this evening," she exclaimed wearily. "You'll have to rustle up real magic to make me interested in anything at this moment."

"Gin." I said, tasting the metallic bite of the mica dust on my palate. "Gin. And lime. And lots of ice."

"The penalty for that sort of talk on this sort of day is to be made to take off my shoes," she grinned. "If they come off, I'll never get them on again."

Stein strolled over. "Let's gets some wood together for a fire, Captain. This is game country all right. I think we should dig for water, too."

It was better now than later, I decided. I got uncertainly to my feet. Stein was almost friendly as we broke off dry branches and gathered them in a heap.

"We'll start a little later to-morrow morning—a late breakfast won't do any of us any harm," he said amiably. "Miss Nielsen has kept up very well. Now that we're at the river, the going should be easier."

I kept silent.

"You disagree, Captain?" he said quickly.

"I don't know," I replied. "I can only repeat what I said earlier, that if this had been the easy way in, someone would have done it long since."

"Baynes did," he retorted.

"He came in from the other side," I said. "North of Ohopoho there's Swartbooisdrift, but that's a couple of hundred miles upriver from here. There's a hell of a lot can happen in even twenty miles of Skeleton Coast, let alone a hundred."

"If it weren't so late, I would reconnoitre the cataract now," he said impatiently. "But we've still got to dig for water to-night."

We gathered up the wood and threw it down in a large pile

between the two trees. Johann did not stir. He looked at me malevolently.

"That man will kill you without any pretext at all," said Stein conversationally, as if my death were the subject of a confidential little chat. "Remember that, if you have any ideas about me, Captain Peace. You wrecked his whole life. It's really a pity you didn't do the job properly."

I was too tired to argue.

"Look," I said, pointing out game tracks in the sand. "Those may lead us to something."

We followed the hoof marks until they reached the far side of the sand bed. There were deep scratches in the sand, but originally the hole must have been deeper, for fresh sand had blown in. We dug with small folding shovels which had obviously come off the back of a jeep. At about four feet the sand grew damp. By dint of quick shovelling so that the sand did not run back in again, we found a shallow seepage. It seemed drinkable. We filled the canteens, although Stein carried them.

He put a match to the pile of wood as the sun sank. Facing downriver, the great murky mass of the Hartmannberge lay behind me to my left and, although it was already almost dark in the river bed, a peak or two were silhouetted, still. The fire threw a troubled, rosy glow over the white sand. There was absolute silence, except for the crackle of the flames. Anne lay where she had first sat, too weary to move. I flexed my knees and propped my back against the huge tree. Had all this been in company with Mark, the utter peace, the remoteness and the age-old quality of the African bush would have held me enthralled. As it was, my mind crawled with fear, fear because of what Stein was after—it couldn't be just a beetle, I told myself—again—even scientists don't go kill-crazy like he had done just for the sake of one lost species.

The deeper we got into the Kaokoveld, the less became my chances. I was only useful as a guide, a navigator. At what point my usefulness ended was what worried me. Certainly once the beetle had been found. Or was it one of those caches of diamonds real or imaginary, that have lured men to certain death so many times in this wild, untamed region? That was my guess. If so, then Stein must have some notion of the exact spot, but certainly on his map there was nothing to indicate it. He had been quite open about our destination—somewhere in the region of the Otjihipoberge, leaving the river at the Nangolo Flats. Such frankness with me meant one thing only—I wasn't meant to come back.

But why then all this talk about the Onymacris beetle? And why the girl? She obviously wasn't in the plot. Where did she fit into Stein's scheme of things? Looking into the leaping flames, I saw the answer to none of my queries. I only knew that in the Skeleton Coast I must obey the laws of the Skeleton Coast—I must kill or be killed. Johann must be my first objective. To subdue Stein I must have the Remington's range against the Luger's. And to get back, I must have water. I calculated that two days without food or water would see me at the end of my tether. I needed two days from this spot to Curva dos Dunas. Up river there might be more water. It would be suicide to venture from the course of the Cunene. The five-thousand foot peaks of the Hartmannberge were eloquent warning of that.

On the Angola side the Serra de Chela looked even worse. The outline of the massive range on the map looked like some evil animal clamped along the course of the Cunene for sixty miles, with a tail near the Nangolo Flats, where the river bent sharply northwards, as if stepping out of the way of the creature which sucked at its lifeblood on the other side of the Baynes Mountains. Stein had said there was a seven-thousand-five-hundred-foot peak in the Baynes Mountains not far from where we were headed; God alone knows what height they are in the Serra de Chela—no one has ever surveyed them, not even from the air.

I brooded into the gloom. Almost as if reading my thoughts, Johann stirred, and the barrel of the Remington gleamed dully in the firelight. Johann wouldn't sleep.

We ate out of tins, each one of us preoccupied with his or her own thoughts. The water, heavy with minerals, offset the overpowering taste of baked beans and bully beef. Far out in the night distance came the chuffering roar of a lion hunting. Stein looked at Johann and then at me. I suppose the roar of a lion when one is isolated in the bush is one of the most frightening things there is. He must have been miles away. Anne shivered slightly.

"No watch for you to-night, Captain," said Stein. "We shall guard you. But to-morrow night you'll take your whack."

"At least there are some compensations for being held hostage," I replied wearily. I took my single blanket and scooped out a place in the soft sand amongst the roots of the trees. Anne did the same. All the scorpions in the world could not have made me keep my eyes open.

Despite Stein's assurance about a late start, we were shuffling along the course of the river before nine o'clock. The east wind blew down the course of the river into our faces, but the sun was not unbearably hot yet; it had not had time to accumulate the heat of the slopes which makes temperatures in winter on the Skeleton Coast higher actually than in summer, when the seawind brings welcome coolness.

Stein marched alongside me, tensed and anxious. The fringe of the river was dotted with huge ana trees and a load of chattering monkeys made us all feel better. At least there was some sign of life. They stared at the small party in open disbelief and chattered wildly as we passed. We were as much out of place as a journalist at a garden party. The river gorge was narrowing rapidly and a glance ahead showed clearly that the course of the Cunene was the only cleft in the great mountains, and probably the only route through them. Looking at the giant tumble of the Ongeamaberge, which stretch out like a pirate's steel hook from the northern fringe of the Hartmann-berge to the river, I could see that any thought of getting across them on foot was out of the question. There might be game tracks, but even so they would be scarce. Besides, it would only be purely mountain animals which could negotiate the riven clefts and precipices, which I could see through my glasses even at this distance. Another dry stream, the Orumwe, hit the Cunene above the cataract with a wide delta shaped like the roots of a dead tooth, but the cleft ran north and south and was no good to me. I wanted a cleft running east to west. There wasn't one.

The river gorge narrowed and more shrub and smaller trees appeared on its walls.

Then the cataract came in sight.

My reaction was one of extreme disappointment.

"Look," said Stein, jubilantly. "There it is! Why, there's nothing to it."

No need for my glasses to tell me that.

"No," I said quietly, and I felt Anne sagging a little. "It's only about forty feet high. There are plenty of footholds on the rocks."

The rocky shelf stretched up in front of us, the rock polished to a dull gunmetal gloss by water and sand. A schoolboy could have climbed up it without assistance. Stein had brought a length of rope, but we all managed to scale the easy rock slope without it, even Anne. She had become completely silent. Stretching upriver was more sand, but there was more greenery, too, indicating water not too deep down. The sand, softened by the greening banks, looked more friendly.

Stein was full of himself.

"Why, there is absolutely no obstacle if the next cataract is like that," he said. "We'll follow the course of the river and turn off just as I said. All this country needs is a little initiative and a little planning.

I looked at him searchingly. "Famous last words," I retorted.

But he was not to be fobbed off.

"The Skeleton Coast has a reputation and everyone who comes here builds it up, until the whole thing is a mumbo-jumbo of superstition. When someone fails through his own lack of foresight, he adds still another legend to the Skeleton Coast. We've broken it wide open. It's straight-forward going. Nothing to it." He looked at me quizzically. "Not much in the way of navigation required, is there, Captain Peace?"

I knew what he meant. I saw Anne's face go pale. The cruel mouth of the German showed what he meant, too.

"Come on," I said harshly, "let's get on."

Stein called a halt, surprisingly, at about three in the afternoon at a group of huge ana trees near the river's edge. We

had made good progress. Perhaps he was feeling the effects
of the rapidly increasing altitude, discernible even in the bed of
the river. The river, only a couple of hundred yards in width
now, was flanked by cliffs which rose up sheer. Where they
met the river, they had been burnished still brighter by the
water, which, when the river was full, must have cut past them
like a file through the narrow passage. We stopped where a gap
showed to the right, the entrance channel to the Orumwe
River, whose delta splayed out in a welter of white sand. I
remembered that old Simon's chart had marked it " Rio Santa
Maria." Had the Portuguese explorers ever got as far as this?
I couldn't imagine how they would ever have got through the
wicked sand-bars at the mouth of the river, even with surf-boats
and surf crews.

For the hundredth time that day I lifted the binoculars from
their lanyard round my neck and searched the cliffs. I had done
it so often that even Stein took no notice any more. More
greenery, thicker trees to the left. Deep channels from the
Portuguese side into the river, unscalable cliffs. Round and
back. To the right. The wide cleft of the Orumwe, narrowing
within a mile to cliffs not incomparable with the ones on either
side of our river route.

Then I saw the ship.

She was full rigged and lay at anchor. She might be five
miles away.

The sand and the fatigue of the march have created an
hallucination, I told myself. I found my hands trembling.
Stein was watching me idly. There must be no give-away from
me. Deliberately I swept the glasses farther round to my
right. I must not fix on any point or Stein would be suspicious
immediately. I let the lenses sweep back past the ship. She
was still there.

" Satisfied, Captain?" sneered Stein. " No way of escape?"

" Satisfied," I replied, my heart pounding with excitement.
I wanted to shout—a ship! a ship! I must play this one
gently. I gave it fully five minutes before I looked at the spot
where I had seen her. There was nothing. You fool, I said, you
can see her only with the glasses, not with the naked eye.
Stein must have no suspicion that I had seen anything. For
another half an hour I searched about, finding wood for the

fire. Anne smoked, lying back against the trunk of a tree. She hadn't said anything all day. I could see this march to the death—for me at least—was preying on her nerves. I hoped she wouldn't do anything foolish. I have never known half an hour go so slowly. I deliberately checked every movement.

At the end of the time I said casually to Stein:

"Do you mind if I take a walk?"

"Haven't you had enough?" he asked sarcastically. "You remind me of a tiger I once saw in a zoo, Captain. Pace, pace, pace, bumping himself against the bars until his shoulder was raw. You can go and bump your shoulders against the bars if you wish."

I could have rubbed his smug face in the sand.

"I'm going for a walk up this valley for a couple of miles," I replied, keeping my temper under control. "I'll be back by sunset. I don't suppose any white man has ever been up it before."

"I expect it's the same sort of bug which makes you want to do that as made you find your anchorage. Good hunting, Captain. I won't come and look if you don't come back. There'll be another skeleton in a couple of days, that's all."

I wished I could have got my hands on him, but Johann was vigilant with the Remington and Stein was quick, mighty quick, with the Luger.

"Care to come?" I asked Anne.

She looked at me in amazement. "What!" she exclaimed. I had half turned from Stein. She caught something in my face. She was as quick as a needle.

"No thank you," she said almost offhandedly for Stein's benefit. "I've done enough walking to last me the rest of my life."

"Very well," I replied, walking away.

"Wait!" she called after me. "Perhaps I will, provided it's only a mile or two."

"As you wish," I said, also casually indifferent.

We must have gone a mile from the camp before either of us spoke.

I lit a cigarette. My hands were unsteady.

"What is it, Geoffrey? What is it? Tell me quickly!"

" A ship," I said hoarsely. " A ship at anchor."

I half gestured towards the distance.

The eagerness went out of her face. Pity and compassion took its place.

" Yes, of course," she said sadly. " Let's go and look at the ship. At anchor fifty miles from the sea. Is it a nice ship?"

I stopped and grabbed her arm.

" You think I've gone off my mind, don't you? I saw a ship through my glasses. She's lying over there," I nodded with my chin, for I still was wary of Stein and a gesture might give me away.

She shook her head and there were tears in her eyes.

" All right," she said softly. " Go ahead. Show me your ship."

I gave it another half a mile and pulled the lanyard and glasses from my neck. The ship was there, all right.

I gave them to Anne.

" There, take that overhanging reddish cliff as your line. In the sand, at the foot."

I couldn't see her eyes, but her mouth registered her dumb-foundment.

She dropped the Zeiss glasses from her hands and looked unbelievingly in the same direction.

" I don't believe it!" she repeated. " But it's not an ordin-ary ship, Geoffrey. It's—my God!—it's an old-fashioned ship!"

I shared her amazement.

I said very slowly : " It is a very old ship, Anne."

Her knuckles were white where they gripped round the glasses, worn to the brass by my own hands and those of her one-time owner, a U-boat skipper. I'd won them in Malta in a wild orgy in the mess after some sinkings.

She dropped them from her eyes and looked at me. The eyes, coming quickly back to near-focus, added to her air of being dazed.

" How on earth did it get here? Fifty miles from the sea? —why, it looks like, like . . ." she paused uncertainly.

" Say it!" I said. " No one will think you mad except me, and I have seen it with my own eyes."

She said very slowly. " It looks like one of those ships . . .

those ships . . . that Columbus . . . no, it's just too fantastic!"

We were getting closer now and we could see her with the naked eye.

" It would take a sailor's sight to have spotted her from where we were," said Anne, still gazing ahead of her in disbelief. " Anyone else would have thought they were just bare branches of a tree."

" She could never have sailed up here," I said, still more shaken as the three masts, with the mizzen awry to take a lateen sail, became clearly visible. " The coast must have changed radically some time during the past centuries—some enormous volcanic upheaval, perhaps. Just think of all the flat, low-lying country we have come through—perhaps this was a bay once, hundreds of years ago."

" It could be, behind these mountains," said Anne. " Perhaps the seabed was thrown up and created all those dunes. Maybe the true coastline was here where the mountains and rocks are. It's quite feasible."

" I've heard strange stories about a ship in the desert," I said. " But they're the sort of yarn one hears when the drinks have gone round a few times. No one ever substantiated them. I've heard stories of an Arab dhow and a galleon—but all of them were so surrounded with mist and legend that one simply couldn't credit them. It's a strange coast this—anything can happen."

" Is she a dhow?" asked Anne. As if we had not trudged all day, we stumbled, sometimes half at a run over the harder patches, towards the ship that had lain dead there for centuries.

" No, never," I said. " She's European. A caravel. Look, you can even see the deadeyes and the cordage holding up the mizzen truck. How those masts have stood. . . ."

" Don't become nautical, I'm just a simple land girl," she grinned back. " What I just simply can't understand is how she has never rotted away."

" The sand and the dry air have unique properties of preserving things," I replied. " I remember reading somewhere that the first British warship which surveyed this coast before the turn of the century found a mummy in a coffin down the coast from Walvis Bay. They took it home and sold it to a sideshow in Blackpool, I think. It was the hit of the place for years."

"A body might be mummified on purpose," said Anne frowning. "But a whole ship. . . ."

"There's a church in Dublin where Robert Emmet is buried," I said, searching for a rational explanation of a medieval caravel, intact, fifty miles from the nearest sea, perfectly preserved after centuries. "I myself saw a Crusader in the crypt who'd been buried since Richard the Lionheart's time. The sexton told me that the ground had some unique chemical property of keeping bodies indefinitely. As we descended the crypt there were coffins everywhere and they looked like new. It must be something similar here—but on a gigantic scale."

"It seems so utterly impossible!" exclaimed Anne.

We stumbled over a low dune about a quarter of a mile from where the caravel lay, facing south and her starboard bow towards the high cliff another quarter of a mile farther on. Although I was looking at her, a glint like a mirror caught the corner of my eye. I put my hand on Anne's arm.

"If I'm not mistaken, I see water—a pool of it, there to the left, look!"

"It *is* water, Geoffrey! It's only a small pool, and I shouldn't think it's more than a quarter of a mile away."

"Not a word to Stein," I said. "This may well be our salvation, Anne."

The idea hit her.

"It's simple, then," she said. "We have water here and we can strike back to the coast. He'll never be able to catch us."

"With nothing to carry water in, no food, and—that?" I gestured towards the formidable mountain barrier on our right, for we were facing up the valley. "We'd be half dead by to-morrow afternoon and completely dead by the next afternoon. It's only useful knowledge, this pool. We may be able to use it in the future, though."

The pool of water had distracted our attention, but now we paused in amazement at the sight of the old ship. The anchor rope was down, lost to sight in the deep sand. The gunports were open and the puny muzzles pointed defiantly. A good deal of the lower rigging was intact, although the foremast was broken off short above the truck and lay over towards the cliff. The mizzen stays, brown instead of their original tarred black, looked firm enough. She was bedded in sand almost up to the row of gunports. The gilding, or "gingerbread work," round her stern was tarnished and faded, but still clearly visible. I could make out the spokes of the helm on the high poop. I would not have felt surprised if a figure in an old-time helmet had paced her deck and called on us to declare our business.

"Let's go aboard," I said huskily.

"It's like—the past coming alive," whispered Anne. "What is she—Spanish, Portuguese, Dutch?"

"I should say Portuguese, but that's only a guess," I said. "Perhaps we'll find some identification when we get on deck."

"Isn't there a name?" asked Anne, her voice still low, as if in the presence of the dead. Dead she had been for centuries.

"All I can make out is something ending in ' az '," I said. "We may be able to decipher it close up."

The maindeck wasn't more than six feet from the level of the sand. I reached up and was about to haul myself through one of the gunports towards the poop when Anne stopped me.

"Geoffrey," she said urgently. "Don't go aboard. Let's go back. We've seen enough. I feel—there's something sacred aboard . . . perhaps, we should respect the dead. Don't let's pry. Please don't go. I have the strangest feeling. . . ."

I laughed reassuringly.

"This is a secret and a mystery. How could I ever forgive myself in the future if I stopped now? Sooner or later someone is bound to find her. I want to be the first aboard since she sailed from Lisbon in fourteen something-or-other. Think, the first sailor to come aboard in five centuries!"

She looked at me and the tears welled in her eyes.

"You're assuming you've got a future," she said sombrely. "I've got a premonition, a hunch, call it what you like."

The right eyelid was rumpled. Her sweater, stained with sand and sweat, looked years, instead of weeks old. Her face was thin and drawn with inward tension.

"Come," I said, testing the wood to see whether it would hold my weight. "You're coming too. If there's any sudden death, or bolt of lightning, we'll share it."

I hauled myself past the cannon's mouth, which was not very

rusted, and gave a quick glance round the deck before reaching for Anne's hands. The port side guns were all run out and a curious-looking culverin on the rail of the poop pointed the same way. The starboard broadside was secure and the gunports on that side were closed. By each gun was a neat little pile of shot, some no bigger than a cricket ball. Some leather buckets, hard as iron with age, stood grouped round each gun. Of the crew there was no sign. A fine carpet of sand coated the deck.

"Nothing spooky here," I called cheerfully to Anne. "Give me your hands."

I leaned over the rail and pulled her up. She glanced round and shivered.

"What happened—to them?" she said with a sweep of her hands at the guns.

"Probably escaped ashore when the catastrophe struck," I said. "See, they were obviously expecting trouble. All the guns are run out, but on one side only. It would support our idea, too, that this was the seaward side and the other, the starboard side—maybe that very same cliff there—land. Something happened out to sea which made her captain run out a full broadside."

"We'll never know what it was," said Anne, with no change of mood.

"There are no bones about," I said. "That means they must have got away. Let's take a look below."

She glanced round again reluctantly.

"I can't get rid of the feeling that we're intruding, somehow," she said in a low voice. "All right, if you wish."

I tried the small door leading under the port side of the poop rail. I thought it was locked at first, it was so stiff, but it yielded about a foot. We edged in. The passageway was narrow and so low that I had to stoop. I led. Another door.

I opened it.

A man and woman were making love on the big bunk.

I was too dumbfounded to speak. I gestured to Anne. She squeezed past me and looked. She didn't draw back or make a sound. She just stood looking and, without turning round, drew me in by the arm.

The two lovers, naked, were dead.

He lay on top and slightly on her right side. Her face looked up into his. Her lips were slightly parted, a little lopsidedly to the right, and I could see the line of her white teeth. The hair, dark as passion, lay back across the pillow, filmed with sand. The eye sockets were full of sand. In the erect nipple of her left breast the sand had gathered in the runnels of flesh. Her other breast was somewhere under him. Propped on his left elbow, he looked down—as he had done for five centuries —into her eyes. His hair was dark and the hollow of his back was filled with sand. Below the waist, their two bodies were fused—for ever.

Anne was crying. She took me by the arm.

" Come," she said.

She led me back over the side and we dropped down into the soft sand near the stern. The sun was falling behind the mountain barrier.

She let a handful of sand run through her fingers.

" That is the most beautiful thing I have ever seen," she said. " That is how I would wish to die. I'd like to be buried near them."

I took her in my arms. I never knew her more than in that moment. The right eyelid was quite smooth.

A last shaft of light blazed into the big locked stern windows above us. Their stained glass bore the arms of Aragon and Castile.

FOURTEEN

The Secret of Curva dos Dunas

I THOUGHT it only a gigantic black shadow against the rock— until it moved. The face, cased in black hair to the end of its square, blunt nose, peered at us in concentrated animosity.

Johann raised the Remington, but Stein spoke swiftly in German. It was a long shot, and upwards as well into the long ledge which ran along the left side of the gorge.

" What is it?" Anne asked me in a whisper of fear.

" Back a little," said Stein.

The four of us withdrew from the gloom of the narrow defile

towards the brighter light where the sand of the river still caught, whitely, the sun from overhead, despite the tree-lined banks. It was about ten the next day and we had marched since eight. Stein had had nothing to say when we returned to camp the previous evening from the old ship. I had lain awake long with my own thoughts, and now and then I had heard Anne turning restlessly, too.

For the two hours of the morning's march the river bed had gained altitude considerably, and the gorge narrowed sharply. Now, at a point which I estimated to be half-way between the previous night's camping-spot and our turn-off point down the Nangolo valley flats, a huge spur of the Ongeamaberge threw itself, as if in despair to link up with peaks on the Portuguese side, right into the course of the river, leaving a passage so narrow that in floodtime the water must have shot through with the velocity of an open faucet.

We had come upon the narrow gap after rounding a steep bend.

Now we fell back towards some huge trees a couple of cables' lengths from the gap.

Stein turned to me venomously.

"You never mentioned this," he said furiously. "Is there still another cataract? What is that—that animal?"

I shrugged my shoulders.

"Let's go and have a look," I said ironically. "Give me the gun."

Johann burst into a cackle.

"If there's any shooting to be done, we'll do it," he snapped. "What is that animal—is it dangerous? Can we get past without its tackling us?"

"How should I know?" I retorted.

"You soon will," he said. He spoke to Johann in his own language again. Reluctantly the U-boat sailor passed him the Remington. Stein carried all the arms now. But he wasn't going to take any chances. He took the Luger in his right hand and swung the rifle under his left.

"Forwards," he said to me. "You and the girl wait here, Johann. If there's any shooting, come after us."

I led. We rounded the bend again, gloomy and over-hanging. The giant shadow moved. He was standing sentry.

I looked up the gorge and my heart froze. The river bed had narrowed until it had cut its way through solid rock. There must have been another sharp bend a little higher up, for the water had swathed away the rock on our left until it looked for all the world like the last lap of the Cresta run, smooth, polished rock instead of snow, with a shallow runnel above extending for maybe three hundred yards. If a toboggan can touch ninety miles an hour on the Cresta, my guess was that the Cunene in flood came round this bend with the speed of *Nautilus*. Above the gigantic furrow of rock was a ledge running the whole length of the bed. I thought it was in black shadow.

The shadows were gigantic black lions.

Stein drew back in amazement and fear.

" A lion!" he exclaimed. " But it cannot be! There is no living lion as big as that!"

The sentry beast got to its feet from a crouching position and looked over at us, measuring the distance. For the first time I saw the tawny coat as well as the enormous black mane which enveloped not only its head and shoulders, but its back and chest. It was the size of an ox, though not as tall.

" Not one lion, Stein," I said. " Look, the whole ledge is crawling with them!"

I laughed in his face.

" Now find the ace," I sneered at him. " Remember what I said—' famous last words.' You'll have to go back, Stein."

" Never!" he shouted. " I'll shoot every one. . . ."

" Don't be a bloody fool," I said. " How many do you think you'd get before they'd get you? Look at that, man!"

There were stirrings on the ledge and a whole troop of eyes swivelled on to us. The great brute at the mouth of the rock tunnel opened his mouth and purred softly. It was the most frightening noise I have ever heard. The great black heads, majestic, contemptuous, watched lazily, vigilantly, every muscle at the ready.

" It's the Cape lion!" screamed Stein. A quiver ran through the beast when he heard the noise of the human voice. " My God! It's been extinct for over a century. The old Cape hunters said it was the most dangerous animal in Africa! They shot it out on the plains. Now—the Skeleton Coast is its last retreat."

I gazed in fascinated awe at the huge beast poised on the ledge. Stein's was the only explanation. I was looking at history, looking at antiquity. Deadly, hellishly dangerous antiquity! The Skeleton Coast guarded its gateway with the world's oldest and deadliest animal! I felt weak at the knees. I also knew that Stein and his crazy expedition was at an end.

I said so.

"This is the point of no return, Stein," I said roughly. "You couldn't get past that lot, even with a tommy-gun. I doubt whether a high velocity two-two would even halt one of those brutes."

Stein rounded on me so savagely that I thought he would use the Luger.

"You capitulate, Captain Peace, but I don't! We go on, even if we have to go round the mountains."

"What is it you're so keen to find there in the Otjihipo mountains?" I said bluntly. "Not some piddling beetle. Is it a cache of diamonds?"

He looked surprised. He wasn't lying.

"No, Captain Peace, not a cache of diamonds. Something much more valuable. The Onymacris beetle. Found only in the Gobi Desert and North Borneo once. No longer."

He must be mad, I decided.

"Let's go back and talk this over with the others," he said, and there was nothing irrational in the way he said it. "But understand, we are going on—at whatever cost."

We retreated cautiously again, with a careful eye on the huge black-covered face.

We were starting to emerge when I heard the noise at our backs.

"Listen!" I rapped out. I heard it again.

"Sounds like thunder," he said uncertainly. "But there's no cloud about——"

"Run!" I yelled. "It's the river coming down! The highest trees farthest up the bank—quick!"

I grabbed his shoulder as he stood hesitantly. The narrow

gorge funneled the sound. Anne and Johann saw us come sprinting towards them in amazement.

"Quick!" I yelled. "The river's coming down! Listen! It's like distant thunder! Those trees over there!"

We scrambled up the steep bank, slipping and scrabbling. The noise sounded like an approaching Underground train. We hoisted each other wildly into the branches, praying that the water would not reach as high.

The flood broke through the narrow tunnel and spread into the sand.

It wasn't water. It was thousands of zebra.

They came through the rock-lined gap at full gallop, packed so close together that they sprayed out like water as the river bed widened. The thunder of thousands, tens of thousands, of hoofs on the rock, was deafening.

"It's a mass migration," I yelled above the uproar. "It happens once in a lifetime. They'll tear on for scores of miles. Fifty years ago a magistrate in South West Africa saw the same thing happen with springbok. They threw themselves into the sea and drowned by the thousand. Mass suicide——"

"Look!" screamed Anne.

The huge sentry-lion dropped like a stone off the rock on to the mass of animals below him. His victim staggered under his weight, but was borne remorselessly clear of the narrow section under the impetus of the herd behind. Almost without effort, it seemed, the black-maned brute struck the zebra across the head and together they tumbled into the sand. Terrified, those behind opened out around the lion and the prostrate zebra. Another huge lion dropped among the herd from above and was carried out into the sand by the flood. Like experienced paratroopers, lion after lion catapulted himself into the mass of thundering animals passing below. Soon the white sand was dotted, black and white stripes on the ground and huge black forms kneeling over them. Once the thundering zebra overran a lion and his victim. He rose savagely and struck out. I heard the dull sickening thud even above the other noise. I saw the outline of his gigantic paw across the rib-cage of one crazed creature which had overrun him, the mark outlined against the black and white stripes in scarlet blood. It was so swift and sudden that the zebra ran for fully thirty yards before it pitched head over heels in the sand, a shattered, bloody corpse.

The slaughter went on for half an hour. Then, like magic, the thunder of the hoofs stopped. The white bed of the river was red as the lions ripped at their victims. There must have been more than a hundred, each with his own kill. The nearest was perhaps fifty yards from our tree. He tore open the zebra's stomach and pawed among the bowels, still quivering with latent life. We watched fascinated, sickened. He scraped them on one side and then plunged his whole head into the hole in the carcass. The black mane emerged, soaked in blood. The black and scarlet looked like a flamenco singer's costume. He chewed some inner delicacy with gusto, uttering that same low purring.

The silence, except for the chewing noises like tearing sacking, was complete.

Stein's voice broke it.

" Down, all of you!" he rapped.

He was sitting on a branch below us. I looked at him incredulously.

" Hurry!" he went on.

" I'm staying," I said. Anne nodded in agreement, white-faced.

He made a faint gesture with the Luger and smiled.

" This is our moment," he said. " This sort of thing happens once in a generation. You said so. I'm playing my luck on this migratory compulsion complex of the zebra, as our American friends would call it. For once the rock passage is clear. All the lions are feeding. We can get through—now. There's nothing to stop us."

He was right. Dead right.

But he'd forgotten something.

" How about the return?" I asked.

His eyes gleamed.

" That's *my* problem," he replied shortly. " Get down!" he rapped.

We climbed down silently to the foot of the tree. Anne took my hand and her fingers were shaking. There was no avoiding the great beasts. Stein took the lead. I give him full marks for his guts. We passed within twenty-five yards of one of the huge animals, but it didn't even look up. Clear of the carcass-scattered sand, we broke into a run. We kept it up right through the gloomy tunnel with its overhanging ledge of death. The stench was unbelievable. I could see that the water never reached quite as high as the ledge, but when the river foamed through the gap, it must have been a stupendous sight.

We ran on, panting and slipping.

Then we were through. In front the mountains drew back their fangs and I could see that we were not far from the Nangolo Flats, our turn-off point into the forbidding mountains.

It froze that night when we made camp among the high peaks at an altitude of nearly seven thousand feet. As if relenting, the going had been easy all day. We left the river where the broad shelf of the combined Kapupa and Otjijange rivers meet the Cunene, striking south now instead of east. The view of the Baynes Mountains on our left as we rose steadily upwards, following the course of the Kapupa, was superb. About twelve miles from the river the Kapupa strikes down from the heart of the massive Baynes range and joins the Otjijange, which steps out from behind a huge dun peak, isolated, at the head of the valley. We followed the lead of the Kapupa—dry like all rivers in this territory—into the heart of the Otjihipo peaks, which are not ten miles from the Cunene as the crow flies. But between lies such an inextricable tumble of peaks and valleys, fretted with razor-edged kranzes and unscaleable cliffs, that it would be quite impossible to venture through them.

Stein pushed on eagerly. At the sharp easterly swing of the Kapupa into the mountains I would have liked to have had time to have studied a great fissure running south and east from the sentinel peak at the head of the valley, but Stein would not even pause. If the gap persisted, it must run roughly towards the Kandao Mountains which could—might—lead to the Orumwe valley where the caravel lay. I took careful mental bearings on the key peaks. It might be a way of escape. Even as sunset came and we were all panting at the unaccustomed altitude, Stein pushed on. Superb in all its primitive wonder, the great seven-thousand-five-hundred-foot Baynes Mountain, dusted chalk-rose by the flaring sunset at our backs, stood as magnificently captain of the peaks as the huge lion at the rock tunnel entrance.

Even Stein was moved by the splendid panorama.

' We'll be right at the spot, or very nearly there, to-night,'' he enthused. "We'll start looking for Onymacris to-morrow."

Anne had scarcely spoken all day. She shrugged.

Now, with the coming of night, it was bitterly cold. The easterly wind, blowing in our faces all afternoon, had dropped. Anne sat by my side. Orion hunted over the Baynes Mountains and the Southern Cross hung lopsidedly over the Onjamu peaks towards Walvis Bay.

A slow light trailed across the frosty sky.

" Meteor or sputnik?" asked Anne. She felt for my hand. There was premonition in the cold flesh. Stein sat immobile, staring into the leaping flames. Half a dry tree was burning. It was the loneliest fire in the world. Anne and I sat close, scarcely exchanging a word. There were no words for what we felt, anyway. Her face was drawn in the light, not with fatigue, but with some inward tumult. Occasionally she glanced at me and smiled.

I rolled out her bedroll next to mine, our feet pointing at the flames. She squeezed my hand and pulled the blankets round her hair. I did likewise.

In about ten minutes she called softly.

" Geoffrey !" she said.

" Yes, Anne?"

The voice dropped until I could scarcely hear.

" Remember, I forgave you—everything?"

I reached out, but she had withdrawn her hand.

Stein took Anne away with him after an early breakfast. I was left in the care of the sullen Johann. My usefulness seemed to have come to an end as far as I could see. Except that Stein might not feel himself able to find Curva dos Dunas again. My plans were complete, now that I was alone with Johann. He was target number one. I occupied myself about the camping spot, finding more wood, washing up dishes. Anne and Stein set off to go higher up the steep path—obviously a game track—round the shoulder of the mountains, below which the camp was pitched on an open, flat clearing. As she reached the turning she turned and waved.

The next two hours were a torment. The tension inside me knotted every nerve. It was far worse than waiting for a depth-charge attack to start. I kept myself from glancing at Johann. When I struck, it must be as swift and deadly as a black mamba. There would be no second chance. Therefore I waited until I could be sure that Stein was well clear of the camp in case there was a shot. The sound would carry far among the echoing peaks. He and Anne were lost to view since the path wound steeply upwards.

I was dumbfounded when Stein appeared, alone, before ten o'clock.

"Captain Peace!" he shouted as he turned the last bend in the path. "Captain Peace! Onymacris! Onymacris! We found it! Look! Look!"

He came forward at a slight run, holding his hand outstretched.

My hopes regarding Johann fell to the ground.

"What is it?" I asked dully.

"The Onymacris!" he said, scarcely able to contain himself. "Right where I said it would be! It's the biggest scientific find of the century? Look, man, look—pure gold!"

He was obviously speaking metaphorically, for the two dead beetles in his hand were an undistinguished off-white. To me they looked no different from any common beetle crawling round a suburban backyard in Windhoek or Cape Town.

"The Gobi, North Borneo and now the Skeleton Coast— living!" he cried. "Congratulate me, Captain Peace! I congratulate myself. I am rich, richer than my wildest dreams!"

Two putty-coloured beetles didn't seem worth all that.

He slapped me on the shoulder.

"Congratulation to you, too, Captain Peace! The navigator of my hopes! Congratulations to Johann, the watchman! You have all played your part nobly! You shall be rewarded as is your due!! And now," he turned to me and I was again struck by the ray-like gash of the mouth and jaw, "you must go and congratulate Miss Nielsen. She is waiting up the path for you. She asks if you will go and join her—soon!"

There was a curious inflexion about his last words. But if Anne wanted me to join her alone, there it was.

I set off up the steep track, which narrowed to a spine across the back of a huge, eroded peak; it ran clean across the summit. It was well defined. There was no other way, for the ground fell away on both sides to a colossal drop. On the left it must have been every bit of fifteen hundred feet, and slightly less on the right. The wind tugged at me as I strode forwards. Thank God there was less sand, although I could still feel the rasp of it on the wind's breath.

The path struck across the peak and converged at two great boulders. There was no sign of Anne. She must have remained pretty far up, I thought. I strode between the two boulders and in passing my eye caught something on my right.

Anne was sitting with her back against one of them.

" Anne. . . ." I started. Fear ran like ice down my spine. She was dead.

The eyes were half shut and her face had a curious look of resentment—resentment as if she had been taken away from something which meant more than the loss of her life.

I could scarcely distinguish the bullet hole from the bright scarlet of her sweater.

I wrenched up the sweater and saw the neat surgical incision of the Luger bullet. There was scarcely any blood. It had crushed in the left nipple. A few strands of ragged nylon from her brassière fringed the hole. It might have been passion, not death, which stared at me. She was sitting neatly. Stein must have shot her as she sat.

There was almost no violence about the whole scene. Only the expression of resentment. Only the puckering of the right eyelid. I knelt down and kissed the rumpled lid. I pulled the sweater down and straightened the unseemly dent on the outside. Only then, a great blind rage overwhelmed me. I have killed men with weapons—with torpedoes, with fire, with machine-guns—but now I longed for the feel of killing with my fingers, the gurgle of life being choked out, of hot blood reeling under pressure to make it eternally cold. It was so overpowering that it made me icy-cool in caution. I saw it all—she had found his precious beetle, and, her work done, he had killed her with as little compassion as he had had for the Kroo

boy. Why murder for a blasted beetle? It kept going through
and through my mind. He had sent me up here to be killed.
He wouldn't do that himself, not only because I think he was
frightened, but because of Johann. Johann would kill me and
Stein would kill Johann. Then he would beat it for Curva dos
Dunas with enough food and water and a plausible story.
There couldn't be any search—not in this forbidden country.
John Garland's hands would be tied. He might be as sus-
picious as hell, but he'd never be able to prove anything.

I edged forward on my knees and peered round the rock.
As sure as clockwork, there came Johann. He was coming
quickly, the Remington under his arm. His head was swaying
like a hound's on the scent.

I drew back farther, sheltering half behind a huge bolder.
I had no plan. I was as kill-crazy as he.

Johann rounded the rock and stopped short when he saw
Anne's body. He wasn't fifteen feet from me. Now or
never.

I sprang forward. In a flash Johann covered me with the
rifle.

"She died very easy," he said. "I died very hard all those
years with the little black men; I died. I died over and over.
You will die slowly, Captain Peace." He swung the Remington
back without taking his burning eyes off me and threw it sideways over the cliff. I felt a brief feeling for him; I, too, wanted
to kill with my hands. He pulled a sailor's knife from his belt
and we faced each other like wrestlers. He wasn't afraid. He
was fearful only lest he would do it too quickly.

I moved so that the rock was on my left and slightly behind
me. He saw I was unarmed and grinned, a fiendish, satisfied
grin. He was going to enjoy the fight, like a sailor fights a
harlot in bed. As he reached forward with the knife, I whipped
my right hand out of my pocket and extended the palm. It was
my faintest hope. As he saw *Trout's* little mascot hand he
blenched and I whipped forward and grabbed his knife hand
with my left and slipped my right under his armpit. It was the
same grip which had torn Hendrik's arm out of its socket.
Johann struck punily at my kidneys with his left, but there was
no force in the blows—there never can be, with that fearful
hold.

I twisted his arm. He held on with the strength of a maniac, but he said nothing. I felt one tendon start to tear. The knife moved back from three inches from my right eye to six. I threw myself against his weight. I felt his muscles tear. But he wasn't going to get away with it as Hendriks did. I forced the arm still farther back. His eyes were frantic with terror. I marched him remorselessly back past the dead woman towards the precipice at his back. The knife now hung back over his right shoulder in a grotesque parody of a strike. I knew exactly what I was going to do. Like a released spring, I ducked back, freeing my arm and shoulder, in one movement and kicked him in the stomach. I give him credit. Any other man, with the bite of that heavy seaboot in his vital parts, would have fallen over backwards. Johann stood swaying, his face grey-green with terror and pain. For a second we stood panting in great gasps facing one another. Then I stepped forward and administered the *coup de grâce*. I hit him twice with my right forearm across the side of the neck. He pitched and rolled dustily backwards. I never heard the final crump of the body far below. The dead woman gazed at me sightlessly.

I picked up the knife from the path and sagged down on a rock, my breath coming in frantic inhalations. I felt no remorse, no sorrow, no triumph even. My mind kept saying : Stein ! Stein !

What had she said? " I would like to be buried there."

It came to me like fire amid the icy clarity of my lust to kill. I looked down at the quiet face and eyes whose pupils I would never see again. I'll carry you there, I vowed. You'll lie for ever beside those other lovers. And then, like a scream of taut nerves : but I'll kill Stein first ! Give him time, and he would come looking for either Johann or myself. He came, hours later. I caught the glimpse of sun on metal before I actually saw Stein himself. He was making sure. He had the Luger out. I crouched down as low as I could and withdrew from boulder to boulder until eventually on my right I found a slight cleft, wide enough to take a man's body. I balanced the heavy knife. At least I had something on my side. I stood sweating between the hot rocks. I reckoned he'd take another half an hour to reach Anne's body. I'd lost my cap in the struggle and the sweat poured off me, as much reaction and anticipation as heat.

I'd never thrown a knife before, and it's a tricky business at the best of times. He'd see me yards before he reached the cleft, and there was no hope of an ambush from above. I forgot all about that. I clutched the knife until my fingers ached.

I flicked a glance down the path and then jerked my head back. Stein was coming on like a cat, holding the Luger. There was a jagged boulder which I judged would be my best marker for a throw before he saw me.

I whipped out of the cleft and cast the heavy knife. The shot followed simultaneously. I reeled back streaming blood as the bullet tore through my right shoulder.

I bit down the searing pain.

Then Stein's voice came. It was strained.

" Step out of that hole, Captain Peace, unless you want me to come and ferret you out."

I remained where I was. But he had courage, had Stein. He came forward until he could see me propped against the hot stone wall.

The knife projected from his left arm. It must have bitten deep, for his face was grey, but it was low and anything but fatal. That fact passed through my mind with quick, bitter realisation.

In the other hand he pointed the Luger steadily at me.

" So you killed Johann at last," he said. " At least I presume you did?"

There was no point in denying it. I nodded.

The voice gained some of its earlier sneering quality.

" Brave, resourceful Captain Peace!" he said. " No histrionics on my part about shooting you, I assure you, Captain. No confessions, no deathbed gloating."

He raised the Luger and fired. But I saw him flick the barrel aside from me as his finger whitened on the trigger. I saw his face contort and he fired again and again and again.

The first zebra galloping down the path stumbled as the heavy bullets struck home, but its impetus swept both itself and Stein over the precipice beyond. It was a small group of about fifty and they thundered by without a pause. How many of them went over the edge with Stein I do not know. In less than a minute the path was clear and the dust was filtering down into the red-gold hair by the rock. The animals had not touched her as she sat back from the pathway. I could hear their clatter down the mountains towards the camp.

I was oblivious of the pain from my shoulder until I reached camp, carrying Anne over my other shoulder. Of the next days, in fact, only salient points remain with me now, interspersed with some completely trivial. I remember how fresh her lipstick was and I was at infinite pains not to blur it. She would have liked it that way. By the remains of the camp fire I cut lengths of rope and tied her hands and feet for the long carry back to the caravel. I had no rational thought. My movements were automatic. There was no gap in the remorseless vacuum of grief which encased me. I rummaged among her things and found a scarf. I tied her jaw firmly and bound a handkerchief across the half-closed eyes. I wrapped the dufflecoat round her head. I feared the sand would tarnish the brightness of the lovely hair. It was not until later that I found I had made a careful selection of food and one nearly full canteen of water.

I set off down the bed of the Kapupa river. I set course as automatically as were my other reactions. Perhaps something instinctive came to my rescue. I might have fumbled or hesitated had I been conscious of what I was about, but I wasn't. Instead of branching northwards towards the Nangolo Flats up which we had trudged from the Cunene, I struck left at the sentinel rock up the gigantic break in the rock towards the Kandao mountains, which are the southern outposts of the great crag which juts into the river to make the lions' tunnel. The sun struck into my face as it dropped in the afternoon. The sweat poured off me. I had nothing to protect my head. I could smell the sweet woman-smell of the body as my sweat soaked through her jersey. I followed blindly a track not dissimilar to the one on which she had found the fatal Onymacris. It ran too much to the south for my liking, but it had a lot of west in it. And I must get to the west. My one thought was not to return to Curva dos Dunas, but to get my burden to the caravel. My right shoulder where the bullet had pierced it—

high and by no means dangerous—ached like hell. With my left cramped with the weight of the dead woman and the wound in my right, it felt as if someone had strapped a red-hot poker across the base of my neck.

I stopped at evening when it was too dark to stumble on. The great valley of the Otjijange lay at my back. I camped where a slab of eroded rock lay spreadeagled on the edge of a mile-wide drift of sand. In front lay the highest peak of the Kandao range, almost directly opposite me, four tiny peaks on the right and one sloping summit attached to them—like four little warthogs running after their mother. I could see the track stretching round the left flank of the peak—but I was getting anxious about the way it continually bore south. I must get more north. I reckoned, roughly speaking, that on a line to the coast I would now be twenty miles south of Curva dos Dunas.

I have little recollection of the next morning. Perhaps I was a little delirious for the wound hurt more than ever. I became fully aware of things when my sailor's instinct told me there had been a change in course. The track was now veering north-wards, and I saw the Kandao peak was a dozen miles behind me. It was also downhill. I stumbled on. I scarcely noticed that the sun had burned the skin off my forehead and face. The smell of sweet sweat from Anne's clothes drove me on. Death and corruption were holding back. I knelt in the burning sand to drink from the canteen and blessed the Skeleton Coast for that mercy. I staggered on into the afternoon sun.

Like the lift of fog off the Skeleton Coast, my consciousness cleared. I was heading due north, but something else had penetrated. I rubbed my sweat-soaked eyes against the rough hair of her duffle-coat. The pool! Away to the left against the cliff was the caravel. In half an hour it would have been in shadow. The thought that I might have stumbled past and missed it woke me to full realisation like an injection of adrenalin. I knew what I had to do. I skirted the pool, my mind numb with memories. I pushed the body through the open gunport, when I reached the ship. There was no rigor mortis. The Skeleton Coast was pouring its balm still. I swung myself up, and cried aloud at the pain in my shoulder. I carried her through the doorway. I didn't go into the lovers' cabin. There was a smaller one on the left.

The bunk was bare and I laid her on it. I unwrapped the head and jaw.

I leant down and kissed the rumpled eyelid.

I stood back and tossed a lighted match into the red-gold hair.

It was all over in an hour. The old ship crackled like a chord from Ravel while I stood and watched the blaze. Before the moon came up there was scarcely even a glow among the ashes.

I decided to have some food and try to sleep.

The food and the water canteen were missing. I had left them aboard in my agitation. I was alone in the Kaokoveld without food or water.

The realisation took a long time to sink in. Panic really only assailed me next day when I tried to dig for water in the bed of the Cunene. The going was easy enough and I had traversed the Orumwe valley and was following the main course of the Cunene downhill towards the first easy cataract. My half-conscious strike along the zebra path over the formidable peaks of the Kandao range had made a wide detour of the lions' barrier. I panicked when I found that I couldn't get the hole for the water more than eighteen inches deep. The sand poured back far quicker than I could scoop it out with my hands. It was like playing seaside sandcastles—but death stood by and laughed. It had seemed so easy with one of the small spades Stein had brought. I clawed frantically. The sand returned mercilessly. The tips of my fingers were wet. I sucked them frantically. Then a wave of panic swept over me and I threw myself at the flaccid hole like a rabid dog. The gritty stuff tore the skin off my fingers. I plunged my face into the damp sand and only got a caking like a custard pie across my face. I knew, then, how weak I was. I had tapped my strength across those high peaks. A muscle kicked spontaneously in my left arm above the elbow which had been crooked round Anne's body. The exertion brought a faint new trickle of blood from the wound in my shoulder.

I sat back and weighed the chances. I must take it easy, I told myself. Imagine you're playing golf, I told myself.

Swing easily, never force the swing, I kept repeating. If I could get at the water a couple of feet down, I could make it to the sandy delta where we had first encountered the Cunene on our way in. I'd drunk as much water as I could at the pool before leaving the site of the old ship. I was only thirsty now, not really in desperate need of water. Assuming I could get to the seaward turn-off, I would have another two days' march to Curva dos Dunas. It might be a bit longer in my present condition. I had no food. Nor was there the slightest chance of finding any. We had seen on our way in that game hid itself pretty thoroughly during the day. Even a rifle would be a particularly big asset. I made up my mind. I'd dig for water farther down where the river bed looked firmer. I'd strike out for the turn-off. I'd drink as much water as I could and then try and make Curva dos Dunas. . . .

I got as far as the turn-off when the north-westerly gale started. Had I been in better shape my mind might have registered the fact that the wind, instead of being behind me from the east, had backed rapidly into the north-west. At sea a sudden backing into the north-west in winter time means only one thing. An enormous sea builds up and chops against the great Benguela current. For miles the sea bucks like a tormented thing. The winter north-west gales have twice the lash of the perpetual south-westerlies; the most remarkable thing about them is that the wind, blowing one moment high up in the Beaufort scale, will suddenly end, as if cut off by a knife. The sea remains anguished, while complete calm prevails. Then comes fog—the thickest fog I have ever encountered at sea.

I might have tried for water sooner had it registered that the wind had changed. But I was pushing mindlessly for the turn-off. The full realisation struck me when I emerged from the sheltering funnel of the cliff-bound river into the open. A solid curtain of sand struck me. I couldn't see where I was. The sun was hidden in the murk of white, gale-lashed sand. The gale seemed to bring every particle of sand with it which lay between me and the mouth of the river, ten miles away. I retreated a quarter of a mile the way I had come, but it was too late. The gale was now funnelling up the narrow bed and, if anything, the sand was even worse than in the open. Eyes smarting and streaming, my nose and mouth blocked with sand, I staggered back into the open delta, keeping as far to my left as I could. I sank down and tried to make a small cup in the sand—anything to get water. It was hopeless. I couldn't even get a wet finger-tip. I remembered how we had had to go down almost four feet, Stein and I, for water here. My mouth was so full of sand that I retched weakly. It made things worse. Now I couldn't get rid of either the sand or the vomit in my mouth. Turning my back to the sand-driven whiteness, I scooped the muck out of my mouth with my fingers. This is where I had counted on one last long drink before my trek to Curva dos Dunas. If I stayed, I might wait for three or four days before the gale blew itself out. They seldom last less than that. I knew I'd be dead long before then. The only thing was to strike south—if I could find the elephant track along the edge of the sand delta, the wind screaming and plucking, bitter with sand. Now I knew why the feel of the sand had tormented Johann.

After about three hours I found the track. I stumbled southwards.

By sunset I knew I was finished.

Blind with sand and heat, my knees sagged and I fell full length off the right hand side of the track. The bright white sand of the Cunene had given way to grey, gritty filth. My ears, eyes, nostrils, mouth and throat were encased in one remorseless band of sand. The wind was an invisible thug choking me with a thong of sand. I fell clear of the path. I regained consciousness perhaps half an hour later as darkness fell. I felt strangely detached. My hair was half sunk in sand now. I was a dead man for all intents and purposes. I watched a small beetle suddenly shoot out from the sand not a foot in front of my eyes. Then another, and another. They catapulted up as suddenly as a submarine with her tanks blowing.

Then my detachment, the detachment of approaching death, vanished. I struck out hysterically, blindly, madly, at the half dozen or so tiny grey beetles.

Onymacris! I was so weak that I only succeeded in crushing them into the sand without doing them any real harm. They swarmed out of reach of my feebly striking hand.

Onymacris! The name was a curse. Why, I raved, had we not found them here, here within reach of Curva dos Dunas? My sense of grief and of helpless rage jerked me into a sitting position.

The big hyena, as tattered and sandblasted as myself sat ten feet away looking at me. We gazed at one another. So the scavenger had arrived even before his victim was dead. I threw a handful of sand at him in impotent rage, but he simply paid no attention. Unable to rise to my feet, I dragged myself twenty yards farther away, off the path. The foul animal followed. I thought I could detect the stink of him—then a shock of realisation ran like a drink of life-giving water through me.

The wind had stopped.

I dragged myself farther from my tormentor. It was almost dark. The hyena advanced, and then stopped the same distance away. I saw two other smaller forms behind him. Jackals! I prayed that I would be dead before they started in on me.

The moon rose. I kept on dragging myself away, but the animals followed. I saw to my horror that there were now about half a dozen of them, all in single file behind the hyena. He kept the same distance between himself and me. I let my head drop weakly. It didn't crunch on sand. It was packed hard. It was some sort of minor game track I had been dragging myself along.

I got semi-consciously on to all fours and struggled onwards —away from that dreadful queue of scavengers. They kept station on me with the precision of a destroyer line. I half got to my feet, but my knees would not hold me and I rolled down the slope. My tormentors followed at a slow trot. My head struck against a rock. I was beyond caring. I rolled over to avoid it.

The small conical tower, about four feet high, was silhouetted against the moon.

It was made of tiny flints, each one worked with infinite care, morticed together. I dragged myself into a sitting position. The little tower was firmly fixed in a concave rock structure. It was against the side of this that I had struck my head. The flints all amalgamated into one larger pattern, a long fluted spiral which twisted round like a fire escape to the top of the structure. The concave rock in which it rested must have been about six feet across.

The animals, still in Indian file, kept station behind me. I cursed them for not putting an end to it all.

Then everything went blank.

I thought I had passed out again, but it was fog. Thick, enveloping fog, so tightly woven of land heat and sea-cool that I couldn't even see the strange conical tower a hand's-breadth away.

I heard the tinkle of water. I knew then that I was dying. Yours was a much easier death, Anne, I said aloud. A bullet is neat and swift. Johann has had his revenge. I am dying more slowly than he could ever have wished.

The hyena came right up to my feet. I stared fascinated into the reddish eyes. He stank worse than anything I have ever smelt, before or since. I wondered if my breath was as bad. I debated how he would begin, and what the first bite would feel like. But he wasn't looking at me. He was looking past my head at the conical tower. The other animals crowded closer, but still didn't move out of position.

Water was dripping down the conical stonework, gathering momentum as it accumulated more from the lower flints, and was dripping into the stone basin. There must have been a cupful even as I watched. I didn't wait. I thrust my head under the stone funnel and felt cold, pure water pour into my parched throat. As it dripped across my face and mouth I saw that the fog was condensing against the stones and precipitating into the stone basin. What dead race—for this was human construction—had made this ingenious drinking fountain? The principle was simple : adiabatic warming. The flints had been heated in the same way as a bicycle pump heats up when used; by a change in air pressure. The air pressure in this case changed steeply between mountain slope and sea level, heating itself. The stone flints absorbed it, retained it, and when the cold sea fog struck the little tower, pure moisture condensed. The simplicity of genius!

For how many centuries had this ingenious source of life in a country of death been working? The heavy sea fog was miraculously converted to channelled, life-giving water. The water was running in a steady stream and I let it wash away the sand from my head and face.

The animals stood and watched, crowding, but none came forward to drink. I realised with amazement what was happening. They were waiting for me to finish! I had been first in the queue. The life-giving liquid was so precious that it had impressed a code of behaviour even on these savage animals. They were waiting in line while the one in front drank from the fountain! I took another long drink and pulled myself to one side. The hyena came forward eagerly and drank. He paid no attention to me or the other animals. Water had declared eternal truce among the wild creatures. He drank long and eagerly, waiting for the water to accumulate in the stone basin. He must have taken a quarter of an hour over it.

Then he withdrew and one of the jackals came forward. The ritual was repeated as each reached the basin. There was no hurrying, no jostling, no fighting for place. The priceless fluid dripped from the tooled flints. I waited until all had drunk, and then I drank again, as much as I could take. If I kept going all night, I would be on the beach in the morning.

As I left the ancient drinking-fountain another stinking animal passed me. He took no notice, but his tongue was almost black with thirst and he was panting heavily. A strand-wolf! A savage, nomadic animal called a wolf which wanders the surf-line of the beaches preying on carrion swept up by the sea. He took no notice of me and brushed past as I regained the main track.

I found the surf-boat at sunrise. The sea was shrouded in fog. *Etosha* would be out there all right. The tide was receding from the causeway. I could imagine John's surprise when a scarecrow emerged, literally from the sea! It was perfectly calm.

I went across to the boat to see if there was anything left of the Kroo boy. There wasn't. A narrow pathway of sand stretched out in the grey light, pointing out to sea. I started to walk out along the causeway. The sea was a curious metallic grey. A wave slopped over my feet and I stopped to straighten the torn boot. My hand came away oily and sticky.

Oil!

With the clarity of mind which follows complete fatigue, I saw it all in a flash.

The charts—they all said " discoloured water."

Discoloured—with oil!

Onymacris—the oil beetle of the North Borneo and Gobi oilfields!

NP I—she didn't have to refuel, she was atomic driven! I had set the sea on fire round her. And the sea had burned because it was—oil! Natural oil!

The Onymacris beetle—that is why Stein was prepared to do murder, anything, to find it. He knew the connection. Everywhere Onymacris is found, there is oil. It's a surer pointer than any wildcat. And they'd struck oil in Angola, only a couple of hundred miles north of the South African border.

Oil! The whole of Curva dos Dunas anchorage was oil! So much oil that it filled the sea as it burst up from its untapped billions of gallons beneath. And Curva dos Dunas was mine! Except in the Sahara, they'd never struck oil richly in Africa. And here it was, the same kind of pitiless desert, bursting with oil! Stein went for the mountains first—he must have had a strong hunch—but if only Anne had seen the Onymacris as I had done within five miles of the sea! The whole sand had seemed to crawl with them as I lay there.

I limped slowly out towards where *Etosha* lay with my seaboots coated in oil.

THE END

Alistair MacLean

His first book, *HMS Ulysses*, published in 1955, was outstandingly successful. It led the way to a string of best-selling novels which have established Alistair MacLean as the most popular thriller writer of our time.

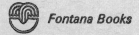 *Fontana Books*

Desmond Bagley

'Mr. Bagley is nowadays incomparable.' *Sunday Times*

The Freedom Trap *35p.*
The hunt for a notorious Russian agent leads to Ireland and
Malta. Now filmed as *The Mackintosh Man*, starring Paul
Newman. 'Unbeatable for sheer gripping excitement.'
Daily Telegraph

Running Blind *35p*

The Spoilers *35p*

Landslide *35p*

The Golden Keel *35p*

Wyatt's Hurricane *30p*

High Citadel *35p*

The Vivero Letter *35p*

 *Fontana Books*

James Jones

The Ice-Cream Headache 30p
A collection of thirteen powerful stories by this best-selling author. 'Each story is perfectly constructed and rich in over-tones.'
Times Educational Supplement

Go to the Widow-Maker 60p
A superb novel about the war between the sexes, set in the world of rich men and those who cater to them. In Jones's tale of dangerous living, love is for men and women are for sex. 'Jones is the Hemingway of our time . . . There is savage poetry in his descriptions of spear-fishing and treasure-hunting.'
Spectator

The Thin Red Line 50p
His novel of the Marines on Guadalcanal—a gory, appallingly accurate description of men at war. 'Raw, violent, powerful and terrible, the most convincing account of battle experience I have ever read.'
Richard Lister, Evening Standard

From Here to Eternity 75p
The world famous novel of the men of the U.S. Army stationed at Pearl Harbour in the months immediately before America's entry into World War II. 'One reads every page persuaded that it is a remarkable, a very remarkable book indeed.'
Listener

The Merry Month of May 50p
Paris in the spring of 1968: students on the rampage and their effect on a wealthy American family living in Paris. 'Very gripping . . . a novel of our time which takes the reader into the heart of the Revolution. The atmosphere is splendidly conveyed.'
Financial Times

Fontana Books

Fontana Books

Fontana is best known as one of the leading paperback publishers of popular fiction and non-fiction. It also includes an outstanding, and expanding section of books on history, natural history, religion and social sciences.

Most of the fiction authors need no introduction. They include Agatha Christie, Hammond Innes, Alistair MacLean, Catherine Gaskin, Victoria Holt and Lucy Walker. Desmond Bagley and Maureen Peters are among the relative newcomers.

The non-fiction list features a superb collection of animal books by such favourites as Gerald Durrell and Joy Adamson.

All Fontana books are available at your bookshop or news-agent; or can be ordered direct. Just fill in the form below and list the titles you want.

FONTANA BOOKS, Cash Sales Department, P.O. Box 4, Godalming, Surrey, GU7, 1JY. Please send purchase price plus 7p postage per book by cheque, postal or money order. No currency.

NAME (Block letters) _____

ADDRESS _____

_____

_____